Praise for th
of John S

The Wishing Trees

"John Shors's *The Wishing Trees* is an affecting and sensitively rendered study of grief and loss, the healing power of artistic expression, and the life-altering rewards of travel to distant lands. I was deeply moved by this poignant and life-affirming novel."

—Wally Lamb, #1 *New York Times* bestselling author of *She's Come Undone* and *Wishin' and Hopin'*

"Beautifully written, *The Wishing Trees* is a fascinating tale of a father and daughter on a spiritual and emotional journey—where they find love and forgiveness in the most unfamiliar but amazing places. The trials and triumphs of these characters serve to paint an emotionally resonant picture of their voyage as they're able to miraculously transform their shared sorrow into acts of hope, kindness, and affection."

—Mahbod Seraji, author of *Rooftops of Tehran*

Dragon House

"A touching story about, among other things, the lingering impacts of the last generation's war on the contemporary landscape and people of Vietnam. In a large cast of appealing characters, the street children are the heart of this book; their talents, friendships, and perils keep you turning the pages."

—Karen Joy Fowler, bestselling author of *Wit's End*

"John Shors has written a wonderful novel about two American lives shaped by an encounter with the lives of the Vietnamese people in this present age, decades after that country has faded from the ongoing clamour of news in this country. For that very reason, Shors transcends politics and headlines and finds the timeless and deeply human stories that are the essence of enduring fiction. This is strong, important work from a gifted writer."

—Robert Olen Butler, Pulitzer Prize–winning author of *A Good Scent from a Strange Mountain*

"In *Dragon House* John Shors paints such a vivid picture of the lives of Vietnamese street children and the tourists they need in order to survive, you would swear it was written by one of them. I loved this book, and cared deeply about the characters brought to life by Shors's clear sensitivity to the plight of the unseen and unwanted in Vietnam."

—Elizabeth Flock, bestselling author of *Sleepwalking in Daylight*

"Amid the wreckage of what's known in Vietnam as the 'American War,' Shors has set his sprawling, vibrant novel. All of his characters—hustlers, humanitarians, street children—carry wounds, visible or otherwise. And in the cacophony of their voices, he asks that most essential question: How can we be better?"

—David Oliver Relin, #1 *New York Times* bestselling author of *Three Cups of Tea*

continued . . .

"There is a tenderness in this moving, deeply descriptive novel that brings all those frequently hidden qualities of compassion, purity of mind, and, yes, love—the things we used to call the human spirit—into the foreground of our feeling as readers. This is a beautiful heart speaking to us of the beautiful world we could and should find, even in the darkness that so often floods the world with fear."

—Gregory David Roberts, bestselling author of *The Mountain Shadow*

Beside a Burning Sea

"A master storyteller. . . . *Beside a Burning Sea* confirms again that Shors is an immense talent. . . . This novel has the aura of the mythic, the magical, and that which is grounded in history. Shors weaves psychological intrigue by looking at his characters' competing desires: love, revenge, and meaning. Both lyrical and deeply imaginative."

—Amy Tan, bestselling author of *The Joy Luck Club*

"Features achingly lyrical prose, even in depicting the horrors of war. . . . Shors pays satisfying attention to class and race dynamics, as well as the tension between wartime enemies. The survivors' dignity, quiet strength, and fellowship make this a magical read."

—*Publishers Weekly*

"An astounding work. Poetic and cinematic as it illuminates the dark corners of human behavior, it is destined to be this decade's *The English Patient.*"

—*Booklist*

"Shors has re-created a tragic place in time, when love for another was a person's sole companion. He uses lyrical prose throughout the novel, especially in his series of haiku poems that plays an integral role in the love story, and develops accessible, sympathetic characters. . . . A book that spans 2½ weeks, set on a deserted island, easily could become dull and redundant. But Shors avoids those turns by delving into the effects of war on each character, causing readers to attach themselves to the individuals yearning for home and the ones they love."

—*Rocky Mountain News*

"In *Beside a Burning Sea*, Shors has combined the classic desert island adventure with touching stories of love among the castaways. These elements provide an irresistible pull; Shors makes the reader a willing accomplice on this rewarding journey."

—*BookPage*

"Fiery romance raging in the tumult of war. . . . Emotional structures are powerfully built. The story is rescued from a softening of narrative by strong doses of brutality. Against the vast theater of war, each character experiences a private drama. . . . This story of redemption, love, and friendship is placed against a hideously distorted, morally arid world, one where the prophets, saints, and deities of the great religions have been silenced, but where human decency, even heroism, survives in small, fertile patches."

—*The Japan Times*

Beneath a Marble Sky

"[A] spirited debut novel. . . . With infectious enthusiasm and just enough careful attention to detail, Shors gives a real sense of the times, bringing the world of imperial Hindustan and its royal inhabitants to vivid life." —*Publishers Weekly*

"Jahanara is a beguiling heroine whom readers will come to love; none of today's chick-lit heroines can match her dignity, fortitude, and cunning. . . . Elegant, often lyrical writing distinguishes this literary fiction from the genre known as historical romance. It is truly a work of art, rare in a debut novel." —*The Des Moines Register*

"Agreeably colorful . . . [with] lively period detail and a surfeit of villains." —*Kirkus Reviews*

"An exceptional work of fiction . . . a gripping account." —*India Post*

"Highly recommended . . . a thrilling tale [that] will appeal to a wide audience." —*Library Journal*

"Evocative of the fantastical stories and sensual descriptions of *One Thousand and One Nights*, *Beneath a Marble Sky* is the story of Jahanara, the daughter of the seventeenth-century Mughal emperor who built India's Taj Mahal. What sets this novel apart is its description of Muslim-Hindu politics, which continue to plague the subcontinent today." —*National Geographic Traveler*

"[A] story of romance and passion . . . a wonderful book if you want to escape to a foreign land while relaxing in your porch swing." —*St. Petersburg Times*

"It is difficult to effectively bring the twenty-first-century reader into a seventeenth-century world. Shors accomplishes this nicely, taking the armchair traveler into some of the intricacies involved in creating a monument that remains one of the architectural and artistic wonders of the world." —*The Denver Post*

"[Shors] writes compellingly [and] does a lovely job of bringing an era to life . . . an author to anticipate." —*Omaha World-Herald*

"A sumptuous feast of emotional imagery awaits the reader of *Beneath a Marble Sky*, an unabashedly romantic novel set in seventeenth-century Hindustan, inside the warm sandstone of its Mughal palaces." —*India West*

"This sweeping love story takes place in seventeenth-century Hindustan during the building of the Taj Mahal. Princess Jahanara, the emperor's daughter, tells her parents' saga and shares her own story of forbidden love with the architect of the legendary building." —*St. Paul Pioneer Press*

"Shors . . . creates a vivid and striking world that feels as close as a plane ride. Most important, he manages to convey universal feelings in a tangible and intimate way. Shah Jahan's grief isn't just that of a man who lived centuries ago; it's a well of emotion felt long before Mumatz Mahal ever lived, and is still felt today. Shors's ability to tap into that well, and make it so alive, renders the novel as luminous a jewel as any that adorn the Taj Mahal's walls." —*ForeWord Magazine*

ALSO BY JOHN SHORS

Beneath a Marble Sky

Beside a Burning Sea

Dragon House

the Wishing Trees

JOHN SHORS

NEW AMERICAN LIBRARY

NEW AMERICAN LIBRARY
Published by New American Library, a division of
Penguin Group (USA) Inc., 375 Hudson Street,
New York, New York 10014, USA
Penguin Group (Canada), 90 Eglinton Avenue East, Suite 700, Toronto,
Ontario M4P 2Y3, Canada (a division of Pearson Penguin Canada Inc.)
Penguin Books Ltd., 80 Strand, London WC2R 0RL, England
Penguin Ireland, 25 St. Stephen's Green, Dublin 2,
Ireland (a division of Penguin Books Ltd.)
Penguin Group (Australia), 250 Camberwell Road, Camberwell, Victoria 3124,
Australia (a division of Pearson Australia Group Pty. Ltd.)
Penguin Books India Pvt. Ltd., 11 Community Centre, Panchsheel Park,
New Delhi - 110 017, India
Penguin Group (NZ), 67 Apollo Drive, Rosedale, North Shore 0632,
New Zealand (a division of Pearson New Zealand Ltd.)
Penguin Books (South Africa) (Pty.) Ltd., 24 Sturdee Avenue,
Rosebank, Johannesburg 2196, South Africa

Penguin Books Ltd., Registered Offices:
80 Strand, London WC2R 0RL, England

First published by New American Library,
a division of Penguin Group (USA) Inc.

First Printing, September 2010
10 9 8 7 6 5 4 3 2 1

Cover photographs: Photo of man and girl courtesy of Fotosearch; photo of fortune paper by Zenshui/Laurence Mouton/PhotoAlto Agency RF Collections/Getty Images; photo of envelope courtesy of Shutterstock Images; photo of cherry blossoms by Lynn James/Photonica/Getty Images; back cover background photo © Maxxxur/Shutterstock Images.

NAL REGISTERED TRADEMARK—MARCA REGISTRADA

LIBRARY OF CONGRESS CATALOGING-IN-PUBLICATION DATA:

Shors, John, 1969–
The wishing trees/John Shors.
ISBN 978-0-451-23113-0
1. Fathers and daughters—Fiction. 3. Americans—Asia—Fiction. I. Title.
PS3619.H668W57 2010
813'.6—dc22 2010016227

Set in New Caledonia
Designed by Ginger Legato

Printed in the United States of America

PUBLISHER'S NOTE
This is a work of fiction. Names, characters, places, and incidents either are the product of the author's imagination or are used fictitiously, and any resemblance to actual persons, living or dead, business establishments, events, or locales is entirely coincidental.

The publisher does not have any control over and does not assume any responsibility for author or third-party Web sites or their content.

For my family.

Allison–Thank you for wandering with me. I love you.

Sophie and Jack–Nothing makes me happier than your smiles.

the Wishing Trees

AMERICA

Two as One

"When one door closes, another one opens."

—American saying

Ian watched Mattie sleep, her body curved as if still pressed against his, her arms resting on a pillow that he had carefully positioned alongside her torso. The pillow acted as his body double on many nights, comforting her in his absence, offering her warmth and the remnants of his scent. The king-sized bed made his ten-year-old daughter seem so small. She looked too fragile and lonely, as if she might come unbound without him beside her.

As it often did, the sight of Mattie sleeping brought tears to Ian's eyes, since in most every way she was an image of her deceased mother. Several years earlier, Mattie had compared herself to what she saw in a nearby park. Her hair, she said, was the color of an oak tree's bark. At some point the sky must have dripped into her eyes, she was certain, because they were the same hue as what she saw above. Her mother had then asked Mattie where her freckles came from, and Mattie had paused, glancing around the park. She finally replied that her freckles were tiny pieces of leaves that had fallen onto her face while she napped.

Ian reflected on how Mattie and Kate had often spoken like that—

as if they shared the same mind and view of the world. Mattie didn't try to copy her mother, to make her mother's characteristics her own. Rather, Mattie just seemed to be a miniature Kate, as if Kate's DNA had been neatly sorted and stacked into Mattie's mannerisms and thoughts. Like her mother, Mattie was artistic and curious. Her heart was filled with her mother's love and laughter. Most everywhere the three of them had gone together, Mattie and Kate held hands—even when Mattie's friends became too old for such public displays of affection.

Ian lowered himself to the edge of the bed nearest Mattie. This had been Kate's side, and he ran his fingers over the sheets that had once warmed her. Even though ten months had passed since he'd last touched her skin, the ache of her loss was as intense as if she had died the day before. He still felt empty and incomplete, as if his soul had tried to travel with hers but had been tethered to the world of stone and dirt. His soul remained trapped within him now, bereft of the magic that was once so sustaining. Through his will, and his love for Mattie, he had managed to repair parts of this trapped soul—fitting its pieces together as he might patch up a broken vase. But this element of him, he feared, would never soar again. At least not the way it once had. An injured bird might relearn how to fly, but never with the same sense of unbridled freedom. Whatever had brought the bird down would always loom in the distance.

Mattie stirred in her sleep, dislodging the sheet and blanket that Ian had pulled to her neck. He carefully repeated the process, then bent to kiss a freckle on her forehead. Glancing to make sure that both night-lights were on, he stood up and stepped toward the doorway. He reached an antique mirror that Kate had hung opposite their bed, and paused. His reflection had changed so much over the past year. His six-foot frame was now slightly stooped. His hair, recently the shade of shadows, had patches of gray near his temples, a color that was slowly spreading over him, as if it were ice subjugating a pond. He had lost twenty pounds, his body now more like a college student's than a middle-aged man's. Even his eyes had changed—still brown, but the flesh beneath them appearing bruised.

Ian shook his head, disliking his reflection. He left the bedroom. The rest of their brownstone was almost exactly the way Kate had arranged it. Every nook and open space rekindled memories, and he wondered if their real estate agent had fielded any calls that day. Ian couldn't stay inside these walls much longer. And he didn't think that Mattie could either. Their home, he felt, had been murdered. Nothing remained but a skeleton.

His office gave him little comfort—only some of Mattie's colorful sketches provided solace. He glanced at Kate's photo, but for once his eyes didn't linger on hers. Instead he opened his closet and picked up a neatly wrapped present, which Kate had given him ten months earlier, just three days before she died. She had asked him to promise not to open it until his birthday. And he'd kept his promise, despite many temptations.

Ian sat on a chair and placed the package on his lap. He smelled the wrapping paper, hoping that a trace of Kate might remain. He imagined her tying the bow and he kissed the neat little knot of fabric. A tear raced down his face, dropping next to the bow. Maybe her tears fell in the same spot, he thought, wishing that he could kiss her damp cheek once again.

The box carried no card, which he had thought about often over the past ten months. It wasn't like Kate to forget something like that, as she had always loved letters. She'd detested e-mail and text messages, refusing to write to him in such a manner unless it was absolutely necessary. Her notes had come to him via pen and paper.

After taking a deep and measured breath, Ian moved his fingers to an edge of the wrapping paper. His heartbeat quickened. The back of his neck tingled. His right thumb edged back and forth as if it were on the dial of his BlackBerry. He was afraid that Kate's gift, through no fault of her own, would wound him. And he didn't have the strength to withstand being wounded again.

The wrapping paper resisted him. The paper was like a flag draped over a coffin, and he treated it with respect. Kate had been careful with it, and he needed to be as well. "What's in here, my luv?" he asked softly, his thick Australian accent at odds with the sounds of Manhattan seeping through a nearby window.

A box was soon revealed—a red shoe box that he had seen her use on other occasions. He removed the lid, moving faster, and saw an envelope first. Below it were about a dozen black film canisters. Ian pursed his lips, opening the envelope, which contained a letter. The sight of her elegant handwriting made him cry. She had always written in cursive, and even facing death, and in substantial pain, her hand had been steady and unrushed.

> *Ian,*
>
> *Did you know that you take your love with you, when you die? I am so certain of this, because during the last few months, as I've lain here and deteriorated, my love for you and Mattie has been growing. Nothing, these days, grows within me except my love for you two. And that love rises like a tropical grass, overshadowing everything beneath it, reaching for light and warmth. A year ago I didn't think that I could love either of you more. But I was wrong. I was looking at a tree in front of me, a gorgeous tree for sure, but not as lovely as the forest that surrounded it. I love you. I love you. I love you.*
>
> *I feel so blessed to have stumbled upon you, though surely fate brought us together. Why else would we have both decided to teach English in Japan? Me, a girl from Manhattan. You, a boy from rural Australia. The heavens must have conspired for us to meet. That was the beginning of our story. The end will never be written. The middle saw us travel the world together, create a loving daughter together.*
>
> *Do you recall when we were at the Taj Mahal and our guide told us about the emperor and his wife? He loved her so much. And as she lay dying, he wondered*

if she needed anything. She asked him for one wish—to build her something beautiful and to visit that place on their anniversary and light a candle. That dying woman's wish became the Taj Mahal.

Well, I have a last request, too. It may be simpler than what she asked for, but it won't necessarily be easier. You see, I want you and Mattie to be happy. That is my last wish. I want you both to be happy after you've mourned me. I can't rest in peace if either of you is miserable, so please do this for me. Be happy. Learn to laugh again. To joke. To wrestle together like you once did. Learn to be free again.

Remember how, before I got sick, we were planning to retrace our steps around Asia? To celebrate our fifteenth anniversary? Only this time, Mattie would be by our side. We were all so excited, so full of life, of joy.

I want you, my love, to take her on that same trip. See what we were all so eager to see, feel what we wanted to feel. Will you do that for me? Please? Please visit the places you and I so adored, walk the paths that we planned to walk again. Let me hear you laugh. Let me see you smile. Teach each other how to experience joy once more. Please go sometime soon, and open these film canisters when you arrive in the country that I've marked on the front of each canister. There are six canisters for you and six for Mattie, representing the countries on our original itinerary. Please don't open any of them until you arrive at the proper destination.

Take my life insurance money and use it for this trip. You've already sold your company, and I hope that you haven't started another one yet. There will always be time for work.

Please go on this journey. Please. I wish I could

travel with you. I'm sorry I had to leave. I tried so hard to stay. I fought until I began to become a different person, until rage tainted my thoughts. Only then did I give up the fight.

Do you remember, my love, how we used to write each other poems? When you're overseas, step outside, look at the stars, and think about those poems. I was bound to you when you wrote your first poem for me. You didn't know it then, but you bound me to you and we can never be unbound.

Please grant me my final wish. It won't be easy, I know. But take this trip for me, for Mattie, for yourself. Leave your footprints in foreign lands, and cherish each other along the way. You both used to joke and laugh and smile so much. One of the greatest joys of my life was watching you two laugh together. And you need to laugh again. You will laugh again.

I love you, Ian. Remember what I wrote—that we are bound together and nothing can unbind us. Not time. Not distance. Not physical separation. The love I feel for you both can't be pulled apart, because that love is like an ocean, and you're both the salt and the water of that ocean.

I will love you and Mattie forever.

Your Kate

Ian put his head in his hands and began to weep.

Only much later was he able to trace her words with his forefinger and think about them. He didn't want to travel to Asia without Kate. In so many respects, such a journey would be hollow, bereft of color. And yet their little girl seemed so lost, such a shadow of her former self. He'd tried in countless ways in countless moments to shine a light on her, to purge her of this shadow. And though sometimes his light settled on her face, these moments were as fleeting as the flight of falling leaves.

Ian reread the letter again and again until exhaustion rendered him nearly incapable of thought or emotion. Lying down beside Mattie, he pulled her close, kissing her, closing his eyes, letting darkness come to his rescue.

JAPAN

Memories Awoken

"One kind word can warm three winter months."

—Japanese saying

"It's not so bloody bonkers in here, is it?" Ian asked, helping Mattie to her seat, relieved to be free from the press of bodies on Tokyo's sidewalks.

Mattie studied the mini conveyor belt in front of her, which carried servings of sushi to customers lining a long table. Different-colored plates held the sushi, and Mattie glanced from one to another. "Why are there so many colors?" she asked, exhausted from the lengthy flight, her voice slow and steady—so different from her father's, with its Australian accent and his tendency to run words together.

Ian nodded to a passing waitress. "Well, each plate represents a different amount of money, my little ankle biter. The green plates hold the cheapest sushi, I reckon. The blues ones might be in the middle, the red ones the most expensive, and so on. That's how they do it over here—keeps things moving fast and efficient."

"Oh."

"Care to have a go at it?"

"Sure."

The waitress, dressed in a black T-shirt and skirt, asked if they wanted something to drink. Ian tried to remember Japanese, pulling a few phrases from his past life. After the waitress had taken his order and left, he put his arm around Mattie, who was rubbing the end of one of her long braids against her chin. "She must think I've got kangaroos loose in the top paddock," he said, seeking to put a smile on Mattie's face, a task that had become an obsession of his. "I don't know if I ordered us water or told her we fancied a swim."

Mattie kept watching the plates, thinking that she might like to sketch them. "Did you ever come here with Mommy?"

"No, luv, I reckon not. Tokyo has something like thirty million people. It's a heap bigger than even New York. And restaurants like this one are on about every corner, so stumbling upon the same place twice would be like finding your favorite needle in a mountain of needles. Plus, we lived in Kyoto and didn't come to Tokyo but two or three times."

Nodding absently, Mattie studied the various offerings of sushi. Rectangular cuts of pink, red, white, and orange fish occupied most plates, though piles of roe, octopus tentacles, slices of shrimp, and bottles of beer and sake were also moving from her right to her left. She was surprised to see that a man two chairs down from her had a stack of almost a dozen plates in front of him. How could someone so small eat so much? she wondered.

As Mattie studied the man, Ian watched her. Since Kate had died, Mattie didn't talk as much as she used to. She still asked lots of questions but seemed more interested in answers than conversations. Once Mattie had been nine going on nineteen, so eager to tell her parents how the world worked. But now, a year and a half after her mother's death, she seemed to have lost interest in sharing her knowledge.

"I reckon it's no help being an octopus in these parts," Ian said as a nearby customer devoured some tentacles. "Having eight arms didn't do him much good."

A smile spread across Mattie's face. Her smile was like a sunrise, warming him. "Don't be silly, Daddy," she said. "You'll embarrass me."

"Embarrass you? The lass who used to run around naked on our deck?"

"Daddy!"

He leaned over to kiss the side of her head. "Ah, you're best off to ignore my yammering."

The waitress brought them water and Ian thanked her. Mattie continued to watch the food flow past. She picked up her chopsticks, remembering when her mother had tried to teach her how to use them. Her mother had taught her so many things—how to ride a bike, how to plant tulip bulbs, and, most important, how to draw. They had often gone to Central Park and sketched together. Sometimes her mother read her a story and Mattie drew what was happening in it. At first her sketches weren't more than simplistic collections of uneven lines and colors. But as the seasons played hopscotch, Mattie's creations became more complex and refined. With her mother's encouragement, she learned to draw with emotion, to put her hopes and loves and happiness into whatever she was trying to bring to life.

Mattie glanced out a window into the chaos called Tokyo. The city was an infinite assortment of moving parts. She saw elevated trains, thousands of people moving like rivers, and lights of every color that blinked, pulsated, and seemed to be alive. Suddenly Mattie missed her room. She was disoriented in Japan, and even with her father beside her, she felt alone.

"Daddy?" she asked.

"Yeah, luv?"

"Do you think Mommy really sees us? Even with all these people around?"

Ian pursed his lips, her words echoing his own thoughts. "Your mum always saw you, Roo. She always watched over you." He sipped his water, trying to keep his voice steady as memories of Kate flooded into him. "One night, only a few months after you were born, I came home, quite late, from work. You were in your crib, and she was asleep on the floor, still reaching through the crib's rails to hold your hand. You two looked like a couple of angels."

"We did?"

"You were a couple of angels."

"Did you take a picture?"

He shook his head. "I've been a dimwit a thousand nights of my life and that was one of them." Seeing that Mattie was huddled low, as if cold, he moved his chair closer to hers until their legs touched. She was wearing a T-shirt with one of her earliest sketches on it—a shirt that Kate had ordered—and it was wonderful, but hardly warm. "I'm dead cert that your mum's watching you now," Ian said, putting his arm around her.

"I miss her so much."

"I know. So do I."

Mattie reached for his free hand, a tear tumbling from her eye. "Daddy, will . . . will I always be sad?"

He brushed away the tear. "No, luv. You won't. That's why your mum asked us to go on this walkabout. She wants us to laugh like we used to. You remember laughing, don't you? We used to laugh so bloody hard."

"I remember."

Ian leaned toward her, kissing a freckle near her nose, seeing pieces of his wife within his daughter. "Will you try to laugh with me? Like your mum wanted you to?"

"She really said that? She wanted me to laugh?"

"That's what she wrote. In her letter to me."

Mattie tried to remember her mother's smile. "Aye, aye, Captain, I'll laugh."

He squeezed her shoulder. "That's my first mate. That's the spirit. Let's have heaps of fun together, like we used to, like we always will."

She reached for a plate that held thin slices of cucumbers. "Can you tell me a story? About you and Mommy in Japan?"

"Something to tickle your funny bone?"

"No. Tell me about something good she did. How she helped someone."

Ian nodded, walking through memories. He picked up a plate of tuna but didn't touch the perfectly cut fish. "One day, luv, your mum and I were outside, eating our lunch, taking a break from teaching. We were in downtown Kyoto, near the train station."

"And what happened?"

"I'll tell you in a tick, Roo. But have a go at those cucumbers first."

"Tell me."

He used his chopsticks to place a slice of cucumber in her mouth, thinking that her lips had grown fuller in recent months. "As you know, luv, your mum fancied helping people," he said, dipping a piece of his tuna in soy sauce. "People who couldn't help themselves. And we were out there, on that lovely day, and there was a homeless man, and he was drunk, so legless that he couldn't stand. Well, a heap of people had gathered around him, and these three businessmen came up and started to pester the bloke. The dimwits were laughing at him, mucking around, knocking over his bag. And then they began to kick him. And soon more people came to watch the spectacle—a bunch of bloody cowards if you ask me, because no one did a thing to stop it, even when those three mongrels started kicking him."

"Did you stand there?"

Ian smiled, remembering how Kate had stepped forward. "Your mum, she dropped her food and ran right up to them. And I had no choice but to do the same. By the time I got there, she was already yelling at the businessmen. She had two of them on their heels. I reckon she had them beat, but one of those mongrels stood his ground. At least until I showed up. At that point he scampered off like his backside had been set afire."

Mattie picked up another cucumber. "And what did Mommy do?"

"Your mum bent down and helped that homeless chap to his feet. And then she gave him some money. A proper sum of money, if I remember right."

"Wasn't she afraid?"

"I don't know. I was. If something had happened, we might have been deported. And I'd only been in the country for a few months. I didn't have anyplace to go."

Mattie nodded, not surprised by the story. "I want to be like Mommy. I want to help people."

"And you will, luv. You will. Just don't be in a rush to grow up. You can still help people when you're young."

She finished her cucumbers and picked up a pink plate that held thin slices of shrimp. "Daddy, should we open our messages from Mommy tomorrow?"

"Tomorrow?"

"I think we should."

Ian added wasabi to his soy sauce, giving himself more time to think. He didn't know if he was ready to read Kate's words again. He was afraid she might ask him to do more than he was capable of. Already she had pushed him to his limits, pressuring him to return to Japan, to the place where he had fallen in love with her. A part of him hadn't wanted to come back to Kyoto, as sometimes it was best not to stir up the repertoire of his memories. Such memories weakened rather than strengthened him, and he needed to be strong for Mattie's sake. He couldn't let her know about his demons, about the sorrow that threatened to suffocate him. He had to be an actor, convincing her that he wanted to go on this trip when he sometimes resented Kate for begging him to do so. She had asked too much. How could he walk through memories that would never be relived? How could he make Mattie laugh and smile when so many joys had been stolen from him? He would try, of course, but feared that he would fail. He'd never been as strong as Kate, and she should have thought about that before asking the impossible.

"Can we wait, Roo, until after tomorrow?" he finally answered. "How about that? You and I will do a Captain Cook tomorrow, and the next day we'll open the canisters."

"A real Captain Cook?"

"Sure, luv. A real look around. Let's explore Tokyo. Let's have some fun. And then we'll read your mum's notes."

"Aye, aye, Captain," Mattie replied, trying to smile, aware that her father was worried about the canisters. She knew that he thought he could hide his feelings from her, but she'd seen too much of his suffering. She'd pretended not to, but he couldn't fool her. Not when she watched him stare at her mother's photo, not when he paused in midsentence as a smell or sight reminded him of his loss. And especially not at night, when he went into the bathroom, turned on the shower, and cried.

Mattie understood her father. She understood him because she'd seen his face in happier times. She knew how he liked to laugh, to tickle her, to play jokes. Now he rarely did such things and didn't do them nearly as well as he once had. On occasion she'd glimpse his old self, but these glimpses were as infrequent as her own feelings of happiness.

"I love you, Daddy," Mattie said, placing another plate of tuna in front of him.

Ian managed to push his thoughts of Kate aside, at least for the moment. "I love you too, Roo. I love you so bloody much, I don't know what I'd do without you."

THE MATTRESS FELT LIKE A BOARD BENEATH Mattie. She stirred, turning away from her father, who was wearing his plaid pajamas and had finally fallen asleep. Their first full night in Japan hadn't been a restful experience, especially for Mattie, who had never been overseas and who wasn't used to such a drastic time change. She felt physically exhausted, yet her mind raced, churning with a speed that she couldn't control, try as she might.

Even though the hotel room didn't appear much different from what might be found back home, the small space made Mattie anxious. The writing on the door was strange—ancient and unknown. The toilet, she'd discovered in the middle of the night, had a heated seat. A sliding, frosted-glass door separated the bathroom from the sleeping area. Two steel stools sat in the corner. Mattie thought that the entire room, except for the toilet, couldn't have been more uncomfortable.

Careful not to wake her father, Mattie moved out of bed. She unzipped his immense traveling backpack, picked out her jeans and an old soccer T-shirt, and dressed. Upon entering the miniature bathroom, she slid shut the door and turned on the light. Her hair, which fell well below her shoulders, was a tangled mess. She picked up a plastic hotel comb and began to pull at the knots. Within seconds, she was reminded of how her mother had brushed her hair. They'd sit outside when the weather was nice and look for things for Mattie to sketch. And as they looked, her mother would run a damp comb through Mattie's hair until each strand was untwisted from its neighbor.

Mattie gazed into the mirror, longing to glimpse her mother behind her, but seeing only the white bathroom wall. Her eyes started to tear and she set down the comb, turning from her reflection. She didn't want to see herself standing alone, crying in a strange place, and so she left the bathroom. Noticing that her father was still asleep, Mattie opened her blue backpack—a smaller version of what he carried. She removed a piece of paper the size of a playing card, which she'd drawn on several years before. Her sketch was done in colored pencils and showed a little girl in a dress holding hands with her mother. Mattie had written "I love you, Mommy" beneath the image. Her mother had taken the drawing to a store and had it laminated. She'd carried it with her until she'd become ill. Then it had lain on a table beside her hospital bed. Mattie had kept the picture ever since her mother's death. Sometimes she put it under her pillow. Sometimes she used it as a bookmark. It was never far from her.

Thinking about the happy faces on her drawing, Mattie looked around the stark room and began to cry. With her forefinger, she traced the outline of her mother, trying to remember how she had looked with a comb in her hand. But instead of seeing her mother's comforting grin, Mattie saw her in the hospital bed, with tubes running into her nose and wrists. Her mother's face was pale and pained, her arms thin and weak. And her smile was a mirage, containing neither joy nor hope, but suffering, sorrow, and despair.

Mattie didn't want to remember her mother in the hospital bed, to think about her steady decline, how her strength vanished, how the light faded from her eyes when painkillers were pumped into her system. Continuing to stare at the picture she'd drawn, she sought to recall her mother during a happy time—when they went camping or played Monopoly. But no matter how hard Mattie sought to remember those moments, she always ended up picturing her mother at the end, with the tubes in her nose.

Pressing the picture against her lips, Mattie closed her eyes, unable to stop crying, tears racing down her cheeks, falling near a stain on her soccer shirt. She wrapped her arms around herself, as if her mother were giving her a hug. Rocking back and forth, she wept, still trying to imagine her mother during joyful times.

Suddenly her father knelt before her, pulling her close, kissing the tears on her cheeks. *"Sssh,"* he said softly. "It's all right now."

"No."

"Let me hold you."

"It's not all right."

"I'm here."

"But, Daddy . . . I can't remember. I don't want to remember."

"Remember what?"

"Her face. I only remember the tubes. At the end."

Ian kissed her forehead, her eyes. He silently assailed himself for letting Mattie see Kate during her last day. That had been a mistake. Mattie had wanted to say good-bye but had erupted in tears at the sight of Kate's nearly lifeless body. It hadn't been a farewell, but a session of horrors for everyone present. The tubes and needles were the instruments of a torturer.

"I don't want to think about her like that anymore," Mattie added, still clinging to her drawing.

"Easy on, luv," Ian said. "Easy on."

"I can't think like that!"

"And you don't have to," he replied, wiping away her tears, lifting her onto his lap.

"But that's all I see! She's in the bed, with the tubes, and her eyes are so red and tired."

Ian held her close to his chest, trying not to let his own misery surface, wounded by the sight of his weeping daughter. Nothing hurt him more than the spectacle of Mattie in tears. A young heart, he often thought, shouldn't endure such pain—better that he take her pain and somehow make it his own. But he didn't know how to steal her misery, and so he continued to simply hold and comfort her.

"Let me show you something," he said, lifting her, stepping toward the desk where his wallet lay. He sat down on one of the steel stools and opened the wallet, sorting through it until he produced a dog-eared photo of Kate lying on their hammock. He'd taken the photo just a few weeks before Mattie was born, and Kate's belly rose from beneath her sundress. Her face, in so many ways like Mattie's, was dominated by a wide smile. Her eyes were locked on Ian, and her hands cradled her belly.

Ian handed the photo to Mattie. "Your mum loved being pregnant with you. Most of her friends, to be honest, weren't so keen on the experience. But she adored it."

"She did?"

"She fancied your kicks, which were so strong. That's why I nicknamed you 'Roo.' I'd seen so many kangaroos down in Oz. And you reminded me of them."

"But, Daddy, I don't remember Mommy looking like that. Looking so happy. All I see are the tubes."

"You have to try and—"

"I do try."

Ian kissed her forehead, his thumb making its back-and-forth motion on a BlackBerry that he no longer carried. His stomach ached as if he hadn't eaten in days. He wished he knew what to say, the way Kate had always seemed to. "Sometimes that happens to me," he said, kissing Mattie again. "I see those tubes. But then I take out this photo, and I look at it, and then that's how I remember her."

"You do?"

"I remember how, on that day, she was knackered and needed a rest. It was a warm spring day. A real beaut. And I got out the hammock, put it on our little deck, and she lay down for a spell of reading. I surprised her with the camera, and when she smiled and wrapped her arms around you, I took the shot. And whenever I want to remember what she was really like, I take out that photo and have a good gander."

"But I don't have a—"

"Take that one, luv. We'll tape it to the back of your drawing. That way you can look at them both."

Mattie shook her head. "But then you won't have it."

"We'll share it, Roo. You and me. Like everything else."

"You don't mind?"

"Not a bit."

She hugged him, resting her chin on his shoulder. "Sorry for waking you up. I was cold. And that bed's too hard. I can't sleep on it."

"No worries, luv, about waking me up. I needed to get off my backside anyway. I'm going to take you on an adventure today. A real Captain Cook."

"Promise?"

"Absobloodylutely."

"Should I bring my pencils?"

"Aye, aye, First Mate," he replied, kissing her on the forehead and standing up, drained from the acting, wondering if either of them could manage this trip, wishing that Kate hadn't sent them on it. He went into the bathroom, sat on the toilet, and thought about Mattie's tears and shudders. He had to make her laugh today, he told himself time and time again, his eyes tightly shut, his fists squeezing so hard that his fingernails left imprints on his palms. If she didn't laugh, then he would have failed her once again. She needed him, needed to hope for better days, even if he could not.

Turning on the shower, he tried to keep his own tears at bay until the water fell on him. When it did, he leaned against the tiled wall, his strength ebbing, flowing down the drain, disappearing from light. For a while it felt as if he were drowning, suffocating in a millimeter of water. He longed for help, but no one could help him. He yearned for tomorrow, yet the day had just begun. His every plea seemed to rebound from the nearby walls, to reenter him unanswered. Cursing himself for once working like a madman, for being gone so much of Mattie's life, he wondered how he might meet her needs and repress her fears. He wanted to lift her above the muck and misery of life but felt incapable of such a task. To lift her, he had to be a part of her, as Kate had been. But he didn't feel a part of her. Sometimes she was like a foreign language on his tongue.

Afraid that Mattie might knock, he willed himself to stand up straight, his legs trembling, his fingers reaching for the soap. He started to hum, pretending to sing, bubbles forming on his skin. He scrubbed harder, as if soap might purge him of memories, of failings, of weakness.

Thinking more about Mattie, about what she needed from him, he continued to scrub and hum, formulating a plan. Today he would make her laugh. That was a start.

AFTER A LATE BREAKFAST AND AN HOUR of studying Mattie's math workbook, adding fractions, Ian and Mattie left the hotel. They were dressed the same, in colorful T-shirts, jeans, and tennis shoes. He wore a green and black baseball cap that she and her mother had bought for him during a trip to the Statue of Liberty. He had braided Mattie's long hair, and secured the ends with purple bands.

Stepping out of the lobby was like moving into a flooded river. The wide sidewalk appeared incapable of holding any more people. Businessmen and businesswomen wearing dark suits walked briskly, inches from one another. Everyone seemed to be in a hurry, most carrying umbrellas even though the sky was only partly cloudy. Many of the pedestrians headed toward a discreetly marked subway entrance, vanishing into it like water being sucked down a drain. The water was without end.

"Ready, First Mate, for our walkabout?" Ian asked, holding Mattie's hand, determined to put a smile on her face and keep it there.

"Aye, aye, Captain."

"Then let's have a go at it."

He led her forward, noticing that she practically disappeared into the people around her. Mattie wasn't used to walking alongside hundreds of others. If Ian moved too quickly, she bumped into the people in front of her. If he slowed down a little, her heels were stepped on. She looked up at him, her face flushed, and without a word he bent down, lifted her up, and set her on his shoulders. "There you go, luv," he said, heading toward the subway entrance. "It's time you had a proper view."

The stairway, perhaps twenty feet wide, seemed ready to burst from the presence of so many people. Ian had to stoop with Mattie atop him, which caused his back to ache. But he wasn't about to put her down. "How's my lookout?" he asked, wondering how far down they would descend.

"It's a lot better up here."

"I reckon you'll be ready to trade places in a tick. Just let me know when."

"No way, Captain."

They finally reached the bottom of the stairs, emerging into an underground world. Mattie gasped, having never seen anything like it. She might as well have been Alice falling into the rabbit's hole, for she found herself in the middle of a subterranean city. Though the ceiling was only about twelve feet high, this city stretched as far as she could see. There were restaurants, banks, shops, movie theaters, and what she thought was a supermarket. And the people—she spied tens of thousands of them: schoolchildren in blue-and-white uniforms, college students wearing fashionable attire, and legions of businesspeople.

"I feel like an ant in an anthill," Mattie said, as Ian walked steadily.

"You reckon? I don't think even ants are jammed together like this. See those numbers ahead?"

She looked into the distance and noticed a row of numbers that ran from one to forty. "What are they for?"

"Well, each of those stairways leads to a train platform. And each of those trains is going somewhere different in the city. I want you to pick a number. We'll get on that train and see where it takes us."

"Any number? Are you sure?"

"Ever met an Aussie who wasn't sure about everything?"

Mattie smiled. "Mommy would have liked this."

"She did like it. She invented the game."

"Twenty-three. Let's take number twenty-three."

"Twenty-three it is," Ian replied, walking toward the number. He descended a flight of stairs, emerging into another level, this one full of platforms and trains. Platform number twenty-three was crowded with people. "Our train must be almost here."

"Why?"

"Look at all these blokes. They're waiting for it, all in their own little worlds." Ian moved to a large electric sign that displayed a departure schedule. The information was written in both Japanese and English. After glancing at their platform number on the schedule, he found the next departure time and then looked at a digital clock. "I'll wager you an ice-cream cone to a kiss that our train will be here in about . . . two minutes and five seconds."

"No way."

"Yes, way," Ian replied, moving to the middle of the platform.

Mattie looked into the distant tunnel, unsure what to expect. "Aren't trains late here? They're always late at home."

"If I remember right, which is less likely than catching a two-headed cockatoo, this station serves three or four million people a day. It's the busiest in the world. And you don't get three million people somewhere by being late."

She pointed to a light that appeared in the tunnel. "Is that it?"

"I reckon."

A blast of warm wind preceded the train, which pulled quietly alongside the platform. Dozens of doors simultaneously opened in front of orderly rows of people.

"You'd best do some hopping here, Roo," Ian said, setting her on the ground. They followed the people ahead of them and crammed into a gleaming train car. An automated voice came on, making an announcement as the doors closed. The train moved forward, rushing past the platform, darting into a tunnel. "You picked an express train," Ian said. "A real cheetah. Grab hold of that pole beside you."

Mattie watched as the train flew past another group of platforms and into a new tunnel. The scenery alternated between tunnels and other underground stations for a few minutes before the train abruptly emerged into the light, rising on top of an elevated rail system. Dozens of skyscrapers passed by the windows as if they were fence posts along a highway, blurring as they came and went. Mattie saw thousands of people walking on pedestrian bridges that seemed to float above the streets. Electronic billboards the size of mansions blinked and changed colors. Another train flew past in the opposite direction, seemingly inches from their windows. Just as Mattie was growing used to the view of the city, the train descended underground, passing a few more stations before finally coming to a smooth stop.

"Should we hop off here and explore?" Ian asked.

"Let's hop."

The automated voice announced the station name as the doors all opened. The majority of the passengers got off, and Mattie and Ian joined the exodus. This underground station, while not as large as the one where they had boarded, was still immense and featured a variety of shops and restaurants. Ian held Mattie's hand and walked toward an exit gate, inserting their train passes into a machine, which prompted a pair of small plastic doors to open. Ian led Mattie forward, retrieved their passes, and followed a stairway up, emerging onto the sidewalk near a busy street. Cars, buses, motorcycles, and a surface train rumbled past. People were everywhere.

Mattie and Ian started moving down the sidewalk, passing a life-sized bronze statue of a samurai. A group of schoolchildren approached, many of them holding hands. The children appeared to be Mattie's age, and were led by a middle-aged woman.

"Fancy meeting some new friends?" Ian asked, seeing an opportunity to make Mattie smile, believing that she'd enjoy an exchange with some local children.

"What?"

He grinned and approached the group. "G'day, lads and lasses," he said, waving.

At first the children stepped back, unsure what to think of this tall stranger. The woman leading the group nodded and bowed slightly. "May I help you?" she asked.

"Ah, your English is lovely," Ian replied. "You make me sound like it's my second language, or maybe even my third. Are you their teacher?"

The woman bowed again as students began to giggle behind her. "Yes, I am their English teacher. Are you lost?"

Ian looked at Mattie, reminded of having such conversations years ago. "Well, not exactly. But we're wondering what we might do around here. Is Tokyo Disneyland nearby? Or an aquarium? Or maybe we can watch a good sumo match?"

The teacher, dressed in a uniform similar to her students', suppressed a laugh. "Tokyo Disneyland? Here? I am so sorry, but you are on the wrong end of the city."

"I must have had my map upside down."

"Unfortunately, there are not activities for tourists in this area," she said. "I am sorry that I cannot help you."

Ian shrugged, winking at Mattie, wanting to surprise her, to make her focus on something new. "I used to teach English in Kyoto," he said to the teacher. "For two wonderful years. How about my daughter and

I go back to your school with you and help teach your class? We'll all have heaps of fun, I promise."

Mattie shook her head. "Daddy, don't be silly."

The woman glanced at her students and then back at Ian. "You would like to help me? Teach English?"

"I enjoy teaching," he replied, smiling at a girl who was staring at him. "In Kyoto I taught elementary school students, and students at the uni. They were all lovely. And I reckon that my daughter, Mattie, would fancy helping out. She led us here, after all."

"And you would really like to teach my students?"

"Sure thing."

The teacher looked again at her students, who nodded and giggled. "I am Akiko," she said. "And if you would like, you may come to our school with us. Please follow me."

As several of the children clapped and others held hands in front of their grinning faces, Akiko proceeded along the street, at the edge of the sidewalk. Businesspeople were everywhere, talking on cell phones, rushing to catch trains while carrying briefcases and umbrellas. At the next corner, teenage girls dressed in pink tights handed out plastic-wrapped packets of tissues that carried advertising messages.

While Akiko waited for a light to turn green, Ian pointed at thick white stripes that had been painted across the street. Turning to the schoolchildren, he said, "In Australia we call that a zebra crossing. Though ours aren't as big as this one."

The children looked at the crosswalk, repeated his words, and began to laugh. Mattie laughed with them. For the first time since the encounter had begun, she didn't feel embarrassed about her father, which she often did. Before her mother had died, he used to joke constantly. Her earliest memories, in fact, were of giggling on his lap. And while she liked to giggle, sometimes he said too much.

"Of course, we don't have zebras in Australia," he continued. "But if you ever want to see a kangaroo, Mattie and I will take you out into the bush. And we'll watch them hop around like their backsides are on fire."

When the light turned green, a pulsating beep punctuated the air, letting anyone blind know that it was time to cross. Akiko led the group forward, entering a tall building and proceeding down a hallway that might have been found in a Western bank. Mattie realized that she was in a school, since she saw students in classrooms. But this school didn't look like any other she'd experienced. No drawings or banners hung from the walls, nor did rows of lockers span the sides of the corridor.

Akiko led her students, followed by Ian and Mattie, into a classroom. As the students sat down at two-person desks, chatting excitedly, Mattie moved partly behind her father, who stood near a blackboard.

"Your mum used to teach children like these," Ian whispered into her ear, sensing her disquiet. "And I reckon she's watching now. Let's give her a laugh."

Mattie instinctively looked up, her gaze dropping back to the students as Akiko began to speak in Japanese. Mattie realized that the teacher was older than she'd first thought. Some of Akiko's hair had started to gray, and deep laugh lines surrounded her mouth. As she spoke, the students nodded attentively, sitting motionless, something Mattie's classmates wouldn't be able to easily duplicate.

Akiko turned to their visitors. "Well, Mr. . . ."

"McCray. I'm Ian McCray. But please call me Ian. And my daughter here is Mattie."

"We are lucky, students," Akiko said. "First we enjoyed our field trip to *The Japan Times*, and now Ian-san and Mattie will help us for the remainder of our class. About fifteen minutes. Now please open your English conversation books to page thirty-four."

Ian leaned closer to Akiko. "Could we play a game instead?" he whispered.

"A game?"

"Something to make them laugh."

She smiled, brushing hair from her face. "Certainly, Ian-san. That would be fine."

Ian took Mattie's hand and looked at the students. "Your lovely teacher, Akiko-san, is going to let us all play a game," he said, exaggerating his Australian accent, believing that the children found his dialect funny. "Have any of you ankle biters ever heard of Chinese Whispers?"

The students smiled and shook their heads.

"Codswallop," he said, shaking his head, feigning disbelief.

Akiko laughed, instinctively putting her hand in front of her face. "What does . . . codswallop mean, Ian-san?"

"It means that I can't believe you've never played the telephone game," he replied, remembering how Kate and he used to play the game with their students. "It's quite simple," he said, looking again at the children. "I'm going to whisper a sentence to Mattie. She'll whisper it to Akiko-san, and then Akiko-san will whisper it to one student, who will whisper it to the next, and so on. We'll go through everyone. Then the last student will stand up and repeat the sentence. And we'll see if it's London to a brick. I mean . . . we'll see if it's just right."

The students nodded and smiled, understanding the game. Ian closed his eyes for a few seconds, formulating a sentence. He then leaned down to Mattie, cupped his hands around her ear and whispered, "I love you, Roo. And I always will. Now here's the sentence. Twenty-six giggling zebras crossed a street in Tokyo today."

Grinning, Mattie stood on her tiptoes as Akiko bent down, and quietly repeated the line. Akiko smiled at her, then walked to a student who sat in the first row. The teacher leaned over and whispered. The student laughed, repeated the line to herself, and twisted toward a boy beside her. This process was duplicated until all the students had participated. The last student to receive the sentence smiled and stood up.

Ian shrugged. "So? What was the sentence?"

The girl beamed, glanced at her teacher, and then at Mattie. "Twenty-six wriggling zebras ate a treat in Tokyo today," she said, doing her best to properly pronounce each word.

Ian laughed and told the students the original words, while Akiko wrote both sentences on the blackboard. The students joked and spoke in Japanese, shaking their heads. "Fancy another round?" Ian asked.

"Please, Ian-san," Akiko replied, setting the chalk down.

"Mattie, why don't you start it out this time?"

Nodding, Mattie tried to think of something that the students would find amusing. When she did, she stood on her tiptoes and whispered to her father, "I love you too, Daddy. Now here's my sentence. My father, Ian-san, once kissed a walrus."

Ian pulled back from her, grinning. "Good onya, Roo," he said, and then turned to Akiko and repeated the sentence.

Akiko looked at Mattie, smiled, and walked to her students. After a few minutes the message had traveled from one end of the classroom to the other. A different student was the final recipient, and he stood up and bowed slightly, trying to remember the right words. "My mother, Ian-san, once missed his walrus."

Smiling and shaking her head, Mattie said her original line, and Akiko wrote both sentences on the blackboard. The students laughed, a few clapping at her cleverness. Akiko started to speak when a bell sounded, prompting the students to groan. "We will play this game again," she said, dusting her hands of chalk. "Please, each of you, write a sentence tonight in English, and we will remove several from a box tomorrow. Now kindly thank Ian-san and Mattie for joining us today."

The students offered their thanks, both in Japanese and English. They then organized their books and filed out of the classroom. Akiko turned to Ian and Mattie. "Thank you both so much," she said, bowing.

"You're welcome," Ian replied, pleased that Mattie had experienced a game that her mother had enjoyed. "It was our pleasure. A real treat."

"Are you in Tokyo long?"

"No. Just a tick really. Tomorrow we buzz off for Kyoto."

Akiko glanced at the blackboard, which still displayed the sentences. She smiled. "Would you do me the honor of eating dinner at my house tonight? It is not far from here, and I should repay you for your kindness. You are visitors to my country, and I would like to be your host."

Ian looked at Mattie, who nodded. "That would be lovely," he replied. "Just lovely."

Akiko walked to her desk and wrote on a piece of paper. She handed the paper to Ian, bowing toward him. "You can take a taxi, and show the driver this note. Perhaps you could arrive about seven o'clock?"

"We'll be there. We look forward to it."

The trio said good-bye. Mattie and Ian left the classroom and the school. They walked outside, the sounds of the city once again rising up to drown out any noise from nature. Mattie took Ian's hand, smiling up at him. "You played that game with Mommy, didn't you? With your students?"

He nodded. "We played heaps of games like that. We were always getting in trouble for it, actually. The dimwits who ran our company didn't want us to stray from our textbooks. But stray we did."

"Mommy got into trouble?"

"Getting into trouble wasn't exactly your mum's bowl of rice, but sometimes she did it, just to make a point."

Mattie played with one of her braids, twirling it around her forefinger. "I liked Akiko, and her students."

"So did I, luv. You know, teaching here was a bloody good time. It made me want to see the world. And it did the same thing for your mum."

"And what did you see?"

Ian bent toward her as a pair of businessmen walked past, talking on their cell phones. "Everything looks different, Roo. Japan is full of giant cities and bullet trains. Cows walk the streets of Kathmandu. India is . . . Well, it's India." He slowed his pace, remembering how Kate would chastise him for walking too fast. "But under all that difference, luv, if you really look, people are basically the same. That's what your mum and I learned on our travels. That's what I hope you'll learn. I reckon it's one of the reasons she sent us on this walkabout. I'm sure she wanted to show you herself. But she couldn't. So she sent us."

Nodding, Mattie looked down the street. "What are we going to do now?"

"Well, we've got some ticks to run off the old clock. Why don't we find a park, and you can sketch for a bit? And we'd best get a present for Akiko. In Japan, you always take a gift to your host."

"What should we get?"

"I don't know. But let's have a gander and you can find her something. Something that will make her happy." Still holding Mattie's hand, Ian skirted a square machine that used solar energy to compact garbage. "Maybe some sake."

"Daddy?"

"Yeah, luv?"

"Thanks for showing me Mommy's game."

"No worries."

"I'm glad you showed me, and that I'm here with you."

"You are? It's not too hard?"

She shook her head, her braids rising and falling. "No."

"What if that changes?"

"Was it hard for you and Mommy? Going from country to country?"

"Sometimes."

"Then that's okay."

Ian squeezed her hand, proud of her, but still wondering if he should be taking her to places like Nepal and India. Wasn't she too young for such a journey? Would the sorrows of such countries do her more harm than good? How could the sight of so much suffering help her, especially now, when she carried such a heavy burden?

SEVERAL HOURS LATER, MATTIE AND IAN SAT in a taxi. They had come from a large park, where a dozen cherry blossom trees were in full bloom. Mattie had used her colored pencils to sketch the trees, which bordered a traditional Japanese garden. Ian had told her that he believed the garden to be relatively new, as the trees were middle-aged, and most of Tokyo had been destroyed in the war. The blossoms were beautiful, however, despite the thinness of the branches that bore them. Mattie had studied the blooming trees before sitting down to sketch them. After drawing almost every day for the past five years, her hand was able to re-create the loveliness around her. Focusing on three trees that leaned toward one another, Mattie brought life to the pink blossoms that filled the air with their fragrance. As she worked, Ian wondered why she'd chosen the three trees to duplicate, when so many others were present.

Now, as their taxi drifted down Tokyo's streets, Ian asked if he could look at her drawing again. Mattie opened her sketch pad and flipped to the middle. He studied her trees, aware of how her strokes were growing more graceful. The trunks of the trees were perfectly imperfect, drawn in black and brown, reaching skyward. The cherry blossoms were like pink clouds that encircled the upper halves of the trees.

"You're getting so good, Roo," Ian said. "You're a real Rembrandt."

Mattie smiled but said nothing, which didn't surprise Ian. Kate and Mattie had always shared a special bond when it came to her drawings. They had spoken about them every day, Kate asking questions, offering encouragement. Ian had tried to do the same, but wasn't home enough to create a pattern of such support. As their taxi sped through a yellow light, he wondered if Mattie would ever open up to him about her drawings.

"Why, luv, did you use three trees?" he asked. "Is it because of our family? Because there are three of us?"

"There are two of us, Daddy. Just two."

"That's not true."

"It's only a drawing."

Ian decided not to pursue the subject. It had been a good day, and good days hadn't come often since Kate's death. He carefully closed the book and handed it back to Mattie. "Are you knackered, Roo?"

"A little. My pillow felt like a rock."

The taxi turned into a residential area. The homes, so close together that they seemed connected, were two-storied. They didn't look like the houses in Kyoto, many of which were old and had tiled roofs and miniature gardens. These dwellings resembled small offices. Only a few of the homes had a car parked outside. Such vehicles were miniature, practically toys that had been backed into carports.

The uniformed and white-gloved driver muttered to himself and turned again, soon coming to a stop. He pushed a button and the door next to Mattie opened. Ian glanced at the meter and handed several bills to the driver. The man said thank you in Japanese. Ian and Mattie got out of the car and looked at the house in front of them, which was almost identical to all of the other nearby dwellings.

As Ian stepped forward, the door to the home slid open. An old woman, bent over as if she'd spent a lifetime working in rice fields, smiled and gestured at them to come in. Ian didn't speak much Japanese but said hello and asked the woman how she was doing. She laughed, nodding her head, cackling to herself. "Is Akiko-san home?" Ian inquired, holding a blue bottle of sake in one hand and Mattie's fingers in the other.

"She cooking," the old woman replied in broken English. "Come. Come here."

Ian stepped inside the doorway, pausing to remove his shoes. The woman handed Mattie and him sandals, laughing when she saw that the sandals weren't nearly big enough for his feet. He bowed and gave her the bottle of sake, for which she thanked him profusely. Beyond the entryway, a narrow hallway was dimly lit, pictures hanging at odd angles from its walls. As she led Ian and Mattie forward, the woman chirped like a sparrow might if it could speak Japanese. She didn't stop talking for an instant as she entered a relatively large room. The floor was composed of traditional tatami mats made of tightly woven straw. In the center of the room was a low table surrounded by cushions. The only other notable item was a small wooden altar placed below a black-and-white picture of a somber-looking man.

"Please, you sit, Ian-san," the woman said, still smiling. "Akiko come soon. She cooking and cooking and cooking."

Their hostess bowed and left. A flurry of Japanese ensued from an unseen room. Before a minute had passed, the woman returned, carrying a tray full of refreshments. "Drinking time," she said, setting a glass of beer before Ian and some pineapple juice in front of Mattie. Lifting up her own beer, she said, *"Compai!"*

Ian repeated the word, clicking his glass against their hostess's, explaining to Mattie that compai meant cheers. The woman emptied most of her glass, set it on the table, and left. Mattie sipped her juice, looking around. Nodding toward the altar, she asked, "What's that, Daddy?"

"A shrine."

"What do you mean?"

"I reckon the man in the photo," Ian answered softly, "is Akiko's father, who must have passed away. And this is how they remember him. And honor him."

Mattie nodded, studying the picture, wondering how old Akiko was when her father died. The teacher seemed so happy. Mattie didn't understand how she could act that way when one of her parents was dead. She was about to ask her father what he thought, when Akiko appeared, carrying a lacquer tray. "I am so sorry for keeping you waiting," she said, smiling, using tongs to give a steaming white washcloth to each visitor. "Please refresh yourselves after your long day."

"Thank you, Akiko-san," Ian replied, wiping his hands with the cloth. "And don't be sorry. Your mother is taking good care of us."

"She is so excited that you are here. She has been cleaning for hours."

Mattie shifted her position on a cushion. "What should we call her?"

Akiko put her hands to her face. "I am so sorry. I forgot to introduce you. My mother's name is Chie." Akiko refilled their glasses to the brim. "Please excuse me for a moment. I am almost finished preparing our dinner."

As Akiko left, Chie entered, carrying a large book. Sitting down next to Mattie, she opened the book and gestured toward a map of the world. "Your house?"

Mattie studied the map, then pointed to New York City. "This is where I was born."

"U.S.A.," Chie stammered, spitting out the letters like a jackhammer.

"Yes."

"Good. Big sky. Big country." She traced the borders of America with a bony finger. "You live New York? Near Golden Gate Bridge?"

"I was born in New York," Mattie replied, smiling. "I've always lived there. In Manhattan."

The old woman nodded repeatedly, as if her head were tethered to her neck by an invisible spring. Bringing her hands together in a single clap, she bowed to Ian and topped off everyone's drinks. *"Compai!"*

"Compai," Ian and Mattie echoed, glasses clinking together.

Mattie watched as Chie took a large gulp from her beer. Their hostess couldn't have weighed more than ninety pounds, and Mattie was surprised to see her drink so quickly. Grinning, Chie stood up and vanished once more. A few heartbeats later, the sound of traditional Japanese music emerged from the kitchen. Chie returned, once again filling the glasses, even though they were almost full.

"Bath?" Chie asked, pretending to vigorously scrub herself.

Ian remembered how the Japanese loved to bathe at night, sometimes before dinner. He and Kate had often gone to a local bathhouse in Kyoto, splitting up into the men's and women's sections, sitting under squat showers to clean themselves before sliding into tubs full of naked strangers. "Fancy having a go at it?" he asked Mattie. "That's what they do over here."

Mattie glanced at Chie, who again pretended to scrub herself. "No . . . that's okay. But thank you."

Chie smiled. "You beautiful eyes," she said, kneeling to sip more of her beer. She moved her arms as if swimming. "Your eyes, ocean, same blue."

"Your eyes are pretty too."

"Ah, my eyes, like dirt. No can swim in mud."

Mattie giggled as Chie pretended to get stuck while swimming.

"You just have to try harder," she said, prompting Chie to dig herself out of the ground.

"Me too old. No can see. No can hear. No can swim."

"If you're too old, why do you sit on the floor? Doesn't it hurt your bottom?"

Chie pursed her lips, shrugging. "Bottom?"

"Right here," Mattie replied, touching the underside of her hip.

"My bottom gone. Disappear. So no hurt."

As Mattie smiled, a new song emerged from the unseen stereo. Akiko entered the room carrying a large porcelain pot. "I am sorry for keeping you waiting," she said, placing the pot on the table. "I hope that my mother has been behaving herself."

"She's lovely," Ian replied, helping Akiko place plates on the table.

"I have made you some *nabe*. A traditional Japanese food."

Mattie leaned forward as Akiko removed the pot's lid. Inside, a dark, steaming broth contained cabbage, bok choy, boiled eggs, mushrooms, shrimp, clams, and fish. Though Mattie had never seen such ingredients in the same dish, the smell emanating toward her couldn't have been more savory. The clams were opening slowly, as if Akiko had just put them into the boiling soup.

"Eating nabe together is an old Japanese tradition," Akiko said. "We believe that sitting close together, and eating from the same pot, will make us even better friends."

"A beaut of a tradition," Ian replied, lifting a beer bottle to refill Chie's glass. *"Compai."*

"Compai."

The glasses clinked and the new acquaintances began to eat, using oversized chopsticks to pluck morsels from the stew. Chie appeared to drink more than she ate, her laughter growing louder. She often swayed to the music and was continuously handing Mattie more food, treating Mattie as if she were her granddaughter. While Mattie and Chie smiled and bantered, Ian and Akiko spoke about how Japan had changed over the past fifteen years. Some of the changes, like equality for women, Akiko spoke about with pride. Other transformations, such as increasing crime, she lamented. She asked many questions about Ian's time in Kyoto and was fascinated by his experiences. As they spoke, Ian noticed that Mattie often glanced at Akiko, and sometimes at the nearby shrine and portrait. The pot of nabe was finally emptied, and Chie stood up, bowed, and disappeared into the kitchen.

"We should help her," Ian said, starting to rise.

Akiko shook her head. "Please sit, Ian-san. She will be much happier if you remain here."

"But I'm sure there's a heap of work to do."

"You are right. But she wants to contribute to our house. If she does not, then she will worry that she is a burden to me." Akiko smiled and refilled their glasses with green tea, which they had begun to drink. "Are you excited for your trip tomorrow to Kyoto?"

Ian nodded, though he wasn't looking forward to visiting the city where Kate and he fell in love. Too many memories resided there, memories that would bring him more pain than pleasure. "I reckon Mattie will fancy her first bullet train ride."

"I am sure that she will."

Mattie sipped her tea, studying their hostess. "Thank you for inviting us for dinner, Akiko-san."

"It is our pleasure to have you. And thank you for teaching my class today. I am sure that my students will be talking about you for a long time to come. My students work so hard. It made me happy, to hear them laugh."

"Akiko-san?"

"Yes, Mattie-chan?"

"Can I ask you something?"

Akiko set down her tea. "Of course. Anything you wish."

"Is that your father?" Mattie wondered, pointing to the picture.

"Yes. Although he was a much happier man than he looks to be in that photograph."

"How old were you . . . when he died?"

"That was twelve years ago, Mattie-chan. I was thirty-four years old."

Mattie shifted on her cushion. "You seem . . . so happy now. How are you so happy?"

Ian had told Akiko about his wife's death, and the Japanese woman nodded to Mattie. "Not a single day goes by without me seeing my father's photograph and wishing that he was here," she said. "I will always miss him. But I have my mother and my students. My life is good."

"It is?"

"Yes. I am content."

"That's nice," Mattie replied softly, looking down, wondering why she felt so lost without her mother, why she couldn't be content like Akiko.

"Now may I ask you something?"

"Okay."

"Do you know what I see, when I look at you?"

"Me?"

"I see a girl who will soon be a young woman. And that woman, I am sure, will be like her mother. She may have her own children someday. And I think she will be so pleased."

Mattie looked up. "You do?"

"Yes," Akiko said, smiling. "My own life, I know, has been a changing of the seasons. My mother and I have spoken of this many times."

"How was your life . . . a changing of the seasons?"

Akiko glanced at Ian, who bowed ever so slightly to her. "I was a child in the spring," she said, "when the cherry blossoms filled the trees. And then the rains and typhoons of summer came, and sometimes I had to be careful. That is what I tell my students now—do not be afraid to splash in the puddles, but also do not forget to watch the sky." She paused to sip her tea. "In autumn, when the leaves yellowed and fell, I went away from home and studied. And then, years later, my father died. That was the winter of my life. I felt so cold. But my winter did not last forever. It is once again spring. And I am as happy as the songbirds."

Mattie looked to her father, her eyes tearing. He reached for her fingers and held them tight.

"May I tell you something else, Mattie-chan?" Akiko asked.

Nodding, Mattie looked at Akiko's big brown eyes. "Yes."

"Now, I think, you are in the winter of your life. But spring always follows winter, no matter how deep the snow."

"It's deep. As deep as a house."

"But it will melt. And after it does, remember that just as the seasons come and go, so will smiles and tears. What will you learn from the tears? How do you share the smiles? How can you honor your mother by being a good person? Those are the questions that we must all learn the answers to. And I am sure that you will learn them."

Again Mattie nodded, her fingers still within her father's grasp.

"Thank you, Akiko-san," Ian said quietly. "Your students are lucky to have you."

"Oh, I do not often share such thoughts at school. But here, among new friends, after a pot of nabe, it seems right to do so, yes?"

Mattie sniffed and turned to where she had set her blue backpack. She opened it, leafed through her sketch pad, and came to the picture she'd drawn of the cherry blossoms. Her small fingers carefully pulled the edge of the drawing, tearing the paper from the pad. "This is for you," she said, handing her drawing to Akiko.

Akiko bowed, taking the offering, surprised by Mattie's skill, delighted by her gift. "It is beautiful, Mattie-chan," she said. "You do me a great honor by giving such beauty to me. I am undeserving of it."

Mattie shook her head. "I'm glad you're happy, Akiko-san. And that you like my drawing."

"Your drawing reminds me of all those wonderful spring days. And I am going to put it somewhere special in our home. Where my mother and I can look at it and smile."

"Really?"

"Yes. And, Mattie-chan, please trust me when I say that you will be happy. That the snow will melt."

Mattie looked at her host, wanting to believe Akiko's words, repeating them in her mind. But she didn't know if happiness would find her again. She'd always longed to have a little sister, and that now seemed unlikely. She'd wanted to show so many more of her drawings to her mother but now never would. It was as if each of her childhood dreams had been turned into a glass bottle and thrown from a moving car.

Still, Mattie wanted to try to be happy, even though these days she was far more familiar with tears than smiles. And so she thanked Akiko again, sipped her green tea, and pretended not to notice that her father felt and acted the same way she did.

THE NEXT MORNING, A BULLET TRAIN LEFT downtown Tokyo, accelerating with breathtaking speed and grace. The interior of the train car that carried Mattie and Ian hardly seemed to move. Nothing rattled. No bumps or sways were felt. A girl walking down the wide aisle didn't have to hold on to anything. The train glided forward in an almost magical fashion, seeming to hover above the rails instead of rolling over them. Outside the long windows, Tokyo rushed past, cars becoming blurry, people nearly impossible to discern.

"It's like being on a plane, isn't it?" Mattie asked.

Ian stretched out in his chair, looking around, impressed with the mode of transportation. "It's better than a plane, luv," he said. "It's always right on time. There's no turbulence or danger. It's a heap more comfortable. And it'll get you anywhere in a tick." He pointed to an electronic sign at the end of the long, gleaming cabin. "See those numbers? That's our speed. When we reach the countryside those numbers will jump like roos in the bush. I reckon we'll hit two hundred miles an hour."

"Wow," Mattie replied, looking outside, then about the cabin. She couldn't believe how large the interior of the train car was. "It's like being in a spaceship."

"Kind of wallops the subway back home, doesn't it?"

"Oh, yeah."

"How about a bit of homework, luv? Remember, you're supposed to study three hours a day. That's the deal we made with your teacher."

"No, not now, Daddy. Please not now. I want to draw the train."

"We'll be in here for a while."

"Please."

He reached into his day pack and removed her history book, putting it on his lap. "Fine, luv. But when you're done, we're going to have a go at this. Joan of Arc, of all people, isn't going to run away and hide."

As Mattie got out her sketch pad, Ian glanced at the city. Skyscrapers were no longer everywhere, but scattered about. The train continued to accelerate, quietly powered by electricity. A pair of businessmen seated behind Ian and Mattie started to speak in Japanese, the sound of their voices pulling Ian into the past. He had overheard such voices a thousand times on the train, returning from work or dinner with Kate. They'd often eavesdropped on the conversations around them, trying to decipher nuggets of information.

Thinking about Kate, about nearing the place where they met and fell in love, made Ian's pulse quicken. He was afraid of what he would see. His days in Kyoto by Kate's side had been among his best. On their mountain bikes, they'd explored the city. On foot, they'd made almost daily climbs into the mountains behind their apartment.

Ian didn't believe that he would be strong enough to walk through Kyoto and constantly maintain his composure in front of Mattie. How could he look at something that Kate had touched and not be affected? Such self-control would be impossible. Perhaps years from now, when his memories had dulled, he'd be able to walk past the past. But not now. Not when he still awoke reaching for her. Not when she dominated so many of this thoughts.

Please give me strength, he said silently, closing his eyes, his thumb moving back and forth. Mattie needs me to be strong. Like I used to be. So please, when we're in Kyoto, don't kick me in the teeth. Don't let me fail her. I've failed her before, and I can't do that again. I need a fair go this time. Please give me a fair go.

Ian opened his eyes and glanced outside, surprised that they were already in the countryside. Shimmering rice fields dominated the floor of the valley through which they sped. Lush mountains rose in the distance. The mountains moved slowly to Ian's left as he looked at them, unlike everything nearby, which rushed past as if comprising a colorful tapestry that spun around the train. Ian felt that he was moving forward at the speed of light toward pieces of Kate, for to him memories were pieces of the people who made them. He mused over the letter she'd written to him, still unsure what he thought of her request. A part of him continued to resent her for sending Mattie and him on this journey. It seemed too demanding—both physically and mentally. What if Mattie became sick in India? What if she got hurt or lost? Why in the world had Kate asked so much?

A bullet train going in the opposite direction suddenly appeared. Even though the other train was well over a thousand feet long, it vanished in the blink of an eye. The view of the lush countryside once again filled the windows. As Ian glanced at an electronic map showing their progress, he realized that he was sweating. He swore to himself, pulling his shirt away from his stomach, which ached. He took off his black and green Statue of Liberty baseball cap and hung it from the seat in front of him. Trying to move his mind from their destination, he turned to Mattie, who was drawing a rice field with mountains behind it. "Good onya, Roo," he said, forcing a smile. "That's going to be a beaut."

Mattie looked up at him. "Thanks, Daddy."

"You're a bloody good artist."

She nodded, but said nothing, picking up a lime-colored pencil so that she could add a different hue to her rice field. Hoping that her father was still watching, she tried to move the pencil the way that she'd seen older artists sketch, her hand in almost continuous motion. When Ian turned his gaze back to the window, Mattie's pace slowed. She knew that her mother would have asked her questions about the drawing, wondering perhaps if the water in the field was cold, or if Mattie had thought about adding birds to the image. Her mother always asked such questions, always applauded Mattie's ideas as well as given her new ones. Her father usually just said that her pictures were pretty. He didn't have much else to offer, which made Mattie want to create fewer and fewer sketches. Drawing had given Mattie and her mother joy. And with her mother gone, that joy had been halved.

Mattie put down her pencil. "I'm hungry."

Ian turned toward her. "Oh. Well, can you wait for lunch? We'll be there in an hour."

"Mommy would have packed me a snack. She wouldn't have forgotten that."

"She what?"

"She wouldn't have forgotten some food for me."

"Easy on, Roo. There's a dining car down the way. Want to have a go at some sushi?"

"I don't feel like sushi."

"How about some noodles?"

"We had noodles for lunch yesterday. And they tasted like paper."

Ian sighed, glancing again through the window. "Do you want to eat or not? There's a heap of tasty treats on this train. Or we can wait and have a proper lunch in Kyoto."

"Let's wait."

"But you're hungry. I could get something for you."

"No, I'm okay."

Ian massaged his brow, aware that Mattie was upset about something but not knowing what. He could ask her, of course, but knew that she probably wouldn't tell him. Some pains she kept to herself, just as he did. "Do you want to open the notes, Mattie?" he asked, nodding. "Do you want to have a gander at what your mum wrote to us?"

"But I thought you wanted to wait until we got to Kyoto."

"Ah, I've waited too bloody long as it is," he replied, thinking about how Kate had asked him to open their canisters when they arrived in each country. "I've been mucking around, afraid of what I might read. But I reckon it's time for me to stop being a dimwit."

"You can be a dimwit, Daddy."

"Too right."

"You really want to open them?"

Ian reached into his pocket and removed two black film canisters. Both had "Japan" written on them in gold-colored permanent marker. One carried his name, the other Mattie's. "Here you go, luv," Ian said, handing Mattie her canister.

"Maybe you should read yours first."

"No worries, Roo. You go ahead. I'll wait."

Mattie nodded. Her fingers, darkened from the colored pencils, pulled the gray top off her canister. Inside was a narrow but long piece of paper that had been rolled up like a little scroll. Mattie studied the paper, her heart thumping faster. She didn't know what she hoped her mother would say, or even if it were possible for her mother to say anything that would make her feel better. Her colored fingers trembling, she unrolled the paper and squinted at the small, elegant words.

My Lovely Little Lady,

If you're reading this note, then I know you've gone on our trip, the trip that we were planning before I got sick. I'm so proud of you for going, Mattie. I know that it won't be easy. I haven't walked the road that you are walking, but I can imagine how it might be.

Now, as I lay here, I am imagining your sketches, your freckles, the way you can laugh as if everyone in the world were tickling you. I imagine everything about you. And when I think of you, I think of goodness, of a girl who makes me smile, both as a mother and as a fellow human being. I don't believe I've met anyone, Mattie, who has your heart. You're so young, yet you already know how to share your compassion, how to share yourself. You're far beyond your years when it comes to sharing, to so many things.

I love you so much. I loved you from the moment I felt you growing inside me—a miracle that I held in my belly and then in my hands. I've always loved you, and I always will. Some things might have been stolen from me, but my love for you is not one of those. It is without end.

Would you do something for me, Mattie? There is a trail behind the apartment in Kyoto where your daddy and I lived. This trail was created by monks two thousand years ago. It's beautiful and spiritual. We walked it almost every day we lived in Japan. I still walk it in my mind. Will you please take your daddy's hand and walk it with me? I'll be right beside you. You won't see me or hear me, but I'll be there.

And then, when you reach the top of the mountain and look down on Kyoto, will you do something else for me? The Japanese have an old tradition of writing their wishes on a piece of paper and tying that paper to a tree so that their wishes or prayers might come true. I remember seeing hundreds, maybe thousands, of white notes attached to sacred trees in Kyoto. The Japanese call these "wish trees," and they are as lovely and powerful as anything you'll see.

Please write down a wish, and tie it to a tree that overlooks Kyoto. I'll read your wish and do my best to make it come true. Ask for something fun, for yourself. And maybe also leave a drawing for me to look at. That would be wonderful, Mattie. That would make me so happy. Wish for something beautiful and draw something beautiful, and know that I'll read your words and see what you've created. I'll be smiling, wherever I am. And I'll love you as much as I always have.

Mommy

Mattie bit her lower lip, trying not to cry. She brought the paper to her face, holding it against her cheek. She shuddered, still remaining silent, but powerless to keep her tears at bay. Perhaps a time would come when she wasn't so often on the verge of tears, but that time wasn't now, not when, even with her father beside her, she felt so alone. She missed her mother so much that sometimes she felt as if she had died as well. Parts of her certainly had.

Her father kissed her on the forehead, drawing her tight against him. She could see that he was also crying, not because he'd opened his note, but because she had reacted to hers. He kissed her again and again, and she wrapped her arms around him and quietly wept. He whispered in her ear of his love for her. And his words helped. Sometimes he knew what to say. When she felt his scratchy face against hers and heard the sorrow in his whispers, she understood that he shared her feelings, and somehow this shared pain made her feel better. As the bullet train continued to dart to the east, her tears and shudders stopped.

"I love you, Daddy," she whispered.

His fingers traced the contours of her jaw. "I'm so lucky to have you," he replied, smiling, his eyes still red. "Do you know how lucky I am to have you?"

"No."

"When we go to Oz, Roo, on our next walkabout, I'll take you into the bush. And we'll look up at night, and you'll see so many stars. You'll see an ocean of them. And I reckon you'll want to reach up and touch that ocean. I know I did." He tucked her unbraided hair behind her ears. "To me, you're like all the stars that fill the sky. I'd be lost without you."

She stopped his thumb from moving. "Do you want to know what Mommy said to me?"

"Only if you want me to. Maybe we shouldn't . . . read each other's notes. But you can tell me what she said."

"Are you going to open yours?"

"Should I? Right now?"

"I think so."

Ian nodded, suddenly needing to see his wife's words. He opened the canister, which contained a note as well as a seashell that resembled a robin's egg. The shell was speckled with bits of orange and amber and was as smooth as a newborn's cheek. The note, written in her elegant hand, read:

Ian,

Thank you, my love, for going on this trip. I know that I've asked much of you, perhaps too much. And I'll be honest—I'm not through asking. In the days ahead I'll implore you to do more. And you may not like these requests or agree with them, but please think them through. I love you so much, and I'm trying to help you. The greatest regret of my life is not being there to make you and Mattie happy. That thought causes me so much sorrow. So, please do these things for me, because the thought of you doing them gives me some solace now, at the end, when I face the prospect of losing so much.

Will you please take Mattie and have a picnic along the Kamo River, like we used to? Knowing you, I'd guess that you've gone to Japan during the cherry blossom season. Maybe you can sit under a big tree beside the Kamo and watch the blossoms fall. Remember how we used to try and catch them on our tongues? I loved those days.

I've been thinking of you all night. I even wrote you a poem. I've got so many painkillers in me now that it's hard to know if my poem is worthy of you, but here it is. Hold the shell in your hand, and think of me. I love you.

The Story of Me

Fifteen years ago,
I rested on a reef
In the South China Sea.

One perfect day—
When the sky was but
A continuation of the sea—
A Girl found me.

This Girl dove deep to grasp me,
As she always searched for beautiful things,
And when she saw me
I became the focus of her world.

I traveled with the Girl after this day.

We climbed mountains.
We slept in rain forests.
We listened to ancient cities.

Much later,
The Girl gave me to
A Boy she had discovered.

Like me,
He was beautiful and wise and good.
Like me,
She'd found him deep down,
Where she least expected to.

When she saw him
She wanted to place him

In her pocket—
As she had me.

And now that he holds me
I am his.

Ian studied the shell, envisioning Kate diving down, into the warm waters of the South China Sea. He imagined her spotting the shell, grasping it, bringing it into the light. She had always loved such discoveries, and when she made them, he'd been reminded of the child in her.

Thinking about her touching the shell, Ian brought it to his lips and held it against them. He knew then that he would carry her gift until he could walk no farther. And even then, the shell would stay with him, a treasure she had found and passed to him, another part of herself that she had shared.

AFTER IAN AND MATTIE HAD ARRIVED IN Kyoto, they checked into their hotel and spent the day visiting some of the city's sights. Thinking of her mother's wish, Mattie had sketched one of Kyoto's most famous attractions—Kinkaku-ji, or the Golden Pavilion Temple. The top two levels of the three-story pavilion were covered in pure gold leaf. Two distinct rooflines separated the sections, curving upward at their ends. In front of the structure was a pond, which the Japanese called the Mirror Pond, because Kinkaku-ji's reflection was as elegant as the pavilion itself. The grounds beside and behind Kinkaku-ji were dominated by a lush Japanese garden.

Mattie had been startled by Kinkaku-ji's beauty. She thought that it resembled a painting, a wondrous image dreamed up by a mind long since gone. Two hours passed before Mattie finished her sketch. Beneath it, she wrote "I love you" and signed her name. As she'd worked on her sketch, Ian had sat nearby, watching her draw, knowing that Kate had asked her to create something beautiful.

They had been tired that night and had eaten dinner in their hotel, something Kate never would have done. Afterward, they went to the business center, and Mattie read while Ian checked his e-mails. Even though he had sold the company he founded, his former colleagues and customers occasionally had questions that he could best answer. And he often wondered whether his Realtor had anyone interested in their brownstone.

Sleep had come fast for Mattie, but not for Ian, who had drifted between conscious and unconscious thought. He'd dreamed about Kate several times and, upon opening his eyes, had tried and failed to keep the vision of her within him.

Breakfast the next day had been a hurried affair. Both Ian and Mattie were eager to walk the trail behind the old apartment. Though Ian harbored reservations about seeing the place where he and Kate had spent so much time together, he hoped to sense her on the trail. She had loved hiking to the top of the mountain and watching the city below.

Mattie didn't share his concerns about the day. She longed to see what her mother had seen. If her mother had loved the trail, Mattie knew that she would too. She was also impatient to leave her drawing and a wish in a tree. The night before, as she'd taken a bath, she had thought about her wish. Did her father even know that she still thought about having a little sister? Since her mother wasn't able to undergo another delivery after the trauma of her birth, they had often spoken about adopting a girl. In fact, they'd even researched how they might adopt a girl from China or India. They had spent several months studying the process by the time her mother had gotten sick. Then conversations about adoption had ceased, though Mattie continued to want a sister. That desire had only strengthened when her mother died, when she felt the weight of loneliness almost suffocate her.

Now, as Mattie and her father rode a surface train toward Yamashina, the neighborhood in Kyoto where her parents had once lived, she thought about the sister she'd lost when her mother died. In all likelihood, if her mother hadn't gotten sick, they would have adopted a little girl by now. They'd be a family of four. Instead she only had her father. And though she loved him as much as she could imagine loving anyone, she wished that she had a sister. With a sister at her side she would be so much less afraid of what might happen to her if her father became ill.

The train climbed, following the contours of a mountain. Mattie watched thousands of homes below, individual dwellings with blue tiled roofs and miniature gardens. Moving at the speed of a car on a highway, the train shifted from side to side on the curving tracks as Mattie studied people on the street below. Many children were present, clad in navy blue uniforms, moving together in packs. Mattie looked for a school, saw children filing into a large building next to a baseball field, and wondered what it would be like to be a child in Japan. Would she feel alone here too? Was there a girl in the city below who had also watched her mother die? Did that girl cry more days than not? Did she have a little sister?

Mattie glanced at her shoulder, aware of the weight of her backpack, thinking about the two pieces of paper inside. Would her mother really be able to see her drawing of the temple? Would her wish for a little sister somehow come true? Please, Mommy, she thought. Please let my wish come true, like you promised.

The train approached the station, slowing as an automated voice announced their arrival. Mattie tried to smile at her father but realized that his eyes weren't on her. Instead he looked toward the mountains, his face as blank as paper awaiting her pencils. He took her hand and led her from the train, following hundreds of passengers into the station. A few minutes later they emerged into the suburb. Convenience stores, a bank, and restaurants flanked the train station. There was also a slender five- or six-story parking garage that contained a few dozen cars and thousands of bicycles. The cars could be lifted upward on a giant revolving belt that allowed vehicles to be practically stacked on top of one another.

"Which way, Daddy?" Mattie asked, eager to walk the trail.

To her surprise, he still didn't look in her direction. "Straight ahead, luv," he answered softly.

They walked on a narrow road leading toward the mountains. Businesspeople and schoolchildren approached them on bicycles, darting toward the train station. Mattie glanced at the children and then back at her father. He'd been uncommonly quiet all morning, and she felt his hand perspiring against hers.

She tugged on his fingers. "Are you okay?"

His gaze finally dropped to her. "I reckon so," he said, his smile fake and forced.

They proceeded up the hill, passing women who swept doorsteps with old-fashioned straw brooms. No sidewalk existed, so they kept close to the edge of the street, aware of approaching cars. The street was too narrow for vehicles moving in opposite directions to pass one another, so one car would pull over to allow the other an opening. Drivers were efficient, maneuvering their vehicles within inches of concrete telephone poles, homes, and stone privacy walls.

The mountains above were lush, highlighted by blossoming cherry trees. Mattie saw that her father's gaze was fixed on a three-story apartment building ahead. The white building was dominated by rows of balconies, on the railings of which futons and blankets were draped. She watched an old man emerge from the top level and beat a hanging futon with a wooden paddle.

"What's he doing?" Mattie asked.

Ian didn't seem to hear her. "That's . . . that's where we lived," he said, his words almost obscured by a passing car.

"You did?"

"Your mum and me."

Mattie scanned the building. "Where?"

He pointed toward the middle of the second level. "There. I moved in with her. She found the place first."

"Can we go up?"

"No, luv. I reckon I can't do that."

"Why not?"

Ian felt his heartbeat quicken, a bead of sweat running down his chest. His thumb twisted and turned. His stomach ached. "Because that little room was our first home. And sometimes . . . sometimes there's just no going back."

"Oh."

He wanted to say more, but the power of speech seemed to have abandoned him. And so he led Mattie forward, passing the building, treating it the way he might Kate's tombstone. He remembered moving into her room, carrying his bags up the cement stairs. She'd met him halfway down and had kissed him, despite a Japanese taboo on such a public display of affection. They had entered her room, set down his bags, and made love as distant trains rumbled past.

Kate's apartment had been about five paces across and ten paces down, but its limitations only served to bring them closer together. They had fallen in love in those cramped quarters, brought together by walls and want and a world that had somehow conspired to make their paths cross.

Ian increased his pace, leading Mattie toward a canal that ran along the base of a mountain. The canal was lined with blossoming trees, and he was reminded of walking alongside it, arm in arm with Kate. Instead of turning so that he and Mattie might retrace those steps, Ian kept on the street, soon veering down a paved walkway. In a few minutes the alley ended, leaving them at the bottom of a mountain, near a bamboo forest.

He pointed to a trail ahead. "This is it, Roo. This is where your mum and I went on our little walkabouts."

"Let's go."

And so they went, following a trail that monks had hewn out of the mountain two thousand years earlier. The grove of bamboo soon disappeared, replaced by a combination of maple and evergreen trees. Rays of sunlight pierced the thick canopy above, revealing ferns, moss-covered logs, and a stream that the trail crossed over back and forth.

Moisture hung in the air, as if they'd climbed into the belly of a storm-producing cloud.

Mattie followed her father, pausing suddenly when she saw how a shaft of light fell to illuminate a series of stone steps in front of her. Above the steps, the forest loomed, lush and almost luminous. "Wait, Daddy," Mattie said, unzipping her backpack. "I have to draw this for Mommy."

Ian looked around, nodding slowly, becoming aware of the beauty that surrounded him, a beauty that Kate would have pointed out, just as Mattie had done. "Good onya, Roo," he answered, knowing that a part of his wife would always be in his daughter.

She looked at him, her brow furrowing. "Are you all right?"

"Let me see you draw."

Sitting on the decaying trunk of a long-dead tree, Mattie opened her sketch pad. She used a gray pencil to create the path, three different shades of green to fashion the forest, and a series of other colors to add the sunlight and the stream. Her skill as an artist was limited in that she accidentally exaggerated the contrasts of colors, as well as the features of her surroundings. A fern was too green. Tree trunks were too straight. But, still, a replication of the beauty in front of her began to emerge. And though the rays of her sunlight were too bold and bright, that boldness and brightness brought a sense of warmth to her drawing that might not otherwise have existed.

Ian watched his daughter's small fingers guide and discard her colored pencils. He stepped closer to her, putting his hand on her shoulder. "That's lovely," he said, bending down to kiss the top of her head. "And she's going to adore it."

"You think?"

"Since when didn't your mum love anything you did?"

"She'll see it, won't she?"

Ian glanced up through the treetops. "I don't know, Roo. But your mum, she believed that she would. And she was closer . . . to something . . . to an end, to a beginning . . . than we are. So maybe she understood something that we don't. And if she believed, well, then I reckon we should too."

"I believe."

"I know you do," he said, sniffing, his eyes growing moist. "And I'm glad you do."

Mattie finished her drawing, put her sketch pad in her backpack, and stood up. "Let's go."

The path led them upward. An hour passed before they reached the summit of the mountain, which offered an unobscured view of Kyoto. The city sat amid a lush valley, swaddled by mountains. Though much of modern-day Kyoto was uniform and ugly, other parts were dominated by ancient temples, shrines, and gardens. The Kamo River ran from north to south, spanned by a series of bridges that bore trains or cars. Even from a distance of several miles, the trains could be seen moving ahead, shimmering steel snakes that disappeared into tunnels or behind buildings.

Ian walked to a nearby clearing, remembering how he and Kate had picnicked here, drinking wine as the afternoons passed. Looking for traces of her presence, he sat atop a smooth rock into which monks had chiseled a series of Japanese characters.

"Do you know what it means?" Mattie asked.

"Yeah, luv. I read about it once. And I never forgot. 'Live to be content.' That's what it says."

Mattie nodded, studying the trees around her. "Which one would Mommy like?"

"You decide."

Her gaze swept from tree to tree. Though many pines were present, she was more interested in the maples, because they carried new leaves. They had survived the winter and were growing, were reaching toward the sun. Mattie walked over to a big maple that leaned in the direction of the city. "Does this look like a wishing tree?"

Ian stepped beside her. "If it's not, I don't know what is."

"Can you lift me, Daddy?"

"I'll climb with you."

He raised her to the bottom branch, which she grasped and pulled up on. When she had moved out of the way, he jumped, grabbed the branch, and followed her. She moved cautiously, having climbed only a few trees in Central Park. Not looking down, she continued on, careful not to break twigs or dislodge leaves. Finally, when she was about twenty feet above the ground, she sat on a large branch and reached for her father's hand. Ian positioned himself beside her, watching her face.

"Do you have the string?" she asked.

"Why don't you give me your papers, luv, and I'll tie them on?"

Mattie did as he asked, handing over her two drawings and her wish. Ian took the three sheets of paper, aligned them, and carefully rolled them up. He then used a piece of string to tie the rolled paper so that it looked like a scroll. Pointing to a wrist-thick branch that sprouted bright green leaves, he asked, "How about this spot?"

"That's good, Daddy. She'll see it there."

Ian tied her drawings and her wish to the branch. He used several pieces of string, so that no breeze would sever the bond between the papers and the branch. He thought of Kate, dying in her hospital bed, wondering how her daughter might send her wishes. And this thought provoked a new pain in him—an immense sense of love, loss, and legacy. He glanced at the sky, debating if the words Kate had written might be true, if she could see Mattie and him as they sat in a tree above the city. If there was a time when she could see them, this time was it. If there was a single moment when he wanted to sense her presence, that moment was now. It had followed him around the world, climbed this mountain beside him, and now shared the branch with him and Mattie.

"I love you, Roo," he said softly, kissing the back of Mattie's head, but continuing to look above. He tried to keep his grief at bay, but the emotion was too strong. He didn't feel Kate's presence when he wanted to feel it most. And so he cried. As did Mattie. He held her tight against him and they clung together, father and daughter, weeping for a woman who had loved and left them.

Ian wanted to believe in Kate's words, in the wishing tree, but try as he might, he couldn't. How could he believe in such goodness when that very goodness had been ripped away from him?

He knew, though, that Mattie needed to believe, that she couldn't soar if she didn't have faith. So, as he cried, he whispered to her about how much her mother must love her drawings. And about how her wish, whatever it was, would surely come true.

NEPAL

To Climb and Fall

"One who doesn't know how to dance
says the floor is crooked."

—Nepalese saying

Five days later, Ian and Mattie had seen most of Kyoto and its surroundings. They had visited Todai-ji Temple, the largest wooden building in the world. On the banks of the Kamo River, they'd picnicked and watched cranes hunt for crayfish. They had followed kimono-clad women who strolled on wooden sandals down cobblestone passageways. Days were spent sharing smiles with strangers, hiking to ancient shrines, sketching sights both new and old. To Ian, much of Kyoto had changed. And yet so many corners and crevices carried memories. They'd walked past a famous bar, outside of which Kate and he had first kissed. They'd traveled to Lake Biwa, where Kate and he had swum and camped. Unfortunately, the rebirth of such memories sent Ian careening into black holes from which he struggled to escape.

They had left Japan two days ahead of schedule. Though he enjoyed the country as much as any he'd visited, Ian simply couldn't stay in Kyoto. Staying in Kyoto was like setting himself on fire. And he couldn't do that with Mattie by his side.

The next stop on their itinerary was Nepal, a land through which he and Kate had hiked and climbed, yet a place where his memories weren't so crisp and common. They had only spent three weeks in Nepal, and though those three weeks had been wonderful, the Himalayas had overshadowed everything they'd done there. Ian didn't fear returning to Nepal as much as he had Japan, though he did worry about taking Mattie to a developing country. He felt irresponsible for doing so, given her age.

Now, as they sat in the back of a well-traveled plane, heading deeper into the heart of Asia, Mattie opened her film canister. She didn't know what to expect and was surprised when a diamond ring set in silver tumbled onto her lap. "What's this?" she asked, picking up the ring.

Ian smiled. "I know whose it is, luv. But I'd rather have your mum tell you."

"What?"

"Read her note."

Mattie held the ring in her left hand and opened a rolled-up piece of paper with her right.

My Marvelous Mattie,

What you hold in your hand was your great-grandmother's wedding ring. She wore it for thirty-nine years. When she died it went to my mother, and then to me, and now I'm passing it along to you. I know that it's too big for you to wear properly, but someday it won't be.

Your great-grandmother was a remarkable woman, as was your grandmother. They may not have made newspaper headlines, but they were extraordinary nonetheless. Do you know, my precious girl, that your great-grandmother aided in the war effort? She worked in a factory, painting jeeps, touching them up and adding white stars. And your grandmother volunteered her whole life, helping those less fortunate than she. I had planned on following in her footsteps, but this illness has derailed those ideas.

Someday, Mattie, you may have your own wedding ring. Choose it wisely, because I hope it will spend a lifetime on your finger. And choose your husband with even more care. Take your time. Pretend that you're walking with your eyes closed. Love should be savored, not rushed.

Do you know why I fell for your daddy? Well, it wasn't because he was handsome or powerful or rich. He was average-looking and as poor as a church mouse. But inside, Mattie, inside he glowed. He knew how to make me happy. From our very first encounter he made me happy. Think of all the times he prompted me to smile and laugh. Haven't you always known how much he loved me?

There is a famous saying about love, Mattie. It says that we were given two legs to walk, two hands to hold, two eyes to see, two ears to hear. But we were given only one heart. Why? Because our other heart was given to someone else. For us to find. I found your daddy, and he found me. And the same will happen to you.

I wanted, so much, to talk to you about boys and love. But I can't. So instead of those conversations I want you to have this ring. Remember who wore it, and what it means. And don't be afraid to talk with your daddy about anything. He's a wonderful listener, Mattie, if you need him to be, if you let him know that you'd like to take his hand. He'll help you. So, please, always go to him.

Did you know that when your daddy and I were in Nepal, we made up poems for each other as we hiked? Most of them were funny, but a few talked about those two hearts. When you're there, climb as we did, and be happy. Sketch something beautiful and smile at the sky. I'll be watching, as always.

I love you.
Mommy

Mattie held the ring against her chest. She reread her mother's words, then tucked the canister safely away in her pocket. She didn't cry. Instead she studied the ring, imagining her great-grandmother painting white stars. "Maybe, Daddy," she said, "I like to paint because my great-grandmother did too."

Ian nodded. "I reckon paint . . . it gets into your blood and stays there. And her blood is in your blood."

"Could you put this ring on a string for me, so I can wear it around my neck?"

"Sure, luv. I'll do that when we get back to New York. You can wear it and we'll go to a fancy restaurant."

"Thanks, Daddy."

"No worries."

"Are you going to open yours?"

"You want me to?"

"I think you should. Before we land."

Ian glanced out the window, looking for the Himalayas but seeing only clouds. He sighed, his stomach starting to ache as his heartbeat quickened. He thought about taking an antacid but, instead, opened the canister, and unrolled the little scroll.

My Love,

So, you've come to Kathmandu. Remember when we climbed the pass? We were so tired, so spent. We could hardly breathe. But the Himalayas made a circle of white castles around us. We were alone, and on top of the world. How lucky we were.

I worry about you both so much, Ian. I worry about Mattie because I know how she must be hurting. And I can't help her. I want to remind her of her blessings, of the gift that is you. But I can't. So, will you do that for me? Let her know that she's not alone, not in her suffering, not in her yearning. Maybe it would be good for her to see the poor in Kathmandu. Maybe she could learn from the collective angst that is a part of the human experience. I don't know. I'm lost. I've never been so lost in my life. Dying is like being in a maze while blindfolded. It's overwhelming. One of my few consolations is that I know you'll do this trip together, and that it will bring you closer together. She loves you so much, Ian. She wants to make you proud. Remember to tell her how you feel.

I wish I could visit those wonderful mountains with you both. Sometimes, Ian, sometimes you forget the beauty around you. I've had to show you, which has been one of the greatest joys of my life. But you can't forget now, because I won't be there. And you need to see the beauty that remains in the world—the beauty of the Himalayas, of the strokes of Mattie's pencils, of the people you will come to know in the future. So, please, go discover something beautiful.

Here are a few words to leave you with:

Beside You

Walking beside you,
I've heard music that stirred my soul,
Seen sights fit for the eyes of gods,
Touched you and known that my loneliness is gone.

Walking beside you,
I've laughed.
I've cried.
I've bled and loved and dreamed.
I've lived a thousand lifetimes,
Each one as precious as a child's smile,
As poignant as my earliest memories.

Do you know, my love, what I feel now,
as I approach my next journey?
I feel pain and sorrow.
I feel regret.
I am tormented by the echoes of roads untraveled.

But I would not trade away this suffering
if it meant never meeting you.
Because walking beside you is what I've always done best.
I've reached such summits,
Realms of light and wonder and joy.
And those moments and monuments will never be taken from me,
Not in this life,
Not in the next.

So, please, blow me a kiss from a high place.
And know that I'll be beside you—
Then,
Now,
Always.

Kate

KATHMANDU WAS AS IAN REMEMBERED IT—A CHARMING yet unornamented city located in the gentle hills outside the Himalayas. From above, the city looked like a rambling collection of three-story brick buildings. From the ground, Kathmandu's contrasts were more apparent. Colorful rickshaws carried tourists and locals. Blue tarps fluttered above stalls. Dark-skinned people clad in multihued robes and dresses hurried down narrow streets. Cows, monkeys, and countless pigeons were everywhere. The cows—sacred to many Nepalese because of their belief in Hinduism—wandered about without a care in the world. The monkeys gathered near temples, leaping to and from ancient rooftops, oblivious to the people below who photographed them.

Near the heart of downtown, where tourists tended to congregate, hundreds of Nepalese peddled their wares. Much of the goods catered to climbers. Though these offerings were almost inevitably knockoffs, no one seemed to care, as the quality was still good. There were rows of fake North Face jackets, piles of phony Columbia sleeping bags, and box upon box of hiking boots. As it was still early in the trekking season, most of the stalls were bereft of customers, which made proprietors even more aggressive than usual.

The foreigners in the city tended to be young, either students or adventurers. Ian studied them, noting how fit and strong and sunburned they were. These weren't tourists, he knew, but travelers. They carried battered backpacks and wore shorts and tank tops that revealed their muscles and tattoos.

As Ian and Mattie walked, hand in hand, near downtown, he glanced at her small frame and questioned the wisdom of taking her to such a place. He felt torn—pulled in one direction by his need to fulfill Kate's wishes, but tugged in the opposite way by his desire to shelter Mattie. What if she got sick here? he wondered, scratching at his week-old beard. What if something happened to him?

One of Ian's biggest fears was that he would die, leaving Mattie alone. Of course, he had reworked his will after Kate's death, and Mattie would be taken care of by his sister-in-law. Mattie would be loved.

But she'd suffer, no matter how much Kate's sister tried to make her happy.

Ian watched Mattie as they walked around a sleeping cow. Her brown Mickey and Minnie Mouse T-shirt made her freckles even more pronounced. A pair of blue shorts revealed slender legs that seemed to have recently sprouted from her tennis shoes. Her braids weren't as tightly woven as they'd been when Kate had worked her magic. Unfortunately, try as he might, Ian had never mastered Kate's skill of plaiting three strands of hair. And Mattie didn't seem to want to learn.

To Ian, Mattie looked so vulnerable. She was young and thin and innocent. What right did Kate have to ask her to travel to Nepal? Was Kate's mind clear at the end, with so many drugs swirling within her? How could it have been clear? If it had been she wouldn't have asked them to come here, where they were so far from help.

Though Ian and Kate had rarely fought, their few arguments had tended to be about risk taking. Kate had always pushed him, sometimes too hard. It was she who wanted to climb mountains, to travel like nomads, to move to New York without jobs. He'd always been more cautious. He didn't mind a degree of risk, but many of her desires seemed too perilous. And while some peril might have been fine when it was just the two of them, Ian wasn't pleased that he and Mattie had been led to Nepal, a place with few doctors and many dangers.

As they walked closer to the center of Kathmandu, the streets narrowed. Hundreds of black electrical wires ran from building to building, as if an immense spider's web had been dropped on top of the city. Ian glanced down an alley and saw a pile of trash the size of a minivan. Children were sifting through the pile. Ian started to turn away, but Mattie tugged on his hand. "What, Roo?" he asked, pulling her closer as honking cars maneuvered through the foot traffic.

"What are those children doing?"

"I don't know. Probably sorting through all that rubbish for food."

"For food?"

"Yeah, luv," he replied, bending lower so that he was at her level. "I reckon we're going to see a heap of that on this walkabout. A heap of suffering."

Mattie looked at the children again and shook her head. "But why?"

"Because the world isn't always a fair place. And those children might not have parents. They might not have homes. They're doing what's necessary to survive."

She bit her bottom lip, thinking about how it felt to be alone. "Can we help them, Daddy?"

"How do you want to help them?"

"I don't know how. But I want to."

Ian nodded. Since Kate's death he had wanted to help others, to share his wealth, to generate some good from the rewards of his work, which had kept him away from his family. Holding Mattie's hand, he led her into the stinking, closed-in alley. Three children stood atop the trash pile—two girls and a boy—sorting through the most recent additions. Their clothes were stained and ragged. They moved like little robots, tossing trash aside with economical, practiced motions. Ian guessed them to be about Mattie's age, maybe a bit younger.

"G'day," he said, stepping to the edge of the pile.

The dark-skinned boy paused in his work, then climbed down. "You lost?"

Ian started to say no but changed his mind, trying not to gaze at the boy's thinness, which made it appear as if nothing resided within his tattered shirt. "That's right, mate. We're looking for . . . for Thamel Street. We want to have a gander at the Rum Doodle."

"The Rum Doodle?" the boy asked, grinning.

"Might you show us how to get there?"

"Me?"

"All of you. You three."

The boy spoke in Nepali to the girls, who smiled and climbed down the trash pile. Ian was glad that they could still smile. He'd seen children who couldn't. Still holding Mattie's hand, he followed the children back to Thamel Street. They took a left, walking alongside battered cars stuck in traffic. The boy drifted back, closer to Ian and Mattie. "Your first time to Kathmandu?" he asked, pointing out a pile of cow dung that they should avoid.

"Not for me," Ian answered. "But for my daughter, Mattie."

Mattie glanced at the boy, smiled, but said nothing.

"Be careful of brown piles on the street," the boy said. "Stepping on one will destroy your day." Pretending to beep like a car, he passed a broken motorcycle and its passenger. "You need guide for mountains? I could take you. I could carry your pack."

"Oh, no worries. If you can just get us to the Rum Doodle, we'll be happy."

"You be happier after the Rum Doodle."

Ian followed the children, wondering if he should be taking Mattie to a pub, even if it was famous. "Will you do me a favor, mate?" Ian asked the boy. "Will you tell my daughter here about the Rum Doodle?"

"I never go inside before. I try once, but . . . but that was not so smart."

"That doesn't matter. I reckon you know all about it, and we might as well chew the fat a bit."

The boy picked at a bug bite on his arm. "People tell me Sir Hillary sign his name there. On the wall. So do Uemura, Tabei, Rob Hall. Many of the people who climb Everest. They have wall for them to sign. Even Jimmy Carter go there. But his name not on Everest wall. Jimmy Carter fly over Everest in his golden plane, but he not climb up it."

Ian looked at Mattie. "Tabei was the first woman who climbed Everest. She wasn't even five feet tall, but she climbed that bloody beast." He shook his head, remembering the story, which their guide had told as Kate and he had approached the world's highest pass. "She was Japanese," he added.

"Was she from Tokyo?" Mattie asked.

"No, luv. A small town to the north. When she was a little girl, people said she was weak. Quite weak, really. And so she began to climb mountains."

"And they still thought she was weak?"

"I reckon they changed their tune after she topped Everest."

She smiled and he squeezed her hand.

Their guides turned a corner, eased their way past a group of backpackers, and pointed to a nondescript door. "The Rum Doodle," the boy said. "You have good day, and no get lost on mountain. Then they have to rescue you, and everyone know, and you never get to go into the Rum Doodle again."

"Wait," Ian replied, reaching for his wallet, pulling out some Nepalese bills. He gave two thousand rupees, roughly twenty-five dollars, to each child. Their eyes widened at such wealth. "You're top-notch guides," Ian added. "And we'd like to thank you for showing us the way."

The boy glanced around, closing his fist quickly, hiding the money. "Thank you, mister," he said, shaking his head, not fully understanding how such luck had befallen him. "My friends thank you too."

"Good-bye, then," Ian said.

"Good-bye, mister. Thank you. So much. I will pray, every day, that you and your daughter have the long and happy life."

Ian watched the children hurry away, chatting excitedly. "That was a great idea, Roo," he said, playfully tugging one of her braids. "A real stroke of genius."

"We helped them, didn't we, Daddy?"

"Aye, my first mate. I'm dead cert of that."

"I'm glad."

"Me too."

He leaned down and lifted her up, hugging her tight. "Are you ready to go into that waterhole? Into a real pub? Do you want to see where Sir Edmund Hillary and Tabei wrote their names?"

"Can I get a Sprite? I'm thirsty."

"Sure, luv." He kissed her cheek. "We'll get two Sprites. But before we do that, might I ask you one more little question?"

"What?"

"Are you glad that you're here? In Nepal?"

Mattie glanced around. "I want to see the mountains. Where you and Mommy went. I want to draw something and leave it for her in another tree."

"You do?"

"In a tall tree. On a tall mountain."

He kissed her other cheek, loving her more than himself, wanting to show her the mountains but afraid of what the mountains might do to her. "Just don't get sick, luv. Or hurt. You stay hopping like the little roo you are, and we'll find a tall tree on a tall mountain."

THE BUS RIDE OUT OF KATHMANDU WAS exactly as Ian had feared, and without question it placed Mattie in danger. The interior of the bus was crammed with eighty or ninety people. Only the elderly were allowed to sit. Everyone else stood, shoulder to shoulder, swaying with the movement of the vehicle. People were so close to one another that they might as well have been the colored pencils bundled together in Mattie's art kit. Ian had taken one look at the compact mass of humanity and decided that Mattie wouldn't fare well. She'd only rise to the bellies of the passengers, most of whom were men. And he hadn't wanted to make her endure such an experience for the hour it would take to drive to Kakani, the starting point of their four-day trek.

With some reservation, Ian had decided to sit atop the bus, along with about thirty other travelers. A two-foot-high metal railing had been welded to the roof, providing passengers with a pretense of safety. Thinking that the railing was about as useful as an ashtray on a motorbike, Ian had been the first to climb up and had positioned his backpack at the front of the roof, directly over the driver. He'd strapped his pack to the railing and had let Mattie sit with her belly against it, almost as if she were hugging it. His pack contained all of their possessions and was about three feet long and two feet wide. Most of it was filled with clothes. If they were in a wreck, he figured, the backpack would protect her, acting like an air bag. He'd taken her much smaller backpack, as well as his day pack, strapped them to the railing, and sat behind them.

Many of the rooftop passengers had copied Ian's tactics, and soon the railing was padded with an assortment of packs, suitcases, bundles of wool, and rolls of carpets. Most people sat in the middle of the roof, spreading out on blankets. The Nepalese drank tea as the bus idled, filling the air with the scent of diesel fuel. The foreigners took pictures and tried to get comfortable. Three Western women sat near Ian and Mattie, applying sunscreen to one another as the bus finally got going.

Though Ian had continued to fret about the safety of the drive, Mattie's face brightened as they left Kathmandu. She'd never ridden on top of any vehicle, and the sensation of the bus moving beneath her was liberating. From fifteen feet up, the streets of Kathmandu had taken on a new perspective. She told her father that she felt like an adventurer, and feeling invulnerable as only a child might, she smiled as the bus dipped and rose amid the city's hills.

It had taken about twenty minutes to leave Kathmandu behind them. Now, as they started to climb into a low range of mountains, Mattie repositioned herself against the pack, holding on to its straps as her father had asked. The road began to wind its way up, following the contours of a river far below. The nearby vegetation was thick and unruly, dominating hillsides. Occasionally, parts of the forest had been cleared and were peppered with roadside stalls. Scooters and motorcycles tended to congregate at these stalls as people sipped on sodas or shared cigarettes.

The traffic on the road was an odd collection of smoke-belching vehicles. Ancient buses tried to pass one another on the descents, casting cars, tractors, and scooters aside. The buses were inevitably filled far beyond capacity and carried passengers on their rooftops. Some were occupied mainly by tourists. Others ferried Nepalese to and from Kathmandu. At one point, Mattie looked far below, toward the bottom of the valley, and saw the carcass of a bus that had careened down a cliff. Suddenly aware of how close their bus came to the edge of the road, she grabbed her father's hand.

Though the scenery continued to mesmerize Mattie, she was equally intrigued by the three young Western women who sat near her. They seemed at ease on top of the bus, moving in rhythm with it, the way they might ride a horse. The women wore shorts and tank tops, as well as a variety of rings and necklaces. Two had blond hair that they'd pulled back into ponytails. The other's dreadlocks bounced whenever the bus hit a pothole.

Pretending to study the landscape, Mattie watched the women. She was impressed that they didn't seem scared or uncomfortable. They were covered in mosquito bites, yet they hardly scratched them. Wearing oversized sunglasses, they laughed, studied a map, and spoke about their time in Nepal. Mattie listened intently, trying to follow their conversation despite the frequent honks of the bus or passing cars.

Mattie wondered if any of them had seen their father or mother die. They seemed so happy and confident. So strong. Though she tried not to be, she was envious of their smiles and laughter. If the nearby cliffs made them nervous, they didn't show it. If someone they loved had died, they had somehow managed to not feel older than they were. The women were everything Mattie wanted to be.

Finally, as the bus swooped down a mountain, the woman in dreadlocks saw Mattie looking at her. "Hi, there," she said. "Like it up here?"

Mattie glanced at her father, thinking that he might respond. But he only smiled, and so she answered, "I feel like a bird."

"A bird? How so?"

"Well, we're flying through these mountains."

The woman smiled, her white teeth contrasting with her black skin. "I'm Leslie. And you?"

"Mattie."

"Where are you from, Mattie?"

"New York City."

"Really? You're a long way from home, aren't you?"

Mattie nodded. "Can I . . . can I ask you a question?"

"Ask away."

"Does it hurt to have your hair like that?"

Leslie vigorously shook her head, as if she were a dog stepping from a lake. "See that? Doesn't hurt at all. It would only hurt if I tried to comb it."

"And your mother, she doesn't mind?"

"You know, she actually likes it," Leslie replied, scooting closer to Mattie.

"I like it too."

The bus rounded a corner, and Leslie reached forward to grab the bottom of Ian's day pack. "Sorry about that," she said.

"No worries," he answered, smiling. "Thanks for keeping my daughter company. I think she's a bit knackered of listening to me yammer away."

The stranger extended her hand. "I'm Leslie."

"Ian. A real pleasure."

Leslie looked at Mattie. "What brings you to Nepal?"

"I want to . . . to draw something for my mother. And climb a tall mountain."

"Well, you've come to the right place. I've been here fourteen months, and I've seen so many tall mountains that I don't know what I'll do without them."

Mattie nodded, not wanting Leslie to turn away. "Do you go to school here?"

"School? No, I'm with the Peace Corps. And so are my friends. I'm stationed in a city called Pokhara. Tiffany works in the mountains, in a village. And Blake, she's in Kathmandu."

"And you all . . . what do you do here?"

"We're here to help the Nepalese. I teach English. Tiffany helps villagers understand sustainable farming. Blake runs an AIDS-awareness campaign. We all started out together in Kathmandu, in our orientation program, and we've been friends ever since."

"And you like living in Nepal?"

"I like it, and love it, and hate it. Totally depends when you ask. Back in Pokhara, I might as well live in a zoo. My apartment is full of bugs and geckos. Hundreds of them. And I miss my family. And, you know, the Nepalese can be frustrating. Really frustrating. But still, coming here was the best decision of my life. Makes up for a lot of bad ones."

Mattie looked at Leslie's necklaces, which swung to and fro as the bus continued to snake up the mountains. To Mattie's surprise, a Nepalese woman sitting behind Leslie began to nurse her crying baby, holding the swaddled child against a swollen breast. Mattie lowered her gaze. "You miss your family . . . and you still like it here? Why?"

"Just a second," Leslie replied, turning to her friends. She spoke to them and then twisted back to Mattie. "When you're in the mountains, you'll see why. Are you doing the Shivapuri trek?"

"I don't know. Are we, Daddy?"

Ian, who had been listening to every word of the conversation, leaned forward. "That's right, luv."

Leslie nodded. "Want to trek with us? Sometimes it's better to travel in a group, you know. In case something happens. It's a lot safer."

"What do you think, Roo?" Ian asked, gripping her arm as a turn approached. "You fancy doing a walkabout with these ladies?"

Mattie glanced up at her father, not wanting to hurt his feelings. "If it's all right with you, I think it would be nice."

"Then I reckon we've found our traveling companions."

Leslie motioned for her friends to introduce themselves. Tiffany was slight, with an almost boyish body. Big-boned and tall, Blake held a guitar case on her lap. The women swayed to the contours of the road like palm trees in a strong wind.

The bus reached a summit. In the distance, much larger, snow-capped Himalayas rose to touch the sky. Mattie glimpsed the mountains, in awe of their proportions. Even as she smiled and said hello to Tiffany and Blake, her eyes wandered back to the peaks, and she wondered if her mother might be up there, atop one of them. Did her mother know that she was making new friends? That she would soon climb high so that they might sense each other?

Mattie hoped her mother knew the answer to such questions. She wanted her mother to see her, especially now, when she was trying to be brave, when so many parts of her were scared, when, despite the presence of her father and the three friendly women, she felt so alone.

IAN LAY IN THE DARKNESS, EYEING THE small room they had rented. The day's first light crept into this space, illuminating stone walls that had been painted white. A faded poster of orange-robed monks studying a bronze Buddha was taped to the far wall. A frayed ornamental rug covered the cement floor. The room was otherwise unadorned.

Turning to his right, he faced the same direction as Mattie, who was about a foot away. He'd zipped together two sleeping bags that they had bought in Kathmandu, creating an oversized bag that they could share. For months Ian had wondered if they should still be sleeping in the same bed. He was sure that most people would say she was too old to share a bed with her father. But most people hadn't seen their little girl lose her mother, and if sleeping with him kept Mattie from crying at night, from being scared, well, then he would gladly sleep with her. And, if truth be told, he enjoyed their nights together. He often read to her in bed, or made up a story. And when she rested her head on his chest and fell asleep, his sorrows were momentarily pushed away.

Mattie mumbled, still half asleep, instinctively reaching for him. *"Sssh,"* he whispered, easing closer to her, putting his arm over her shoulder. He thought she would go back to her dreams, but instead she turned to him, opening her eyes. For a few heartbeats she looked around the room, clearly confused. "No worries, luv," he said, stroking her brow with his thumb. "We're in Nepal, remember?"

She nodded, looking so young, far too innocent to have seen so much. He kissed a freckle on her nose. "Daddy," she said, "your breath stinks."

"Oh, sorry about that. Shall we get up and have a go at our teeth? Mine need a bath."

"One of mine's a teeny bit loose."

"Really? Reckon the tooth fairy could find you up here?"

Mattie scratched at her scalp. "She couldn't find me up here because she isn't real. I've known that for two years."

"For two years? No, not that long. A year, tops."

"For that long, Daddy. For at least that long."

He stretched his legs, enjoying the cool fabric of the sleeping bags. "Well, anyway, I disagree. About her being real, that is."

"What do you mean?"

"Your mum and I always slipped you a dollar, putting it under your pillow and taking your tooth. Just because we didn't have wings doesn't mean that we weren't fairies. A few times your mum even sprinkled a bit of glitter on the floor, leaving her magical dust. So if she wasn't the tooth fairy, I reckon I don't know who could be."

Mattie smiled. "Do you think Leslie is awake? Let's go have breakfast with her."

"You fancy that lass, don't you?"

"She's nice. And I like her hair."

He twisted Mattie's locks around his finger. "You want hair like that?"

"Would you let me?"

Sitting up, he pulled the sleeping bag down from his chest. "Well, dreadlocks aren't exactly my bowl of rice, but I want you to be whoever you want to be. Whoever makes you happy. You know, my mum and dad weren't too keen on me leaving Australia. And we fought about that. Fought like three cats in a sack. They're still quite vexed about it, actually. So I'm not going to tell you how to walk in your own shoes."

"But you don't like her hair?"

Ian smiled. "I think she's a beaut of a person, Roo. And because of that, yeah, I fancy her hair." He reached for his toothbrush. "Now, how about cleaning up, and getting a bit of chow so that we can start looking for our mountain?"

THE PEAKS THAT IAN HAD BEEN THINKING about loomed large above them. He'd climbed the Himalayas once, following Kate as she summited the highest pass in the world. That day remained vivid in his mind. He remembered singing marching songs to kill time as they rose higher and higher, into air that didn't seem to fill their lungs. A time came when they weren't able to sing, or even talk. And so he stepped where she stepped, their shadows merging when their voices could not. The world fell away beneath them as they climbed into the sky.

The trek with Mattie was far different from his last journey through the Himalayas. Now he followed her footsteps, and Kate was gone. And these mountains bore little resemblance to the barren peaks that had encircled the pass. The world he saw now was lush, as if grown in an infinite greenhouse. Deciduous trees of every shape and size bordered the trail, which skirted the contours of a large valley. Flowering azaleas grew in clumps around boulders and next to streams. The flowers were red and violet, and Ian knew that Mattie would have paused to sketch them had she not been beside Leslie and Blake. Tiffany walked alone, behind Ian, at the end of the column. The women all carried large backpacks and used worn walking sticks that Ian was sure had accompanied them on other treks. Tiffany and Blake wore bandannas over their hair. Blake had tied her guitar case to the back of her pack. Mattie was dressed in a khaki-colored hiking outfit that Ian had purchased in Kathmandu. He wore shorts, a T-shirt, and an olive-colored nylon and mesh traveling hat.

Mattie had been talking with Leslie and Blake for almost an hour and had been able to keep up with them surprisingly well. Ian wasn't used to staying silent around her but was glad to do so. Since Kate had died, he'd often worried that Mattie didn't spend sufficient time with women. He knew enough about fatherhood to understand that, try as he might, there were some things he couldn't teach her. And the closer she got to being a teenager, the more he worried about failing to provide her with a balanced childhood. The fact that she seemed so eager to talk with Leslie confirmed his suspicions.

Though Tiffany walked right behind him, and sometimes next to him, Ian hadn't spoken much with her. She seemed forlorn, unlike the previous day when she was first reacquainted with her friends. Ian was certain that something troubled her, but he didn't want to ask. And so he simply kept near her, sometimes glancing at her face, which was soft and unlined. Her sun-bleached hair was barely visible beneath the bandanna.

When Mattie started to laugh alongside Leslie and Blake, Ian felt awkward walking in silence beside Tiffany, who seemed smaller than her pack. As she came to an immense log that had fallen on the trail, he extended his hand, which she took until crossing the barrier. "It's lovely here, isn't it?" he asked, breathing in the scent of the mountain flowers.

She nodded, her walking stick in constant, practiced motion. "Usually."

"Leslie said that you live in the mountains. Is that right?"

"For more than a year."

"How's that going?"

She waved to a boy in the distance, who sat on the roof of a stone home. "It's going okay. The Nepalese are good people. And they live in a beautiful place. But life's hard here. Really hard. It's still winter in my village. The pile of firewood on top of my roof, which was six feet deep, is almost gone."

"Crikey."

"What?"

"Oh, sorry. 'Wow' is what you would say."

The trace of a smile alighted on Tiffany's lips. "This beautiful place makes for a hard life. That's what a local once told me, when I first got here. And he was right. And a hard life leads to some terrible things."

"Like what?"

"You don't want to hear about it. Trust me. Better to look around and enjoy the day."

"I can do both. Three things would be a real stretch for me, I reckon. But I can manage two."

Tiffany glanced up at him and adjusted her bandanna. "A couple of months ago, a woman in my village, who I was friends with, got married. And then her family didn't pay her dowry. And so her husband . . . he killed her. With oil and fire. And I . . . I was by her side when she died. And that was as ugly as these mountains are beautiful."

Ian looked again at her face, thinking that, like Mattie, she was too young to carry such a burden. "I'm sorry," he said. "That's bloody awful."

"It was. It is."

"Did you think about going home?"

"More than half of our original group already has. A lot of people can't take . . . certain things. Just a few weeks ago, a girl from Atlanta was found naked and screaming in a tree. Her parents came and took her home."

"But you're staying?"

"Yeah. I'm staying. This is something . . . something hard but good. And I won't leave until my tour is up."

She dropped her walking stick and he picked it up, which wasn't easy with the weight of his pack. "What you're doing," he said, "what all of you are doing is lovely. When I was your age, I was teaching English in Japan. For piles of loot."

"There's nothing wrong with that."

"No, but I wasn't out saving the world."

"Neither am I. Not by a long shot."

A herd of yaks approached—buffalo-like creatures that Ian remembered seeing at much higher elevations. The yaks were kept in order by three boys in dirty clothes who carried bamboo poles. The biggest yak had a shaggy brown coat, immense curved horns, and a rusty bell the size of a grapefruit that hung from its neck. The bell rang to the rhythm of the animal's footsteps.

Ian nodded to the boys. *"Namaste,"* he said, pressing his hands together and bowing slightly.

The boys grinned and returned the greeting. After they'd left, Tiffany turned to Ian. "You did that just right. How did you know how? I thought you just landed in Kathmandu."

"I've been here before. My wife and I did the Annapurna trek, fifteen years ago."

"Really?"

"My knees were a lot younger then. I doubt I could do that walkabout today. Reckon I'd have to hire a porter to carry me up."

"And your wife? Is she in New York?"

Ian looked to the sky, to Mattie. "She passed on. A storm blew in and wouldn't leave her be."

Tiffany put her hand on his elbow, squeezing it. "I'm so sorry. I don't know what to say. I'm sorry."

He kept walking, staring at the distant mountains, wondering if Kate could see them. "Might I ask you something?" he wondered.

"Sure."

Stepping closer to her, he whispered, "Do you think my little girl seems happy? I try—I try bloody hard—to make her happy, to give her hope. But I'm not always good at it."

"Is that why you came here? To make her happy?"

"Her mother wanted her to come. Us to come. But I'm not so sure. It's a lot to ask of a ten-year-old."

"Well, look at her now. She seems happy."

Ian watched Mattie as she spoke with Leslie and Blake. "I think . . . with her mother gone . . . she wants to grow up too fast. And I don't want to see that happen."

Tiffany nodded, a bead of sweat running down her cheek. "I grew up faster when I saw my friend. Saw what the fire did to her. So I know what you mean. Sometimes I wish I hadn't seen it. Sometimes I think that if she had to die, I'm glad I could be with her."

"So what should I do?"

"Let's catch up to them. How about a game? Something fun to pass the time?"

"A game. That's always a good ticket, I reckon. Many thanks, Tiffany. It's been a real pleasure."

"For me too."

Ian increased his speed, trying to remember one of the many diversions that he and Kate had used while climbing all day. He greeted Leslie and Blake, and took Mattie's hand, determined to make her giggle like a little girl. "Do you mind if I teach you a game?" he asked the older women. "It's something you Yanks invented, but I fancy it just the same."

"What is it?" Leslie said, looking for a walking stick for Mattie, as she had promised.

"A marching song. A trick to pass the time. Any dimwit can do it, which is perfect for me. All you have to do is repeat whatever I say."

Mattie looked up at him. "Please don't embarrass me, Daddy."

"Embarrass you? Like you did to me in Tokyo with those students?"

"Daddy!"

"No worries, Roo. I'll spare you. Now, ladies, shall we have a go at it?"

Leslie smiled. "Let's have a go at it."

Ian moved to the head of their column. "Remember, repeat after me. All together. And lift those knees high and swing those sticks. We're a bunch of soldiers, all right?"

"Yes, sir," Blake said, slowing down so that Mattie could follow her father.

Ian took a deep, melodramatic breath. "I don't know, but I've been told!" he shouted, trying to sound and move like a drill sergeant.

"I don't know, but I've been told!"

"That my jokes are getting old!"

"That my jokes are getting old!"

"My little Mattie, she tells me these things!"

"My little Mattie, she tells me these things!"

"She pulls me along with rubber strings!"

"She pulls me along with rubber strings!"

"Did you hear she likes Leslie's hair?"

"Did you hear she likes Leslie's hair?"

"One day they may have to share!"

"One day they may have to share!"

"Now someone take over this song!"

"Now someone take over this song!"

"My tired lungs are none too strong!"

"My tired lungs are none too strong!"

Still longing to hear Mattie laugh, Ian pretended that no strength remained in him. Gasping for air, he stumbled, spun around, grabbed at her, and collapsed to the trail. Mattie giggled, falling on top of him, instantly reminding him why he continued onward, when so much of him longed to close his eyes and rest forever. He hugged her tight, tickling her sides—her laughter an answer to his prayers, a constellation in the dark of his mind. Soon he laughed with her, rolling in the dirt, his pains forgotten. His little girl was begging him to stop, laughing so hard that she could barely speak, and few sounds had ever filled him with such joy.

THE DINING AREA OF THEIR HOTEL LOOKED to have been built more than a century earlier. The walls and floor were composed of crudely cut stones that had been cemented together. The once white but now smoke-stained ceiling was supported by thick beams that ran from one end of the room to the other. In the far corner, an immense stone hearth sheltered a fire that filled the room with warmth and light. A battered wooden table occupied the center of the area, holding candles, as well as Ian and Mattie's dinners. The two travelers were the only guests of the restaurant. Leslie, Blake, and Tiffany had opted for another hotel across the street, as a room there cost two dollars a night instead of the four that Ian had paid.

Mattie eyed the food in front of her, unsure what to think of it. She'd ordered *dal bhat*, one of the most popular dishes in Nepal. The meal consisted of steamed rice and a spicy soup fashioned from lentils, onions, chilies, tomatoes, ginger, coriander, and turmeric. She'd debated asking for pizza, which was on the menu, but her father had promised that the local food would be better than anything Western. The pizza, he was sure, would be little more than spaghetti sauce and yak cheese poured over flatbread.

"How far are we going tomorrow?" she asked, eating a spoonful of the soup, wishing that she'd ordered the pizza.

Ian sipped from a scratched bottle of mineral water. "A bit farther than we hiked today, I reckon. We'll head higher too."

"How much higher?"

"Oh, it should only be a few hops for you, Roo. A thousand feet up, so the guidebook says."

Mattie had managed to finish about half of her dal bhat when the hotel's proprietor—a woman who looked a decade older than she was—carried two pots to the table and scooped more rice and soup into their bowls. "You big girl," the woman said, her English as rough as the walls of her restaurant. "Must eat more to walk higher."

"Thank you."

The woman, who was dressed in brightly colored robes and wore her hair in a bun, smiled. "I have girl like you. Three girl. But now they old. Now they have babies. So many babies."

"How many?"

Their proprietor's smile revealed several missing teeth. "Fifteen," she said, rolling her eyes. "Before, I help daughters. But one day, my husband go into mountains to get wood. Big avalanche that day. Husband no come home. So I work alone in his hotel."

Mattie nodded, unsure what to say. "Your soup is good. Thank you."

"In Nepal, we eat dal bhat. Breakfast, lunch, and dinner."

"Really? That much?"

"Dal bhat make you strong."

"I'm . . . feeling strong."

The woman smiled again, patting Mattie's shoulder. "You have more. Then you sleep nice tonight."

Ian and Mattie finished eating, paid their bill, and returned to their room. The hotel was a rectangular building with the restaurant on one side and six rooms on the other. The stone-walled hallway was clean, its wooden floors polished smooth by the passing of countless feet. Ian walked past the communal bathroom to the last door on the left and inserted a key into the padlock below the doorknob. Their room was small and nondescript. They'd zipped their sleeping bags together once again, and the purple bags dominated the bed.

"Shall we read a bit, luv?" Ian asked, removing two flashlights from his pack.

"Sure."

"You change first. I'll go outside."

"Okay."

Ian stepped out into the hallway, the scent of smoke still reaching him. He wondered how the woman got her firewood, now that her husband was gone. Did she have to gather it herself? She probably couldn't afford to buy it. Perhaps one of her sons-in-law helped her with the wood. He hoped so.

After Ian reentered the room, Mattie eased into the sleeping bag and closed her eyes while he changed into his pajamas. He then used bottled water to brush his teeth, spitting carefully into a tissue that he then dropped in a rusted bucket serving as a trash can. Picking up an old copy of *Newsweek* that he'd purchased in Kathmandu, he lay beside Mattie and turned on his flashlight. She already had hers out and was reading the fifth book in the Harry Potter series, a heavy work to haul up the side of a mountain.

"Is our brave lad getting into his usual mischief these days?" Ian asked.

"He had a really boring summer, and now he's back at Hogwarts, which should be good, but he's fighting with his friends."

"Fighting with his mates? Why?"

"No one else believes that Voldemort is back."

"But Harry does?"

"Of course."

Ian smiled, pleased that Mattie was so engrossed in the series, which sometimes they read together. "It's not getting too scary, is it?"

"Well," she said, partially shutting the book, "maybe you can tell me a story later. A happy story."

"No worries, luv. You let me know when."

Ian leafed through his magazine, scanning letters to the editor, political cartoons, and an article about rising sea levels. Occasionally he glanced through the room's sole window, watching darkness creep into the world. Now that Kate was gone, darkness affected him differently. He thought about her more often at night, for once Mattie had been born, night had brought them together in ways that the day could not. If he wasn't working late at the office, after putting Mattie to bed they had often sipped wine and recounted the highs and lows of the day. Sometimes he needed to catch up on e-mails, and she paid bills by his side. But even in silence, they'd been together, keenly aware of each other's presence, grateful for the solace that this presence provided.

Mattie set her book aside. "Daddy, will you tell me that story? I'm tired."

"Aye, aye, First Mate," he replied, shutting off his flashlight. She did the same a few seconds later and the room further darkened. "Feels as if I have my eyes closed," he said. "Maybe this is what it's like to be a bat."

"But you can't fly. And you don't have radar."

"No, luv. Not yet. But I'm working on it."

"Why don't they have electricity?"

"I reckon they will, in a few years. That road we came up here on, one day I figure it will run straight through this valley. And then they'll have lights and idiot boxes and all that other nonsense."

"You like it better like this, in the dark? That's better than watching television?"

He pulled the sleeping bag higher up on him, careful not to move it past her face. "Sometimes it's good to remember our roots," he answered, feeling her feet brush up against his shins. "And idiot boxes don't remind us of that."

"Right."

"You know, your mum never had one. Not even as a girl. So she read books and poems instead. That's why she fancied poetry so much. Why she was always looking at things and describing how they made her feel."

"She was good at that."

"It helped that her mum was a teacher. I reckon they learned a lot together."

"Like Mommy and me."

He tugged gently on her earlobe. "Those toes of yours are like bloody ice cubes."

"They're freezing."

"Sure you don't want your own bag?" he asked, smiling.

"No way."

"So, I get to carry both bags up the mountain, and now I'm your electric blanket as well?"

"Can you tell me a story? Something happy?"

"About what? An animal? A princess? A girl?"

"Just a girl. A girl like me."

"A girl like you? A little ankle biter with frozen feet who tortures her father?"

"Daddy!"

"All right, luv. Just give me a few ticks of the old clock. I'll think of something. And I need to get my radar working here in the dark."

As her father thought about his story, Mattie continued to move her feet around the oversized sleeping bag, trying to warm them up. Somewhere in the distance, a guitar twanged to life. Mattie thought about Blake, and then her own friends back at school, wondering what they were doing. For some reason, she didn't miss them as much as she once thought she would. A part of her didn't want to see them. They seemed so happy. Their mothers were still alive.

Ian turned toward her. "That's a lovely sound, isn't it?"

"It's nice. Blake's nice."

"Ready for that story?"

"Aye, aye, Captain."

"Well, there once was a young girl who was ten years old and carried a sketch pad everywhere."

"Was she me?"

"No, I reckon not. But she was like you. In some ways, very much like you. Though not quite as ornery."

"How was she like me?"

"Well, drawing was her favorite thing in the world. And so she carried that sketch pad everywhere, often pausing in odd places, sitting at a corner to draw a stray dog, walking through a forest until finding just the right tree. Her sketch pad was one hundred pages thick, and almost each and every page was filled with something beautiful, something created from the inside of her heart. Some of her pictures were of people she loved, of her teachers, of her mates. She drew hearts on them and made their smiles too big."

He paused for a moment, listening to the rise and fall of the guitar. "One day she went for a walkabout, way up into the mountains. Her father went with her. They climbed up, higher and higher, through the clouds, looking for rainbows, for something she could draw. And they finally found something just right. A green valley was filled with grazing deer, and the girl opened her backpack, eager to bring the scene to life on paper. Only she realized she'd forgotten her sketch pad at home. She'd brought some colored chalk, but no paper."

"Oh, no," Mattie said, pulling the sleeping bag up to her chin. "How could she have forgotten her paper? She must have been upset."

"She was upset. She was a bloody mess, to tell the truth. And her father was too. He wanted to see her drawing. Her loss was his loss."

"So what did she do?"

"What would any artist do? She improvised, Roo. She wiped away her tears, picked up her chalk, and walked to a nearby cliff, which was made of sandstone. Its walls were like giant red chalkboards. And so she took her chalk and drew that valley and those deer. She worked on her sketch all afternoon. She'd never done anything so big or beautiful. And when she finished, she knew that she'd drawn her first masterpiece. Nothing in her sketchbook could compare. What she'd drawn on that cliff was . . . It was like a song that a musician had summoned to life. Something that had been set free . . . rather than created. And so, her loss that day turned into a gain, into something lovely and unexpected. Like a blue jay's feather found in the city."

Mattie edged closer to him, even though her feet were no longer as cold. "What about the rain? Wouldn't the rain wash away her drawing?"

Ian stroked her forehead. "She thought about that, but she didn't mind, I reckon, because she'd created something beautiful, and beauty isn't something that can be easily taken away. Her drawings, her chalk, would be washed into the earth by any rain. So her drawings would become a part of the earth. A part of forever."

"What happened then?"

"She continued to climb mountains and to sketch. And sometimes she'd bring her sketch pad, and sometimes she wouldn't. Her pad was a part of her, she knew. And it always would be. But she also drew on boulders, on cliffs, on cement. Those were her favorite drawings, because they gave her a sense of freedom. Years later, she became famous, a real beaut of an artist. People traveled from around the world to see her work, which was housed in the best galleries. And though the images she'd drawn on canvas and paper made people smile and earned her a heap of loot, she kept sketching outside too, in nature, where only her loved ones saw the beauty that she created. She would draw something lovely, and then rains would wash it away. And this happened again and again and again."

"She was happy, wasn't she, Daddy?"

"Yeah, luv. She was happy. Not every day, of course. No one can do that. She wasn't a dog with a wagging tail. But she had a good life. And she always drew, even when she was an old woman, when her hands didn't work properly. And her loved ones, those who still lived and those who had gone to heaven, they all enjoyed her work just as much as her father had loved her first drawing on the cliff."

Mattie smiled, resting her head on his outstretched arm. "Maybe I can get some chalk, Daddy," she said, her voice soft and shallow. "Then I could draw on a rock, like she did."

"If you'd like to. Whatever you want."

"Sweet dreams, Daddy. I love you."

"I love you too, Roo. I love you like that girl loved her chalk."

Mattie closed her eyes, imagining the girl in the story, wondering what it would be like to draw on stone, and to sit back and watch water fall from the sky and wash away her creation.

As if prompted by Mattie's thoughts, the rain came early the next day, enshrouding the valley in a mist that made her feel as if she'd woken up inside a cloud. After eating breakfast, she and Ian packed, put on their purple ponchos, and stepped into the elements. Waiting for them across the muddy trail were Leslie, Blake, and Tiffany. The women also wore oversized ponchos that even covered their packs. Leslie carried a red umbrella.

"Morning, ladies," Ian said, tipping his travel hat to them. "Ready for a little walkabout?"

Leslie smiled beneath her umbrella. "How was your night?"

"Well, we were knackered from our hike, and slept like a pair of old shoes. Roo here even snored a bit."

"Daddy."

"Or maybe that was me. Or maybe the snow leopard under Roo's bed. Anyway, shall we buzz off?"

Leslie motioned to Mattie to lead. "We'll follow you."

Mattie tried to smile, said hello, and started up the trail. She gripped her great-grandmother's wedding ring, sliding the ring up and down her thumb. She was glad for the rain, because she didn't have to try to hide her tears. She'd awoken on edge after dreaming about playing soccer with her mother in Central Park. As was true in real life, her mother had let her win, even though Mattie had never been great at sports. In the dream, Mattie had been so happy, laughing with her mother, enjoying her company. When Mattie opened her eyes, she was crushed to discover that she'd been dreaming. The sun and Central Park and her mother were gone, replaced by silence and gloom. Her father had noticed her mood and asked about it, but Mattie didn't want to talk much. Sometimes it was easier to just be quiet, to try to forget the dreams and walk on.

Because her father had worked most Saturdays, Mattie and her mother had often gone to Central Park to take walks, kick a soccer ball, or simply play in the grass and watch the day pass. While her mother had read, Mattie often sketched, trying to capture a bridge, a cloud, a leaf. She'd never been in a rush for those days to end. Sometimes they chatted while she drew. Mattie had always been aware that her mother actually listened to her, unlike so many adults. The questions her mother asked weren't simply ways to break the silence and pass the time, but attempts to better understand her. They'd spoken about everything from Mattie's desire to have a little sister to problems at school to how the great artists saw the world. Sometimes her mother even confided in Mattie—sharing her own desire to have another child, even though she couldn't. It had been Mattie and her mother who had first talked about adopting a girl from another country, something her father supported but might not have actively pursued otherwise.

Now, as Tiffany and Blake walked beside Mattie and chatted about Kathmandu, she watched the trail and imagined her mother climbing up these same mountains. She missed her mother every single day, but she particularly missed her after the dreams—when she awoke and realized that her mother was gone and wasn't coming back, no matter how much Mattie loved her and longed to lie beside her.

The mist thinned, and Mattie caught glimpses of the mountains above, which were green and rolling. She would have liked to draw them but didn't want to get her sketch pad damp or slow their progress. And so she sought to commit the peaks to memory, so that she might draw them later in the day. She wondered what it might be like to look down from such a high place. Can you see me, Mommy? she wondered, staring skyward. I dreamed about you last night. We were playing soccer and you let me win as usual. Oh, Mommy. I miss you so much. I know Daddy does too. We miss you and love you, and I just wish that you'd come back to us. Please come back to us. Please. I don't like being so alone. Daddy tries his best to make me laugh, and sometimes I do, but we're still so lonely.

The sky darkened, obscuring the peaks. Mattie continued on, breathing through her nose, feeling the moisture enter her. Thirty paces behind, Ian walked with Leslie, aware of Mattie's mood—wanting to help her but, at the moment, not knowing how. "Might I ask you something?" he said quietly to Leslie, who was in the process of shutting her umbrella since the rain had lessened.

She hung her umbrella from the side of her pack and turned to him. "Ask away."

"What did you think about . . . as a girl . . . when you were Mattie's age? Reckon you can remember?"

"You know, I don't think I thought that much about anything. I just . . . I played with my friends and went to school."

"Do you remember being sad?"

"No, not really. I remember being hurt, by my friends, by my brothers. But that wasn't the same as being sad."

Ian nodded, watching Mattie, who walked beside Tiffany and Blake, but was silent. "Sometimes I worry that Mattie thinks too much," he said, wiping sweat from his brow. "I just want her to be a little girl, and to do whatever little girls usually do."

"Yesterday she acted like a little girl, when you were on the ground, tickling her."

"I reckon so. But she had a dream last night, a lovely dream about her mum, and now I feel like everything's starting all over, like it always does. She's sad. She's missing her mum. And I can't give her everything she needs. Not by a bloody long shot."

Leslie's walking stick stuck between two rocks and she paused to pull it free. "You know, you shouldn't worry because she went from laughing one day to being sad the next. If she didn't laugh at all, then you'd worry."

He caught the scent of burning wood and glanced around for smoke. "Would you do something for me?"

"What?"

"Would you go talk to her? She asked about you last night, before bed. She fancies you. Quite a bit."

Leslie nodded. "She's a sweet girl. A really sweet girl."

"Maybe you could get her to laugh."

"Sure. But catch up to us. She might fancy me, but it's pretty obvious that she adores you."

Ian thanked her, watching her move ahead. He and Kate had often met such people while traveling the world—strangers whom they soon grew to enjoy and trust. Sharing a trail or a bus somehow bound people, perhaps because the massive, overwhelming complexity of the world had been condensed, bringing strangers together to share a space and an adventure. Kate and he had often reflected on feeling that they had more in common with a pair of fellow travelers from Sweden or South Africa than with their own neighbors in Manhattan. Traveling had always made Ian feel so very human, as if by sharing a trail with a stranger he were sharing part of himself, of his own life's journey.

The path reached a plateau, and the sound of rushing water found Ian's ears. He couldn't see a river but knew that one was nearby. The air, already so laden with moisture, seemed to get even heavier. He walked on, pleased to see that Mattie and Leslie were talking, that Mattie appeared to be moving faster.

After ten minutes of alternating his gaze between the trail and the Himalayas, which peeked at him through the clouds and mist, Ian realized that the women and Mattie had stopped. He saw that the path led across a three-foot-wide suspension bridge that had been somehow slung across the river. The bridge hung from two thick cables anchored into towers of rock and cement. The bottom of the bridge was composed of wooden slabs, while the sides resembled short chain-link fences.

"What a beaut," he muttered.

The river below was gray and full, fueled by runoff from the highlands. Boulders the size of tanks slowed down the mad rush of the waterway, which might have been a hundred paces wide. Moss and ferns covered the shore, making Ian feel as if green blankets had been draped over the entire area. He'd never seen so much green.

"Shall we have a go at it?" he asked, extending his hand to Mattie, gripping her fingers as the women went ahead.

"Can I draw it on the way back?" she asked, looking from one end of the bridge to the other.

"Of course, luv. I'd like to see you do just that."

"Is it safe?"

"You don't fancy a swim?"

"Not in this river."

He stepped onto the moist planks and led her forward, feeling the bridge sway slightly from side to side. "Feel like Indiana Jones?"

"I haven't seen that movie. Remember, you thought the end would be too scary for me?"

"Oh, right. Well, never mind. It was boring anyway."

"Daddy!"

At the center of the bridge, he paused, pointing toward where the river beat against a boulder, casting spray and froth into the air. "Think you could sketch that, Roo?"

"The water would be hard. It's moving so fast. But I could try."

"Maybe you could draw it for me."

"You want another one of my sketches?"

"I'm greedy, you know. Like Captain Cook with all his islands."

She smiled, stepping forward, now leading him. The remainder of the bridge came and went, and soon they stood on firm land. The path continued for a few minutes before turning into a series of steps that had been carved into a cliff. Mattie let go of Ian's hand, following the women up the steps, which were worn and smooth, polished from the passage of countless sandaled feet. Ian turned around, intending to take another look at the river. At that moment Mattie fell, her muddied boot slipping beneath her, sending her tumbling forward, her right knee striking the step ahead. She whimpered as she collapsed, falling and sliding down the stairs. Ian called out her name, catching her before she reached the bottom.

Mattie tried not to cry, but her knee was bloody and bruised and felt as if it had been smashed by a hammer. Ian cradled her, dropping to his backside, keeping her on his lap. She wept and he kissed her brow, kissed her tears. She thrashed against him, wanting his attention, but unable to bear the sight of her knee or the thought of him brushing up against it.

Ian continued to cradle her as Leslie hurried down the steps. Without a word, she opened her pack and found her first-aid kit, removing a large bandage, a bottle of aspirin, and some antibiotic cream. Seeing that Mattie wasn't ready to be attended to, Leslie opened up her umbrella and held it over the father and daughter. "You're a brave girl," she said, watching Ian kiss the top of Mattie's head.

"It hurts, Daddy," Mattie said, crying, arching against him. "It hurts so much."

"I know, luv. I know." He held her tight, blowing on her knee because that was what Kate had always done when Mattie had been injured. "That wasn't a fair match," he said. "Your little knee against that big rock."

"Stop joking."

"Sorry, luv. Just trying to take your mind off it. Do you want Leslie to doctor you up?"

"No, not yet. Don't touch it."

"No worries. Take your time, Roo. Just . . . listen to the river."

"Please don't touch it."

Ian continued to cradle Mattie until she nodded, and Leslie carefully applied ointment to the wound and covered it with a bandage. Tiffany and Blake tried to be as helpful as possible, using Leslie's umbrella to shield Mattie from the elements. "How far is it to the next village?" Ian asked, glancing behind them.

Blake knelt lower. "Maybe another mile or two. Not far."

"I'll carry you, Roo, to the next hotel," Ian said. "You can't do much hopping on that leg. At least for now. Or we could turn around. We could head back down and—"

"No! We can't go back. Not now."

"Are you sure, luv? You're cold and wet. And your knee is—"

"We can't stop! Mommy asked us to get to the top of a mountain. She's waiting for us there."

"But you're hurt."

"No! She's waiting!"

Ian sighed, glancing at Blake. "Another mile or two?"

"It's not far after the bridge. At least that's what the guidebook says."

Leslie started to unzip her pack. "We'll all take some of your stuff and lighten your load."

"You're sure?" Ian asked.

"Yeah. Absolutely."

It took about ten minutes to redistribute most of Ian's and Mattie's possessions into the packs of the Peace Corps volunteers. Ian thanked them, kissed Mattie on the brow, and lifted her up into his arms. "This is just like old times," he said, trying to smile, wounded by the sight of his little girl in so much pain.

"Old times?" Mattie asked, relieved that they would be continuing on, and holding back her tears.

Ian started to follow the women up the stone steps, careful where he placed his feet. "When you were a wee babe, you'd fall asleep downstairs, sometimes lying on a blanket, sometimes on the couch in your mum's arms. And I'd carry you upstairs, just like I'm carrying you now."

"Mommy didn't carry me up?"

"Oh, sometimes she did. But usually it was me. That way I could steal a few extra kisses on the way up. There's nothing more beautiful, you know, than kissing a sleeping baby."

Mattie wiped away her tears, embarrassed to have cried in front of everyone. "Why is that so beautiful?"

"Well, luv, when that baby is your baby, and you're kissing her, you just sort of feel at peace. No matter how hard your day has been, no matter what disasters happened, you realize that the most important thing in the world is in your arms, held tight, and that's a powerful thing."

"And you carried me to bed? Almost every night?"

"I reckon so, Roo. Even when I came home late. Your mum was sweet. She let me do that, because she knew I fancied it."

Mattie glanced below, realizing that he'd already carried her halfway up the steps. "Don't drop me, Daddy."

"Never, luv," Ian replied, glad that she was no longer crying, but worried because her knee seemed to be swelling. He doubted that she'd be able to walk the next day. They'd have to remain in one place and say good-bye to the women whom Mattie seemed to look up to so much.

THE DAY EVOLVED EXACTLY AS IAN HAD feared. He managed to carry Mattie to the next village, but by the time they arrived, her knee was swollen and achy. Fortunately, she could move her leg without much additional pain, so he doubted she'd broken anything. His guess was that she had badly bruised her kneecap and would need several days of rest before tackling the trail again.

Ian paid for a room at the best hotel in the village, which was really nothing more than a collection of stone homes and two-story buildings that bordered terraced wheat fields. The room was like the others they'd stayed in—sparsely furnished, cold, and inhospitable. Ian pushed the two beds together, combined their sleeping bags, and lay Mattie down. Leslie, Blake, and Tiffany were as helpful as possible. Leslie gently cleaned Mattie's wound, applied a new bandage, and gave her half an aspirin. On her guitar, Blake played the songs Mattie requested.

Since it was already past noon, Ian knew that the women would have to continue onward if they were to finish their trek on time. He didn't want them to leave, as he was sure that their departure would sadden Mattie, but he couldn't ask them to linger.

"You ladies should head out," he said, standing up from where he'd been sitting next to Mattie. "If you're going to make it to the next village before dark, you'd best buzz off."

Tiffany glanced at Mattie. "Are you sure you'll be okay? I feel bad about leaving."

"No worries," Ian replied, the taste of antacids dominating his mouth. "You've all been grand. Just lovely, really. We'll be fine. Right, Roo?"

"Right."

Leslie bent toward Mattie. "Is the aspirin helping?"

"A little. Thank you."

"I hate to leave you," Leslie said, straightening Mattie's pillow, "but if we don't get going, we'll never finish our loop. And, you know, we have to get back to our jobs."

Ian put his hand on Leslie's shoulder. "Don't fret about us. We're lucky to have found you."

Leslie removed a digital camera from her pack and handed it to Ian. "Can you take a picture of Mattie and us? I'll e-mail it to you."

"Lovely," Ian replied, waiting to aim the camera until the women had gathered around his daughter. He took several photos, aware that Mattie was trying to smile and that her smile was fake. She looked so small compared to the Peace Corps workers. She shouldn't have been in a dark and dreary room with them in Nepal, but with her friends back home. As Ian handed the camera back to Leslie and told her his e-mail address, he felt guilty about taking Mattie into the mountains, regardless of Kate's request.

The women lingered for a few more minutes before saying goodbye, hugging Mattie and Ian, and stepping from the room. Mattie began to cry. She pulled the sleeping bag up to her chin and turned away from her father. She had liked walking with the women and didn't want them to leave.

Mattie's misery caused Ian's spirits to tumble. Suddenly he didn't want to be in Nepal. He was angry with Kate for sending them here, for asking them to pursue the impossible. "I reckon we should just go home," he said quietly, sitting on the bed to untie his boots. "This trip is too bloody hard. On you. On me."

"What?"

"What if you'd really been walloped today? If you'd broken your ankle or fallen off the top of that bus? You shouldn't be here. You're too young. You're missing school."

"But I've been reading. I've been studying. Just like I promised."

He shook his head. "This isn't right, Roo. You're too little to be here."

"That Japanese woman was little. And she climbed Everest."

"She was heaps older than you."

Mattie moved away from his hand as he reached for her. "But Mommy wanted me to come."

"Mommy was sick. Really sick. She wasn't thinking straight."

"Yes, she was."

"No, she wasn't."

Her tears intensifying, Mattie pushed his hand away. "I'm not afraid."

"I know, luv. I know."

"And I'm not too little. Mommy wouldn't have asked me to come if I was."

"She didn't—"

"No!"

"Easy on, Mattie."

"You don't get to decide!"

"What?"

"You decided everything for Mommy, at the end. And that didn't work. So you don't get to decide this."

Ian leaned closer to her. "I tried my best. Just like I'm trying my best now."

"You let the doctors put those tubes in her! Even when she didn't want them!"

"I . . . I thought they would help. Don't you understand that? The doctors told me the tubes would help."

"They didn't! And you didn't listen to Mommy and you're not listening to me!"

"I am listening. Though I don't want to hear any of this."

"You don't listen!"

Ian rubbed his brow, trying to settle his emotions. "You know, Roo, I listen to you a lot bloody more than I listen to myself. If I didn't, we wouldn't be here. And those tubes . . . I wanted them in because I thought we could save your mum. Would you rather that I did nothing? I wanted to give her a fighting chance."

"She didn't want to fight!"

"You don't know that."

"Yes, I do! She didn't want the tubes! And I don't want to go home!"

Ian glanced toward the door, wishing that they were still walking, that Mattie hadn't fallen. His stomach ached, and he pulled another antacid from his pocket. "I understand that you don't want to go home," he said, chewing the medicine, his thumb moving against his forefinger. "But I still think we should turn around. This trip is too hard. On both of us."

"No, Daddy! It's not."

"But you're hurt. You're cold and crying. How's that good?"

Mattie shook her head, wringing the sleeping bag in her hands.

"I'm not going back! Not until we've finished. Mommy asked us to finish, and I'm going to listen to her. Even if you won't."

"I always listened to her. And to you."

"No, you didn't."

"Mattie."

"You don't."

"I—"

"How can you listen when you're at work? When you're gone all the time? Mommy was home. And she listened. I know she heard everything I said. Everything!"

Ian closed his eyes, wanting to shout but staying silent, feeling trapped in the small, cold room. "I did my best. Maybe I made mistakes, heaps of them, but I did my best."

"You should do what she says."

"I came here, didn't I? Even when I didn't want to."

"You came but—"

"And you know, Roo, this is tough on me too. I've been kicked in the teeth just as hard as you have."

"I'm not going back."

"Why not? Why are you so afraid of going back? We live in a lovely place, in a lovely country. We've got mates who would do anything for us. Don't you miss your soccer team? Your art teacher at school? Walking to the movies with me and stuffing ourselves with popcorn?"

She pulled the sleeping bag over her head. "I don't want to go back because I know Mommy's here. And I'm not going to leave her. I'm not ever going to leave her again."

TWO DAYS LATER, AFTER THE RAIN HAD subsided and Mattie's knee was no longer swollen and stiff, they left the stone room. They'd passed the time by going over her schoolwork, reading Harry Potter, and writing postcards. Through the years, Mattie had often sent Ian's parents postcards and she wanted to continue the tradition. She'd only met them once when they'd visited New York, and she enjoyed receiving their postcards and seeing different parts of Australia, a country her father promised that she would come to know well.

Her mother's parents were both dead, so Mattie didn't have many people to send postcards to—mainly her aunts, uncles, friends, and a few teachers. She sketched miniature sights from Japan and Nepal between her words, bringing her best memories of the trip to life. A bullet train navigated its way around her words on several cards. Mountains rose on others.

Mattie had also whiled away the hours by sketching her father as he leaned against the doorway. Exaggerating his stubble, she drew his face the way she and her mother had liked to see it—a happy face, with dark whiskers that meant he wasn't going to work.

Even though Mattie had been angry at him for wanting to head home, her anger hadn't lasted. They had agreed to continue the trip and had made amends in their own ways. Mattie had done her best not to complain about her knee. She didn't want him worrying about her, as she understood that her emotions tended to dictate what his would be. If she lay there and cried about her knee, he would be just as miserable.

And while a part of Ian believed that the trip was too hard on Mattie, he understood that she wanted to take it, needed to take it. His misgivings didn't vanish with the rain, though. He felt as if Kate was continuing to force his hand, and he resented being pushed in an unwelcome direction. For the first time since she had died, a full day passed without him looking at her picture.

The stress of keeping his emotions at bay affected Ian, though he pretended otherwise. Mattie watched him carefully, and he couldn't let her see his despair. His frustration, bitterness, and sorrow had to be hidden, buried deep behind a bright facade. If Mattie knew how close he was to breaking, what little progress she had made over the past months would be undone.

Ian remembered talking with Kate the day before she died, about how he would raise Mattie alone. He was afraid of doing so and had told Kate as much. What if he couldn't give Mattie joy and hope? What if he failed her as he had Kate? He'd worked so hard to provide for his family, yet his long nights at the office had only hurt them. If he had been around more, maybe he would have been a bigger help to Kate; maybe she wouldn't have gotten sick. And perhaps, as Mattie believed, maybe he shouldn't have pushed Kate so hard to fight. He'd thought that she could beat her illness, that she was strong enough to battle until the end. His love for her had compelled him to press her, but his love had misled him, because she'd listened to him, endured far more pain than was necessary, and died anyway. He had failed her when she needed him most, when he could have made her comfortable. And because of that failing, he didn't want to push Mattie to climb mountains or ace school or be someone she wasn't. He just wanted her to be content, if that was possible.

Now, as Ian and Mattie slowly ascended a mountain that was so lush it could have come straight from Tolkien's *Lord of the Rings*, he followed her up the narrow trail, eyeing fields of flowers near and far. Irises, orchids, and magnolias dominated uncultivated swaths of the valley. Herds of yaks and fields of wheat also loomed in the shadows of the Himalayas. The wheat fields were a light green, and appeared to glow in the sunlight. Bamboo fences enclosed the fields, which flowed from the valley floor to the foothills. Here the land had been cut into terraces, and the fields ascended for several hundred feet until the Himalayas became too steep to farm. The mountains were as lush as the fields, though a much darker green. Ian tried to compare the peaks to the skyline back home but realized that such a comparison was inherently faulty. The mountains were much, much bigger than anything Manhattan had to offer.

Ian lowered his gaze to Mattie. She was dressed in jeans and a purple T-shirt with a smiley face on it. Her hair was in long, fairly tight braids, a product of his determination. She appeared to move without pain, which delighted him. "You know, Roo," he said, "I don't fancy fighting with you."

Mattie's walking stick paused in midflight. "I know, Daddy."

"And when we do fight, I'm not trying to pester you. I'm trying to do what's best for you."

"This trip is best for me."

"Why? Why do you say that? What if one of us gets hurt or sick?"

"Like Mommy?"

"That's right. Like Mommy."

"But that won't happen. You promised me that would never happen again."

Ian glanced to their right, toward a waterfall that dropped from a crevice between distant rises. "Sorry, luv. You're as right as rain. That won't happen to either of us, just like I promised. But still, I reckon it doesn't hurt to be careful."

"I am careful."

"I know."

"So let's not talk about it, okay?"

He sighed and moved ahead. Pointing to the waterfall, he said, "There's a real beaut. Care to stop and sketch it?"

"No."

They continued forward in silence. Ian glanced ahead, knowing that if the day remained clear, they would soon be rewarded with a view of Everest. "I've got a surprise for you," he said, adjusting his traveling hat to shield his eyes from the sun.

"What?"

"Actually, two surprises."

She nudged him with her walking stick. "What, Daddy?"

"Just wait until we get to the top."

The trail, bordered by stalks of wild marijuana, twisted to the left, approaching a vertical section of a mountain that had stairs etched into it. The stone steps, of which there were several hundred, led to a crevice in the mountain. At the base of the steps stood a Nepalese girl about Mattie's age who wore a tattered blue dress. She carried an immense bundle of firewood on her back. A thick strip of canvas encircled the firewood and hung from her forehead. The girl had her hands on the canvas near her forehead, keeping it in place. She leaned against a large boulder near the bottom of the stairs, glancing up the mountain, and then at Ian and Mattie.

"Namaste," Ian said to the girl, placing his hands together and bowing slightly.

She smiled. *"Namaste."*

Mattie studied the girl, noticing how dirty and ragged her clothes were. Her dark hair was matted, long, and disheveled. "Hello," Mattie said, embarrassed to be carrying almost nothing and to be dressed in such clean clothes.

"Hewwo," the girl replied, still smiling, still holding the canvas strap in place against her sweating brow.

"Daddy," Mattie asked, "could you carry that for her? I don't think she'll make it up all these steps."

Ian was glad to hear the request. Though his own pack wasn't light, he felt that he could also carry the firewood. "Reckon I can take that from you?" he asked the girl, gesturing toward the wood. "I'll carry it to the top of these steps and then you can take over."

The girl's brow furrowed. "No understand. No speak English."

"May I take your wood? I'll put your strap around my forehead, like you've done. And I'll carry it up these steps."

Mattie saw that the girl was still confused. Stepping closer to the stranger, Mattie pretended to take the wood and put it on her father's back, on top of his large backpack. "He will carry it up for you," she said slowly.

The girl nodded, her eyes widening. Mattie saw that her knees trembled, probably from the weight of the firewood. Not wanting to waste any more time, Mattie helped the girl lift the strap over her head and set the wood on the ground. Mattie was surprised by the weight of the load, which she knew she could never carry. "Can you do this, Daddy?" she asked. "Maybe I could carry your backpack."

"And if your leg was in proper shape, I'd let you try. But no worries, luv. Just help me get that strap up on my thick head."

Ian dropped to his knees, and Mattie and the girl lifted the bundle of firewood, setting it atop his backpack. The girl took the strap and placed it over his forehead, so that his neck would carry the load, as hers had.

"Be careful, Daddy," Mattie said as he stood up. She did her best to help him lift the firewood, as did the girl.

"Holy dooley, that's heavy," Ian said, straining beneath the weight. He held the canvas strip in place against his forehead, clenching his teeth from the pressure put on his neck. Leaning forward, he stepped on the first stair.

"Maybe you shouldn't do this," Mattie said, pushing up from behind to try and help him.

"Rubbish, Roo. Now let's stop our yabbering and get this to the top."

"But, Daddy . . ."

"Come on, now. I'll race you."

The stone steps were wide and high. Ian watched the ground carefully, aware of the two girls behind him. Despite what he'd said to Mattie, he was worried, as his load threatened to pull him backward. Continuing to clench his teeth, he moved up the steps, glad that they were dry. As he struggled, he thought about the girl, wondering why she wasn't in school. Even though villagers were usually poor, their children attended school as long as crops didn't need harvesting. Ian was surprised that the girl was carrying a load of firewood in the middle of the day. Perhaps her parents were sick and needed help.

"Twenty more steps, Daddy," Mattie said from behind him.

"Is that all?" he answered, sweat emerging from his brow to fall to the stone stairs.

"Your knees are wobbling."

"You must need glasses, luv. I'm as strong as a mallee bull."

"A what?"

"A cow that lives in the Outback. Deep in the bush."

"You don't look strong."

"Well, neither do mallee bulls. But you wouldn't want to tangle with one."

"Only ten more steps."

"Thank goodness."

"But you said you were as strong as a mallee bull."

"That was ten steps ago, Roo. Times change."

"Daddy!"

Ian finally made it to the top of the stairs. He took a few steps forward and dropped to his knees, lifting the strap from his head. The girls helped pull the bundle of firewood from his back and set it aside. He moved his head around in circles, relieved to have taken such weight off his neck. "How far do you have to carry that?" he asked the girl.

Smiling, she shrugged. "No understand."

"Are you going to Nagarkot?"

"Nagarkot. Yes. I go Nagarkot."

He knew from his guidebook that the village of Nagarkot was less than a mile away. "Well, then, we'll see you in Nagarkot."

"Wait, Daddy," Mattie said, moving behind him and unzipping his backpack. She carefully sorted through its contents before removing a blue brush that had a picture of horses on the back. She looked at the brush, remembering buying it with her father before the trip. "Here," she said, handing the brush to the girl. "I think you need this."

The girl took the brush in her dirt-stained hands. "Me?" she asked, pointing to her chest.

"Yes. It's for you. That way, your hair won't get so tangled up."

"Me?"

Mattie smiled, closing her hands when the girl tried to return the brush. "Good-bye. See you in Nagarkot."

"Namaste," the girl replied, grinning. Bowing low, she stared at the horses on the back of the brush.

Mattie said good-bye again and followed her father up the trail, which went into a ravine in the mountain. They walked in silence, glancing behind on occasion to watch the valley below and to see if the girl had begun moving. After a few minutes she started up after them, proceeding slowly. The valley looked even more fertile from high above than it had from below.

"Why did you give her your brush, Roo?" Ian asked, his pack feeling lighter than ever. "I know you fancied it."

"Did you see her hair? She needed it."

"Well, you made her happy. Good onya for that."

"You think?"

"Aye, First Mate. I do."

The ravine they were following opened up. The mountain that had obscured their view for so long was now behind them, revealing the distant village of Nagarkot. The village wasn't much more than a few hundred stone homes surrounded on all sides by terraced farms. Miles behind Nagarkot, a row of snow-covered Himalayas rose into the blue sky. One triangle-shaped mountain stood above the rest.

Ian removed his backpack, set it on the ground, and walked to a nearby boulder, leaning against it. "Do you see that mountain?" he asked, pointing to the tallest peak.

"The big one?"

"It's Everest."

"Really?"

"You made it, Roo. You made it to the top of a tall mountain and you're looking at Everest."

She smiled, glancing around. "Wow."

"Care to see my second surprise?"

"What is it?"

He walked back to his pack, unzipped an internal compartment, and removed a roll of red fabric. He unwound the fabric, revealing two wooden poles connected in the middle by fishing line. Ian rotated them until they formed a cross. He then attached the fabric to the ends of each pole.

"A kite?" Mattie asked, smiling. "Where did you get it?"

"Kathmandu, luv. I had a lad find it for me when you were in bed counting sheep. Fancy having a go at it?"

"Maybe we can fly it as high as Everest."

"Higher than Everest." He patted her on the head, then tied a ball of string to the kite. The wind was strong, and Ian didn't think that they'd have any problems getting the kite aloft. "You hold it, Roo. And when I tell you to, push it up into the air."

"Push it hard?"

"Just let it soar. I reckon you won't need to do much."

"Okay."

Ian unwound the string, moving away from Mattie across the wide, level ground. He walked into the wind, stopping about a hundred feet from her. The wind tugged at the kite in her hands. "Let her loose!" he said, pulling the string taut as she tossed the kite upward. He stepped back, lifting the string above his head. For an instant the kite faltered, and he feared it would crash. But then the wind thrust itself against the red fabric and the kite leapt up. Ian whooped, walking backward, continuing to unwind the string above his head.

Mattie started to run, eager to fly the kite. But suddenly she stopped. She saw her father standing in front of the village, in front of Everest. The blue sky. The red kite. The biggest mountain in the world. And her father. All of these things were bundled together before her and she knew that she had to draw them for her mother. Without a word, she ran back to her backpack and removed her sketch pad. Soon she was drawing, using colored pencils to re-create the scene. Her fingers moved faster than they ever had. She was afraid the wind might stop, that the kite might fall. But neither happened, and soon her hands were stained blue and red and brown. She smiled as she drew, smiled at what she saw on the paper. Because what she saw was beautiful, was what she'd climbed so high to see.

When she finished her drawing, she took out a black-tipped pencil and prepared to write beneath her sketch.

Can you see us, Mommy? We're climbing. We've climbed to see Mount Everest. And it's beautiful. It looks like an iceberg in the sky. And we helped a girl. We carried her wood and we made her smile. We're trying, Mommy. We're doing our best. Can you say hello to us? We love you so much. I was so sad, two days ago in the rain. But I'm happy now, even though I miss you. I'm on top of a mountain, and Daddy is flying a red kite. He's waving at me now. He wants me to fly the kite too. So, I have to go. Just remember how much I love you. I hope you're happy in heaven.

Mattie

She turned around, searching for a tall tree that she had seen earlier. Soon she was running toward the tree, even though her knee still hurt. She passed the girl with the wood, calling out hello. The tree was larger than anything else around it. The Nepalese must have considered it sacred, because colorful prayer flags had been tied to it. Mattie didn't know much about prayer flags other than what her father had told her—that the Nepalese wrote their prayers on little flags and tied them to high places, so that the wind might carry their prayers upward. As soon as Mattie had seen the tree with the prayer flags, she knew it was a wishing tree.

Tucking her rolled-up piece of paper into the front of her pants, she climbed the wishing tree, careful not to disturb any of the prayer flags. She didn't climb higher than the rippling little flags, for doing so didn't seem right. Finding a crevice between two branches, she eased her paper against the tree. Only when she was certain that her drawing was held tight did she descend, pleased to have left such an image for her mother.

Mattie ran toward her father, her lungs heaving from the thin air. He laughed as she approached, and she held out her hand, taking the string from him. She was surprised at the strength with which the kite tugged at the string. "It wants to fly higher," she said, standing on her tiptoes to let the kite do just that.

"Can you blame it, luv?"

"No, I can't. I want to go higher too."

He smiled. "What did you leave in the tree?"

"It's a wishing tree. And I left a sketch for Mommy. A sketch of you flying the kite."

His fingers stroked the side of her face. "That's lovely, Roo. You're lovely."

She let out a gasp as a gust of wind yanked at the kite. "Help me, Daddy."

He leaned down, his hand gripping the string above hers. "You make me very proud, Roo—you know that? I reckon you couldn't make me any prouder. I'm sorry if I didn't always tell you as much. I know your mum did. She was heaps better at that than me. And she was right. She was right and I was wrong, and I'm so bloody proud of you."

Mattie smiled, moving closer to him. "You did your best, Daddy. And you carried me up the stairs every night. Even when you were tired."

"Carrying you up the stairs was the top of my day."

"Mine too."

Ian kissed her on the cheek, lifting her up so that she and the kite might be even higher. He raised her until his arms straightened, until she was closer to Everest and her mother and so many other wonderful things that he wanted her to feel.

THAILAND

The Land of Smiles

"BORROW FROM GRANDMOTHER TO BUY HER SWEETS."

—THAI SAYING

Ian,

Remember our time in Thailand, my love? Those three weeks were some of the best days of my life. You put me on the back of that old motorcycle and we drove around the country. We visited ancient temples. We swam with sharks. We made love on that beach with no name. It was just us—always. And that's when I knew that I really loved you, because I didn't need to talk with my friends or my family or even myself. All I wanted was you.

Will you show Mattie what you showed me? She loves nature so much, even though we were removed from it in Manhattan. Take her for a swim in the South China Sea. Throw a Frisbee on an empty beach. Laugh over a bowl of spicy soup. You can open up her world there. The Thais are such fun-loving people, even though many of them endure hardships. Let Mat-

tie see their suffering and their joy. She can learn from them. So can you.

It was in Thailand where I started to believe in reincarnation. The Thais were so good at that—they saw their ancestors everywhere. So when you're there, know that I won't be far away.

Here's a poem for you to read in paradise.

Within

How can I be pulled from you
When I am a part of you?

Does the sun ever leave the sky?
Or simply travel to illuminate another piece of it?

Does the wind retreat at the end of the storm?
Or depart to blow somewhere else?

Just because I cannot touch you
Doesn't mean that I cannot be with you.

Just because you cannot see me laugh
Doesn't mean that I cannot laugh with you.

I am within you, Ian,
Like the ocean in Mattie's eyes.
Like the unstained rays of the sun brighten the sky.

My death did not make me surrender.
I did not give up the right
To love you,

To be with you,
To watch you from near and afar.

So when you stand on those beaches,
When you feel that light on your back,
Think of me.
And our thoughts and love will mingle.

Kate

Ian rolled the paper up, and closed his eyes, feeling the light on his face. Beside him, Mattie opened her canister and read her mother's words.

My Sweet Mattie,

Remember how, before I got sick, I was teaching you how to snorkel? Well, your daddy is taking you to a place where you can snorkel and see so many beautiful things. It's like swimming in a warm bath, Mattie. And you'll discover a new world below you, a world that you can draw until you run out of paper. Drop a piece of bread in the sea and watch what happens. Watch it underwater. You'll be amazed.

Thailand is called the Land of Smiles and there's a reason for that. I don't think I've met a happier people. The Thais might not have new shoes or fancy homes or straight teeth, but they're happy, Mattie. Like you were. Like you'll be again.

You'll see a lot of statues of Buddha in Thailand. Do you know what Buddha said about happiness? He said, "Thousands of candles can be lighted from a single candle, and the life of the candle will not be shortened. Happiness never decreases by being shared."

Some of the people in your life will light your candle, Mattie. And I know that you'll take your candle and use it to light the candles of others. You'll be happy again, and you'll share that happiness. I understand that right now my words might not seem true. You may have more sad days than happy ones. But all things change, my precious girl, change like the castles in the sky. So when you're in Thailand, try to be happy, try to run free. Draw a picture for me in the sand and know that I'll be watching from above.

I love you,
Mommy

Mattie reread her mother's words, then rolled up the little scroll and placed it in the canister. She leaned back in her chair, watching the ocean below. Sitting near the rooftop pool of their hotel, she had an unobstructed view of the Andaman Sea—an infinite swath of azure-colored water that bordered an immense white-sand beach. Hundreds of red and blue umbrellas lined the near side of the beach, which was packed with thousands of locals and tourists. Though the beach was at least a mile long, very few stretches were free of people.

"What did she say, luv?" Ian asked, looking at Mattie, taking off his T-shirt so that the sun would touch more of his skin.

Mattie pocketed the canister. "She wants me to be happy. She talked about how Buddha said that happiness should be shared."

He nodded, thinking about Kate's poem, wondering if she was right, hoping that she was. "When you see statues of Buddha, Roo, you'll see that he's usually smiling. Even though his life was no picnic."

"What did Mommy say to you?"

"She said that she's still with us. And she wanted us to swim in the ocean."

"Should we go swimming? Right now?"

Ian looked below. The island of Phuket, which he'd grown to know so well with Kate by his side, was hardly recognizable. The dirt roads and water buffalo, virgin beaches and thatched huts were gone. In their place were busy boulevards and bars, cigarette boats and high-rise hotels. Paradise had been found and lost. In fifteen years. Where they'd once listened to crashing waves, horns and screeches now dominated the air, which, depending on the wind, sometimes carried the scent of burning plastic from a distant dump. Perhaps Ian would come to enjoy this new Phuket, this twisted version of what he'd known. But today was not a day for such discoveries. He would never feel Kate here, try as he might, because the world they had shared was gone.

He turned around, looking at the beautiful swimming pool, the lounge chairs, the unfinished drinks on glass tables. At least the mountains behind them seemed unchanged, green rises that mirrored the waves below. "I reckon we should buzz off for a different island," he said, shaking his head.

"Why?"

"Look at that street. There's a bloody Macca's on the corner."

"A McDonald's?"

"And a Starbucks, for the love of God. They've . . . they've kicked this island in the teeth."

Mattie scratched at a bug bite near her ankle. "How did it look before?"

He shook his head, handing her a pair of sunglasses. "You should wear your sunnies."

"How did it look?"

"Well, your mum and I, we used to stay in a little bamboo bungalow near the beach. There was only one paved road, and we'd ride it at night on our motorcycle. We'd maybe see a taxi or two, but that was it. I could switch off the headlamp and follow the street by the light of the stars." Ian reached into his day pack and handed Mattie a tube of anti-itch cream. "I don't blame the Thais . . . for this. They only want to make heaps of loot like everyone else. But still, I reckon we should go. There are islands farther from here, places that I hope are still the same."

"What if they aren't?"

"That would steal the wind from my sails, to tell the truth. Just like last night, when that little boy ran away with our laundry. But the deeper we go into the sea out there, the farther we'll get from all this madness."

"But it wasn't his fault. He was hungry. He needed the money."

"I know, luv. I know."

Mattie smeared the anti-itch cream on her bug bite, aware that her father would have rather given the boy some money, some job than see him steal their clothes. Seeing that had made him feel helpless.

As her father stared into the distance, Mattie thought about her mother's words, about how one candle might light another. "Let's go, Daddy," she said, standing up. "Let's find another island."

FIVE MINUTES INTO THE FERRY RIDE FROM Phuket to the island of Ko Phi Phi, Mattie was reminded of her experience atop the bus in Nepal. Though the ferry was much larger than the bus, most of the passengers had opted to travel on the roof. Almost all of the more than a hundred seats below were empty or filled with crates of Singha beer, boxed televisions, bottled water, pet supplies, and various nonperishable food items.

Since there were no seats on the roof, which had been painted white, people sat on their backpacks or used them as pillows. A few Thais were mixed in with the crowd, but most of the passengers came from Scandinavia, Japan, Korea, Israel, England, and Australia. Many travelers wore nothing more than swimsuits and sunglasses. Beers were consumed, photos taken, books read. Though several passengers listened to iPods, music wasn't heard, and people weren't boisterous. A common respect for fellow travelers seemed to linger, as people from all corners of the world set their personal preferences aside so that they could share an experience and the top of a boat.

While Phuket faded into the distance, Mattie studied the other travelers. She realized that she was the youngest passenger and her father was the oldest. Ages were sometimes hard for her to guess, but most of the people around her might have just graduated from college. There seemed to be many small groups of passengers—three or four friends who laughed together, drank beer, applied sunscreen to one another's backs. To Mattie's surprise, there were at least as many girls as boys. Some of the girls wore shorts and tank tops. Others repositioned their bikinis to take advantage of the sun.

Mattie studied the girls carefully. She watched them smile and laugh together, noting how close they seemed. The girls often had different skin colors but they acted like sisters—eating from the same bowl, looking at digital pictures over one another's shoulders, reading one another's postcards. Suddenly Mattie was jealous of their friendships. She'd always felt closer to her mother than to any of her friends, and with her mother gone, she had no one with whom she might share what these girls were sharing.

As she continued to watch the girls laugh and smile, Mattie's despondency increased. She wanted to be happy for her mother, and brave for her father, but for the moment she could do neither. She felt alone, even though she knew her father cherished her. What if he died? she asked herself, studying the wrinkles on his forehead. Her mother's wrinkles had seemed to deepen when she got sick, and Mattie often looked at her father's face, wondering if his lines of stress and laughter might also thicken.

She turned away from her father, gazing at a distant island that seemed to rise straight up from the sea. The island appeared lonely, with no others around it. Though the land was beautiful, she had little desire to pull out her sketch pad. Instead she removed her great-grandmother's wedding ring from her backpack and slipped it onto her forefinger.

Nearby, a girl lay back and put her head on her friend's bare belly, which had a tattoo of some sort. The friend said something in a language Mattie didn't understand, and the girls laughed. Mattie sniffed and turned back to her father. "Can we get something to drink?" she asked, seeing that almost everyone else on the roof held a can or a bottle. "Something that's not water. I'm tired of water."

"Aye, aye, First Mate. I'll be back in a tick."

"Maybe a Sprite," she said, watching him get up and make his way past the sprawled bodies around him. She noticed that, despite his age, he walked with a grace that most of the younger travelers lacked. They might have been shirtless and muscled, but unlike them, her father moved as if he'd been on a hundred such rooftops before. Mattie wondered how her mother would have looked on the roof. What would she have done if I'd put my head on her belly? Would she have stroked my hair? Would she have talked to me about my drawings?

Mattie was still asking herself such questions when her father returned, carrying two cans of Orange Fanta. "You didn't get a beer?" she asked as he sat beside her.

He smiled. "Why would I fancy a swallow of amber when I could have a Fanta with you?"

"But everyone else is drinking beer."

"And they'll be zonked and falling asleep by the time we hit shore."

"Oh."

Moving closer to her, he touched his can to hers. "Will you do something for me, luv?" he asked quietly.

"What?"

"Don't be in a rush to grow up. I'll miss you if you grow up too fast."

"Daddy."

"You don't rush through your sketches, do you?"

"No."

"Well, life is like your sketches. You'll see the loveliest things, you'll do the loveliest things, only if you take your time."

"I do take my time."

Ian sipped his Fanta, then tightened the drawstrings of his traveling hat under his chin. "My biggest regret, Roo, is moving too fast. Your mum moved at a much better pace."

Mattie nodded, not wanting to talk about her mother. After putting away her great-grandmother's ring, she glanced ahead and saw that a group of islands was materializing in the distance. At first the islands resembled little more than dark fins that rose from the sea. But as the ferry rumbled forward, the islands seemed to blossom. Colors and characteristics emerged, as if dawn were spreading its light on something that had been cloaked in darkness.

The limestone islands were unlike anything Mattie had ever seen. They rose straight from the sea, dominated by cliffs more than a thousand feet high. The islands were the shade of a stormy sky, though tinged with red sediment and partly covered in knee-high foliage. The bottoms of the cliffs were battered by waves and pockmarked with caverns. For a reason Mattie didn't understand, the water near the islands was a brighter blue than the deep sea. She wasn't sure if she'd ever seen such a beautiful blue. It seemed to glow—almost neon.

One island was bigger than its neighbors. This island, low in the center with a large beach, was dominated by an immense series of cliffs on either side. A few two-story hotels sprouted from amid clusters of palm trees.

"We'll do a Captain Cook and climb to the top of that cliff," Ian said, pointing. "From that high, Ko Phi Phi looks like a butterfly. The beach is its body. The cliffs are its wings."

"Can we climb up there right away?"

"Soon, luv. But it's best to go at dawn. We'll go before the sun rises tomorrow."

The ferry approached a cement pier. Ian didn't recognize the pier and thought about the tsunami that had swept over Ko Phi Phi a few years earlier, killing thousands of locals and tourists. He dipped his head and closed his eyes, praying for everyone who had died and those they'd left behind. He would have kept his eyes closed longer but he didn't want Mattie to inquire about his thoughts. And so he looked up and watched the island loom larger above them. Though it had been fifteen years since he'd been here, and the passage of time had dulled his reactions to a great many experiences, the sight of Ko Phi Phi still filled him with awe, for Ko Phi Phi was something out of a fairy tale.

Travelers around them began to gather their belongings. A beer can rolled atop the roof, nearing the edge. Ian started to move toward it, but Mattie was quicker and grabbed the can when it was a foot away from falling into the water. She carried it back to him and tucked it into one of the side pockets of his backpack. He smiled at her.

People began to disembark, and Ian and Mattie climbed down the stairs, made their way past piles of supplies, and stepped onto the pier. A few dozen Thais held signs with photos depicting various guesthouses. Ian had already made a reservation online and walked past the Thais, leading Mattie forward.

At the exit from the pier a different world emerged. Tightly packed within a space of three or four city blocks was a bizarre assortment of shops, restaurants, massage parlors, bars, and mini-marts. There were no streets, just a series of paths wide enough to accommodate baggage carts. Tropical trees, many of them banyans, rose far above the weather-stained structures. The trunks of the banyans—as wide as a king-sized bed—were wrapped in tattered red, blue, and yellow ribbons.

"This way, luv," Ian said, turning to his right and walking past a series of dive shops. Next came a half dozen restaurants perched above the beach. Outside the restaurants, lying in wooden boats filled with ice, were rows of red snapper, tuna, barracuda, mackerel, squid, shark, crab, prawns, lobsters, and mussels. Diners eyed the seafood, setting items on stainless-steel scales to assess their weight and cost.

Electrical wire was strung ten feet off the ground, from shop to shop, restaurant to restaurant. Some of the paths were paved with bricks, while others were just sand. Travelers from around the world shared the paths, many carrying large backpacks, many dressed in swimsuits. Thais hawked snorkel trips, massages, dinner specials, and full-moon parties.

Ian and Mattie passed a crepe shop, and then a bar with European soccer matches playing on three televisions. A variety of cats chased insects or sat in shaded spots. Bordering the paths were irises, birds of paradise, bougainvillea, and delicate white flowers that resembled exploding fireworks. Clusters of bamboo rose like tufts of hair on a giant's scalp. Hanging from many of these clusters were delicate cages containing brightly colored birds.

The air was heavy—full of moisture, heat, and the scent of vegetation. Hammocks were slung between eucalyptus trees. Children rode bicycles with training wheels. The absence of cars, scooters, and engine-powered vehicles helped maintain a sense of tranquility. Looming above everything, the massive wings of the island rose to touch scattered clouds.

Mattie gazed around in wonder. She didn't know what to think. For the second time on their trip, she felt as if she were Alice falling into the rabbit's hole. She followed her father as he turned left, toward the middle of the island. Soon they walked amid rows of wooden bungalows, many of them highlighted by high-peaked roofs that curved and flared out at the bottom. Most of the bungalows didn't look well made. Perhaps they'd already withstood too many storms.

Mattie was surprised by how the locals dressed. The majority were clad in simple shorts and T-shirts, but Muslim women wore robes and head scarves. She'd heard some bad things about Muslims, but these people smiled at her and said hello in Thai. She returned their greetings and walked ahead, feeling lighter on her feet.

Though she didn't hold her father's hand as often as she once did, Mattie reached over and took his fingers in hers. "Daddy?"

"What, luv?"

"I'm not in a rush to grow up. So don't worry about that."

He smiled, pulling her closer. "What made you say that?"

"I like this place."

"Me too."

She spotted an immense, multicolored caterpillar on the ground and was careful to step around it. "Mommy asked me to draw her a picture in the sand."

"She did?"

"Is there an empty beach here? With no people? I want to draw her something big."

Ian nodded, glad that she had reached out to him. "I'm going to show you some sights tomorrow, Roo. Some sights that will make you smile. Then I'll take you to one of the loveliest beaches in the world. And we'll be all alone." He turned right, heading toward a group of newer bungalows. "But how are you going to draw something so big? Won't your feet leave footprints?"

"I'm going to use my feet, Daddy. That's how I'll draw."

"With your feet?"

"You'll see."

He adjusted his backpack, moving the straps away from sore spots on his shoulders. "I'll make you a deal, Roo."

"What deal?"

"We'll check in, finish those postcards we started on the plane, work on your math for two turns of the old clock, and then have dinner on the beach."

"Two hours? But, Daddy, you said we'd do a Captain Cook."

"And we will. But do you think our old mate sailed around the world without being a wizard at his numbers?"

"He—"

"And, speaking of wizards, I reckon that young Mr. Potter knows his figures too."

She shrugged, glancing at the cliffs above them. "How about an hour?"

"How about two, and dinner and dessert on the beach? And then we'll watch the sun wave good-bye."

"Can you fix my braids while I study? Like Mommy used to?"

"Sure thing, Roo. I'd fancy that."

She hopped over a puddle. "Don't you think that doing homework is making me grow up faster?"

He chuckled, raising his hand with hers as she jumped over the next puddle. "I reckon not, luv. But nice try. I may be a dimwit, but I'm not a zero wit."

"Daddy."

"Doing your homework is just preparing you to be a grown-up, so that you can have heaps of fun when your hair starts to turn gray."

"And you think grown-ups have fun? Back home, all you do is e-mail and have conference calls, and I don't think it looks fun. Boring, boring, boring."

"Your boring old father will show you some fun," Ian replied, laughing, continuing to hold her hand as he increased their pace, as he tried to leap over an immense puddle in the middle of the path. His sandaled feet landed about halfway across, splashing their legs with warm brown water. Mattie giggled as he kicked the water at her. She splashed him back, soiling his shorts and shirt. Several passing Thais laughed at the spectacle, prompting Mattie to kick even harder. For the moment she forgot about her homework and her mother and her sadness. She was happy to be playing in a puddle, happy when her father picked her up, threw her over his shoulder, and hurried toward the nearby sea.

THE OPEN-AIR RESTAURANT WAS PERCHED SEVERAL HUNDRED feet from the water, at the edge of the main beach. Almost everything, from the ceiling to the fans to the tables and floor, was fashioned from bamboo. The tables were covered with green silk and held bottles of chili sauce, pepper, and salt. Small paper napkins rose from the tops of plastic tissue boxes. The ceiling rafters were bordered by strings of Christmas lights. American Top-40 music played in the background as waitresses moved around, setting plates of steaming seafood in front of travelers from all over the globe. The seafood was prepared however the patrons wanted—shrimp served with sweet and sour sauce, shark steaks grilled with lemon and butter, squid added to fried rice. Most everyone was dressed in shorts, T-shirts, and sandals. People seemed to drink either Singha beer or fruit smoothies. Birds chirped in a nearby banyan tree while mosquito coils sent smoke wafting into the air. Geckos clung to the ceiling, remaining still until unsuspecting ants approached.

On the beach in front of the restaurant, travelers and locals enjoyed the coolness of the early evening. A group of about twenty Thai boys and a few foreigners played soccer on a vast stretch of sand. Two Thai men threw a Frisbee back and forth, separated by a distance of almost a football field. The Thais were extraordinarily athletic, leaping to kick the approaching Frisbee higher, then tapping it up and up with their heads, their hands, their elbows. They threw and played with the Frisbee as if it were a part of themselves that they could launch and catch with the greatest ease.

On either side of the beach, the immense butterfly-wing cliffs of the island rose hundreds of feet high. The cliffs were almost completely vertical, jutting out of the sand and sea with surreal precision. The sun had started descending toward the distant horizon, a subtle line between blue and blue, separating the sea and sky.

In the middle of the restaurant sat Ian and Mattie. Between them on the table lay a large red snapper that had been grilled. The fish's fins, scales, and eyes were blackened from the flames, but its flesh was white and moist. Ian squeezed an additional lemon on the fish as he carefully pulled back its skin, which was covered in lemongrass and chilies. "Roo, would you hand me that pepper?" he asked, breathing in deeply, enjoying the scent of the fish and the humid air.

"Aye, aye, Captain."

Ian sprinkled pepper, then salt on the fish. "Ready to have a go at it, luv?"

"It looks weird," she answered, sipping on her watermelon smoothie.

"Too right. But that's how they cook fish over here. And I reckon it will taste the same, or better, than any fish you had back home."

"Just don't give me its eyes."

"I thought I'd eat those. Pop them into my mouth like candy. Like those little beauties that Elliott gave E.T."

"E.T. was a lot smarter than you. He wouldn't eat any fish eyes."

"Well, I reckon that's his loss."

"Yuck."

He smiled, cutting up the fish, then placing a piece on her plate. He also served her a scoop of steaming white rice and some grilled asparagus. "Hard to believe that all this costs less than what we'd spend at Macca's back home."

"Do they have Happy Meals here too?" Mattie asked, grinning.

Ian sipped on his Singha beer, remembering how he and Kate used to peel off the damp labels and stick them to the covers of books. He took a bite of the snapper, which was spicy and sweet. As he wondered what other seasonings had been added to the fish, he noticed a Western man and a Thai girl of maybe sixteen sitting in the corner. The girl was dressed in a yellow T-shirt and white shorts. Her shoulder-length black hair was unbound. By any account she was beautiful, her features soft and pleasing. Ian thought it was odd how close the man and girl were sitting together, at least until he saw him caress her leg under the table.

Ian's pulse quickened. He'd witnessed many similar sights in Bangkok and in some of Thailand's other large cities, but never in a place like Ko Phi Phi. The man, gray-haired and appearing to be in his late fifties, had probably come to Thailand to seek pleasure in the company of a teenage girl. Thousands of such men traveled to Thailand each year, pursuing fantasies that they could never experience back home. On their earlier trip, Kate had accosted a sex tourist who was arm in arm with two young girls, and memories of that incident flooded back to Ian. He hadn't been as upset as Kate, but now, as he studied the girl in the yellow shirt, he thought about Mattie. There was a good chance that this girl's parents, likely poor farmers from the north, had been duped by child traffickers. These criminals often paid a small amount of money to parents, promising jobs for their daughters in hotels or restaurants. The girls were trucked to Bangkok and forced into the sex trade. Few ever made it home.

Continuing to watch the girl, Ian thought about Mattie's sadness at the loss of her mother. What would it be like to be so young and taken from both parents? To be made into a prostitute? His stomach began to ache as he asked himself such questions. He wondered if the girl was dead inside. Perhaps she'd only recently entered the sex trade and could still be saved.

Ian pulled an antacid from his pocket and munched on the medicine, answering a question from Mattie, but looking beyond her toward the girl. Sweat beaded on his back and dampened his shirt. He thought again about Mattie, imagining someone stealing her from him and forcing her into such a life. The thought made him angry, and his stomach clenched with increasing intensity.

The Westerner ordered a large Singha and continued to occasionally fondle the girl's leg. Ian's heart raced. He drank from his own beer to settle his nerves. Eating quickly, he tried to engage Mattie in conversation, even though he wasn't really listening. She'd sense his indifference and be upset by it, but for the moment, he didn't consider her feelings. Somehow he needed to help the girl.

Ian finished what remained of the fish and paid the bill. Mattie prepared to leave, but he wasn't ready to go, and removed a deck of cards from his day pack and asked her if she'd like to challenge him to a game of blackjack. She looked annoyed but nodded and began to shuffle the cards. He watched the girl as they played, as Mattie beat him. A second and third antacid were consumed. He wiped sweat from his brow.

After about twenty minutes, the man handed the girl a set of keys. She got up from the table and started to make her way out of the restaurant. The man opened a fresh beer as Ian's heart hammered away at his chest. "Let's go, Roo," he said quietly.

"What?"

"My stomach is throwing a bloody fit. We need to leave."

"But, Daddy, I don't—"

"Now, luv," Ian said, sweeping the cards into a pile and dumping them into his pack. He took Mattie by the hand and led her from the restaurant, following the girl. She didn't head toward the guesthouses along the beach, but toward the interior of the island, where the more worn-down bungalows resided. The girl walked with her head lowered, as if unaware of the beauty around her.

Ian glanced behind to make sure that the man wasn't in sight. Seeing no one, he increased his speed and approached the girl, still holding Mattie's hand. As the Thai walked past an intersection of paths, he caught up to her. "Please follow me," he said, gesturing for her to turn to the right, toward the sea.

"What?"

"Please. Please follow me and my daughter."

The girl glanced at Mattie, who looked back and forth between Ian and the local. Everyone was confused but Ian.

"Please," Ian said again. "Just follow me for a moment. Just a tick."

The girl nodded, turning to the right, away from her intended path. They walked another thirty feet and turned again.

"Daddy, what are you doing?" Mattie asked, tugging at his hand.

"Just trust me, luv. Please trust me. I'm doing what your mum would do."

The trio proceeded for a few more minutes before Ian led the girls into a gathering of small bungalows. His heart thumped so hard it seemed to steal his strength. He understood that he was acting rashly, that his actions might lead to a confrontation that would scar Mattie. But he felt compelled to help the girl. If the man came and found them, Ian would have to deal with him. He wasn't afraid of the stranger. Actually, he wouldn't have minded confronting him, had they been alone. But Mattie mustn't see or hear such an altercation.

Ian turned to the girl, feeling time rush past. "Do you miss your parents?" he asked, watching her eyes.

"What, mister?"

"Your parents? Do you want to go back to them?"

The girl shook her head. "Me have no money."

"What if I gave you money? A heap of it. Would you go back to them?"

The girl's eyes filled with tears. "Go back to them?"

"Right now. Would you hop on a longboat and buzz off this island? Then get on a train and go back to your family?"

The girl tried to speak but couldn't, her tears dropping to the dirt path. She nodded, though, and Ian reached into his day pack and unzipped a secret compartment, pulling out three hundred-dollar bills and some large Thai notes. He handed the money to the girl, who still cried, but also smiled. Ian took off his Statue of Liberty baseball cap and placed it on her head. "Go to the far end of the beach," he said, "away from where you ate dinner. Hire a longboat to take you to another island. And then tomorrow, jump on a ferry to Phuket. From there it should be no harder than hopscotch to get home. Just catch a bus or a train."

"Why . . . why you help me?"

Ian smiled for the first time since he'd seen her. "Because I want you to be with your family. I have my beautiful daughter. I want your father to have his."

The girl pursed her lips. "You think . . . you think he still love me?"

Ian put his hand on her shoulder. "I know he'll still love you."

"Thank you. Thank you, mister."

"What's your name?"

"Jaidee."

"It's been a pleasure, Jaidee. A real honor. Now go. Stay away from where that mongrel . . . Sorry . . . From where that man might walk. Go get a longboat and start the journey back to your parents."

The girl looked at Mattie. "You so lucky," she said, smiling, wiping away her tears. "Your father, he have good heart."

Mattie still didn't understand what was happening but she nodded. "Thank you."

"Good-bye."

Ian and Mattie said farewell and watched the girl hurry down the trail. She disappeared within seconds, and Mattie turned to her father. "Daddy, why wasn't she with her parents? Why was she crying?"

He dropped to his knees so that he could look into Mattie's eyes.

"She was working for that man. She was . . . his guide. And she didn't have enough money to get home. So we gave her some. And in a day or two she'll be back with her parents."

"Why were you worried about the man?"

"Well, he was her boss. And I told her to leave him. To go straight home. So he might be vexed about that. But there's nothing to worry about, luv. She's leaving and he'll never know what happened. I guess he'll just have to find his own bloody way back to Bangkok."

"I hope he gets lost."

"Me too, Roo. Me too."

"Daddy, maybe we should go back to the beach, and see if she gets away."

Ian thought about the prudence of returning to the beach. "How about a game of soccer?"

"With those boys?"

"That's right."

"And we can keep our eye out for Jaidee?"

"I reckon so."

Mattie squeezed his hand, leading him back toward the beach. She still didn't understand exactly what had happened but knew that they'd helped Jaidee. And this knowledge made her feel warm. As they walked past backpackers and banyan trees she began to hum, skipping along the path.

Ian found himself hoping that he'd spoken the truth, that Jaidee would find her family and be welcomed back into it. He longed to ensure such an outcome but didn't know how. No amount of money or advice from him would help Jaidee. Her father would have to look into her eyes and want her back, despite her history and the whispers of his neighbors. He would have to see the gift of her, not the prejudices of others.

A few minutes passed before Ian and Mattie reached the beach. The boys were still playing soccer with several foreigners. Most of those playing wore no shoes or shirts. One red-haired girl kept up with the boys, sending crisp passes to her teammates. Mattie had been on soccer teams for most of her life but couldn't remember hearing players laugh as much as the Thais did. They shrieked as they slid for the ball, stumbled in the sand, and tripped their opponents. Two bamboo poles with fishnet between them composed each goal. The ball was often sent sailing into the water, which stretched along one side of the field.

A Thai boy in shorts scored a goal, did a cartwheel in celebration, and then laughed with his friends. During this break in the action, Ian asked the locals if he and Mattie could play. The boys clapped encouragingly, placing the two of them on opposite teams. Mattie and Ian took off their sandals and were soon chasing the ball, trying to remember which of the many Thais were their teammates. At first the locals were deferential to Mattie, but once they saw that she could pass and defend, they pressed her at almost full speed. Ian was given no leniency. The Thais rushed at him whenever he had the ball, sliding out in front of him, sending him stumbling across the sand. Though Ian hadn't played soccer for years, he had once been good, and long-discarded skills flooded back to him. And as he played, a sense of weightlessness seemed to fill him. His stomach no longer ached. He laughed along with Mattie, chasing the white bouncing ball through the sand. He collided with her and felt her push against him, giggling, trying to trip him.

Every so often, he glanced at a dozen or so distant longboats, which resembled brown bananas floating on the tranquil waters. He saw Mattie look as well, and his pride in her swelled. After fifteen or twenty minutes, just as he started to grow nervous about what might have happened to Jaidee, he saw her, wearing his green and black baseball cap, walking with a Thai man toward a longboat. He helped her into the boat, the bow of which rested at the water's edge.

The soccer ball flew into the sea and Ian nudged Mattie, nodding toward the distant boat. She saw what he did, and a smile alighted on her face. They watched Jaidee settle near the bow. The captain proceeded to the stern, where he started the motor and began to back the vessel out into the glowing waters. The sun was setting behind the boat, and Ian tried to see which direction Jaidee was looking. He thought that she might glance toward the beach, out of fear for the man, but instead she stared toward the dropping shimmering sun. She might have been looking toward home, toward her future. Wherever her gaze traveled, it wasn't backward, into the past.

Finding Mattie's hand, Ian held it tight. The boat picked up speed, sent spray into the air, rose and fell on gentle swells. It headed almost directly at the sun, which was now touching the horizon, spreading its soul across the sea and sky.

Ian waved at the disappearing boat with his free hand, and Mattie waved with him. The soccer ball was kicked again to the sand. The game resumed. But Ian stood still with Mattie, holding her, watching the boat and the girl vanish into the growing darkness, into a world void of light, but not of hope.

KATE LOOKED AT HIM FROM HER BED. Her eyes, once so blue and vibrant, were bloodshot and watery. He didn't recognize them and failed to understand how they had changed so much. They weren't the eyes of his wife, of the woman he had fallen in love with. No, the eyes he looked at now were those of a stranger, of someone who had been wandering in a desert and finally fell into the shade.

Her body mimicked her eyes. She'd once been strong and athletic. Her legs and arms, defined by subtle muscle and smooth skin, had carried little fat. Now she appeared withered, like fruit left too long on a branch. Her skin was wrinkled from her loss of weight. Her legs and arms looked like those of an old woman. Even her hair seemed to have aged, falling from her dying body, covering her pillow and sheets.

Only her mind remained intact. Her memory lingered, as did her ability to focus under most any circumstance. Sometimes she didn't fight her illness as much as he wanted her to, but this change had come near the end, when she was so exhausted that not even the thought of her daughter could prompt her to battle on.

Ian leaned closer, kissing a freckle on her cheek, the same sort of freckle that Mattie had inherited. Kate sought to smile, but strength seemed to have fled even from her lips. When Ian saw her try to smile, and fail, his tears began anew. No matter how much he loved her, how strong the bond between them, she was being taken from him, and he could do nothing about it. He was utterly bereft of power, of hope. Though she was the one dying, he was also being ground to dust. With her gone, he knew, a part of him would go as well. One could not strip his world of color and expect that world to look the same.

"Once . . . I go," she said, tears welling beneath her long lashes, "give all your love to her."

He felt faint, as if he'd just run a race that he hadn't trained for. Nodding, he turned and watched Mattie as she slept on a nearby couch. Midnight approached, and Mattie had finally closed her eyes an hour earlier. She'd cried herself to sleep in Kate's arms, and Ian had later carried her to the couch. He had suffered such pain when lifting her from her mother, knowing that her mother would soon be stolen from her, and that she would grow up with only one parent, the parent she loved less.

"I think . . . I think I'm dying," Kate said, her voice weaker than a whisper.

"No, my luv. Don't tell me that. Please don't tell me that."

"I can't . . . open my eyes. And it's hard . . . to talk."

"That's not right," he sputtered. "That can't be right. You're just knackered."

"I can't feel anything."

His tears fell to her face and he carefully wiped them off. "The medicine . . . it's too bloody strong. That's why you can't feel anything."

"I'm going."

"No, you're not. That's impossible."

"I love you."

He began to breathe too fast, causing the room to twist, his thoughts and vision to blur. "I'll fetch a doctor."

"No."

"No?"

"I want . . . you to be happy."

"I can't be."

Her brow furrowed as tears tumbled down her cheeks. "You have to be. For Mattie. For yourself."

"Please don't go."

"Promise me . . . that you'll make her happy. No matter what. Promise me, Ian. Please."

"I can't pr—"

"Please."

He nodded, his forehead touching her chest. "I promise."

"She's been sad . . . for too long." Kate paused, trying to fill her lungs, to be strong for her family's sake. "Maybe . . . maybe you could remarry, give her a little sister. She's always wanted one."

"I don't want to talk about that."

"It would be good . . . for her . . . and for you."

"No."

She nodded, perhaps to herself, perhaps to him. "Will you . . . tell me the story?"

"The story?"

"Of how you proposed."

Ian closed his eyes, the memory of that day like a bag over his head, suffocating him. He didn't want to relive the event but knew that Kate was desperate to. And so he gathered his reeling thoughts, focusing on the task at hand. "We . . . we'd been in Indonesia for a week," he said quietly, stroking the side of her face. "In the Gili Islands. We . . ."

"Go on, Ian. Please."

"I should get a doctor."

"Please don't stop."

He felt the warmth between them, was afraid of the looming cold. "We had that bungalow with the wobbly ceiling fan. Right on the beach. Right in paradise."

"I remember."

"One morning . . . when you were knackered and reading, I went down to the water, near the reef. I had my mask and snorkel, a secret bottle of wine, and a ring. I swam out to where the water was calm, to a sandy place between the reef and shore."

"Then what?"

He shook his head, longing to turn back the clock to that day, to relive that day a thousand times over. "I had tied the ring, and a weight, to the bottle. I dove down, maybe three meters, and set the bottle on the bottom. And then . . . then I took stones and shells and pieces of dead coral, and I spelled out, 'Will you marry me?' in the sand."

"I remember . . . swimming out with you, hand in hand."

"Me too."

"I was so happy . . . to see what you'd done. I'd never been . . . so happy."

Ian kissed her eyes, her lips. "Don't go, luv. Stay with me. Please stay with me. We'll . . . we'll go back to that reef. Just like we planned."

"I'll stay. But not like before. My body . . . it's shutting down. But something else . . . is opening."

"Oh, Kate. Please don't . . . shut down. Not now. I need more time. A heap more time."

She tried to kiss him but could barely stir. "Would you . . . put Mattie next to me? Please? But don't . . . don't wake her. I don't want her . . . to see me like this."

Ian struggled to stand up. His vision remained blurry. His legs didn't work properly. Still, he lifted Mattie and laid her down next to Kate. He took Kate's arm and put it around Mattie's sleeping form. More tears emerged from Kate's eyes, trickling down her face. Ian caught them with his forefinger as he stroked her cheek. He leaned over the bed, one hand on Kate, the other on Mattie. He tried to keep his family together, even as it was pulled apart, as he felt Kate growing weaker beside him. "Stay," he whispered. "Please stay."

"I will."

His tears fell faster as finally, at the very end, he admitted to himself that she was dying. Once he understood the finality of the moment, he no longer tried to keep her from departing. Instead he thought about how he might make her journey better. "You don't ever have to fret about Roo," he said, touching Kate's face, her hair, her hands. "I'll give her everything possible. And she'll smile. And laugh."

"No one . . . can make her laugh like you."

"And she will. Not next week . . . or next month. But we'll get there, I reckon."

"I love you," she said, trying to squeeze his fingers.

Ian kissed her again. "Will you . . . take a part of us with you?" he asked, his voice strained and cracking. "Of each of us?"

"Yes. And . . . I'll be with you . . . wherever you go."

"I know."

She closed her eyes. "I'm so tired, my love," she whispered as he cried quietly, the beeps of various monitors interrupting her. "Will you tell . . . tell me another story? Of the day Mattie was born?"

He nodded, glancing at their sleeping girl, seeing Kate in her face. But instead of telling Kate the story of Mattie's birth, he told her what he saw in their little girl, for he saw so many beautiful things. He saw Kate's eyes, her mouth, her nose, her freckles. Even better, Kate had somehow infused her best qualities into Mattie, who was generous and loving, artistic and bold.

Ian continued to whisper as Kate's breathing weakened. From time to time, the trace of a smile alighted on her face. Ian kissed these smiles, holding them with his lips until they left. He spoke about Mattie's birth, their first family trip, and his love for them both. He told Kate a story about a boy from the Australian Outback who fell in love with a girl from Manhattan, whose soul merged with his. They began their life together with no money or power or wisdom, but they hadn't needed such things. They were content having nothing but each other. Nothing else had mattered, he said, not when their love prompted them to write poetry, talk about creating a life together, feel each other's pain.

He was blessed to have discovered her, he said, trying not to weep. She'd come to him from afar and he would never let her go.

IAN AWOKE FROM THE DREAM, QUIETLY WALKED into the bathroom, sat down on the toilet, and cried. He wept as the sun slowly chased away the blackness of night, pushing light into the world, but not into him. As he thought about his dream, he realized for the first time why Kate hadn't sent Mattie and him to Indonesia. He'd proposed to her there, of course, and she wasn't willing to send him to such a place. It was too sacred, and some memories were best left unvisited.

After plucking three antacids from a bottle, Ian began to chew, the salt of his tears falling to his lips, to his mouth, and mingling with the taste of the medicine. He clutched at his stomach, needing to stop the pain, the tears. Soon Mattie would awaken, and he had to settle his emotions so that he could crawl back in bed with her.

Rubbing his face with a towel, Ian managed to calm himself, though he still felt overwhelmed, both from the responsibility of raising Mattie alone and from the weight of his sorrow. So much of him was dead.

But as he always did when he was in the depths of his sorrow, he reminded himself of Mattie. His love for her was what kept him going, through the cold, into the warmth of day. As he opened the bathroom door and reentered the sleeping area, he saw her face. She looked so beautiful—a reincarnation of her mother as well as a perfectly unique being.

Ian eased back into bed beside her, continuing to watch her face, hoping that her dreams were happy ones. He kissed her forehead lightly and tried not to grimace from the pain in his belly, a pain that had been growing worse as the days passed.

I love you so bloody much, Roo, he thought. You keep me steaming ahead when no one else could. And I'm going to keep my promise to your mum. You'll be content and fulfilled. You'll laugh. I don't know how the bloody hell I'll do it, but I will. So just sleep, and dream about lovely things, about whatever makes you smile.

THE LONGBOAT WAS ABOUT THIRTY FEET FROM bow to stern, composed of long wooden planks that once had been varnished but were now weather-beaten. The bow curved dramatically upward, as if preparing to face a phalanx of approaching waves. Dangling around the bow were wreaths of plastic flowers. Wooden planks spanned the boat, serving as seats. A canopy that sheltered only a small portion of the craft was held upright by rusting steel rods. At the stern, a large unenclosed motor was operated by a simple throttle and steering pole. Emerging from the back of the engine, a rod, perhaps fifteen feet long, ran almost parallel to the water. At the end of the rod was a propeller. The design of the engine and the prop allowed the boat to be driven into shallow waters.

Ian saw that the longboat had only two haggard-looking life jackets but he wasn't worried. Mattie was a strong swimmer, and they weren't going out far. They both sat near the bow. A red, white, and blue Thai flag rippled in the wind beside them. The boat rose and fell as it met gentle turquoise-colored swells. Their guide, Alak, stood in the stern and used the steering pole to navigate his craft around reefs and the contours of Ko Phi Phi. They were now near one of the island's vast butterfly wings. Waves crashed against the limestone cliffs, booming like distant fireworks.

As they neared the cliffs, Mattie studied the formations of rocks, wanting to sketch them later. The morning hadn't started out well for her, as she'd heard her father crying quietly in the bathroom. His sadness had made her shed a few tears as well, but she had dried them by the time he crept back into bed and put his arm around her. She'd felt safe at that moment—sad, but at least safe. He had tried to make her smile over breakfast, and now, as they rounded a bend and entered a placid stretch of water, she wanted him to forget whatever he had been thinking about.

"Did you and Mommy snorkel here?" she asked, twisting a long braid around her forefinger.

"I reckon so, Roo. I recognize some of it."

"Is this where the sharks were?"

"The sharks?"

"Daddy, you know what I'm talking about. You and Mommy told me all about Ko Phi Phi's sharks."

Ian nodded, impressed with her memory but wishing it wasn't so keen. "Those critters, luv, are a bit farther around the island, at a place called Shark Point."

Though Mattie had no desire to swim with sharks, she longed for him to think that she was brave, as her mother always had. "Can we go there? I want to see them."

"No, I reckon that's not such a grand idea."

"But you said they were just black-tipped reef sharks. That they'd never attacked anyone."

"You remember that?"

"Of course, Daddy. You told me all about them, how you sat still in the water and they circled around you."

"Well, there are other places for us to snorkel, where the reef is just as lovely."

"But that's the best place. Please, Daddy. I'm not scared. Really, I'm not."

He looked away, wishing that he hadn't told her so many stories about their earlier trip to Asia. What else would she remember? "I know you're not scared, Roo. But that doesn't mean we should go swimming with a bunch of bloody sharks."

"I want to draw them."

"And you're not afraid?"

"No."

"You promise?"

"Mommy said they were as safe as cats. So why would I be afraid?"

Ian motioned for their guide to slow his longboat. Alak eased back on the throttle, and the noisy engine quieted. "Is Shark Point safe?" Ian asked. "Safe for Mattie?"

The Thai, who was dressed in a sun-stained U2 concert T-shirt, nodded. "Shark Point very safe. Sharks never attack anyone. Never. They afraid of us. Only if you stay still do they come. If you move, they swim away."

"You've swum with them?"

"I used to. Almost every day."

"Used to? Why not anymore?"

Alak, who was probably in his early thirties, shut off the engine and stepped closer to Ian and Mattie. "Maybe someday I go back in ocean. But not yet."

"Why not?" Mattie asked.

"Because of tsunami," he replied, wiping excess sunscreen off Mattie's nose. "Too much lotion . . . it make your mask fog up."

Mattie shifted on the wooden seat. "But what about the tsunami?"

"The waves kill my wife. My children." He looked back toward the main part of Ko Phi Phi. "Now I have new family," he said, smiling. "New baby. But I not ready to swim yet. Maybe when my boy is ready, I am ready."

Ian nodded, knowing that the tsunami had devastated Ko Phi Phi, killing a third of the island's inhabitants. "I'm so sorry, mate, to hear about your wife and children."

Alak's smile faded. "Two waves come at Phi Phi. From both sides. Before the waves come, the water go down, and all the children rush out, laughing. They go out too far. And then the waves come. So big. Maybe five meters high. I out in ocean. In my old boat. We tip over and have to swim. Two people die from my boat. Then, three days later, I find my wife's body on another island. My children I never find." He paused, carefully wiping the excess sunscreen onto the tops of Mattie's ears. "We rebuild Phi Phi. We still rebuilding."

"And you married again?" Ian asked, wondering how he could have gone on if Mattie and Kate had died together.

"Yes. Just last year. And we have baby boy. He make me so happy. My life start again. I think . . . maybe my other boy . . . he in the new one. Their smile the same. Their laugh the same. I think my other boy come back to me. That what Buddha say, you know. And I think Buddha is right."

Ian studied Alak, believing that the man was much stronger than he. "I'm glad you think your boy came back."

"Me too," Mattie added.

Alak patted her shoulder. "My daughter, she no come back yet. But I hope she soon do. My wife already pregnant again, so maybe my daughter come home, follow her little brother."

Mattie nodded. "I think she will."

"Thank you," he said, smiling. "Now, I take you to Shark Point? I promise, everything fine there. Nothing to worry about."

Ian looked at Mattie, then Alak. "Thanks, mate. I reckon we'll give it a go."

Mattie sat down beside him as Alak went back to the engine. Soon they were plowing through the azure waters once again, headed toward a distant beach. Mattie glanced at Alak, glad that they had chosen him and his boat. Though his story about the tsunami had saddened her, she was warmed by the knowledge that his new family pleased him, and that he planned to one day go swimming with his son.

The journey to Shark Point took only a few minutes. The area, maybe a hundred paces offshore, was protected from waves by a reef that rose several feet higher than the surface of the sea. Above the water, the reef was dark and pockmarked. Mattie looked over the edge of the boat and was surprised that she could see all the way to the bottom. The water was almost perfectly clear.

"You sure, luv?" Ian asked, her snorkel and mask in his hand.

Mattie's heart had started to quicken its pace, but she nodded. "Aye, aye, Captain."

Ian helped her put on her fins and other equipment. He looked at Alak, who'd come to the bow to help. "Reckon you'll take your boy here?"

Alak nodded. "As often as he like. Do not worry, friend. She will be fine. When you get into water, move closer to reef. Then wait, very still, and sharks will come."

Ian smiled at Mattie, shook his head, and eased himself into the water. He looked down, surprised by the many varieties of fish that were so close by. He scanned the bottom for sharks, maybe ten feet down, but didn't see any. Alak helped Mattie over the side of the boat, setting her gently in the water. "You're really not scared, Roo?" Ian asked, ready to help her back into the boat.

"Just hold my hand, Daddy, while we swim to the reef."

"Don't leave me alone out there. I'll wet my swimsuit."

Mattie grasped his fingers as they kicked away from the boat, toward the reef. The water was remarkably calm and clear, reminding her of what it felt like to swim in a pool. But unlike a pool, the water here wasn't rendered dead by chlorine. Layers of life dominated everything below her. Sea grass twisted to and fro. Clams the size of ovens were partly opened, revealing the purple flesh of the creatures within. Mounds of coral rose from the seafloor, covered with urchins and anemones and fan-shaped objects that moved in tandem with the sea grass. Most prominent were the hundreds of fish that darted about. She didn't know their names, but they came in all shapes, sizes, and colors. Many seemed painted with colors, rainbows re-created on scales and fins. Some of the fish were long and gray, and possessed sharp teeth. Others resembled the angel fish that Mattie had seen at her dentist's office, though the fish below were much larger and more vibrant.

When they reached a sandy area near the reef, Ian stopped kicking, and Mattie did likewise. She continued to watch the beautiful fish, but also scanned the water for sharks. At first she didn't see any creature longer than her arm, but then gray shadows appeared above the faraway sand. Her heartbeat pounded in her ears as the sharks approached, moving with grace and leisure. The four sharks she saw looked the same, different only in size. They were completely gray, except for the black tips of their dorsal fins. Three of the sharks were smaller than she, but one was much bigger, and clutching her father's hand with increasing strength, she watched it approach.

The large shark neared them, about ten feet down and twenty feet away, swimming as if it were gliding on ice. Mattie had never seen anything move with such elegance. The shark was in constant motion, its tail fin swishing back and forth, its body an inch above the seafloor. Though the shark was almost as long as her father, Mattie began to grow less fearful of it. The creature didn't seem to be interested in her whatsoever.

Mattie continued to breathe through her snorkel, wishing that her mother could see her. Her mother had tried so hard to teach her how to use a snorkel and mask, and Mattie was sure that she'd be proud of her. Here she was, swimming with sharks, and hardly afraid, hiding behind her father only a little.

New sharks came and went, immune to the tide, which gently drew Mattie toward the open sea. The smaller sharks moved the fastest, she realized. The big ones didn't seem to have a care in the world. They swam and circled, never seeming to look up. The sharks kept a respectful distance from her, none approaching closer than the first big one.

Mattie thought again about her mother, suddenly missing her. She wanted to tell her all about the sharks, about how she was only a little scared, and how she breathed so easily through her snorkel. She longed to be between her mother and father, with each of them holding one of her hands. Then she'd be laughing, and they'd follow the biggest shark as it moved around this beautiful world.

She remembered Alak's words—how the wave had come and taken his family away. She didn't understand why waves came to some families and not others, why her friends complained that they didn't have iPods when her mother was dead. It isn't fair, she thought. Mommy was taken away and I didn't even get to say good-bye.

Tears formed in Mattie's eyes, and because she couldn't wipe them away, they began to sting. She tugged on her father's hand, pointing toward the longboat. He nodded, twisting, kicking in that direction. She took a final look at the sharks and then watched the boat draw nearer. Because she didn't want her father to think she was afraid, she took off her mask and splashed water on her face. Alak put an iron ladder over the side, and she tossed her fins into the boat and awkwardly climbed the ladder, followed by her father.

"What a bloody bunch of beauts!" he said, his grin wide and pure.

"I know!" Mattie replied, also trying to be happy, to be what he needed.

"They were just mucking around down there. Like a bunch of blokes in a pub."

"Did you see that big one? With the scar on his fin?"

"See him? I reckon he was about to kiss me."

Mattie looked into the water but couldn't find the sharks. "Thanks, Daddy. Thanks for showing me what you and Mommy saw."

"You're welcome, Roo. My pleasure."

She rubbed her eyes, which still stung from the salt of the sea and her tears. "Can we go to that beach? The beautiful one where no one is? I want to draw something for Mommy."

He set her sunglasses in her hand. "Put on your sunnies, luv. They'll help."

"But, Daddy, can we go to that beach?"

Looking more closely at her, he searched for how she was feeling. "Here," he said, patting the plank beside him, "have a seat by your captain."

"Aye, aye."

Ian put his arm around her and turned to Alak. "When my better half and I were here, years ago, there was a beach, on another island. It was lovely, with cliffs on almost every side."

"I know this beach."

"Can you take us there?"

Alak smiled, nodded, and moved back to the engine.

Ian continued to hold Mattie as the longboat sped up. Even though the day was warm, the wind produced goose bumps on her flesh, and he wrapped a towel around her. "Are you thinking about your mum?" he asked, noting how her gaze had become expressionless.

"Yes."

"You know, it's all right, Roo, to feel down. Even though we're in a beautiful place. Even though we had fun with the sharks. Sometimes that happens to me too."

"It does?"

"More than I want."

"Will I ever be happy again, Daddy? Like I used to be?"

He wrapped his arms around her, lifting her up and setting her on his lap. She'd grown almost too big to hold in such a way, but he leaned his back against the side of the boat and pulled her snug against him. "You'll be happy, Roo. So bloody happy. Like a kitty chasing a cricket."

She shook her head, thinking about how she never used to cry, back when her mother was alive. "I don't believe you."

"Life is hard, luv, full of ups and downs. We're down now, but we'll come up. Remember what Akiko said about the seasons? How we were in the winter of our lives? I reckon she was right. And one of these days the snow will melt."

"I just . . . I want to go back to the way it was."

He kissed the top of her head, wiping a tear from her cheek. "I know you do. I feel the same."

"I try to be happy. I really do. But I'm not."

"But, luv, it's not a race to be happy. You can't rush it."

"It's not fair."

"I know," he replied, her tears causing his stomach to ache. "You have a wound, Roo. And it won't ever completely heal. Never. But someday you'll have your own family, your own loves. And the . . . the sorrows of today will make you appreciate the loves of tomorrow even more." He kissed the top of her head again as waves crashed into the bow.

"I heard you crying this morning," she said, putting her fingers on his restless thumb.

"Oh. Sorry about that."

"It's okay."

He closed his eyes, wishing that he could be stronger, knowing that his pains weren't helping hers. "Two things get me through this, luv."

"What?"

"Well, you, of course. My love for you . . . it fills so much of the hole in me. And each day it fills more."

She nodded, resting her head against his shoulder. "What else?"

"Helping people. Your mum . . . she let me work hard. She took care of you so beautifully. I never had to worry about either of you. And because of that I made a fair bit of loot. Now, I'm not proud of that, and I'd do things differently if I could hop back in time. But at least that loot will let me . . . will let us help people. And that helps me, because a speck of good has come from me being gone so much. Away from you and your mum."

"What do you mean?"

"I mean, I survive this because of you, and because of things like we did yesterday, like helping out that girl. She's probably halfway home by now, and that makes me feel good."

Mattie nodded again, glad for the girl, but sad for herself. "But what if something happens to you, Daddy? I'll be all alone. Just like Jaidee."

He watched a longboat pass in the opposite direction, wishing that she didn't have such thoughts. He shared her concern, often worrying about his health, about why his stomach hurt so much. *I can't ever leave you*, he told himself. *Not until you're much, much older and you've got a family of your own.* "I'll be fine, Roo," he said. "I'm from the bush and as tough as a dingo."

"No, you're not."

"I just swam with a bunch of bloody sharks, didn't I?"

"You can't die, Daddy. You just can't."

"And I won't, Roo," he said, hugging her tight. He kissed her forehead, and then turned her to the side, so that her eyes could meet his. "And do you know what else? You're like that bloke behind us. You've been kicked in the teeth, kicked so hard, but you're going to end up all right. You're going to be happy. Just like he is."

Mattie watched Alak, thinking that he did look happy. He stood in the stern, steering his boat toward an island that appeared to be little more than a gathering of limestone cliffs. As they approached, Mattie saw a break in the cliffs, one that created a narrow entryway. Alak pushed his steering pole to the side, and the boat turned right, toward the channel of turquoise water that led to the interior of the island. Once they were past the towering cliffs on either side, a lagoon was revealed. A white-sand beach stretched for several hundred feet at the far end of the lagoon. Behind the beach was a jungle full of immense tropical trees but still dominated by the much larger cliffs.

Since her mother's death, Mattie had often heard people talk about heaven, about its beauty. She wasn't sure that such a place existed, but if her mother could go to one place to rest, Mattie hoped it was a place like this beach. She could hear birds calling to one another within the jungle. Flowering vines climbed the trunks of trees. And the lagoon was as clear as glass.

Alak turned off the engine and his boat slid quietly into the beach. Mattie hopped from the bow into the deep sand. She studied the beach, which was flat and mostly free of debris.

"It's like a giant wishing tree," her father said from behind her.

A half smile formed on Mattie's face. "It's perfect."

"Shall we tidy it up a bit, luv?"

"Good idea."

The two of them started to pick up leaves, sticks, and pieces of sun-bleached coral. Within a few minutes, they had cleaned a large swath of sand. Mattie then dropped to her knees and, moving backward, rubbed the sand smooth with her hands. Ian worked beside her, leveling the sand, wondering what she was going to draw but not wanting to ask. By the time they finished, they had smoothed out a section of sand as large as a basketball court.

Mattie stood up and studied the area, debating if she'd best be able to draw with her feet, as she'd said to her father, or if a stick might work better. She finally decided on her feet. "Daddy," she asked, "will you get as much of that coral as you can? The coral on the beach."

"What should I do with it?"

"Walk where I've walked, and sprinkle the coral behind you."

Mattie envisioned the scene she wanted to create. She knew she couldn't be too elaborate, but she wanted to draw something that her mother would enjoy. The waves will be first, she decided, beginning to shuffle through the sand, creating what looked like a giant snake. Once she finished the waves, she carefully made her way back to the middle of her wavy line and turned toward the island, dragging her feet, fashioning the bow of her boat. She then twisted to the right, and shuffled forward, making the top of the boat, adding a canopy and an engine. She wasn't sure how to insert people into her creation and decided to leave the boat empty.

As her father started to line her footsteps with pieces of white coral, Mattie jumped outside her picture, then moved above it. She began to shuffle again, her feet creating oversized, somewhat misshapen letters. Several times she paused to smooth out the sand and start over a letter, so it took her quite a while to write, "We love you, Mommy. Please show us the way."

After Mattie had finished her drawing, she helped her father sprinkle more coral within her footsteps. Alak also assisted, gathering coral and placing piles of it near the edges of her creation. The three of them filled the troughs made by her passing feet until the entire image, and the words, were highlighted in white.

Mattie wasn't sure what to think when she stepped back and looked at her creation. She knew that it was one of the most beautiful drawings she'd ever done, and that her mother would be proud of her for bringing it to life. But what if her mother couldn't see it? What if her mother had gone to a place so far away that she'd never again see any of her drawings? Mattie despaired at such a thought. She wanted to feel her mother, to know that her mother could see the boat and the words. Just knowing that her mother could observe the drawing would shine such a light on her.

"It's lovely, Roo," Ian said, taking her hand.

Mattie nodded, not wanting to talk, knowing that talking would make more tears tumble.

"Should I snap a photo?" he asked, as he pulled a small digital camera out of his day pack.

"No."

"No? Are you sure?"

"It's for Mommy. I only want her to see it."

He put the camera back. "I'm dead cert she's smiling right now, at what you've drawn."

"I hope so."

"It's a beaut, Roo. A real gem."

"Thanks."

He looked up at the sky, at dark clouds to the north. "I hate to say it, but I reckon we should buzz off."

"It's going to rain, isn't it?"

"Aye, aye, First Mate."

Mattie walked to the longboat and climbed over the gunwale. She sat on the front bench, near the bow. Alak told her how much he enjoyed her drawing and she thanked him for his help. His smile revealed crooked and crowded teeth. "I'm glad your boy came back to you," she said, taking a final glance at her boat.

Alak shrugged. "I still miss my first son. So much. But now my heart, it is not as empty as before."

"Do you think your wife and your children, the ones who died in the tsunami, do you think they can see you?"

"I am Buddhist, so I believe what Buddha say, that everyone wander through many births."

"Many births?"

"Everyone born and die many times. Like how the sun goes and comes each day. My family, the waves take them away from me. For long time, I want to die too. But then my new son is born, and I feel lucky to have him. I see my old son in his smile, so my hurt not as bad as before."

Mattie saw that her father was also listening to Alak's words. "Thank you for taking us here," she said.

"You are welcome."

She watched him move to the back of the boat and start the engine. Soon they were out in the open sea, headed back to Ko Phi Phi, which was shrouded in mist and storm clouds. Despite Alak's words about rebirth, Mattie was afraid for the first time on the trip. She felt so alone, so little. Her mother hadn't come back to her.

Mattie imagined the sea rising to create the tsunami that had killed Alak's family. This wave picked her up, carrying her forward, plunging her into darkness. She searched the sky, looking for signs of her mother, looking for something. But the world seemed to have turned black.

She reached for her father's hand, holding it tight. He must have sensed her fear, for without a word, he lifted her up once again and positioned her on his lap. He kissed the back of her head, then carried her, moving backward, under the canopy.

He put his arms around her as the longboat plowed forward, into rising waves, into shadows and doubt and a cold rain.

INDIA

A Tear on the Cheek of Time

"When you were born, you cried and the world rejoiced.
Live your life so that when you die,
the world cries and you rejoice."

—Indian saying

"I have a surprise in store for you," Ian said, patting Mattie's knee.

"What?"

"You're about to be a princess, Roo. Imagine that."

"I don't understand."

"Just look out your window and watch. You'll see."

Mattie did as he suggested—staring out of their decrepit taxi, studying the countryside of southern India. She hadn't expected things to be so open here, at least not after the mayhem that dominated the city of Bangalore.

Their itinerary allowed for only two weeks in India, and they had decided to hit the major cities and travel between them by train and plane. Though Bangalore wasn't on the circuit of many tourists, Ian's former company employed four workers who lived in the area. Feeling compelled to express his gratitude for the Indians' hard work, he had met with them two days earlier.

Now, as Mattie sat on the cracked leather seat of the old taxi, she watched the rolling hills outside the city of Mysore, which was a three-hour train ride from Bangalore. The hills were void of tall trees and were green, but not lush. They'd been told of a drought affecting the area, so Mattie wasn't surprised. Much of the land they passed had been sculpted to accommodate rice and wheat fields. Teams of oxen pulled plows in the fields or wooden carts on the street. The carts seemed to overflow with bursting burlap sacks or bales of hay or disheveled workers, and shared the pavement with buses, trucks, rickshaws, cars, and people.

Their taxi driver was small and impatient. Whenever something slowed him down, he honked at the culprit and muttered to himself. Unfortunately for Mattie and Ian, perhaps one out of four times that he honked, the horn stuck, continuing to sound as he drove on and pounded at it. The man would strike the horn with his right fist, cursing, wiping sweat from his brow. Sometimes the horn quieted, though more often than not it continued to sound until the man stopped the car, put up the hood, and temporarily disengaged the wiring. Despite the fact that this process took several minutes, the driver honked the horn at almost everything they passed.

Soon Mattie was able to predict what he would honk at. A trio of Hindu monks on bicycles was overtaken in silence. A farmer and his water buffalo received a furious barrage of beeps, as did a disabled ambulance, a group of schoolchildren, a sari-clad woman picking up a spilled crate of apples, and a three-wheeled motorcycle that looked to have been assembled from a dozen different vehicles.

Mattie smiled as the man continued to honk, pound the wheel, and pull over to fix the screeching sound. She wondered why he just didn't drive in silence. Certainly all of the stopping and starting wasted more time than simply waiting to pass people. And surely he'd be happier if he didn't have to pound his horn every minute or two. She came to realize, however, that most of the drivers honked as much as he did. They all seemed to have a love-hate relationship with their horns.

The taxi continued to climb the gentle hills outside Mysore. Their driver turned off the main thoroughfare, following a well-maintained road that was almost devoid of traffic. Soon landscaped gardens replaced the endless farms. The gardens were ornate and geometrical in nature, rows of cypress trees flanking rectangular reflecting pools.

Mattie looked ahead as a beautiful white building came into view. The two-storied building was dominated by a pale dome, which rose from the center of the structure. Stretching from either side of the dome was a series of columns that ran from the ground to the roof. Mattie had visited the U.S. Capitol once and thought that the two buildings resembled each other.

"Where are we?" she asked, as the taxi came to an abrupt stop beneath a covered roundabout.

Ian thanked their driver and handed him a short stack of rupee notes, the amount of which they had previously agreed upon. "Your mum and I stumbled onto this place," he answered. "And now I want you to enjoy it."

A man wearing a green suit said hello while opening an oversized door. Mattie stepped inside the building, stopping as a new world blossomed before her. She'd never seen such opulence. The walls and floor were white marble, highlighted by mosaics made of semiprecious stones. Gilded and massive frames held paintings of turbaned men firing guns at British soldiers. Silver and golden chandeliers hung from the vaulted ceiling. Arrangements of fresh-cut violet irises sprouted from immense porcelain vases.

Ian led Mattie forward. "Mysore used to have a king," he said. "This was his summer palace. And now it's a hotel."

"A hotel?"

"Fancy that, luv. And we're going to have lunch here. In the room where the king and queen used to eat. That's why I asked you to wear your best threads this morning."

Mattie glanced down at her red dress—which was too small for her—sorry that she'd argued with him about wearing it. "But I didn't know where—"

"No worries, Roo. I don't blame you a bit. Now, shall we dine?" he asked, offering her his arm.

She smiled. "Sure, Daddy."

"No, luv. You must speak like a princess to dine here."

"A princess?"

"Indeed."

"Are you the king?"

"Yes, my firstborn. I am your father, the king. Now I say again, shall we dine?"

"Yes. Let's dine."

He grinned and led her forward, delighted that she seemed to be having fun. Though returning to the palace caused painful memories to rise within him, he forced them aside, focusing on Mattie, on how he might make her happy for an afternoon. As they walked down a long corridor, he greeted other guests formally, trying to sound British rather than Australian.

The dining room was magnificent. Silk carpets covered marble floors. The walls and vaulted ceiling, which was about forty feet high, were painted a pale blue and featured white columns that ran from bottom to top. Along one side of the room a series of oversized windows revealed an elegant garden.

As soon as Ian and Mattie stepped into the room, a woman in an emerald-colored sari greeted them, asking about their day. Her English was as impeccable as her coifed hair and painted nails. Mattie thought she moved like the wind. The hostess seated them, pulling back ornate wooden chairs with silk upholstery. After handing Ian and Mattie menus that were bound by beaten silver covers, the woman left.

"My lady," Ian said, opening his menu, "what delicacies might you covet today? Curried lamb? Lentil soup? Shrimp with coconut?"

"They all sound . . . lovely."

"Ah, but not as lovely as you."

Mattie smiled, sitting straight in her chair, surprised and pleased that no one else was in the restaurant. "What should . . . What shall we do this afternoon?"

"What shall we not do is the more pertinent question, for we shall enjoy so many brilliant excursions. Why, our elephants await, and upon the conclusion of this fine feast, we might explore our forest."

"I would like that."

"As would I."

Their waiter, a tall man whose pants and jacket were also an emerald color, introduced himself and spoke about the specials of the day, recommending a combination of curries, meats, and vegetables. Ian and Mattie followed his advice and ordered accordingly, prompting him to smile. They continued to banter back and forth as a king and his daughter might.

"Shall we have champagne, my lady?" Ian asked, pointing to an elegant glass.

"Champagne? Really?"

"Just a sip, of course, to cleanse our palates."

"Yes, to cleanse our palates."

Ian ordered a bottle of champagne as their food was served on oversized silver platters, segmented into round and rectangular sections. In the round sections were a variety of curries, while the rectangles were filled with small servings of chicken, shrimp, cauliflower, beans, and okra. Indian flatbread, or naan, completed their meal. Soon after the food arrived, the waiter returned with champagne and carefully filled their glasses.

"Cheers, my princess," Ian said, raising his drink.

"Cheers, my king."

Ian grinned, adoring her smile, thinking of her beauty, both inside and out. "You know, my firstborn, someday you shall make a lord quite happy. You shall give him the most glorious gift in the world."

"What gift?"

"You."

"I don't care about lords."

"I know, but someday you shall. And when that day comes, you will make an old king proud. As you do this day."

Mattie sipped her champagne, swirling it around in her mouth. "This is good."

"Will you promise me something, my princess?"

"What?"

"When that day has come and gone, after you have moved into that lord's house, shall you be so generous as to not forget the old king? Shall you still hold his hand and whisper secrets in his ear?"

Mattie looked more closely at her father, realizing that he was talking about the two of them. She set down her champagne. She remembered her mother reading her English poetry, and she tried to think of the words these poets used. Her mother had once written poems for her father, she knew, and she wanted to say something that would make him smile. "This daughter, my king, shall always tell secrets to her father."

Ian laughed, bringing his hands together in a soft clap. "I love you, my princess."

"And I love you, my king."

"Shall we eat?"

"Yes. Let us eat and be merry."

THE TRAIN THAT CARRIED THEM TO AGRA looked as if it had traveled around the world a thousand times. The third-class cars were battered, overcrowded, and inundated with the scents of sweat, spices, and smoke. People sat on wooden benches, holding children and chickens and dirty canvas sacks on their laps. Since the train cars were so packed, many passengers were forced to stand—invariably the young and strong, who often half climbed out the windows. Though a dozen steel fans hung from each ceiling, very few of the fans worked, ensuring that the train's interior felt like the inside of a clay oven.

Ian and Mattie's sleeper car was also worn, but much more spacious. The green vinyl seats could be converted to beds, and many Indians already slept, curtains drawn shut around them. Since the sun had only just set, Ian and Mattie sat next to each other and read. She had started the next Harry Potter while he mused over *Shogun*, a novel he'd already read once. Beyond their window, India passed—a vast and never-ending assortment of villages, farms, forests, and humanity.

Though Ian was once again caught up in the story of Blackthorne and his Japanese lover, his thoughts frequently returned to the canisters in his pocket. Because the past two days had been good, he'd been reluctant to open Kate's next letter. He hadn't wanted anything about their trip to India to change. Mattie seemed content and had drawn sketches of sari-clad women, a mosque at sunset, and children chasing monkeys.

Ian wasn't sure why Mattie appeared to be doing better. She could be moody, but he didn't know if such moodiness stemmed from her mother's death or was normal in a girl her age. Though he couldn't remember her emotions waxing and waning so much before Kate had been taken, he hadn't been around her as much either.

In any case, Ian was reluctant to alter Mattie's good mood, despite the temptation to open Kate's note. After weighing the pros and cons of doing so, he set down his novel and turned to Mattie. "I reckon it's time for me to see what your mum says."

"Okay."

"That's all right with you?"

"Sure, Daddy. I was wondering if you'd forgotten."

He reached into his pocket, his heartbeat quickening, his stomach tightening. As sweat beaded on his brow, he thumbed the lid of the canister for a few seconds, glancing up to see a man dressed in white robes make his way down the aisle. After the man passed, Ian opened the canister. Inside was another rolled-up piece of paper—one of Kate's scrolls, as he liked to think of them.

Ian,

Thank you for traveling to Thailand, my love. I doubt it was easy, as we made so many memories there, but I hope you created some new ones that put a smile on your face.

As I lie here and think of India, I find myself in a state of flux. There is so much beauty and love in that country. Remember how we wandered around the Taj Mahal in awe? Like it was too beautiful to really exist? Will you tell Mattie the story of Shah Jahan and Arjumand? About how the Taj was built for love?

We found such joy in India, but we also saw such misery. One of my greatest regrets, and I have few, really, is that I didn't do more to help people. I wanted to. That was my plan. But I ran out of time. I gave everything to our family and very little to anyone else. And that was a mistake.

Will you right that wrong for me, Ian? Please? My letter to Mattie is similar. I've asked her to find someone to help in India. But you'll be the one who actually decides the form of that help.

I'm sorry, my love, that I seem to be pushing so many of my problems in your direction. I'm sure that I must sound awfully selfish. I sent you on this trip for yourself, for Mattie, and for me. There it is. I'll be honest with you now, at the end. I sent the two people I love on this trip because I thought it would help them, but also because I knew it would help me.

I didn't do enough while I was on this Earth. I was given so many gifts but shared so few of them. How did I make the world a better place? I didn't, at least not very much. But maybe through your actions I'll be redeemed. That is one of my many hopes, and it comforts me to know that you and Mattie will help someone in India, that our family will succeed in places where I did not.

I love you, Ian. So much. Now, as I'm writing these words, I'm thinking about how we held hands and walked through the Taj, in the footsteps of an emperor who lost his wife, in the footsteps of millions of travelers who loved and lost and loved again.

You can love again too, Ian. Don't forget that. You deserve to have light in your life.

Always,
Kate

Ian carefully rolled the letter back up and put it in the canister.

"What did she say?" Mattie asked, her book closed, distant lights passing by the window.

"Yours should be similar," he said, thinking of Kate's last words. "She said our letters are alike."

Mattie opened her canister, suddenly needing to see what her mother had written.

Dear Mattie,

What did you think of Thailand, my beautiful girl? Did you swim in the sea and watch a new world? Were you reminded of us snorkeling together at the YMCA? I had such fun tossing those coins into the pool and watching you dive down to pick them up. You made me so happy. You won't know how happy until you have your own children. Then you'll know. Then you'll toss coins and you'll smile.

Not long after you land in India, you'll see that it's a very different place. There is incredible beauty, but also incredible ugliness. There is infinite joy, but also infinite sorrow. India is a kaleidoscope of hopes and fears, strength and weakness. Most countries, of course, are the same. But in India these things can seem very pronounced. So be prepared, my sweet girl, to have your mind opened.

When your daddy and I went to India, so long ago, we met a homeless woman who couldn't see well. She was filthy and poor and wonderful. She collected cow dung, patted it into pancakes, dried it out, and sold it as kindling. She crawled along the street, looking for piles of fresh dung. Because her eyes were so bad, she often cut her hands and knees on pieces of glass. Your daddy and I saw her get hurt, and later took her into a shop and bought her two pairs of glasses. She was so happy, Mattie. She was bleeding and hurt, but I don't think I've ever seen anyone so happy.

Will you do something like that when you're in India? Please find someone in need, and help them. Doing so will give you a feeling that you'll never forget.

Some people don't believe in helping the poor. They think that the poor are poor by choice, that they've decided not to work and shouldn't complain when they suffer. And while that might be true on occasion, a woman collecting cow dung in Delhi works every bit as hard as the president of a huge company. Don't ever let anyone tell you differently, Mattie. The people who say such things have never scooped up cow dung, have never seen their children go hungry. They haven't suffered, and they never really stop and think about what causes suffering, about how we're all the same, but how some are born into better worlds than others.

I want you to be happy, Mattie. And your daddy.

If you can help someone else find joy, you'll find it as well.

I wouldn't ask so much of you if I didn't think that you were good and strong and brave.

Enjoy yourself in India. It's a beautiful country. Sometimes you have to look beneath the surface, beneath the grime, but the beauty is there, just like it is when you put on a mask and jump into the sea.

When you gaze at the Taj Mahal, when you study its beauty, know that I love you as much as the emperor loved his wife.

Mommy

Mattie reread the letter, nodding as she came to certain parts, wondering what she would do. The train rolled on. She stared out the window and thought about the world she was born into, and the worlds that she had seen and knew were so very different.

THE RICKSHAW THAT CARRIED IAN AND MATTIE was a testament to the strength of steel. Basically a large tricycle, the rickshaw featured a forward wheel, a seat for the driver, and then a much larger padded bench for passengers. Beneath this bench were two wheels, complete with fenders. A colorful yet ragged canopy could be pulled over the passengers.

Ian thought that he and Mattie would be a significant load for their driver, but over the past few minutes he'd seen rickshaws encumbered with much more weight. One such contraption had carried a family of eight. The father had sat on the driver's seat while the driver leaned forward over his pedals, somehow willing his rickshaw to move ahead. The mother and her children had been crammed together on the bench, sitting on one another's laps, one girl poised over the side of the rickshaw, her legs resting on a fender. The siblings were dressed in typical fashion—the girls in red, green, and purple dresses, while the boys wore shorts and collared short-sleeved shirts.

Though dawn was not long past, the city of Agra already teemed with life. The streets were inundated with rickshaws, cars, trucks, scooters, bicycles, cows, oxen, and donkeys. Sidewalks were likewise filled with every sight imaginable—snake charmers who entertained tourists, men who sat on crates and had their faces shaved by enterprising barbers, turbaned fruit sellers who looked as worn as the wood of their decrepit carts.

Three-story buildings seemed to lean over the streets, which were littered with newspapers, plastic bags, and rotting food. The buildings were stained a shade darker than their original colors from pollution and the passage of time. Balconies dominated the front of nearly every building, level with one another, so that someone might jump from one veranda to the next. Below the balconies, canopies protected stalls from the elements. Wooden and steel signs advertised repair shops, restaurants, bookstores, post offices, and police stations.

Thousands of people seemed to occupy every city block. Hindu women wore colorful saris while their Muslim counterparts were clad in robes and head scarves. Schoolchildren were dressed in green and maroon uniforms. None of the men wore shorts, opting instead for light-colored pants and collared shirts.

The city was like an infinite supermarket, with vendors spreading piles of produce alongside the street. Women haggled with shopkeepers while men hurried past. Because cows were sacred to Hindus and had free reign of the city, one or two often rested in alleyways or sometimes even in main thoroughfares.

Ian and Mattie absorbed the sights as they had during the past few days. Ian often looked at his watch, wanting to reach the Taj Mahal when it first opened, before the hordes of tourists arrived. He and Kate had been lucky enough to see the Taj by themselves, if only for a few minutes. And he wanted Mattie to have the same experience.

The rickshaw driver continued to navigate the chaos as if he were a snake making its way through tall grass. Finally the driver eased in front of a bus and glided to a stop at what seemed to be a particularly dense and crazed part of the city. Ian vaguely recognized the area. He climbed out of the rickshaw, paid the driver, took Mattie's hand, and led her toward one of the wonders of the world.

The main entrance to the Taj Mahal was a hundred-foot sandstone structure that resembled a giant red-and-white door. Dominating this door was an archway inset into the sandstone that served to please the eye, though it was solid except for a small arched opening at ground level. Above the main arch, semiprecious gems formed Hindu motifs—red lotus flowers, vines, and leaves. Verses from the Qur'an set in black stone and based on the work of the most famous of Arabic calligraphers paralleled the rectangular border of the main entrance.

Ian glanced at his watch again and was pleased to note that the Taj Mahal had just opened. He paid a nominal fee and with Mattie stepped through the main gate. Inside, everything instantly changed. Gone was the chaos of modern-day Agra. Instead, lush grounds—highlighted by rows of cypress trees—stretched toward the faraway Taj Mahal. The gardens were geometric in design, divided into squares by two marble canals. An inordinately long reflecting pool stretched toward the mausoleum, giving life to an inverted image of the Taj Mahal.

"Oh, my God," Mattie whispered, squeezing her father's hand.

The sky behind the mausoleum was surprisingly clear and blue, which made the white marble of the Taj Mahal seem to glow from within. The mausoleum, still blocks away, appeared almost like a mirage in the desert. The structure was too perfect and pristine to rest on the same soil as the shops outside. Though the Taj Mahal was the height of a twenty-story building and much bigger than Mattie had expected, it didn't dominate her view by the sheer magnitude of its size. Rather, it entranced her with its grace and elegance. To her, the Taj Mahal looked like a dream, an illusion of light.

"It was built, luv, in an age of patience," Ian said, walking slowly forward. "When architecture was spiritual in nature."

Mattie nodded. Her father's voice, which she normally adored, seemed somehow out of place in the presence of the mausoleum. She continued walking along the edge of the reflecting pool, wondering who had imagined such a thing, embarrassed by the pride she took in her sketches.

As Ian gripped her hand, he mused over how the Taj Mahal appeared to be almost human in its demeanor—reflective and ambitious and original. Yet unlike any human, the mausoleum seemed perfect, in terms of both its design and its dimensions. One could not look at the Taj, he thought, and suggest ways to make it better.

His eyes continued to wander from one side of the mausoleum to the other. The bottom half was rectangular, filled with wondrous arches. Its top, of course, was crowned by a single white dome. A minaret, resembling a vast column, rose beyond each corner of the main structure, adding symmetry.

Ian pointed to the minarets. "Did you know, luv, that the architect designed those towers so that if an earthquake ever occurs, they'll fall away from the mausoleum?"

"Wow."

"A bloody genius, I reckon."

Mattie realized that they were getting too close to the Taj Mahal. She wasn't ready to lose the view from afar and she led her father to a nearby bench. "Can you tell me its story, Daddy?" she asked, sitting down.

"Sure, Roo. It's a wonderful tale. A real dazzler."

"What happened?"

He adjusted his traveling hat so that its brim kept the sun off his neck. "There once was a man named Shah Jahan. And he ruled India."

"How long ago was that?"

"Oh, I reckon three or four hundred years ago," Ian answered, watching her face as she studied the Taj Mahal. "He had a slew of wives, but his favorite was named Arjumand. It's said that they were madly in love, and she went with him everywhere. She was his most trusted adviser."

"Like Mommy and you?"

He smiled. "Like Mommy and me."

"And what happened?"

"Well, she died in childbirth, which happened a lot in those days. And as she died, she asked him to grant her one wish, and that wish was to build her something beautiful, and then to visit this place on their anniversary and light a candle."

Mattie's forefinger started moving on her skirt, as if she were sketching. "And he built her the Taj Mahal?"

"That's right, luv. He wanted to build her the most beautiful place the world had ever seen. Unfortunately for him, as soon as he finished, one of his sons overthrew him and locked him up for the rest of his life in a small room with one window. And through that window he could see the Taj Mahal, where Arjumand was buried. When he finally died, he was buried beside her. And they've lain together ever since."

"Can I sketch it, Daddy? Before all the people come?"

"Absobloodylutely. Though I want to watch."

"Aye, aye, Captain."

Ian turned his gaze back to the Taj Mahal, remembering how Shah Jahan had wanted the mausoleum to mimic the loveliness of a woman. And it certainly did, reminding Ian of Kate in so many ways. He thought of her note, of how she had asked him to remember walking hand in hand through the structure. He wondered if somehow she could see them now. Might the world be so magical, so benevolent? Were Shah Jahan and Arjumand ever reunited, as he so wished?

Can you see us, my luv? Ian asked, pulling the shell she'd given him from his pocket and rubbing it between his fingers. *Do you know how far we've come? I miss you. I feel like I'm trapped in a little room too, looking out through a single window. I'm trapped and I'm tired and I miss you so bloody much.*

Tourists started to walk past, people from all corners of the world, most everyone talking softly, somehow hushed by the sight of the mausoleum. Ian turned to watch Mattie draw, following her fingers as they gripped a light blue pencil and she re-created the structure, making it appear as if it were reflecting the light of morning, which, Ian now realized, it was.

"You've got such keen eyes," he whispered, not wanting to distract her. "You make me feel blind."

She smiled but said nothing, her fingers turning blue and white. She filled the paper with the mausoleum, with its reflection in still water. Ian had seen hundreds of photos of the Taj Mahal but didn't recall any as charming as Mattie's drawing.

"I think Shah Jahan would love it," he said. "And I know your mum would."

"Daddy?"

"What, luv?"

"Last night, when you told me about what Mommy said in her letter, about how she wished that she'd helped more people, you said that you didn't agree with her, that she'd actually helped a lot of people."

"She did. A heap more than she ever gave herself credit for."

"I think you're right. And I want to tell her that."

Ian pointed to a white space at the bottom of her drawing. "So have at it."

Mattie nodded, thinking about what to write. She picked up the green pencil that she'd used to draw the cypress trees. Beneath her sketch, she wrote, "You helped everyone, Mommy. We love you."

Kissing her brow, Ian said, "Perfect."

"Daddy?"

"What, my little question asker?"

"Why do I . . . feel so close to Mommy here?"

He put his arm around her, pulling her to him. "You know, Roo, I've traveled around the world, and I've seen a heap of lovely sights. I've seen mosques and temples. And churches as big as a city block. But the Taj Mahal, it's the only thing I've seen that was made to celebrate love, to cherish love forever. That's why I reckon you feel your mum here, because Shah Jahan understood love. It was the best and most beautiful thing in his life, just like it is in ours. And the Taj Mahal . . . captures everything we feel about love . . . and makes us feel closer to everyone we cherish."

She closed her sketch pad. "Is it as pretty when you're standing next to it?"

"It's at least as lovely. You can't see them from here, but millions of semiprecious stones cover the exterior. They form flowers and vines and . . . I think even lines of poetry."

"I want to see them. And where the emperor and his wife rest beside each other."

He pocketed the shell, took Mattie's hand, and stood up. "Let's go."

"One other thing, Daddy."

"What?"

"I want to put my picture in a wishing tree, where Mommy can see it. But not near here. Can we find a good tree? Maybe tomorrow?"

"India is full of good trees."

Mattie smiled, stepping toward the Taj Mahal, toward a source of beauty through which she could feel her mother. She started to increase her pace, eager to touch what her mother had touched, to see what her mother had seen. The Taj Mahal grew larger, a single jewel from an unknown stone, a dream of a dying woman, a sight so profound that Mattie wondered if it were real. She called for her mother quietly, looking up, above the great dome.

After taking off her sandals, Mattie began to ascend the white marble steps leading to the mausoleum. She thought of Shah Jahan, of Arjumand, of her mother and father, of her father's pain at having lost such love. She squeezed his hand and let him lead the way inside, into a place that would surely stir his memories.

Please look down, Mommy, Mattie thought. Please look down right now and let Daddy know you're here. He misses you so much. Just let him know you're here and I think he'll feel a little better.

ABOUT SIX HOURS LATER, IAN AND MATTIE walked back toward their hotel. Though they were tired from a busy day, they didn't try to catch a ride in a taxi or rickshaw, as the streets were jammed with traffic. Walking, it seemed, might be faster. They moved along the edge of the sidewalk, near the street, where they encountered fewer obstacles. This strategy was far from original, however, and countless locals hurried home from work via this same river of humanity. Even in the early evening, the heat was oppressive, and many of the men had unbuttoned their collared shirts to their sternums. The shirts might have been white at one point but had been yellowed by sweat and pollution. The vibrant colors that the women wore were more resistant to the elements, but mothers and grandmothers still sweated and wiped their faces, still turned the other way as buses belching diesel exhaust lumbered past.

The crowds on the sidewalk were hard for Ian to navigate. He was taller than most locals, but being able to see ahead didn't make it much easier for him to locate his hotel. Only in Tokyo had he ever felt such a press of people. And the crowds in Japan, while claustrophobic, were at least orderly, following long-established patterns of movement. Japanese walked and stopped as one. They waited in lines. In India, no such concepts seemed to exist. Businessmen, women in saris, beggars, schoolchildren, monks, and vendors darted this way and that, often cutting one another off. The horns and foul fumes from nearby traffic didn't help matters.

"Reckon we should hail a taxi?" Ian asked Mattie, who held on to his belt and walked beside him.

Mattie tried to look around but could hardly see the road. "We'd just sit in that traffic jam. And I'm so thirsty. Can't we find something to drink?"

"At least we could relax in a taxi. Then we'll wet our throats at the hotel."

"Let's just get some water. I really, really need some water."

Ian nodded, reaching into his day pack to remove a guidebook. He flipped to a map of Agra and tried to get his bearings. They were near their hotel, he was certain. But despite the thousands of banners, signs, and posters touting nearby businesses, most of the streets were unmarked. Ian remembered how, during World War II, Russians had often removed their street signs to confuse invading German armies. He wondered if people in Agra might have the same mind-set when it came to outsiders.

A large man with a thick beard bumped into Ian, almost knocking the guidebook from his hand. Ian muttered to himself, glancing again at the map, trying to avoid what seemed to be an onrush of people. He walked another twenty paces before putting away the book. "I reckon we're almost home, Roo," he concluded, twisting toward her.

Only she wasn't there.

"Mattie?" he said, turning around in a full circle, his heart thumping like a series of fireworks. In every direction, Indians hurried past. Ian jumped up, looking toward where they'd come from. "Mattie!" Only horns and the confused stares of passersby answered him, and he hurried over to a pile of slabs of broken pavement, climbing up, holding on to a streetlamp. "Mattie!" he shouted, spinning on the cement, peering in all directions. He ran his hands through his hair. "Oh, God. Please don't do this."

He shouted her name again and again, continuing to look for light hair amid the sea of locals. Swearing, he scrambled down the pile of cement slabs and began to retrace their footsteps, bumping into passersby, asking if anyone had seen an American girl. As soon as people shrugged or looked around, he moved on, running now, jumping over obstacles. He hopped onto an idle bus, climbing up the ladder at its rear, rising to the roof, and looking again in all directions. "Mattie! Mattie, I'm up here! Look up!"

A nearby Mercedes honked, and the bus edged ahead. Ian slid down the ladder and jumped to the street. He ran back to the sidewalk, tripped over a shredded tire, and hurried toward where he'd last been with her. Arriving at the approximate spot, he called out her name again and again, asking nearby vendors if they'd seen her. People seemed eager to help, but no one recalled seeing her walk past.

"No, no, no, no, no!" Ian muttered, spinning around, jumping up. He continued to retrace their steps, peering into shops, wiping sweat from his eyes. "Mattie, luv! I'm here! Right here!"

The city seemed to grow louder—honks and screeches and distant jackhammers blending together to form a constant assault on his ears. Ian ran along the edge of the sidewalk, climbing higher when possible to get a better view. His stomach began to ache, filling him with a pain that normally would have doubled him over. But he paid this pain no heed. Instead he tried to corral his scattered thoughts, to formulate some sort of plan.

Realizing that Mattie had money, he wondered if she might have hopped in a taxi and gone to the hotel. Normally, she'd do just that, but he had a hard time recalling the name of the place they were staying—the Hotel Amar Yatri Niwas. Would Mattie remember that?

Deciding she might, he turned and ran toward the hotel. He moved from the sidewalk to the street, darting around idling cars, trucks, and buses. His day pack was banging against him, slowing him down, and he reached inside and tossed out his guidebook and a bottle of antacids. Running faster, he tried to ignore the distress of his body, but had a harder time doing so. Not only did his stomach ache, but his vision had begun to blur. He couldn't seem to get enough air, coughing as he inhaled the stench of diesel fumes.

Ian rushed to an intersection, saw their hotel, and ran into it. The lobby was small and nondescript. He thought he might find Mattie by the door, but she wasn't there, and the sight of that emptiness made his heart tumble. Cursing, he hurried to the front desk. The sole receptionist, a balding man who wore an old suit, looked up from a passport. "May I help you, Mr. McCray?" he asked.

"My daughter. Have you seen her?"

"I . . . I do not believe—"

"Have you seen her?"

The man shook his head. "No. Not since this morning. Is she missing?"

Ian closed his eyes, leaning against the wooden counter, the room threatening to spin. "I lost her. Ten, fifteen minutes ago. We were walking together and I lost her in the crowds." He slammed his fist against his thigh. "Bloody hell! She's gone!"

"We will find her, Mr. McCray," the receptionist said, pulling out a map of the city. "We are here," he added, pointing to the middle of the map. "Now, where were you when you lost her?"

"She's all alone."

"Where were you? Sir, I must know where you were."

Ian ran his hands through his hair as, squinting, he studied the map. "Here," he answered, putting his finger near the receptionist's.

"Are you certain?"

"Between those two streets."

"I will call the police. They will start looking in this area."

Ian shook his head, struggling to maintain his composure. "I've left her all alone. Oh, Christ, what have I done?"

"We will find her, sir."

"No, no, no."

"Mr. McCray, she will be found."

"You don't understand. Her mother's dead. I need to find her. Right now."

The receptionist took off his glasses. "I am also a father, sir. I know what it is like to lose a child. And I will help you locate her."

Ian clutched his side, the pain finally dominating him. "I'm going back out there," he muttered, writing down Mattie's name and description on a piece of hotel stationery.

"Wait, Mr. McCray," the man said, putting his hand on Ian's elbow. "Please take my business card. Call the number for the front desk if you need me. And here is my cellular phone." The receptionist then held up his forefinger and went through a doorway behind the front desk. He quickly returned, pushing an old-fashioned bicycle beside him. "Please use my bicycle," he said. "You can see much more of the city this way."

Ian grabbed the man's hand and squeezed it hard.

"Your daughter, sir, she will look for something familiar. And we have many Western restaurants nearby. If you see one—a Kentucky Fried Chicken or a Pizza Hut—you should go in."

Turning the bike around, Ian stepped toward the doorway. "Please hurry and call the police," he said, and rushed outside. "Tell them she's all alone."

Agra seemed busier than ever. Traffic in the nearby street was almost at a standstill. Ian ran to the edge of the sidewalk and hopped on the bicycle, which was too small for him. Standing up, he pumped the pedals, weaving between vehicles of every shape and size. He didn't want to panic but couldn't help it. The thought of Mattie alone and terrified was too much for him.

"Mattie!" he shouted, riding near the sidewalk. A motorcycle suddenly pulled over to the curb in front of him and he almost crashed into it. "Mattie! Can you hear me? Mattie!"

Please, God, he thought, please don't let anything happen to her. Please, please, please. She's so good. She's been nothing but good her whole life and she doesn't deserve any of this. Now, please. Let me find her.

He passed a Burger King and jumped off the bike, then hurried inside. He called her name and asked patrons if they'd seen her, but everyone shook their heads. Grunting from the pain in his stomach, he ran back outside and started to pedal once again. He knew that child prostitution was a monstrosity in India, and the thought of someone getting hold of Mattie made him weep.

His tears blurring his vision, he sped down the street, ringing a bell on the handlebars to warn pedestrians of his approach. "Mattie! Where are you?"

A cow lay on the pavement before him, and he swerved into the curve to avoid it. People pressed against him from every direction and he realized that he'd never find her like this. He had to be more strategic, though reasoned, calm thoughts flew in the face of his panic.

Where would I go, he asked himself, if I were her? I have money in my pocket. I could get a taxi, but . . . but I don't know the name of my hotel. Would I find a police station? Maybe. Maybe not. What about a big hotel?

Bugger this! Think! Use your bloody brain! Where would she go? To the American embassy? To the airport? Or to something she knows?

Wait, he thought, gripping the handlebars, his heartbeat resonating in his ears. "The Taj," he whispered. "She'd go to the Taj!"

He jumped back on the bike and pedaled as he never had, passing rickshaws and taxis and trucks. Agra revolved around the Taj Mahal, and signs pointed in its direction. He stood upright, putting all his weight on each pedal as it crested, forcing it downward as if it were a demon he was trying to keep from rising upward. The city flew past, the sun dropping, vehicles turning on their lights. People who saw him seemed to sense his desperation and stepped aside to let him pass. Though Agra was a city of a million horns, no one honked at him, even when he cut them off.

"Please, dear God," he said, straining, smashing over a broken pallet.

He turned to the right, saw the main gate to the mausoleum, saw her talking with a security guard. The bike fell as he leapt from it. Her name emerged from his lips. He ran ahead, sweeping her up in his arms, holding her tight, their faces pressing against each other's, her tears falling to his cheek, his hands running through her hair. She wept and shuddered against him and he held her as if someone were trying to pull her away. Kissing her brow, he told her that everything was fine, that he'd never lose her again. She cried in his arms, curling up against him, wanting to be encircled by as much of him as possible.

Over the previous year and a half Ian had spent so much effort hiding his true emotions from her, his feelings of grief and fear. But now, as she held on to him and wept, it was as if he were standing on a stage and the curtains had been pulled up in front of him. He was exposed, rendered naked by the spotlights. His joy and relief at finding her eclipsed his strength to remain levelheaded, and he began to shudder, disintegrating beside her like a glacier warmed by too much sun. While parts of him toppled, he clung to her as much as she did to him, his tears incessant. He kissed her again, telling her how much he loved her, that though she might have been missing, he was the one who was lost without her.

The sky continued to darken. Ian's stomach still ached, and he thought that he might vomit. Now that he'd found her, his nausea and pain were much more pronounced. Trying to slow his breathing, he stroked the back of her head and whispered reassurances. He looked up and said silent prayers of thanks. Never had he been so thankful. Not even on his wedding day.

He thought about how the trip was a mistake, how he was insane to take her to Asia. She could have been kidnapped, he told himself. Some mongrel could have grabbed my little girl. An image flashed in his mind of Mattie being forced into a truck and the landscape began to sway. He closed his strained and aching eyes, rubbing them.

"Do you want to go home?" he asked quietly, hoping that she would nod. "Back to all the beautiful things in America? Back to—"

"No."

"Why not, Roo? After what just happened?"

"Because . . . if it was time to go home, Mommy would send us home."

Mommy is gone, he thought, kissing the top of Mattie's head. She's been gone for nineteen months. "But, luv, Mommy doesn't know how hard this is. She doesn't—"

"No! I don't want to go home. Stop talking about it. Please stop talking about it!"

He pulled her back toward him, cradling her once again. "Easy on, luv. Easy on. I'll stop yammering about it. I will. But . . . but you can always change your mind."

"I won't. So stop your yammering."

"Just think about it."

"No."

Ian sighed, remembered the hotel receptionist, and called the man using his cell phone. He explained everything, hearing the happiness in the stranger's voice. Ian thanked him repeatedly before hanging up. "His blood's worth bottling," he said to Mattie, putting the phone back in his pocket.

"Who?"

"The receptionist at our hotel. He called the police, and gave me his phone and bicycle."

"He did? That was nice of him."

"It was bloody wonderful. He was bloody wonderful."

"I'm glad, Daddy."

Ian kissed her head again, smelling sweat in her hair, continuing to shelter her with his body. "Reckon you know how much I love you?"

"How much?"

He pointed to a slice of the sky between a pair of old buildings. The sky was infused with the hues of the setting sun, as if it were a tapestry dyed in the most beautiful of Indian colors. "When I look up there," he said, "I see a lovely sky. I see something that reminds me of you."

"What?"

"I still hurt, Roo. From your mum's death. You know I do. But I can also see beauty in the world. And that's because of you. That's the gift of you."

"It is a pretty sky."

He saw that tears had dried some of her lashes together and he gently rubbed her eyes. What would make her feel better? he wondered. What would give her the comfort of home without taking her home? "That bicycle is fast," he said. "A real storm in the bush."

"It is?"

"It's a beaut, Roo. And there's a bar on the back of it, and you can stand while I pedal."

Mattie looked at the busy street. "Should we go back to the hotel?"

He lifted her from his lap as he stood up. "I think I passed an ice-cream store a few blocks back. How about a big, fat, dripping scoop of cookies and cream? Something to cool us off?"

"Aye, aye, Captain."

Taking her hand, he led her toward the bicycle. He thought about losing her, about how she was the light of his world. Suddenly he needed to feel her again, and so he lifted her up, kissing her cheek as her arms and legs wrapped around him. "I love you so much, Roo. That was hell for me, to lose you like that. I was dropped straight into hell. I'm so bloody sorry."

She continued to hold on to him, trying to be brave, afraid of getting separated again, but also of going home. "When I was lost," she said, "I thought about Jaidee."

"Who?"

"The girl in Thailand. She was all alone, so far from her parents. I remembered watching her on that boat, going home. I wanted to get on a boat and go to you."

"Well, you did, Roo. You did."

"I love you too, Daddy."

"I know."

"Maybe tomorrow, when we walk, we can hold hands."

"I'd fancy holding hands. And later, back in our room, we'll talk about ways to make sure that we never get separated again."

She smiled, fleetingly. "Is that the bike?"

"Yeah. And do you know what? That man at the hotel, who helped me as much as we helped Jaidee, I think we should do something nice for him."

"Let's bring him some ice cream."

Ian set her on the ground and picked up the bicycle. She placed her feet atop a pair of bars that jutted from either side near the back wheel's hub, then held on to Ian's shoulders as he sat down and started pedaling. Though an hour earlier she'd been terrified of the streets, of the chaos, her fear had mostly subsided. She leaned closer to her father, happy that he'd compared her to a sunset, that she made him think of beauty. She'd always known that her mother had thought as much, but to have her father say such words made her feel safe, and she didn't regret getting lost, because he'd rescued her, as he always would.

Agra swirled around them, the city such a blend of hope and sorrow, of love and loss. Feeling blessed for the first time in days, Ian pedaled on, pausing several times to hand out bills to beggars, eager to share his good fortune.

TWO DAYS LATER, IAN AND MATTIE SAT on a train bound for Varanasi. They once again had paid for a sleeper car. Though the day had been hot, the train's windows were open, and a refreshing breeze tumbled from car to car. The clatter of the steel wheels on the tracks was soothing—a combination of gentle movement and soft, constant noise. Ian thought that riding on a train like this one must be similar to being in the womb. The warmth, the background noise, and the movement merged together into a sensation that could hardly have been more pleasing. For the first time since he'd lost Mattie, he felt completely relaxed.

The sun had set, and scattered lightbulbs illuminated the train. Mattie and Ian sat on one side of a stainless-steel table, while an Indian couple occupied the other seats. The woman was dressed in a red sari with blue trim. Her hair was pulled back into a bun, her nose and ears pierced with gold jewelry. A red *bindi* dotted the spot above and between her eyes. Sitting beside her, a balding man in black pants and a white collared shirt put down his newspaper and looked out the window. His companion carefully unfolded a misshapen box of aluminum foil. Inside were small yellow cakes. She handed a cake to the man, then looked at Mattie. "Would you like one, dear?" she asked in well-spoken English, holding out a cake. "This is mango *halwa*, really nothing more than mango puree mixed with a little sugar syrup."

Mattie glanced at Ian, unsure if she should accept food from a stranger. He nodded and so she smiled and extended her hand. "Thank you."

"And you, sir?"

"I'd fancy a go at one," Ian replied, the smell of the treats making his mouth water.

"I made these from fresh juicy mangos," she said. "Not like those monsters grown from fertilizer that you buy in the city."

Ian smiled, biting into the dessert, which was sweet and soft. "Crikey. That's quite good."

"She's a good cook," the man said, reaching for a second helping. "Of course, her cooking makes me fat, but I'm not complaining."

"Do you live in Varanasi?" Ian asked. "Or are you on holiday?"

The woman adjusted her sari, pulling the garment higher. "Our son is an engineering student there. We visit him every few months. And you? Where are you from? Why are you in India?"

"My wife asks too many questions," the man said, though he smiled.

Ian finished his sweet. "No worries, mate. My daughter, Mattie, and I are from New York. We're in India for a few weeks."

"What have you seen in India?" the woman asked, looking at Mattie, handing her a napkin.

Mattie wiped her hands. "We saw the Taj Mahal."

"What time of day was that?"

"Morning."

"Morning is good. But on your next trip to India, visit the Taj at night, under a full moon. Then your knees will really grow weak."

The man nodded to a uniformed attendant who pushed a cart down the aisle. Words in Hindi were exchanged before the passenger handed over a few bills. The attendant put two beer cans, a bottle of Sprite, and a glass of tea on their table. "For our companions," the man said, handing Ian a beer and Mattie the Sprite.

"Thanks, mate," Ian said, feeling as if he should have done the same.

"It is our pleasure," the man replied. "We are your hosts in our country, after all." He opened his beer, then lifted up his newspaper and pointed to a picture. "We are very excited that your president will be coming to visit us next week."

"I reckon he'll have a lovely time," Ian said, sipping his beer.

The man smiled. "America is the place where all dreams can happen."

"And what about India?"

"Someday, India will be the same. We are getting closer but still have a long way to go."

"I think you're doing well."

The man shrugged. "We are trying. But educating, feeding, and taking care of more than a billion people is not easy. Our son is lucky. We could afford to send him to a university, and he has studied hard. But too many sons and daughters will never go to such schools. In that way, India has not changed so much. The class system is gone, on paper anyway. But really, it is not gone."

Ian nodded, sipping his beer, noticing how the man's wife had grown quiet once the political discussion began. The train's horn blew ahead into the darkness. "I reckon every country has a class system of sorts," Ian answered. "Though back in the States, our skin color doesn't matter as much anymore. And that's a real rags-to-riches story."

"It is," the Indian replied, rapping his knuckles on the table. "And what is your dream? You do not sound like you are from America."

"Well, it's my adopted country, you could say. I married into it and am glad I did, because you're right; it's a good place for dreams. The best place, I reckon. Six years ago, I started a little company, a little company that sold Japanese foodstuffs online to those of us who acquired a hankering for their treats. You know—dried noodles and spices and so on. Anyway, when I recently hung up my hat, we had more than twenty employees. Even a few blokes in Bangalore were working for us."

"Really, in Bangalore? Did they perform well for you?"

"Like wheels on a wagon."

The man nodded, finished his drink, and set the can aside. "You will enjoy Varanasi. Be careful, for there are thieves and pickpockets. But when you take off your shoes and put your feet in the Ganga, you'll feel like you have come home."

"We've heard as much."

"Well, enjoy your trip. And the Ganga."

Noticing that Mattie looked tired, Ian smiled, thanking the couple for the food and drinks. He then helped her climb a small iron ladder that rose to a padded bench above their seat. A curtain could be strung around the bed, and Ian pulled it shut, surprised that the mattress was covered in a clean white sheet. Though the bed was designed to accommodate one sleeping passenger, Ian knew that Mattie would want him to rest beside her. "Reckon there's enough room for us both?" he asked.

"Sure, Daddy," she said, moving over as much as possible to make room for him, her great-grandmother's ring held tight in her hand.

Ian lay next to her, settling on his back. She put her head on his chest. The train rocked to and fro beneath them, the rhythmic thump of the wheels on the tracks obscuring conversations below. "Fancy a story, luv?"

"Can you tell me a new one?"

"About what?"

"About . . . about a girl who finds a little sister."

He stroked the back of her head, wishing that she didn't ask to hear such tales, for she wanted happy endings, and happy endings in a story were easier to create than those in real life. "There was once a brown-eyed girl," he began, "who lived all alone on a train."

Ian continued to tell the story, wondering what words might make her smile, if she ever would have a little sister. He wanted more than anything in his life to give her such a treasure but he couldn't imagine marrying again. And as a single man, adoption was out of the question. No agency would grant him a child.

At the end of his story, the girl found a little sister, which brought a smile to Mattie's face. She thanked him, handed him the ring, and closed her eyes. He remained awake, his mind churning, his fingers turning the ring over and over. He didn't know if ultimately he could offer her hope, as he so wanted to. At some point their trip would be over, and he'd have to find work, to be pulled from her. She'd need him, and he would be at a meeting, perhaps just a few miles down the road, but a span too far for him to bridge.

The night aged, but sleep eluded Ian. For the first time since their journey began, he didn't want it to end.

FROM THE WATER, VARANASI LOOKED SERENE. ALONG the cement-lined banks of the Ganges River, two- and three-story temples, shrines, and palaces rose like colorful castles. The temples often featured a rectangular base and a colorful pointed top. In courtyards below the temples, near the river, Hindus wearing ceremonial robes prayed, often gathered around a body covered in flowers. Rows of shallow steps descended from the temples directly into the Ganges, allowing people to pray and wash with equal ease. Mattie had once been to a New York Giants football game, and thought that the side of the river in some ways resembled the rows of bleachers at a massive stadium. Pink and red temples dotted the riverbank, and thousands of Hindus walked up and down the stone steps, pilgrims who had traveled from all over the country to swim in the Ganges and be cleansed of their sins.

The Ganges was much larger than she would have guessed. Blue-hulled boats bobbed in the current as fishermen cast nets into the murky water and tourists snapped photos. Mattie's father had told her that Varanasi was one of the oldest cities on Earth, and that Buddha had given his first sermon here after becoming enlightened. A stone pier jutted out into the water, and children leapt from it into the air, spinning and somersaulting before landing with a splash.

Sitting at the front of their boat, Mattie had her sketch pad out, and though she was tempted to draw the children, she focused on the temples and the worshippers. She'd never seen people dressed so colorfully and wondered why everybody in America who went to church seemed to wear black or gray. She asked their guide this question and he paused from rowing.

"The Ganga is the most sacred place in India," he said, his English quick and precise, much like his oar strokes. "People come to Varanasi to die, and this makes them happy, their families happy. If you are Hindu and you die in Varanasi, then you have much to smile about. You have won the lottery for death."

Next to Mattie, Ian studied her face, wondering if they should be here. He wasn't certain what she would think of such a place. She'd asked to walk along the river, among all the people, but he hadn't wanted her to get such a good view of the dead bodies. Better to watch such things from afar on the river.

Though Ian feared letting Mattie see the dead up close, he'd been reluctant to skip Varanasi. He believed Hindus possessed an acceptance of death that didn't often exist in the West. They saw death as a spoke that made up a wheel of life, believed death led to rebirth. And while Ian didn't seek to remind Mattie about death of any sort, he hoped that somehow a trip to the Ganges River would show her that some cultures associated death with hope.

"Can we go closer to shore?" she asked, a yellow pencil moving incessantly in her hand.

The man adjusted his turban. "My oars will take you anywhere you like. Except north to the mountains. I have enemies there."

"Enemies?"

"A girl," he said, smiling. "It all began with a girl."

Mattie nodded, not understanding, and wanting to finish her sketch. As she worked, Ian turned around, looking across the river. In the distance he saw what he thought was a bloated body floating past. The poor, he knew, couldn't afford to burn the bodies of their loved ones and simply set them free in the Ganges. Glad that Mattie hadn't seen the corpse, he turned back to her.

Their guide pointed to a stone outcropping below a pink temple. The outcropping extended above the water and held a group of people dressed in orange and yellow robes. Near the river, a fire burned, twisting in the breeze, sending the scent of sandalwood in all directions. "This is a ghat," their guide said, pointing.

"What's a ghat?" Mattie asked, pausing at her work.

"A place where Hindus burn the bodies of their loved ones. The body is burned, and the ashes are swept into the Ganga by a relative. Hindus believe that since the body has been burned to ashes, the journey toward rebirth will be easier. And that journey happens in the river."

Mattie watched a man in white robes add more wood to the fire. Looking up and down the banks of the river, she saw dozens of other fires on similar structures. As the man in white used a long pole to poke at the nearby fire, another man, dressed in colorful robes, began to move his hands and chant.

"He is the priest," their guide said.

"Might you tell us about rebirth?" Ian asked, edging closer to Mattie along the bench.

The man shrugged. "I am a Muslim, so I do not understand everything that the Hindus believe. Muslims believe that we go to Paradise after death. That is our jackpot. The Hindus believe that one is reborn, and this makes death not such a bad thing, because the soul . . . changes its direction at death . . . and then returns to Earth in a new body to continue its journey."

Mattie looked from fire to fire, thinking of her mother's funeral. "What if you were buried? Could your soul still be reborn?"

The Indian picked up his oars and rowed a few times, his lips pursed. "I do not know for certain what the Hindus would say. But I think they would nod their shiny heads. They would believe that the soul could never be caged. The Ganga, of course, makes rebirth easier. But the ground is not so different."

On the nearby shore, the fire appeared to be losing its strength. The man in white continued to poke with his long pole, sifting through the remains.

"If it is a man they have burned," the guide said, "his ribs may remain. If it is a woman, her hips may be left. That man is seeing if everything has been burned enough. If it has, a relative of the dead will use a broom to push the ashes into the Ganga."

Mattie thought about her mother being reborn. She didn't know if she wanted to imagine her mother in heaven, or if being reborn might somehow be better. If she was reborn, maybe Mattie would meet her again. Maybe they could somehow take a walk together or kick a soccer ball.

A mosquito landed on Mattie's arm, and she brushed it away, then pointed to a boy swimming in the river directly below the funeral pyre. "What's he doing?"

"He is homeless," the man answered, rowing again. "Many people would call him an untouchable."

"Why?"

"Because he swims in that water, looking for gold teeth and jewelry."

"For gold teeth?"

"From the burned bodies. He finds the teeth and sells the gold. That is how he lives."

Mattie watched the boy, grimacing as she thought about swimming through the polluted water, looking for teeth. "Where are his parents?"

"Sick, maybe. Dead already. In another city. I have watched this boy every day for more than two years. He goes deeper than the other boys. Even deeper than the big ones. He is a good boy, I think. Once I dropped my oar in the water and he brought it to me. And once I brought him to shore, when he had a fever and the river was too strong for him."

Ian saw that Mattie was troubled and took her hand. "Maybe we should go, luv. I reckon we've seen enough."

Mattie thought about her mother's letter. "Do people really say that he's . . . an untouchable?"

"Yes. He deals with the dead, and that makes him an untouchable."

She turned to her father. "I think we should talk with him."

"He would run away from you," the guide replied, shaking his head. "The bigger boys steal from him."

Ian watched Mattie nod silently. "Will you take us to shore?" he asked. "Right in there, between those ghats?"

The guide shrugged, turning the boat and rowing quietly. Within a few minutes the boat's bow touched cement steps leading into the water. Ian handed the man some bills, thanked him, and helped Mattie jump ashore. Many Hindus were present on the steps—bathers, pilgrims, men carrying wood. Ian and Mattie walked along the water toward the boy. He was about thirty feet from shore, swimming downstream from the large ghat. Mattie realized that he was younger than she'd thought, maybe even younger than she was.

Ian sat on a step directly across from the boy's position. "Is this who you want to help, luv?"

"I think so."

"Why him?"

"Because he's an untouchable. And no one should be that."

Ian nodded, patting her knee. "Don't let anyone ever put you in a box, Roo."

She looked up from the boy. "What do you mean?"

"I mean, people call him an untouchable. They don't stop and think what he's capable of. And someday, some dimwit might tell you that you'll never be a great artist, never amount to a pile of beans. So, if you hear that, don't listen to it. Think about the Japanese girl who people thought was weak. Think about her climbing Everest."

"Daddy?"

"Yeah, luv?"

"Why would people call him an untouchable?"

"Because doing so makes them feel better about themselves. Because they're the weak ones."

"Where do you think his parents are?"

"I don't know, Roo."

The boy surfaced, raising his fist above the water, appearing to look at what he gripped. Continuing to hold his hand high, he struggled against the current, swimming toward shore. Mattie glanced to her left and saw a pair of old sandals and a dirty shirt on a nearby step. The boy seemed to swim toward these items, his head disappearing at times beneath the water. Soon he could stand and began to walk toward shore. He wore dark shorts, but nothing else. His ribs resembled curved sticks. His knees and elbows seemed oversized, stretching his skin taut. The boy's hair was cropped close to his head and cut irregularly, as if he'd found some old scissors and used them on himself.

Mattie watched him emerge from the shallows. He paid her no heed, sitting on the step beside his clothes. He opened his fist, and placed a plastic blue triceratops beside him. Raising his fingers toward the sun, he studied whatever he had found, then rubbed the item on his shirt.

Ian wasn't sure if Mattie would break the silence, so he waved to the boy. "Did you find something good?"

The boy glanced at Ian, then turned around, looking to see if someone was behind him. Seeing that he was alone, he pocketed the small item and picked up his toy dinosaur.

"We've been watching you," Ian continued. "You're a magnificent swimmer."

Shaking his head, the boy looked down at his feet.

"What's your name?" Mattie asked. "I'm Mattie. I'm ten and a half years old. And this is my daddy. His name is Ian."

The boy studied Ian and Mattie. He stroked his dinosaur. "Rupee," he said softly. "I Rupee."

"Is that your friend?" Mattie wondered, pointing at the blue triceratops.

Rupee covered the toy with his hands but nodded. "He Prem."

Mattie smiled. "How old are you?"

Shrugging, Rupee put on his sandals. "Bye-bye."

"Wait," Mattie said, standing up. "Do you want to go to lunch with us? We're about to have lunch."

Rupee looked around again, his thin toes moving back and forth in his sandals.

Ian sensed the boy's fear. "I promise we don't want anything from you. Nothing at all. Mattie just hopes to make a new mate. A new friend, I mean."

Rupee's eyes narrowed and he bit his lower lip. "Me no have money."

"We know," Ian answered. "We don't want your loot. And we'll buy you lunch."

"Whatever you want," Mattie added.

Rupee was confused. People had stolen from him so many times before. He'd been beaten, thrown naked into the river. He was afraid of most everyone—of the bullies who also looked for gold teeth and tried to take whatever he found, of the gangs that preyed on the homeless. Only his dinosaur, Prem, had always remained faithful, had never hurt him.

"Please come with us," Mattie said, nodding. "We only want to have lunch with you. In a nice restaurant where you can get really full."

Rupee wasn't sure what she meant. He had never been in a restaurant. But he watched her eyes and they did not seem to be the eyes of someone who would hurt him. They reminded him of Prem's eyes.

"You look hungry," Mattie continued. "Don't you want some food?"

For two days Rupee had been hungry—he hadn't eaten for longer than that. He longed to trust this girl, who smiled at him, who didn't turn away.

Mattie nodded. "Will you be my Indian friend? Please?"

Rupee had never been asked to be anyone's friend. He dipped his head, his heartbeat quickening.

Ian smiled and walked up the steps, followed by Mattie and Rupee. The smoke and heat from a nearby funeral pyre drifted over him. He smelled flowers, incense, sandalwood, and the scent of a body being transformed by fire. As he increased his speed, Ian glanced behind him, unsure what to do with the boy, but glad that Mattie wanted to help him.

Forty or fifty steps brought them to a funeral procession—a body covered in layers of marigold flowers, surrounded by a few dozen relatives. Ian turned to his right, avoiding the procession, stepping up and up until the riverbank plateaued and the city stretched away from him.

Holding Mattie's hand, he led them forward, pleased that Rupee hadn't run away. Varanasi appeared far different from the interior than it did from the river. People had been living on this stretch of land for three thousand years, and buildings looked to be about that old—stained and crumbling, covered in faded advertisements and draped with electrical wires. Where the buildings met the streets dozens of beggars congregated. Lepers held crying children. Cows lay in filth. A woman with no legs had tied herself to a tire and moved by putting her hands on the pitted pavement and lifting herself up. Hundreds of middle-class Indians also filled the alleys, as well as a few tourists with their digital cameras and oversized traveling hats.

Rupee knew how to speak some English but was afraid to ask anything of these foreigners. He didn't want them to leave him, not when he was so hungry, when his stomach felt as if two snakes were fighting inside it. He followed the tall man down the streets, wondering where they were headed. His hand in his pocket, Rupee felt Prem and the silver nose ring that he'd found on the bottom of the river. The nose ring, he believed, would feed him for a few weeks. He'd been lucky to find it hidden beneath an old tree trunk that had shifted in the silt. He would have to hide it well, for the gangs would search him.

As Rupee walked, he studied the girl beside him. She was dressed in simple but nice clothes—red shorts and a T-shirt with dolphins on the front. She often smiled at him, and he liked the way her freckles moved as the corners of her mouth turned up. She was beautiful, he thought, more beautiful than anything he had ever seen.

Rupee followed her into a narrow but towering building. He had never been inside such a place. Normally, he wouldn't be welcome here, but the presence of the foreigners changed everything. A woman said hello to the tall man and led them toward a stairwell. Rupee trailed the girl up the stairs, his fingers rubbing Prem, his nervousness causing him to miss a step and stumble.

The stairs finally ended, revealing a rooftop restaurant. They walked to a table near the edge of the building, overlooking the Ganges River. Rupee had never seen the river from such a high place, and his eyes widened. The river shimmered, fires along its shore, boats dotting its surface. The man pulled out a chair and motioned for Rupee to sit. He did as asked, moving closer to the table and smiling for the first time since meeting the strangers. They weren't going to hurt him, he decided.

"What a marvelous view," Ian said, motioning toward the river. "And what a marvelous day." He looked at Rupee. "We're glad to have you with us. It's a real pleasure."

Rupee grinned again, nodding at Mattie.

"I like your name," she said.

He fingered Prem beneath the table, remembering how the bigger boys had named him Rupee because he was small, like a coin, and was always begging for rupees. "My name, like Indian money," he said, his feet swinging back and forth.

A waitress wearing a yellow T-shirt and black pants emerged from the stairway. She said hello, placed three menus on the table, and asked what they might like to drink. Mattie saw Rupee's confusion, and she ordered them each an orange Fanta. Ian asked for a bottle of water.

Rupee opened his menu, but since he couldn't read, it was no use to him. He decided to order whatever Mattie did. He felt silly to be looking at a menu, as he was used to trading trinkets for bowls of rice or pieces of bread. Ordering from menus was something reserved for the rich.

The waitress returned with their drinks. Rupee saw the straw in his Fanta and smiled. He'd never used a straw and wasn't certain how it worked. After watching Mattie sip from her drink, he put his lips to the straw and tried to suck. Unfortunately, he pulled the sugary drink into his lungs and started to cough, surprised to see Fanta dripping out his nose. Though his nose burned, Rupee saw Mattie grin and he smiled at his misfortune.

"You have to suck it into your mouth, and then swallow it," she said, slowly drinking more of her Fanta. "You see? Suck it into your mouth and then swish it around your teeth."

Rupee wasn't certain he understood her correctly, but he did his best to copy her movements. The drink was so sugary in his mouth that he couldn't help but smile. He giggled, swallowing the Fanta, slurping through his straw.

A wasp landed on Mattie's arm, and she instinctively leapt up from her chair, knocking the table and causing her father's bottle to topple. Water splashed on the table, running onto Rupee's shorts and legs, prompting him to smile again. "I always in water," he said, as she used a napkin to wipe the table. "No problem."

Ian helped clean up the mess. He watched Mattie and Rupee grin at each other. She seemed younger in the presence of another child, and he felt lucky that Rupee was with them. Though Ian sought to make Mattie laugh, he knew that there were limits to what he could do. He couldn't giggle over straws and spilled water. He could try to be a child, but he wasn't a child.

The waitress returned. When it was Rupee's turn to order, he simply pointed at Mattie and held up two fingers. Understanding his motions, the waitress nodded, then dropped to her knees and lit a citronella candle beneath the table.

"Rupee, were you born in Varanasi?" Ian asked.

Rupee shrugged, smiling. "Me not know. Only remember Varanasi. Me not think I born in Los Angeles, London, or Paris."

Ian chuckled, surprised at how quickly Rupee had emerged from his shell. "You sure? Your accent sounds a bit French."

"Sometimes, Mr. Ian, I beg near river. I talk with foreigners. So I learn to speak little English, little France, little German. That way people give me more money. Other boys call me Rupee because I get so many coin."

"And your parents . . . are they in Varanasi?"

Rupee's smile vanished. "I think the Ganga River is my mother and father. I swim every day, look for pretty things."

"You're not scared?" Mattie asked.

"Prem make me safe," Rupee said, removing the dinosaur from his pocket and putting it on the table.

Mattie could see that Prem was scratched, sun bleached, and missing the tip of his tail. "Where did you find him?"

Rupee stroked the dinosaur's back as he took another sip of his drink. "In Ganga. Long time ago, when I scared to swim in deep water. I find Prem and he always my best friend."

The waitress returned with their food, setting steaming plates of curried chicken and rice before each person. Rupee had never seen so much food. He couldn't believe that one little person like Mattie could eat so much. Wouldn't that be enough to last her for three days?

Rupee started to reach for his rice with his fingers but saw that Mattie was using a spoon. Unsure how to eat with such an instrument, he tried to mimic her movements. The spoon was awkward in his hand, like a steel finger that he suddenly needed to move. He felt silly holding the spoon and once again grinned.

"What's so funny?" Mattie asked, moving up and down in her chair.

"I never eat with spoon. It feel so strange in my mouth. Like a rock."

"A rock? But it's smooth."

"Still feel like rock to me. Maybe I break tooth if I bite too hard."

Ian watched Mattie and Rupee laugh. He was delighted that two children, complete strangers and from such different pasts, could joke together about a spoon. He looked up, wishing that Kate could see their daughter giggling with Rupee. It felt so good to hear her laugh. The pain in his stomach, in his mind, seemed to disappear when he heard her laugh. He felt as if he were undergoing a restoration, like an old sailboat that was being refitted and set out to sea.

As Ian studied Rupee, he thought about what to do with the boy. In two days, he and Mattie would depart for Hong Kong, and they couldn't leave Rupee on the streets. But neither could they take him. Finding an orphanage seemed like the best idea. Surely, some place would accept a bright, happy boy. But how to find such a place? And how to keep from hurting either Mattie or Rupee by splitting them up so quickly?

Mattie finished her lunch, stood up, took Rupee's hand, and led him to the edge of the balcony. They were four or five stories above the ground and had an excellent view of the Ganges. Rupee squinted, studying the funeral pyres. He thought he saw boys diving under the brown water, looking for treasures from the dead. Though Rupee had long ago accepted his fate, he didn't want to go back to the river, at least not yet. He liked the American girl. No one had ever held his hand, and he enjoyed the feel of her fingers against his. She was clean and beautiful, and yet she held his hand, as if he were her friend and not an untouchable.

Rupee squeezed her fingers, not wanting her to let go.

Mattie saw that his smile was gone, that he was afraid she would leave. "Let's get you some new sandals, Rupee," she said, leading him away from the sight of the river. "Those are going to fall off your feet, and you won't be able to show us around the city if your feet hurt."

Ian watched his daughter walk hand in hand with Rupee toward the stairs. She was taking care of him, Ian realized. Though she'd always longed for a little sister, it seemed that she saw Rupee as a little brother of sorts, as someone she wanted to nurture and protect.

As they hurried down the stairs, Ian began to worry about their looming separation, wondering if there was anything he could do to soften the blow.

FIVE HOURS LATER, RUPEE WAS WEARING NEW clothes and sandals. His belly was full. Maybe best of all, at least from Rupee's perspective, was that Ian had opened a bank account in Rupee's name and deposited five hundred dollars. With his new identification card, Rupee could go to the bank and withdraw small sums of money whenever he was hungry. Because of this arrangement, Rupee wasn't worried about having to hide his valuables from the other boys. If he found a piece of jewelry, he could sell it, deposit the money, and then live on his earnings.

Rupee had never understood the workings of banks, but Ian had explained to him in great detail how people went about depositing and withdrawing money. Normally, Rupee wouldn't have been allowed in any bank, but with his new clothes, and with Ian and Mattie at his side, he hadn't experienced any problems. And the bank manager had been happy to take Ian's deposit.

Numerous times during the day, Rupee had looked at the sun and thought about how he'd normally be swimming in the Ganga, fighting the current and the blackness, sifting through the silt to try to discover the treasures of the dead. Most days he found nothing more than bits of wood, stone, and bone. He went to bed hungry, sleeping in a half-sunk fishing boat that rotted at the water's edge. He hid in the boat, lying beside the old wheelhouse, nestled in newspapers, Prem perched on his belly. Rupee always went to the boat well after dark, when the older boys were unlikely to find his hiding place. And he woke up at dawn, returning to the streets or the river.

Now, as Rupee followed Mattie, he couldn't believe how one chance encounter had so drastically changed his life. He'd eaten in a restaurant for the first time, wore new clothes, had a fortune in a bank, and a girl from America called him her friend. Rupee had never been happier. He felt as if he were flying instead of walking. His mind seemed to sing instead of slumber. Even his eyes felt sharper.

Rupee had never been to the small amusement park on the outskirts of Varanasi, but that was where he, Mattie, and Ian were headed. They'd taken a taxi from the center of town, heading only a few kilometers from the river, but driving by sights foreign to Rupee—gardens and three-storied homes and markets with piles of food and goods.

The entrance to the amusement park was little more than an iron gate flanked by a pair of ticket booths. Ian paid a nominal fee and led Mattie and Rupee inside. Both children were excited. Mattie took Rupee's hand and hurried forward, past groups of laughing teenagers, women sitting on benches, men taking photos with their cell phones. Though dusk approached, the day was still stifling. The heat was as noticeable as the balloons that sailed upward from the failed grasp of toddlers.

Mattie led Rupee toward a small roller-coaster ride. A metal frame consisting of iron rods rose fifty or sixty feet high. A few dozen people formed a line that ran toward the ride. Ian looked up and saw a black, bubblelike car rumbling down the rails. The car screeched to a halt near the front of the line.

Mattie, who tended to observe a whole scene rather than its parts, tugged on her father's arm. Pointing toward a rise in the track, she asked, "Daddy, are those people . . . pedaling up that hill?"

Squinting, Ian peered at the car making its slow way up the rise. He saw that no chain or cable ran up the hill to carry the car. In fact, the entire roller-coaster ride seemed to not contain a single engine. "I reckon you're as right as rain," he said, wondering how Indian information technology personnel helped to run his company while their roller coaster didn't have a power supply. "Shall we give it a go?"

"Absobloodylutely," Mattie replied, rising on her tiptoes to try to peer beyond the people in front of her. Putting her hand on Rupee's shoulder, she jumped up. "We're almost there!"

Rupee smiled, giggling at the thought of going on a roller coaster. He'd heard of such rides but hadn't imagined sitting on one. "Thank you, Mr. Ian," he said. "Prem and me, we thank you so many times."

"You're welcome, Rupee. So many times."

Another few minutes passed before the trio stood at the front of the line. An attendant pulled a lever that somehow slowed an approaching car. Four laughing teens climbed out of two rows of seats. Mattie and Rupee got in the front seat, while Ian moved behind them. Sure enough, a pair of bicycle pedals was positioned just above the floor in front of Ian. He chuckled and put his feet on the pedals. "Ready, Roo?"

"Aye, aye, Captain!" Mattie answered, laughing.

"And you, Rupee?"

"Yes, Mr. Ian!"

Ian glanced at the attendant, who motioned for them to get going. Ian started to pedal and the car moved forward with surprising ease. A hill approached, and as soon as the car began to tilt upward, the resistance to the pedals intensified. A click could be heard beneath the car with each revolution of the pedals, and Ian assumed that some sort of safety feature kept the car from sliding backward.

The going was tough and Ian started to sweat. "You ankle biters pedaling up there?" he asked, tousling Mattie's hair.

She giggled. "Let's go faster."

The car continued to lumber upward. "It's like towing a bloody elephant up a hill!" Ian added, sweating profusely.

"Daddy! Stop being such a baby!"

Rupee laughed, peering over the side of the car, surprised at how high they'd already climbed. He pulled Prem out of his pocket and showed him the view. "Don't get too scared," he whispered in Hindi. "I promise we'll be all right."

Finally the car reached the crest of the hill, which plateaued for about twenty feet before descending in a series of rises and falls. "Look around, you two," Ian said, gazing at the distant city. Varanasi seemed to smolder beneath the setting sun. Dead ahead, a pair of naked lightbulbs marked the start of the descent. Encircling the bulbs were hundreds of flying insects.

"Hold on!" Mattie shouted, as the car tipped forward and down.

The descent was faster than Ian would have guessed possible. The car dropped as if free-falling, producing screams from Mattie and Rupee. Ian laughed at the sound of the shrieking children, holding on as the car plummeted and soared. Though the ride didn't have loops like roller coasters back home, for some reason Ian found this experience more enjoyable. The world rushed past, his heart seemed to skip a few beats, and Mattie and Rupee screamed as if they were on Space Mountain at Disney World.

When they approached the line of people on the ground, unseen brakes slowed the car in a start-and-stop fashion. Ian watched Mattie lean close to Rupee and laugh with him. At that moment Ian's joy faded. He thought about how he had never given her a sibling, how she was destined to grow up alone, and how he would die one day and leave her with no one.

As such thoughts dominated him, he felt trapped in the battered car. He saw its age for the first time—the rust on its floor, the frayed ends of the seat belt. He watched Mattie help Rupee from their seat and knew that soon they would be separated. Mattie would leave India, and Rupee would be once again on his own. Ian had already decided to spend the next morning researching and contacting orphanages, but he was worried about being turned away. He couldn't leave Rupee on the streets, but if the orphanages were full or uninterested, what choice would he have?

Mattie took Rupee's hand and hurried toward the next ride—which looked to involve some sort of water balloon fight. Sure enough, a pair of adversaries spaced about thirty feet apart used oversized slingshots to launch water balloons at each other. The participants stood in a chain-link cage, so that errant balloons didn't fly into passersby.

"Rupee and me against you, Daddy!" Mattie said, handing their tickets to an attendant. The man explained the rules in English, gave Ian a bucket with ten water balloons, and handed another full bucket to Mattie and Rupee.

Ian joked with Mattie, laughing, trying to fill her with joy even though he no longer felt joyous. I've become such a bloody actor, he thought, as he held up a balloon and threatened to throw it at his daughter. Kate's dead. And sometimes the future scares the wits right out of me. But I have to smile and laugh and pretend that tomorrow is going to be lovely. But what if it's never lovely? What if I have to pretend for the rest of my life? Soon Mattie will see right through me, and then I'll only make her sadder.

His stomach starting to ache, Ian chewed on an antacid and picked up a red balloon. Placing it in the slingshot, he pulled back and yelled, "Ready to get wet?"

Mattie and Rupee laughed, working together to arm their slingshot. Mattie shrieked as they let go, and their blue balloon tumbled through the air, hitting the chain-link fence above Ian, dousing him with water. "I see ya be declarin' war on me, Blackbeard the Terrible," he said, speaking and snarling like a pirate. "Well, ya scurvy dogs, y'll be walkin' thee plank before this day's dead." Aiming his slingshot, he let go, howling triumphantly when his balloon burst directly over their heads.

The children shrieked, quickly reloaded, and sent a balloon in his direction. Ian could have ducked out of the way but he let it hit him in the chest. "Y've struck a blow," he shouted, pretending to stagger. "But me ain't one to run from a brawl. Prepare to be boarded!" He picked up another balloon, which popped in his hands as he tried to load it. "Curse thee cannon!" Another balloon splattered above him. "Ye think Blackbeard will go down so easy?" he said, baring his teeth.

"Have a drink!" Mattie shouted, as she and Rupee fired another balloon.

Ian smiled, a genuine smile, one that at least temporarily denied his pain and fear. He knew that he would make mistakes with Mattie, that he would fail her, that no matter how much he loved her, he wasn't capable of being a perfect father. And one day he would be gone, leaving her with only memories of him, of their best and worst times together.

He wanted this moment to be one of the best times, something that would give her solace in the years when he was gone. So despite the many aches that compromised his life, he pulled back on his slingshot, told them to fear the wrath of Blackbeard, and launched his yellow balloon.

THE NEXT DAY BEGAN WITH BREAKFAST ON the veranda outside their hotel. Rupee had slept on the floor of their room and now sat next to Mattie, eating from a carton of yogurt. Though usually Ian ordered local food, he'd made the mistake of asking for scrambled eggs and forced himself not to grimace as he ate hunks of watery, half-cooked eggs. Normally, he would have set the food aside and munched on a piece of bread, but in Rupee's presence, he ate every last bite of the eggs.

Though Mattie had spent much of the previous day laughing with Rupee, she was less animated this morning. They were leaving for Hong Kong the following day, and she didn't want to say good-bye to Rupee. He knew how to make her smile, how to laugh and be silly. She had forgotten what it was like to have an aching belly after laughing on and off all afternoon. And she loved how Rupee grinned when she took his hand and led him forward.

Ian was eager to start looking for orphanages and paid the breakfast bill as soon as possible. The hotel had a small business center, and he stepped into it, then settled down in front of a computer and a phone. While Mattie taught Rupee how to draw with her colored pencils, Ian got online and started researching orphanages in Varanasi. He worked hard and fast, as he had before Kate had gotten sick. His fingers beat against the keyboard as if it were an instrument. His eyes read groupings of words instead of individual words. He was unaware of the children beside him.

Within an hour, Ian had a list of four orphanages that appeared to be reputable and well run. He picked up the phone and started making calls, being polite but also succinct and aggressive in his line of questioning. There were some advantages to being a foreigner in India, and he relied on these strengths, asking to speak with managers, pushing people when he felt that they were being evasive.

Once Ian had settled on what he thought was the best orphanage in the city, he tried to convince the man on the other end of the phone that Rupee would be a welcome addition. Though Ian spoke about Rupee's good health and disposition, the man said that his orphanage was filled beyond capacity. Ian reached for an antacid, thinking of a way out. In the end, he promised to make a thousand-dollar donation to the orphanage if the manager would take Rupee. The man was delighted by Ian's suggestion, and the details of the deal were quickly negotiated.

Though Ian felt rushed in his decision-making process, he knew that even if the orphanage wasn't perfect, Rupee would be much better off than he had been a few days earlier. The boy had his own bank account, and the orphanage sounded like an honorable establishment.

Ian was worried that Rupee would be sad to leave them, but on the contrary, he was thrilled by the prospect of having a place to live. After Ian explained the workings of the orphanage, and how he and Mattie would try to find a family to adopt Rupee, the boy started smiling again, as if unbelieving of his good fortune.

Wanting to spend as much time as possible at the orphanage, Ian led the children to a taxi. The streets of Varanasi were predictably chaotic, and the driver punched at the horn like a moth battering itself against a streetlight. It took about twenty minutes to reach the orphanage, a two-story cement building adjacent to a dusty soccer field. Children swarmed over the field, chasing several balls, as if multiple games were occurring on the same patch of dirt.

Ian, Mattie, and Rupee walked past the field and toward the building. They hadn't yet stepped inside when a well-dressed man emerged, introduced himself, and shook Ian's hand. The manager spoke with Rupee in Hindi, and soon both were smiling.

After several minutes of small talk, the manager asked if Mattie and Rupee wanted to play soccer while he spoke with Ian. Mattie wasn't interested, and politely declined, taking Rupee's hand and leading him toward a purple bench near the other children. Ian and the manager stood not more than thirty feet away, watching the children, talking about Rupee's future.

Mattie edged closer to her friend. "I'm going to miss you, Rupee," she said, happy for him but sad for herself.

Rupee smiled, sure that he was dreaming, that an American girl couldn't possibly think of him as a friend, that he hadn't arrived at such a beautiful orphanage. "Why?" he asked. "Why you my friend? Everyone else, they think I dirty. Cannot touch me."

Her hand found his. "You make me smile, Rupee. And you're not dirty. See? My skin is against yours and there's no dirt anywhere. So if anyone ever calls you dirty again, you just think about your hand against mine."

Rupee nodded, remembering sifting through piles of bones at the bottom of the river, hoping that Mattie was right, that his hands had somehow remained clean. "You send me letter? From Hong Kong? I get someone to read it for me."

"I'll send you a lot of letters. A heap of letters, as my daddy would say."

"I no forget you."

"And I won't forget you."

Rupee looked at her skin against his, remembering her words. He didn't have a single memory of being held, of a hand against his. "I so happy," he said.

Despite her sadness at the thought of leaving him, Mattie smiled, reaching into her backpack. She took out her sketch pad and leafed through its pages, coming to the image she had drawn of him. She set the pad on his lap. "Someday, Rupee, I'll come back to India. And I'll draw another picture of you."

He studied her sketch, smiling at his smile in the picture, warmed by the glow of his face. "You so good, Mattie. I think maybe . . . maybe a painter . . . he already reborn into you."

Mattie thought about the river, about whether her mother was in heaven or had been reborn, as the Hindus thought. "Rupee? Can you climb a tree with me?"

"A tree? Why?"

"Because I want to leave a picture for my mother. So she can see it."

Rupee looked around the soccer field, pointing to an immense teak tree at the corner of the building. "Like that one?" he asked, carefully handing her back the sketch pad.

She nodded, then walked to the orphanage's manager, asking him if they could climb a tree and leave a message for her mother. The man's brow furrowed, but then he saw the yearning in her expression, and he nodded. Knowing that her father was watching, Mattie walked toward the tree.

The climb was difficult, as the trunk had been pruned of low branches. Rupee went first, jumping up, grabbing onto the stump of a broken branch and hoisting himself higher. Mattie repeated his motions, her backpack moving from side to side as she climbed. She wondered how high Rupee would go, hoping that he wouldn't stop. Wanting to give her mother the best possible view of her sketch, Mattie climbed higher. She liked following Rupee, liked that he looked down to make sure she was fine. Twice he held out his hand for her, helping her up, their fingers intertwined.

Mattie asked herself what it would be like to climb a tree with a brother or sister. Would they always help each other? Would they be best friends?

Rupee stopped, leaning against the trunk. He pulled Mattie up again and she straddled a nearby branch. They were higher than the top of the adjacent building, and Mattie saw that an immense puddle had formed in the center of the flat roof.

Using her right hand, Mattie unslung her backpack, opened it, and removed her sketch pad. She leafed through the pad until locating her drawing of the Taj Mahal. She studied the drawing, showed it to Rupee, and then carefully folded it and stuck it into a crevice formed within a split branch. She looked up, trying to somehow glimpse her mother's spirit. She spoke silently to her mother, asking her to watch over Rupee, to make sure that he was safe and happy.

"Why you leave picture in tree?" Rupee asked, Prem held tight in his hand.

Mattie put on her backpack, glancing below at her father, who stood near the base of the tree. "My mother . . . she's dead, like I told you. But she loves to see my drawings, and to read my words. So I put them in wishing trees."

"Wishing trees?"

"Places where I feel closer to her, where I know she's looking."

Rupee nodded. "Tomorrow, when you at airport, when you go to new country, I come outside and look for your drawing. If it fall to ground, I carry it back up, put it at top of tree again. Then your mother see it for many days."

Mattie moved her loose tooth with her tongue, not wanting to think of being separated from Rupee. "Do . . . do you miss your mother, Rupee?"

"Me no remember her, so me no miss her. But sometime . . . me see mother with boy, and this make me sad."

"I know. Me too."

"But you take me here, so now I so happy. Maybe someday I have mother."

"We're going to find you a family. My daddy's really great at that stuff."

Rupee exhaled deeply, as if he'd just arisen from the river's murky waters. "Me think me already reborn. When you say hello, when you take me to eat food, that day I born again. Me lucky. No have to get body burned, pushed into water to get reborn. I already reborn. You are like my Ganga River."

"Really?"

"You . . . you do so much for me. Next time I see you, I do so much for you. And Mr. Ian. I make you feel reborn too."

Mattie studied his smile. She was so happy to see it. But her smile was only half as wide. She wasn't ready to say good-bye to the boy who made her laugh, who gave her his hand and helped her climb a tree.

Mattie wanted to be reborn. She understood what he was talking about. She longed to wake up and have everything different, everything the way it had been.

"I'll miss you, Rupee," she said, biting her lower lip so that she wouldn't cry.

Rupee's smile wavered, and he reached out to her, their fingers meeting and clasping, neither of them quite ready to climb down from the wishing tree, from a place where rebirth seemed so near and yet so far.

HONG KONG

Pain and Pleasure

"It is only when the cold season comes that we know the pine and cypress to be evergreens."

—Chinese saying

The hotel rose like a sword into the night sky. The ultramodern building was sleek and soaring, thrusting higher than the half dozen skyscrapers crowding around it. Forty rows of oversized windows provided guests with spectacular views of downtown Hong Kong, which at night resembled its own solar system, replete with brilliant constellations, glowing planets, and setting suns. The city seemed afire with color and radiance. The skyscrapers weren't simply tall rectangles of steel and glass, but sculpted and flowing structures illuminated by millions of green, purple, blue, and red lights that reflected off the clouds, the nearby sea, and the mountains, giving rise to a futuristic landscape that might have been conjured within the pages of a science fiction novel.

Ian stood near the window of their hotel room, peering through a telescope at the world below. Four high-rises fell within his immediate field of view, and all appeared to be apartment buildings. Many featured large windows, and he saw families eating dinner, watching television, gathered around flat-screen computer monitors. Children ran from room to room while mothers washed dishes. Fathers spoke on cell phones, pacing like caged lions. Other telescopes twisted and turned as people studied the scenes around them.

Not sure what to think of such voyeurism, Ian continued to look into the night. The nearby buildings must have housed wealthy families, for many of the apartments contained a variety of large rooms. Ian intensified the strength of the telescope and was able to see children smiling and laughing. He watched a pair of boys make paper airplanes and toss them around a family room. Sitting nearby, a man and a woman, presumably the parents, drank wine and smiled at their children's antics.

Ian turned the telescope, scanning lit and unobscured windows, pausing when he realized that a woman in a nearby building was staring through her telescope at him. He stepped back, fumbled at the buttons of his pajamas, and then once again put his eye to the instrument. The woman wore a black cocktail dress. Her hair was pinned up, dark ringlets held in place by a pair of lacquered chopsticks. She waved to him, then turned her telescope elsewhere.

Twisting to Mattie, Ian started to ask if she wanted to look out into the night but realized that sights of cheerful families would only further dampen her mood. She had been quiet since they'd left India—actually, since they'd left Rupee. Ian was aware of how quickly Mattie and Rupee had formed a bond, a connection based perhaps on the losses they shared. After Kate's death, Ian had often arranged playdates with Mattie's friends, but she'd never seemed to want to be around them. Maybe they had been too happy, their lives too perfect. One day, Mattie had asked Ian to stop inviting her friends. She'd wanted to be with him, or with no one.

Usually when Mattie was feeling low, Ian tried to engage her with humor or games or stories. But tonight he felt too tired. He wanted to surrender for the day. He didn't have the strength to act, to pretend that the moment was grand when he felt as if he'd stepped into a black hole. Watching the families below, he had been reminded of all he had lost.

Ian walked to the couch, where Mattie sat working on a geography lesson. She wore her pajamas, which had been purchased at the Bronx Zoo and featured a collage of African animals. Her hair, unbraided, yet still curled from the memory of being held fast, fell below her shoulders. He kissed the top of her head and put his arm around her. "Need any help, luv?" he asked, kissing her again.

"No."

"What are you working on?"

She closed her book, which had been open to a map of India. "We shouldn't have left him, Daddy. He's all alone."

Ian sighed, rubbing his brow, wishing he had an antacid handy. "Roo, three days ago he was homeless and swimming for gold teeth. Tonight he's sleeping in a bed, with a full belly, and a bunch of nice blokes around him. And he's got his own bank account, which is full of loot. I reckon we shouldn't be too hard on ourselves."

"But what if—"

"And, luv, we're going to stay in touch with the orphanage. We'll make sure that he's all right. And when we get back to the States we'll try and find him a family."

"What about our family?"

"I can't adopt a child, Roo, without a wife."

She turned away. "Then we don't have a family, do we?"

"What?"

"If they won't give us Rupee, then they don't think we have a family."

"Anyone who fancies that notion is a bloody fool," he replied, leaning away from her so that he might see all of her face. "You don't believe that, do you?"

She wiped her eyes. "I don't know. I think . . . maybe we have half a family."

"Half a family?"

"That's what they think. That's why they won't give us Rupee."

"What a bunch of rubbish."

"It's not!"

"We helped him, Roo. Can't you just focus on that?"

"I don't understand. I—"

"You reckon I do? But I'm doing my best, just like you are."

"I miss Rupee."

He sighed, glancing at the ceiling, wanting to curse whatever god dwelled above. "Did you see his smile? He was as happy as a butterfly on a breeze. We made him happy. You made him happy. Just like your mum wanted you to."

"I don't feel happy. We shouldn't have left him. We left him just like everyone else did."

Ian felt anger building within him. Before he raised his voice and said something he'd regret, he stood up, walked into the bathroom, and grabbed an antacid. He looked at himself in the mirror, wondering who he was becoming. He wanted to fall to his knees, lean against the counter, and close his eyes. Instead he chewed the medicine, took a deep breath, and ran his hands through his hair. He squeezed two fistfuls of hair tight, strands falling as he removed his hands from his head. Swearing to himself, he took another antacid and pressed the lever on the toilet as if it were his enemy.

He washed his face, took several minutes to calm down, then returned to his daughter, not wanting to fight with her, memories of his fights with Kate like thorns in his soul. "What if we go shopping for Rupee tomorrow?" he asked, drawing near her. "What if we buy him another set of clothes, and . . . and maybe some more dinosaurs? We could mail him a package and he'd have it in a couple of days."

Mattie looked up at him, her eyes widening. "Really? Could we do that? Could we find him some dinosaurs?"

"In this city? I reckon we could find him anything we want. Have you looked out the window? It's like we're in the middle of a Christmas tree."

She glanced outside, nodding. "Can we go in the morning, before we do anything else?"

"Sure, luv. We'll go dino hunting. Care to be my lookout?"

"Aye, aye, Captain."

He put his arm around her, still thinking about her earlier words, about not having a family. "Let's head for bed," he said, taking her hand and standing up. "I reckon if we're going to rise early and find some dinos, we'd best get some sleep."

"Okay, Daddy."

Impulsively, Ian lifted her up, carrying her toward the bed, laying her down. He crawled in beside her, pulling the sheet over them. She asked him to tell her a story, and stroking her brow, he forced his own thoughts of doubt and pain aside and mused over what tale he might bring to life. He told her a story of a girl who drove a truck, who was supposed to deliver pigs, cows, chickens, and turkeys to cities where they would be eaten by people. But instead of delivering the animals as promised, the girl drove them to a secret valley and freed them within a land of endless grass and lakes. She lived with them for the summer and then returned every summer thereafter, growing older, in time bringing her children with her. The valley, the animals, her children—everything seemed to get more beautiful with each passing week and month and year. And the woman's happiness grew as well, because she was so loved.

Mattie smiled. She put her head on his chest and fell asleep. Ian tried to do likewise but wasn't able to so easily tame his thoughts. He crept quietly from the bed, returning to the telescope. He searched for families within the wombs of light below him. Many people had gone to sleep, but other families lingered, sitting together around tables, using chopsticks to pluck food from colorful platters. These families laughed; they sometimes appeared to argue. They didn't necessarily seem to savor their moments together, but they were together, and in that togetherness Ian saw a certain kind of beauty, something not created by the skill of an artist or the grand design of the world, but by people who loved one another, even if they didn't always recognize that love.

Watching the families—seeing the mothers and fathers interact with their children—brought tears to Ian's eyes. Though he would never admit it to her, he shared Mattie's loneliness; he understood its nuances. He understood it because he needed Kate; he needed her to help make their little girl well again. Without Kate, Ian sometimes felt powerless, no matter how hard he tried. And when he felt powerless, the true loneliness set in, the feeling of being the only person in the world.

Ian wiped his eyes, continuing to watch the families. Seven or eight stories below, a mother put her fingers on her young daughter's face, playfully pinching her cheek. Ian remembered Kate doing the same thing to Mattie. He recalled one Halloween when Mattie dressed as a bumblebee and Kate pinched her cheek again and again. For a moment he panicked, wondering where the costume was, afraid that he'd lost it, that his memories of such times would fade.

The woman below lifted up her daughter, holding the girl in one arm while tickling her stomach. Again, Ian thought of Kate doing the same thing to Mattie, of what Mattie was missing. And that thought put such a weight on him that he slowly fell to his knees, the telescope swinging up toward the starless sky.

Much later, not knowing what else to do, Ian returned to their bed, holding the shell Kate had given him. He wrapped his arms around Mattie and drew her tight against his chest. He listened to her breathe, hoping that she was dreaming about good things, that she wasn't afraid to dream of better times.

"I love you, Roo," he whispered, kissing the back of her head, wondering how he might let her see them as a family, as not just a father and a daughter, but as a family that could smile and laugh and dream together.

THE RESTAURANT LOOKED AS IF IT SHOULD have been at a downtown corner instead of floating in the harbor. The ornamental three-story building was almost as long as a city block. Blue with red trim, it featured a flat roof highlighted by a pair of enclosed, tentlike structures. Most of the diners throughout the three levels were protected from the elements, though about thirty rooftop tables absorbed the sunlight.

Located at the end of a pier, the floating restaurant was accessed by a walkway, but also surrounded by dozens of wooden sampans that ferried people to stairs descending from the lower level of the building into the water. The sampans were in constant motion, shuttling people to and from the shore, various piers, and much larger boats. Many of the vessels were padded with truck tires, as if their captains expected constant collisions.

From their rooftop table, Mattie looked across the harbor. Hong Kong's skyscrapers seemed to rise from the sea, soaring toward the clouds, partly obscuring the much taller mountains behind them. The skyline was as impressive during the day as it had been the previous night. She'd never seen a city that seemed to shine like Hong Kong. The skyscrapers weren't old and stained, but new and sparkling—testaments to boundless human creativity and determination.

The restaurant was populated by hundreds of Chinese, most of whom appeared to be businesspeople. Many of the men wore somber suits and ate quickly. The women also tended to dress in dark colors—blouses and pants that seemed infinitely less inspired than the distant buildings. Since the tables were only a few feet apart, Mattie could listen to the different dialects around her. Though she might normally have felt out of place in her jeans and blue T-shirt, the burlap shopping bag resting against her leg made her happy. Inside were gifts for Rupee—three sets of clothes, a wristwatch, and, most important, a large collection of dinosaurs. Mattie had wanted to find the dinosaurs first, and they'd spent the better part of the morning wandering around downtown, trying to locate a toy store. When they finally succeeded, she had seen the dinosaurs and laughed out loud, running ahead to sort through the brimming bins.

Shopping for Rupee had made them hungry, and they'd taken a sampan to one of the largest dim sum restaurants in the city. Mattie hadn't been sure what to order, but fortunately, the thick menus featured photographs of each dish. As she now looked at their table, she couldn't believe the variety of food. The small-sized entrees came in wooden baskets and plastic plates and bowls. There were steamed shrimp dumplings, rice-noodle rolls, baked buns filled with spicy pork, sweet and sour calamari, deep-fried chicken feet, vegetables wrapped in lotus leaves, egg tarts, tofu dripping in a sweet ginger syrup, and mango pudding. Mattie had tried everything except the deep-fried chicken feet. Their waiter had spoken of how delicious they were, and so Ian had ordered a serving. He'd been brave, finishing half of the plate before moving on to other dishes.

Mattie was eager to find a post office so they could mail their presents to Rupee, and she ate quickly.

Ian watched her, understanding the reason for her haste. He smiled. "These are delicacies, luv," he said. "I reckon the chef wouldn't fancy you sucking them down like spaghetti."

"I like the dumplings. I could eat a whole dinner of them."

"Should we order some more?"

"Aye, aye, Captain."

Ian turned to one of the many waiters hurrying about and ordered more dumplings, as well as another pot of tea. "It makes me happy to see you happy," he said, handing Mattie a plate of sweet and sour calamari.

"Just don't give me any of those chicken feet."

"Why not be bold, Roo?"

She scowled, the freckles on her nose coming closer together. "Are you crazy? Have you seen where chickens walk? Yuck."

Picking up another fried foot, he opened his mouth wide. "You don't know what you're missing."

"That's disgusting, Daddy."

He bit into the crunchy morsel, licking his lips. "Ah, Roo, you just haven't lived until you've eaten chicken feet. And you know what they say: When in Rome, do like the Romans."

"We're not in Rome."

"But we're in Hong Kong, and these cooks . . . their blood's worth bottling. So we should eat whatever they prepare. Chicken feet or lizard lips or eel eyes."

"Lizard lips?"

"Sure."

"Daddy, can we go soon? I want to mail the dinosaurs to Rupee."

"He'll get them in a week or so, luv. It doesn't matter if we mail them now or in a few hours."

"How do you know that? Maybe there's a mail plane leaving for India right now."

He poured her some tea. "Soon, my leaping Roo. Very soon."

"Hurry."

Sipping his tea, he opened a lotus leaf to reveal steaming cauliflower. "You certainly made your mum proud."

"What do you mean?"

"Well, she asked you to help someone. And you did."

Mattie nodded, realizing that they hadn't yet opened their canisters for Hong Kong. "Daddy?"

"Yeah, luv?"

"Should we see what Mommy wants us to do here?"

He glanced at his day pack, which contained the canisters. "What do you reckon? We could open them now. Or wait until tonight."

"Let's open them. While we're waiting for the dumplings and your eel eyes."

Though Ian was unsure if he wanted to open the letters now, while Mattie was happy, he nodded. "Want to read yours first?"

"I think so."

He unzipped his day pack and handed her the appropriate canister. Mattie pushed her food aside and opened the canister, carefully unrolling the little scroll. Her mother's familiar script caused her heart to miss a beat.

Mattie,

What did you think of India, my precious girl? How did you feel when you saw the Taj Mahal? Were you lifted? Did the sight of it make you think about love? About magic? I'm sure that the artist in you was inspired. Maybe you sat down and sketched. Maybe you understood, at that moment, what artists are capable of. How art is one of humanity's most beautiful and lasting achievements. Don't ever be shy about your skills, Mattie. It takes courage, I know, to share things, to open yourself to the world. But really, all that matters is that you love what you make. If your art brings you joy, then your paints and pencils should never go unused.

Do you remember the summer when I tried to get you to jump off that diving board? You'd just learned to swim, and standing at the edge of the board, looking into that deep water, you were so scared. Time and time again, you'd walk to the edge of the board, stare into the water, and decide not to jump into my arms. Sometimes the children behind you laughed, and I know you heard those laughs, but you never stopped going to the end of the board. And I was so proud of you each time you made that journey, because I knew the start of the journey was almost as scary as the end of it.

Remember how that night, at the very end of the summer, we went to the board and talked about the jump? Everyone had gone, and it was just you and me. And you made the journey once more, and you jumped. You flew through the air. You landed with a splash. And you started laughing. You laughed and laughed and laughed. And we jumped so many times that night. At least fifty times. The lifeguard was ready to go home, but he'd seen us on the board before, seen you wanting to jump. And so he let us stay late. We were shivering, and shriveled like raisins, but we kept jumping and laughing and splashing each other.

That was one of the best nights of my life, Mattie. I'd seen you work at something, something that another child might have found easy, but that you found difficult. You struggled and you heard their laughter, and I know how hard those steps were to take. But you finally jumped, and you've never stopped jumping. And I don't want you ever to stand at the edge of a board, look into deep water, and not jump.

If you ever get to that point, remember our night at the pool. Remember how much fun it was to jump into that water, to splash each other as the night grew dark. Don't be afraid to jump, Mattie.

I love you so much. You are the light in my life, and you will always be that light, no matter who you shine on. You will make things grow and blossom. You will make the world a more beautiful place.

I love you like Shah Jahan loved Arjumand. And I have built a place for you, a place like the Taj Mahal, in my own heart.

Mommy

Mattie read her mother's letter twice. Around her, diners came and went; food was eaten or cooled in small bowls. Clouds dissipated, revealing an indigo sky that made the skyscrapers glisten more brightly.

After rolling up the note, Mattie put it back into the canister and looked at her father. "Mommy wants me to . . . to not be afraid."

"What did she say, Roo?"

Mattie watched a sampan head toward deeper waters. "She told me the story of when she taught me how to jump from a diving board. I was so scared. But I finally jumped. Finally. And she doesn't want me to stop jumping."

Ian took her hand. "Neither do I, luv."

"Read your letter, Daddy. See what she says."

He opened his canister, simultaneously eager and afraid to see what Kate might have written. He wanted to see where and how her pen had touched the paper. But he feared being hurt, and of having one less letter from her to read.

Ian,

I am so tired tonight. I feel like an old board that's been walked on by a million feet. I'm worn and exhausted and know that I won't last much longer.

You just left for home, carrying Mattie, who fell asleep in your arms. You're such a wonderful father. Don't ever sell yourself short there. You weren't always around, I know. But you were doing what was best for our family. And you succeeded. And Mattie loves you as much as she loves me. You may not believe that, and she may not always show that, but it's true.

I worry about you, my love. And I want you to do something for me—something that might not be easy. I don't know if you recall these details, but my friend Georgia, and her little girl, Holly, now live in Hong Kong, where Georgia works for her bank. Remember how much fun we had with them on those weekends together? Holly and Mattie had such a fantastic time, and Georgia went from being my best friend to our friend. You enjoyed her company as much as I did.

I'll never understand why Frank cheated on her. He killed a part of her, but she was strong. She moved to Hong Kong, taking Holly with her. She's lived there for two years now.

For the past few months, I've e-mailed her several times a week. She's been a wonderful friend. A lovely mate, as you would say. She hopes to come visit me, but for a reason I can't explain, I don't want her to see me like this.

Anyway, I'm asking you, as your lover and your best friend, to visit Georgia and Holly before you leave Hong Kong. I want you to share a smile with another woman, Ian. I know that you'll avoid such sharing, that you'll run from it. But Georgia and I grew up together. She made me laugh. And I know that she could make you laugh too. And there is nothing wrong with laughter, my love. It doesn't speak of betrayal, of surrender. It makes us all stronger. It means that we have chosen life over death.

I have been working on capturing these thoughts in a poem. Here it is:

Tomorrow

Yesterday I felt your touch,
I heard your joy,
I watched you watch me.
Yesterday my dream was real.
The dream of you,
Of how you and I made us.

Yesterday I never thought about tomorrow.
Only the moment,
The mingling of our thoughts, our shadows, our love.

Today is here.
A new, darker dawn.
A frontier I hadn't wanted to cross.

Today is pain, is suffering.
Many of my dreams are gone.
Shattered.
But many dreams remain.
Like tulips beneath a spring snow.

Today I have hope.
For you.
For Mattie.

Tomorrow you must let go.
Of me.
Of us.

You can hold me in a secret place,
But in the light you must hold another.

Tomorrow you must laugh again.
You must take a hand that is not mine.

Tomorrow your heart must swell,
Must grow large enough to shelter love beyond us,
Must grow strong enough to welcome such love.

You will not forget yesterday.
Love like ours never dissipates, never wavers.
We were one and we will always be one—
Pages within the same book.

But life is long and you should not walk alone.
Please don't walk alone.

Find happiness again.
Find a version of us.

And within that version,
Celebrate what we were,
What we created,
The path that we took.

Only through happiness will you ever again smile at the memory of us.
And I want to watch your smiles from heaven.

I want to see you reborn,
Fashioned together with memories,
With joy,
And with hope.

Remember . . .
Love is a wilderness untamed,
A river uncrossed,
A promise unbroken.

I love you.

Ian held the note, trying to keep his face from revealing his emotions. He knew Georgia well, knew that she was charming and intelligent and attractive. He understood where Kate was trying to take him, but he didn't want to travel there. In fact, he felt betrayed by the mere suggestion of such a destination. The love that existed between him and Kate couldn't be replicated, and he felt that Kate was shortchanging it by mentioning Georgia, as if he could so simply move from one woman to another.

The note went back into the canister. Ian tried to smile, lying to Mattie about what her mother had written. He realized that Kate hadn't mentioned Holly to Mattie or she would have said something. She would be excited. So the decision about whether to meet their old friends was left to him.

He sipped his tea, momentarily hiding his face. She's asking too much of me, he thought. Way too bloody much. It's not right. I don't have a bit of interest in seeing Georgia, even though I've always fancied her, even though Mattie would have heaps of fun with Holly.

"What is it, Daddy?" Mattie asked, her hand reaching for his arm, taking the teacup away from his lips.

"Nothing, luv. Nothing at all."

"What else did she say? Tell me what she said."

Ian sighed, wishing he had more time to think, to sort out the pros and cons of various responses. "It's a surprise. I'm supposed to surprise you."

"What surprise?"

"Stop your hopping, Roo. I'll tell you soon. I promise."

"But why not now?"

He saw a waiter and motioned for their bill. "Let's go mail Rupee's package and do some schoolwork, and maybe I'll tell you over dinner."

"Daddy."

"That's my deal, luv. No negotiating this time. For once."

"More schoolwork?"

"We're supposed to study photosynthesis this week."

Mattie reached down for Rupee's package. "Fine, but I want to draw him something before we mail this. I'll hurry."

"What about the view from right here? Give him a proper look at Hong Kong."

"Okay."

As Mattie cleared a space in front of her, Ian continued to watch her face, weighing the joy of watching her smile at the prospect of seeing Holly against his discomfort at the notion of spending time with Georgia. He knew that Mattie would take delight in an afternoon with Holly. But he didn't want to step toward Georgia, because that seemed to be stepping away from Kate. And the thought of stepping away from her made him feel weak. And he didn't agree with her—his heart had no room for another woman. It never would.

Kate had rarely been wrong during their time together, but she was wrong about his heart. It couldn't welcome new love, whether from

Georgia or anyone else. His heart wasn't like a home—able to open itself to anyone who wanted to enter.

Whatever strength and hope and love remained within him would go to Mattie. His heart would forever stay open to her, and her mother. But the door was closed to anyone else.

THE NIGHT SEEMED TO BE A REALM of contradictions. The hotel room was cold, though heat and humidity continued to dominate the island of Hong Kong. The sun had departed, yet buildings were brightly illuminated, glowing as if covered in holiday lights. Though taxis and trains and ships moved below, from forty stories up, with the windows sealed shut, only the hum of the air conditioner could be heard.

Ian lay in bed beside Mattie, his eyes closed, his mind awake. Though midnight had come and gone, he hadn't been able to sleep. His thoughts moved from Rupee to Mattie to Kate's request. He wasn't sure how to help Rupee further but knew that he must. He wondered how he might make Mattie smile more often. And he remembered how Kate and Georgia had laughed together, how full of life his wife had been.

After ensuring that Mattie was asleep, Ian carefully got out of bed. He saw the telescope next to the large window but decided against looking into people's lives. Instead he walked to the bathroom. Though he would have liked to fill the tub with hot water and soak himself, he didn't want to wake Mattie. And so he took two antacids, walked back out into the main room, and sat down in a chair beside the window.

His wallet rested on a nearby table, and soon a picture of Kate was in his hands. He ran his forefinger around the outline of her face, wondering if he'd take her face with him, once he died. Would he ever see her again? Even in death?

He continued to look at the photo, remembering their wedding day, how his nervousness had been replaced by happiness, how nothing in his life had ever felt so right. The image of her standing beside him, holding his hands, having eyes only for him, tore at his strength. He bent forward, rubbing his brow, longing to relive that day, to travel back in time so that he could spend his life preparing for her illness, figuring out a way to save her. He'd always been smart—gliding through exams, building a company that naysayers claimed couldn't be built. But he'd failed Kate. He had been overwhelmed by the complexity of her disease and the conflicting, convoluted opinions of her doctors. Though he had always believed in science, it hadn't saved Kate. Just as he hadn't. He'd traveled the world, filled a floor with his employees, but failed to save his wife. And he would have traded all of his successes to amend that one failure.

Ian took several deep breaths, biting his lower lip, his emotions a combination of guilt and confusion, anger and sadness. Setting aside the photo of Kate, he ran his hands through his hair, turning to look at Mattie. She lay with the sheet pulled up to her chin, an angel wrapped in cotton.

I'll never leave you, Kate, for someone else, Ian thought, gazing again at the sky. The love we had can't be replaced. You're wrong about that. As wrong as a sunbather in a city. But I'm going to do what you want. I'll e-mail Georgia tomorrow. Mattie and Holly used to have heaps of fun together. And I want to see our little girl be a little girl again. I know you fancy that too. We both fancy that more than anything in the world.

But I have to tell her, my luv, that we can't continue this walkabout forever, that we'll soon go back to reality, back to school and work. She'll need to say good-bye to Holly, just like she did to Rupee. And if she thinks her friends back home have perfect lives, somehow we're going to have to figure out how to live surrounded by that perfection.

I just . . . I can't do everything you want. I'm trying. I'm trying so bloody hard. But I'm knackered. I need help. And that's why I'm going to e-mail Georgia, because I know you're trying to show me the way, even if I don't agree with every step you're asking me to take.

But I'm never going to walk away from you. And whatever love is left in me will go to Mattie. She needs it heaps more than anyone else. She deserves it. And she wants it. And that's all that matters to me now. I reckon I failed you, my luv, but I'm not going to fail her. Whatever becomes of me, I won't fail our little girl. We created her. She's the best part of us. And through her, not through the love of another woman, I'll someday smile at the memory of us. She'll give me that gift. And that's what keeps me moving ahead.

I love you so bloody much, Kate. I'm going to try to sleep now. Please have a go at me in my dreams. Come to me like you used to, with a surprise held behind your back, a flower you found or a handful of ice. I don't care which. Just come.

THE MOUNTAINTOP ABOVE THE CITY REVEALED ANOTHER side of Hong Kong—an immense harbor almost completely surrounded by gleaming buildings. The view was the opposite of what Mattie and Ian had seen from the Himalayas. In Nepal, nature had reigned supreme. In Hong Kong, nature had been subjugated. The sea, the mountains, the sky were brilliant and powerful, yet mere backdrops for the city. Scores of skyscrapers reached toward the sun like trees competing for light in an overgrown forest. Ferries and barges plowed across the harbor. Planes left crisscrossing contrails above.

The park that Ian, Mattie, Georgia, and Holly had traveled to was full of boulders, slides, and swings. Nearby were about a dozen children, most of whom were leaping from one boulder to another. Ian watched Holly and Mattie swing beside each other. The girls had been quiet upon their initial introduction, but that silence had lasted only a few minutes. They now laughed and played as if they'd been doing so for every moment of their lives.

Ian turned toward Georgia, who sat beside him on a granite bench.

She was mostly as he remembered—her straight red hair pulled back into a tight ponytail, her skin pale, her eyes a light green, her body that of an athlete. She wore a sleeveless dress that matched the color of her eyes and appeared to wrap around her waist from the right side to the left. A silver antique bracelet adorned her wrist, while jade set in silver hung from her ears. Ivory-colored low-heeled shoes graced her pedicured feet.

Ian had never possessed any interest in fashion and, glancing at his jeans and his old Hawaiian-style shirt, he felt poorly dressed for the occasion. They were in Hong Kong, after all, one of the world's most fashion-conscious cities. He and Mattie appeared like they were about to go fishing.

"Mattie looks wonderful," Georgia said, her voice slow and smooth, her legs crossed, her lean calves exposed to the sun. "You've got a lot to be proud of, Ian. A lot."

He smiled, delighted that Georgia had held Mattie just minutes earlier, that she'd pushed Mattie's hair back and told her that everything was going to be all right. "And Holly," he replied, "she's like a little you. The apple sure didn't roll far from the tree."

"No, it didn't. Maybe a few feet, but that's good."

Holly laughed, and Ian watched her swing. She was dressed in white tights, a plaid skirt, a maroon blouse, and black patent leather shoes. Her bangs, slightly less red than Georgia's, were held to the side by a clip. Her hair was wavy and short, sculpted the way a model's might have been a century earlier.

Ian continued to watch Mattie and Holly swinging together, talking and giggling as they tried to keep their swings moving in unison. "Holly seems happy," he said, thinking that though she was just a few months older than Mattie, she appeared much more confident and poised.

Georgia sipped from a bottle of mineral water. "She is. Hong Kong's been good for her. Really good. Of course, it was hard at first. But the last year has been wonderful. She loves her school, her friends. She's even learning to speak Mandarin."

As an older couple walked past—the woman shielding herself from the sun with an umbrella—Ian wondered how Georgia had succeeded in bringing such joy into Holly's life. "Do you fancy it here?"

Georgia set the bottle down. "I do. It's new and a start over. I tried to keep everyone happy in Seattle. But . . . but Frank wasn't very interested in that. So when the bank offered me a job here, a great job, I took it. And I don't miss home."

"Why not?"

She looked away, her neck exposed and graceful. "Because home didn't turn out the way it was supposed to."

He remembered talking with Kate late at night, the night that Georgia had called. She'd been near the end of her pregnancy and had discovered that Frank was having an affair with his intern. Kate had spoken with her for most of the night, crying with her, supporting her. Georgia had never considered staying with Frank. But she hadn't known how to leave him either. And Kate had helped her with that.

Ian, Kate, and Mattie had seen Georgia and Holly occasionally over the following years. When the girls turned six, they celebrated together in Disney World. When Georgia's work took her to New York, she often brought Holly, and they stayed with Kate and Ian. In some ways, Mattie and Holly had been raised more like cousins than friends. They'd seen each other during special occasions, never sharing a classroom, but sometimes a bedroom.

"The girls don't miss a beat, do they?" Ian asked, watching Holly lead Mattie to the boulders.

Georgia turned to Ian, her hands starting to reach for his, but dropping to her lap. "I wanted to come to New York, you know. I wanted to help. But Kate wouldn't let me. I don't know why. I asked her over and over but she always refused. And so we said . . . we said good-bye on the phone. And it was awful."

Ian nodded. "I'm sorry about that. I tried to change her mind."

"But why? Why wouldn't she let me come?"

He saw that her eyes glistened, that she was almost imperceptibly shaking her head. "There's no easy answer," he replied. "But Kate was very focused at the end. I reckon all she thought about was Mattie and me. Day and night. She planned this walkabout. She did a thousand other things. She knew she didn't have long, and she just . . . just focused on us. Not her mates. Not her relatives. She told me once or twice to make peace with my mum and dad, but that was all."

A tear fell from Georgia's lashes. She rubbed her eye, smearing her mascara. "Kate was there for me. When Frank . . . did that, she was there. Every day. I needed her so much . . . and she was there. But I wasn't there for her. Even though I wanted to be. And that makes me feel empty inside."

Ian reached into his day pack and handed her a tissue. "You wouldn't have wanted Holly there," he said, lowering his voice. "Believe me, it's better that you didn't come. Sometimes Mattie has nightmares about the tubes . . . about the way Kate withered. And I reckon that's one of the reasons Kate kept you away."

Dabbing at her eyes with the tissue, Georgia shifted her gaze from him. "You know, I e-mailed you once, about wanting to come. And to tell you the truth, it hurt me when you didn't write back."

His thumb moved against his palm. "I . . . I was overwhelmed. I didn't know what to say."

"So you said nothing?"

He waited for her eyes to swing back to his. "I wasn't myself. I'm still not. But I'm sorry. That was bloody rude of me."

She nodded, sniffing. "How's Mattie?"

He apologized again, then watched his little girl climb to the top of a boulder and extend her hand to Holly. "I don't know. This trip—it's been good, I reckon. A real change of speed. But I wish she'd laugh more. I wish she didn't feel so different from her peers, so much older."

Georgia's cell phone rang, but she silenced it. "Different isn't always bad, Ian. Kate was different. You think a lot of girls graduated from college and just hopped on a plane and flew to Japan? She didn't have a job, couldn't speak Japanese. And yet she went. And she met you there."

"Kate's mum hadn't died."

"But Mattie has you. And that's a lot. You think it didn't hurt Holly that her father was more concerned about raising money for his precious museum than spending time with her? That he and I split up? Of course it hurt her. It really hurt her. But children are resilient. More so than adults. And though Holly still sometimes cries about her father, I'm the one who never dates, who won't ever trust another man, who's afraid. Holly moved on a long time ago. Just like Mattie will move on. She'll learn to be happy again."

"She shouldn't have to learn how to be happy."

"No, she shouldn't. But she will."

"But—"

"The days will turn into weeks, the weeks into months, and the months into years. And Mattie's pain . . . most of it . . . will go away. Whatever's left won't slow her down in life. It won't define her. Believe me, Ian. I've seen enough of Mattie to know that she'll laugh again."

Ian wanted to believe her. He wanted to ask her to repeat each and every word, to write her thoughts down so that he might read them every morning. He thanked her, shifting slightly on the bench to watch his little girl, who was hanging upside down at the top of a slide, preparing to descend toward where Holly waited below.

SEVERAL HOURS LATER, IAN, MATTIE, GEORGIA, AND Holly walked toward downtown. Holly was their leader, holding Mattie's hand as they descended a pedestrian pathway running parallel to a series of escalators that carried businesspeople from downtown to their homes in the hills. The escalators didn't have steps but were flat and steep. Glass and steel canopies protected the moving walkways from the elements, though the sides were open.

The tiled steps next to the escalators were broad and spaced far apart. Her feet following a long-ago established rhythm, Holly took four paces and then stepped down, repeating the process over and over. "Each day, Mattie, the escalators run down the mountain from six to ten in the morning," Holly said, her voice as quick as her feet. "And they carry all the workers to their offices. Then the escalators switch directions, and from ten in the morning to midnight, they go up, carrying people home. My mom and I ride the escalators to school and work every day. We hardly ever have to take the stairs like we are now. But since we're going downtown when most people are leaving, we're going in the wrong direction and so we have to walk, walk, walk."

Mattie smiled, watching shoppers and businesspeople on the rising escalator. Many riders read magazines or newspapers. Others chatted on cell phones, sent text messages, or spoke with one another. "I want to take them up," Mattie said. "All the way from the bottom to the top."

"And you can. After dinner, you can go all the way up to your hotel." Holly stepped off the pathway, crossed a street, and then moved on to another set of stairs. She waved to a Chinese girl who was on the adjacent escalator, saying hello in Mandarin. "That's Lian," Holly said. "We go to school together. She's got seven brothers and sisters. Imagine that. I bet they go through a lot of toilet paper."

"You . . . you can speak Chinese?"

"I speak Mandarin. One of the Chinese languages. The most popular one. It's really not so hard when you get used to it. Kind of like talking underwater."

Mattie's gaze swept over Holly's perfectly arranged hair, her white tights, and her plaid skirt. Mattie wished that she could speak Mandarin, that she got to ride an escalator every day to school. She glanced back at her father, who was talking with Georgia. "Do you like living here?" Mattie asked, watching a yellow double-decker bus pass on a nearby street.

Holly nodded, smiling. "Remember when we went to Disney World? Hong Kong's kind of like Disney World. Except there's no Mickey Mouse."

"Or Aurora."

"Or Ariel or Jasmine or Belle or Snow White."

Mattie laughed. "Maybe we should dress up like we used to."

"We could have a dance party. At our apartment. You could borrow one of my Chinese dresses."

"Really?"

Holly called out to a group of girls who had tied a long rope to the middle of a chain-link fence that bordered a parking lot. One girl held the other end of the rope and was swinging it around and around. Two girls jumped over the rope near the middle, while two other girls waited nearby. "Those are my friends," Holly said. "Want to meet them?"

"Okay."

Holly asked her mother if they could play for a minute. Still holding Mattie's hand, Holly led her from the pathway, past a series of open-air restaurants, and to the parking lot. Once in the nearly empty lot, she greeted her schoolmates in Mandarin and then added in English, "This is my friend Mattie. From New York City."

The girls—who wore school uniforms featuring gray sleeveless dresses with blue shirts and maroon ties—stopped jumping and said hello to Mattie in English. Mattie was surprised by how nice everyone looked, with carefully parted hair, white socks, and black shoes. She felt silly in her old jeans, T-shirt, and lopsided braids. Wishing her mother had dressed her that morning, Mattie greeted the girls and moved to the back of the line. Her father, she saw, was watching her intently.

Soon the rope was circling through the air. Holly's friends laughed, jumping on two feet or one, twisting around and around, repeating a phrase in English that made Mattie giggle. When it was her turn to jump, she stepped next to the rope and watched it spin above and behind her. She timed her leap perfectly, and Holly and then the other girls began to chant: "Fire, fire, false alarm. Mattie fell into Bobby's arms. How many kisses did she receive? One, two, three, four, five, six, seven, ei—"

Mattie's feet got caught in the rope and the girls immediately ceased their counting. Holly giggled, touching Mattie's cheeks, which had turned red. "My friends are silly," she said. "We're always doing this at school, always making up new songs. Song after song after song."

"You jump," Mattie said, eager to join in on the chanting.

Holly took her turn, laughing as her friends' voices rose, as the rope spun faster. She jumped until she fell, and the girls began again to take turns. Ten feet away, Ian watched the game, smiling, glad that he'd decided to contact Georgia.

The friends continued to laugh and chat until a woman called from somewhere above. Two of the girls replied, and after saying good-bye and gathering up their rope, they headed toward an escalator. Holly and Mattie bid farewell to the remaining girls and then followed Georgia and Ian back to the pathway. They walked another five minutes down the mountain before the escalators ended. The land had become flat, and skyscrapers were abundant.

Georgia led them to a steel-and-glass building. They took an elevator to a restaurant on the top floor, which provided a partial view of the harbor. Hundreds of well-dressed diners were gathered around lacquered tables, which held soups, whole fish, dumplings, steaming vegetables, deep-fried prawns, and about anything else the mind could imagine.

A hostess took them to a table near the far window. Ian helped Mattie into her seat, wondering if he should have pulled Georgia's chair back for her as well. Seeing the extravagant piles of food around them, he thought of Rupee, wondering how he was faring. Earlier in the day, before they'd met Georgia and Holly, Ian and Mattie had sent Rupee another package. This one contained books for him and his orphanage—books about learning English, about science and math and art. The books were Mattie's idea. She'd included another sketch for Rupee in the package—an image of Hong Kong at night.

The waitress handed them menus, and the girls started giggling about something. "What are you two little ankle biters laughing about?" Ian asked, pretending to scowl.

Mattie bit her lower lip, still grinning. "I told Holly how you ate chicken feet."

He rubbed his stomach. "You did? Well, they were quite lovely. A real treat to the old tummy. In fact, I reckon I'll order another batch."

"Daddy!"

Ian put a napkin on his lap. "You see, Holly, our little Roo here is afraid of such delicacies. Why don't you order her something fun to try?"

Holly nodded, grinning. "How about snake soup? Or a thousand-year-old egg?"

"Snake soup?" Mattie asked, pushing a plate away from her on the table. "No way."

Ian chuckled. "Just order it in Mandarin, Holly. Roo will never know."

As the girls continued to banter, Georgia ordered a glass of wine. Ian asked for a local beer. She smiled at him and he wasn't sure what to think. He felt guilty about sharing a smile with an attractive woman in the wake of Kate's death. Georgia's grin flickered the way a candle might in the wind, and he wondered if she had experienced a similar thought. When her wine came, she lifted her glass to his and took a long sip.

Ian felt compelled to say something to Georgia, to thank her, perhaps. But he was torn. A part of him didn't want to enjoy her company, didn't want any sort of temptation to arise. Another side of him was grateful that they'd experienced a pleasant afternoon together, and he needed to let her know of his appreciation. Tapping his foot under the table, he drank again from his beer, thinking about Kate, wishing that she, rather than her friend, was sitting beside him, asking himself why she'd sent him in this direction.

The waitress returned, and Holly spoke in Mandarin, laughing between words, pushing her bangs from her face. The woman smiled and left. "What did you order, Princess Holly?" Georgia asked, aware that Ian was uncomfortable and trying to lighten the mood.

"It's a secret."

"It's not fair that only you can speak Mandarin," Georgia replied. "Just because I'm an adult doesn't mean that my brain shouldn't be as quick to pick up a new language."

Holly shrugged. "Well, you could study with me more. I'll quiz you tonight."

"Did you order the snake soup?"

"Maybe. Maybe not."

Mattie scooted her chair away from Holly's. "I don't want to see any snakes."

Rolling her eyes, Holly moved her chair closer to Mattie's. "It's not like that, silly. The meat is all cut up. Like pieces of chicken."

"But it's not chicken. It's snake."

"And it tastes like chicken. Cluck, cluck, cluck."

"Yuck."

Georgia turned from the girls to Ian, who held a menu but was looking at Holly's painted fingernails. "Do you know what you want?"

"No, not yet. My mind's as stuck as a cat in a tree."

She opened her own menu, thinking about the time their two families had spent together in Disney World. Ian had been wonderful—entertaining the girls, going on all the rides with them. She had been so happy for Kate, because Kate had found a man like Ian. Georgia didn't believe that many such men existed. Half the fathers she knew would rather spend a Saturday afternoon on a golf course than be with their families. Ian, Kate had always told her, was the opposite. Though running his company often consumed him, once his work was done, his family became the center of his universe.

And yet now he seemed different. Of course, that was to be expected after Kate's death. But he also appeared uncomfortable, as if a part of him regretted being here. Georgia continued to look over the list of entrees as the girls laughed about snakes. For a reason unknown to her, she remembered asking her husband to make love to her when she was five months pregnant. They'd been eating dinner, and her suggestion had caught him off guard. He had avoided her eyes and spoken of unfinished work. At first Georgia had thought that her pregnancy made her less desirable in his eyes. But as the weeks had passed, he'd grown increasingly distant. He came home from work sad and returned to work happy. Nothing had made sense—at least until Georgia met his intern at an exhibition's opening and saw how they looked at each other.

In many ways, Ian now acted the same way Frank had. Ian seemed distracted and distant, glancing toward the skyline, perhaps wanting to be somewhere else. His body leaned away from hers, as if the proximity of their legs was something to carefully heed. He appeared more ill at ease than he had at the park, and she wondered what had changed. She didn't want him to be uncomfortable, and without crossing any lines, she hoped to put him at ease.

"It's okay, Ian," she said quietly, leaning closer to him. "All of this is okay."

Looking up from his menu, he glanced at the girls, and then at Georgia. He didn't know if she was right, but he understood that for Mattie's sake, he needed to brighten up. "I'm sorry," he replied, nodding. "I was just . . . trying to decide whether to order the sea slugs or the bird's-nest soup."

Georgia smiled. "I wouldn't try the slugs. They taste like slimy rubber."

"Did you hear that, Roo?" he asked. "Georgia recommends the sea slugs."

"Far from it," Georgia replied, lifting her wineglass.

Mattie shook her head, her braids rising and falling. "I don't trust anything he says."

Georgia set down her drink. "You're a smart girl."

The waitress came and took their orders. Mattie removed a red pencil from her bag and began to draw a bowl containing live snakes on the paper place mat in front of Holly. The girls continued to laugh, and Ian was pleased to see Mattie acting her age, being silly and immature and a little too loud. This was how she had acted every day before Kate had gotten sick. This was his little girl.

"I reckon you're going to spoil Holly's appetite, Roo," he said. "Should you draw something else?"

"No way, Captain," Mattie replied, handing Holly a blue pencil.

"I'll do the sea slugs," Holly answered. "They can have a party with your snakes."

"Sounds fun."

Ian smiled, inwardly thanking Georgia for reminding him of what was so obvious—that Mattie was enjoying herself. "You're right," he said, lifting his glass in Georgia's direction. "This is good."

She sipped her wine. "We've been friends for a long time," she said softly. "And there's no reason why we can't continue to be friends. That's all I want. So don't worry."

"I've got a thick Australian skull. Sometimes, I reckon, things need to be spelled out for me."

"Kate was good at that."

"She was a bloody genius at that."

"And do you know what else?"

"What?"

"You're a wonderful father. To bring Mattie here, halfway around the world. To do what you're doing."

He didn't turn from her stare. "You did the same thing."

"I ran away."

"No. That's not what you did at all. What you did took a heap of guts. And look at you now . . . all polished and refined. An international banker. A lovely little girl by your side. Whatever you did . . . it worked out quite well. And I reckon that wasn't by chance."

Georgia smiled as Mattie drew a bird's nest. "She's good. Really good."

"You're as right as rain, though I have no idea where that skill came from. Neither Kate nor I could draw a proper stick figure."

"Daddy has two left hands," Mattie said, giggling.

"Watch it, you little bugger."

The waitress returned with steaming appetizers and soon a tray of oversized entrees. The food was set down and split among everyone. Mattie ate the sea bass, the glass shrimp, the sweet and sour bok choy—everything but the snake soup. Like the dozens of families around them, Ian, Mattie, Georgia, and Holly smiled and shared stories, dining on ancient recipes as the sky darkened.

When dinner finally ended, they stepped outside the building, and Mattie and Holly begged to reunite the next day. Since that would be Saturday, Georgia welcomed the idea. Ian went along with it as well, helping to plan their rendezvous. Farewells were exchanged, Mattie and Holly hugging like a pair of best friends. While Georgia and Holly hailed a taxi, intending to swing by a bookstore, Mattie and Ian walked toward the escalators, which were all going up.

Mattie took her father's hand, leading him across a street, stepping onto an escalator. "That was fun," she said, rocking forward and backward on her feet, reminding him of the ants-in-her-pants little girl she'd once been.

"Holly is sweet, isn't she?"

"She makes me laugh."

"I reckon you make each other laugh."

Mattie nodded. "Daddy?"

"What, luv?"

"I think . . . I think Mommy's happy that we're here."

"You do? What makes you say that?"

Mattie pursed her lips as the escalator continued to roll uphill. "Because we've been telling her. We've been leaving our messages in the wishing trees. And I'm sure she's glad to see them."

Ian heard the innocence, the beauty, and the faith within Mattie's words. He wanted to share the same thought, to believe what she believed. He felt the softness of her hand against his, her small palm fitting so easily within his own. She was a part of him and a part of Kate, and the best link to what remained of them. Thinking about this link, he wondered if Mattie understood things that he didn't, if her connection to Kate at that moment was stronger than his.

He squeezed her hand. "I've seen some good wishing trees here, up in the mountains."

"Me too."

Bending down, he kissed her forehead. "Want a lift, luv?"

"Sure, Daddy."

He picked her up, raising her over his head to put her legs on his shoulders. "How about finding some ice cream, Roo? Feel like a little walkabout before heading back to the hotel?"

"You think they have cookies and cream?"

"I reckon they have everything in this city."

"Then let's go."

"Aye, aye, First Mate," he said, holding tight to her legs, stepping off the escalator and into a world that continued to confound and perplex him, as if he were a ten-year-old boy and not a man who'd seen four decades come and go.

AT HALF PAST TEN THE FOLLOWING MORNING, Ian and Mattie met Georgia and Holly atop one of the main escalators. The girls greeted each other with hugs. Ian and Georgia's embrace was much stiffer—a forced merging of two bodies and minds that didn't know what to do with each other. Stepping onto the escalator along with a never-ending stream of locals, the foursome began their descent toward the city. They had decided to shop at one of Hong Kong's most famous markets, return to Georgia's apartment, let the girls take a swim, and then have dinner together.

Ian had spent half the night sitting near the window of their hotel room, Kate's most recent letter in his lap. He had read her poem time and time again, still stung by her words, no longer necessarily feeling betrayed, but certainly disappointed. Did she think that he could so easily fall in love? Would she have dated nineteen months after his death?

Now, as he held a coffee cup and descended into the city, Ian watched Georgia and Holly, noting their fashionable attire. They wore oversized sun hats and sleeveless dresses. Ian didn't remember Georgia owning such nice outfits when they'd seen her in Manhattan, but maybe living in Hong Kong had rubbed off on her. Many of the young women nearby looked as if they were eager to compete in some sort of modeling contest. Deciding that he should take Mattie shopping for a proper dress, Ian squeezed her hand and hoped that she didn't feel out of place.

As Georgia chatted with the girls, Ian thought about her tears after her husband's affair. Ian had seen those tears. He'd heard them. She was ruined but now seemed somehow redeemed. She had a successful career and a happy daughter, and acted confident and poised. How had she come so far? Was she so much stronger than he?

Holly, walking purposefully and holding Mattie's hand, led them from escalator to escalator. Responding in Mandarin to the street vendors who hawked food, clothes, and sunglasses, Holly hurried across a busy street, ignoring a red light. Growing up in Manhattan, Mattie knew that traffic lights were often disregarded, but that her father wouldn't have liked her to run across such a street. Surprised that Georgia didn't say anything, Mattie continued to hold Holly's hand.

Mattie's gaze darted into the stores they passed. She'd woken up thinking of Rupee, feeling as if she had deserted him. Did he miss her? Was he lonely? She worried about him, and after breakfast she and her father had sent an e-mail to the orphanage's director, inquiring about Rupee's well-being.

Seeing the wealth around her, Mattie wondered why some people were rich and Rupee was poor, why most children had mothers and hers was gone. She didn't understand the unfairness of the world, even though she had asked her father about it many times. She wasn't sure that he understood it either. When she asked him such questions, his answers came after long pauses, after his gaze had wandered around and come back to hers.

Deciding to find Rupee something at the market, Mattie hurried alongside Holly, feeling much younger than her friend, even though she wasn't. Holly seemed to act at least thirteen years old, Mattie decided. She knew her way around Hong Kong. She could speak Mandarin. She wore makeup and had her ears pierced.

What Mattie didn't realize was that she and Holly were similar. Since her father had left, Holly had watched other children. She'd wished that she lived with another family. She had hurt. But as the years had passed, she'd witnessed how her mother dealt with pain, and she had mimicked her mother—working hard, dressing nicely, pushing herself to be better and better and above criticism. When they had arrived in Hong Kong, Holly had never felt so out of place. Even with her school uniform, she looked the opposite of her classmates. She felt the opposite. And so she had learned, working on her Mandarin after school, doing her best to talk with locals, attempting to follow their customs and not her own.

To Holly's surprise, after a few months, something wonderful had happened—the locals had accepted her. They'd helped her with her pronunciation. They'd taught her how to haggle, how to use the bus system, where the best hiking trails were located. Her mother had always been with her, of course, but Holly became their leader. And entire weeks passed when she didn't even think about her father. Thinking about him only made her sad.

Holly guided Mattie past a pair of red gates and into an immense outdoor market. The first section they encountered was known by locals as "the dry area." Wanting to shock her friend, Holly walked up to one of her favorite stands, which featured dried seafood. The gray-and-white skin of a large shark hung from a nearby rack, the skin spread open in the shape of a kite.

Mattie looked up from the cobbled street, jumping backward when she spotted the shark. Holly laughed. "It's been hanging there a week. Don't worry."

The shark's skin was perfectly intact, its gills and fins shining in the sun. "Why?" Mattie asked. "Why is that shark there?"

Ian and Georgia moved closer, Ian smiling at the look on Mattie's face. "This man sells dried shark to restaurants," Holly said, pointing to a vendor who appeared to be as old as the worn cobblestones at their feet. "They love to eat shark here. Love it, love it, love it."

Mattie studied the rest of the man's stall, which was covered with dried squid, octopus, fish, eels, and shrimp. She smiled at the vendor, who said something in Mandarin to Holly. Nodding, Holly giggled and replied in the same tongue. "What did he say?" Mattie asked.

"He asked if you like sharks."

"Not to eat."

"That's what I told him."

Holly said good-bye to the vendor and again took Mattie's hand, leading her deeper into the market. Many other stalls offered dried seafood—row after row of headless fish hanging by their tails from thick ropes. Holly turned to her right, proceeding down a different alleyway. Suddenly everything changed—stalls now offered immense displays of fruit and vegetables. Baskets held watermelons, apples, pears, oranges, kiwis, and many fruits that Mattie had never seen before.

"Should we get some fruit?" Holly asked her mother.

"Sure," Georgia replied. "Maybe you can teach Mattie how to haggle Hong Kong style."

Holly smiled, pushing her bangs aside and readjusting her hair clip. "What do you want to eat, Mattie?"

Mattie looked over the options and pointed to a watermelon. "How about that? We can have a seed-spitting contest."

Still grinning, Holly asked the vendor the price of the watermelon. "It's fifty dollars," Holly said, translating for Mattie.

"Fifty dollars!"

"Hong Kong dollars. Not American dollars, silly. There's a big difference, you know."

Mattie nodded. Throughout their trip, her father had given her some local currency, and she was used to trying to calculate exchange rates. "That's about . . . seven or eight American dollars, right?"

"Right."

"What do you think, Roo?" Ian asked. "Reckon that's a fair price?"

Mattie shook her head. "It seems expensive. That's a really little watermelon."

"Hold up four fingers," Holly said.

"What?"

"Tell her that you'll pay forty dollars for it."

Mattie shifted from foot to foot, unsure if she should really ask the woman for a lower price. The lady looked tired and her shirt was frayed. Mattie held up four fingers and then five. The vendor nodded, picking up the watermelon and setting it in a plastic bag.

"Forty-five dollars!" Holly said, laughing. "That's too much. I don't think we'll have you do any more of our bargaining. No way is that a good idea."

Mattie watched her father pay the woman, glad to have given her an extra five dollars. "It looks . . . delicious."

"It's the size of a grapefruit!"

"It's perfect."

Holly rolled her eyes. "Let's go find some fish." She took Mattie's hand and pulled her ahead. "But let me do the haggling."

The market, parts of it housed under canvas canopies, was little more than a series of connected alleys. Thousands of shoppers examined racks of fresh meat, plucked and roasted ducks, tanks full of darting fish, pig heads hooked and hanging by their noses, and buckets of live eels. Holly walked to a woman who held a large cleaver and chopped the bellies from flopping red snapper. After haggling with the woman in Mandarin for a minute, Holly asked her mother for two hundred Hong Kong dollars. Georgia, who loved to watch Holly bargain at the market, handed her the money.

After a few more purchases, the group walked back to the escalators, which by now had switched directions. As they rolled uphill, Ian spoke with Georgia about her job while Mattie asked Holly how to say certain words in Mandarin. Ian watched his little girl struggle with the difficult pronunciation. Though Holly was an excellent teacher, he could see that Mattie wanted to learn faster than was possible. She had never excelled in academics, but she seemed eager to try to keep pace with Holly.

Ian leaned closer to Georgia, lowering his face under her wide-brimmed sun hat. "Might you do me a favor?" he whispered, eyeing the girls in front of them.

"What?"

"Later, will you ask Mattie to show you her sketches?"

Georgia nodded, putting her hand on his shoulder. "Every single one of them."

He remained close to her for a moment longer than was necessary. "Lovely," he said, shifting back to his original position.

Wondering why her ex-husband never had such thoughts, why he'd rather spend an hour at a black-tie event than look at anything Holly created, Georgia nodded. She watched Ian as his gaze traveled back to Mattie, thinking that if Kate hadn't been one of her best friends, she would be interested in dating him, in pursuing what she no longer pursued. "Mattie has her sketches," she said. "What do you have? Your company? Your work?"

"My company? I sold it. I'm done peddling dried seaweed, though I fancied it for a while, to be honest."

"What, then? What do you have now?"

"Roo. She's my sketchbook."

Georgia smiled, watching crates of beer being carried into a restaurant near the escalator. "Well, you have a lot," she said. "Whatever else we do, we're going to leave the world with two beautiful girls."

He turned to her again, surprised and pleased. "That's all I want."

The escalator ended. Holly led Mattie across a street, hurrying to another moving walkway. Carrying their shopping bags, Ian stepped around an idle taxi and followed the children. He wanted to talk more with Georgia, to seek her opinion, to confide in her. Unlike most everyone else in his life, she seemed to understand where he had come from and where he had to go.

"When will you head back to the States?" he asked.

She twisted her silver bracelet, the heat and humidity causing it to stick to her pale skin. "Head home? Not for a few years. Holly's in a great international school. She's doing so well. My job is a lot more ups than downs. And her school and my office are a five-minute walk from our apartment, so I see more of her here than I would back home."

"You don't miss anything?"

Georgia shook her head, though she missed plenty. "I've tried to move on. And Hong Kong is a good place for that."

Another street appeared, and Holly stepped off the escalator, turning right, walking toward a modern black-and-white building that might have been thirty stories tall. The girls skipped with excitement. Georgia smiled, struggling to keep up in her high heels, but glad that Holly and Mattie were having so much fun together.

Ian followed Georgia inside the apartment building, his gaze sweeping over the marble floors, the uniformed concierge. The elevator was stainless steel inside, its walls unmarred by graffiti or scratches. Holly pushed the button for floor number twenty-six, and they began to rise. "Can we swim before lunch?" she asked, wanting to show Mattie the pool. "Please, please, please."

"Please, Daddy?" Mattie added, turning to Ian, her hand tugging on his.

"I reckon we should ask our hostess."

Georgia stepped back as the elevator door opened. "Let's have a snack, girls. And then we'll swim." She winked. "Reckon that'll work?"

As Holly and Mattie celebrated, Ian followed Georgia down a narrow but well-appointed hallway. Georgia walked to the last door, unlocking it and motioning her guests inside. Ian followed the girls, smiling as Holly showed Mattie around. The apartment was contemporary, its yellow walls highlighted by striking examples of modern art, its floor black marble. The top two-thirds of the far wall were dominated by large windows and provided a stomach-dropping view of the city. The living room featured red leather couches, a glass coffee table, and an oriental rug. The adjacent kitchen was small but boasted marble countertops, stainless-steel appliances, and a specialized wine cooler that held about ten bottles. To Ian's surprise, he didn't see a television anywhere. Instead, teak bookshelves occupied opposite corners of the living room.

Mattie walked toward a window, careful not to press her dirty hands against the glass, but drawing close enough to look down. "Wow," she said, watching cars and buses crawl below, wanting to sketch what she saw. "You're like birds up here."

"There's not much room," Georgia said, helping Ian with the shopping bags, "but we sure love the view."

"It's bloody beautiful," he replied. As the girls ran to Holly's room, he unpacked the bags, handing Georgia the watermelon, the fish, and a variety of vegetables. She put the fish into a small refrigerator and everything else on the counter. Then she picked up a remote control and pushed a few buttons, and jazz emerged from unseen speakers. She then began to slice and peel some apples, wanting the girls to eat before they swam.

"Do you need anything?" she asked.

"No. But what can I do to help?"

"There's nothing to do. Though I suppose you could ask the girls to put on their swimsuits. And you could do the same."

Ian thanked her for her hospitality and walked into the hallway, removing Mattie's suit from his day pack. He smiled when he saw how Holly's room was decorated—with green mountains and a castle painted on the walls. The fields around the castle were full of galloping horses, clusters of flowers, and girls in pretty dresses. Mattie stood next to one of the horses, tracing its outline with her forefinger. She was smiling, and he patted her back, handing her the swimsuit.

"I fancy your room, Holly," Ian said, noting a pile of textbooks on a nearby table. "What a lovely place to count sheep."

Holly pointed to her bed, which was high off the floor and covered with a pink spread. "This is where we read at night."

"Looks comfy. Mind if I take a nap?"

"Daddy!" Mattie replied, turning to face him.

"I'm just chewing the fat, luv." He looked again at the castle. "Do you read every night, Holly?"

"We always read."

"No idiot box?"

"What?"

"No television?"

"We don't have an . . . idiot box. We read to each other instead. My mom reads two pages, and I read one. We do that, back and forth, back and forth, until I get tired. Or I study Mandarin and she reads to herself."

"Good onya. That's why you're so smart, why you can speak two languages better than I can one. Now, why don't you little ankle biters put on your bathing suits and we'll go for a dip?"

They nodded and he stepped into the hall. After walking to the bathroom, he shut the door behind him. The space was no bigger than a pair of coat closets nestled together but somehow it managed to contain a compact, deep bathtub that could also be used as a shower. A Western-style toilet was in the corner, complete with a heated seat. Ian undressed, feeling uncomfortable to be naked in Georgia's home. He put on his swimsuit, which looked like a pair of old shorts, and a T-shirt. By the time he emerged from the bathroom, everyone else had gathered in the kitchen. Georgia wore a white cover-up, a red sun hat, and sandals. Holly had on a blue bikini while Mattie was in her faded yellow one-piece. It had never occurred to Ian to buy her a bikini, and he found himself wondering if she wanted one.

After eating the sliced apples and some shrimp-flavored rice crackers, the foursome took the elevator up to the roof, about half of which was covered by a square swimming pool. To Ian's surprise, the pool was empty of people. In the middle of the water rose a circular island surrounded by boulders and tropical flowers. White lounge chairs bordered the pool, and green umbrellas protected some of the chairs from the midday sun. Higher skyscrapers surrounded them on all sides, making Ian feel as if he were in a fishbowl.

He smiled as Mattie and Holly jumped into the pool, but he wasn't sure what to do when Georgia removed her cover-up. After glancing away for a moment, he felt foolish about averting his gaze and turned back to her. She wore a maroon-colored one-piece suit that seemed tailored for her athletic body but wasn't too revealing. Ian avoided looking at anything but her face. His peripheral vision took in her arms, shoulders, and breasts, but he focused on her eyes. And though he saw enough of her to understand that she was attractive, nothing within him stirred. He still remembered Kate's body as if it were his own, and the mere thought of another woman's skin and softness made him feel traitorous.

"Fancy a dip?" he asked, finally removing his shirt.

She shook her head. "I think I'll rest my legs, if that's all right with you."

"No worries," he replied, relieved that he wouldn't have to swim with her. "I reckon I'll frolic with the girls for a tick. If they'll have me."

"They'll have you."

Ian smiled and slipped into the warm water. Mattie and Holly were sitting on an underwater ledge in the middle of the pool. He walked to them, splashing Mattie as he neared her. She laughed and splashed him back, and he dove underwater, opening his eyes, grabbing onto her leg, and gently biting it. Thrashing against him, she beat her fists on his back until he emerged.

"Daddy!"

"Yeah, luv?"

"Don't bite me!" she said, giggling.

"You don't want to play the shark game?"

"No. Not today."

"How about Marco Polo?"

Mattie turned to Holly, who nodded, leaping off the ledge. "You're it!" Mattie yelled, following Holly into deeper water.

Ian closed his eyes, letting the girls draw away from him. He remembered how Kate had played Marco Polo with Mattie and her friends. He had participated a few times, but usually Kate had been the entertainer. She laughed and splashed while he held his laptop and scrolled through e-mails or created presentations. How shortsighted he'd been.

Determined not to let his spirits sink, Ian stepped toward where he heard the girls giggling. "Marco," he called out.

"Polo," came quiet replies.

He smiled, heading in their direction. "Marco."

"Polo."

"I can barely hear you little ankle biters!"

"Polo."

"That's even quieter!"

Laughter floated over the water. Ian heard Georgia's chair moving and wondered if she was watching. He took a deep breath, dove underwater, and swam toward where he thought the girls were. Though he reached out in every direction and kicked hard and fast, he ended up in an empty corner.

"Marco!" he called, pretending to be frustrated.

"Polo."

"Roo, I didn't hear you!"

"Polo."

"That's better. So, you've gone shallow, have you? Well, I'm heading your way." He dove again but this time quickly resurfaced and heard their giggling as they tried to swim past him. "Marco." He spun toward splashes to his right. "I said Marco!" Only laughter answered him, and he dove toward the source, his fingers finally striking flesh. He opened his eyes and saw that he was gripping Holly's elbow. She shrieked and tried to pull away from him, her eyes on his, her smile pleasing him. And he wondered at that moment what it might be like to have another child, to love and be loved by a second little girl or a boy.

Georgia watched them play. Normally, she would have joined them, but she saw their smiles and wanted to leave Ian alone with the girls. Mattie adored him—that much was obvious. But what surprised her was how quickly Holly had warmed up to him. With most men Holly was distant, a wounded soul who didn't dare risk further injury. But with Ian, Holly watched Mattie climb atop his shoulders and dive off, and then Holly did the same thing. She laughed with him, splashed him, and fled his outstretched hands.

Not once did Georgia take her eyes from Holly and Ian. She studied her daughter's movements, her expressions. She saw something emerge from within her. It wasn't just joy or hope, but rather vulnerability combined with a desire to connect with a man her father's age. Of course, Georgia had recognized this desire before, but with Ian, Holly's emotions seemed pronounced. She was paying more attention to him than she was to Mattie.

They played for an hour. Finally, other swimmers arrived, and the games ended. Mattie and Holly stretched out on lounge chairs next to Georgia's, and after Holly found a bottle of nail polish in her mother's beach bag, she painted Mattie's nails. Ian watched the girls, aware of Mattie's smile and Holly's precision. Then he began to swim laps, his stomach pain gone, his body filled with an energy he rarely felt. He swam until his shoulders ached, and then they all relaxed in the sun together.

Later, when their sunscreen had worn off and their skin started to take on a pink hue, they wrapped themselves in towels and headed to the elevator. Back in the apartment, they snacked, then took turns using the two bathrooms. Georgia and Mattie went first, heading to opposite ends of the apartment. When Ian emerged from his turn, he saw them sitting together on a couch, looking at Mattie's sketches. He heard the passion in his daughter's voice as she told Georgia about each sketch, and he smiled. Stepping into the kitchen, he found a cutting board, placed onions and garlic cloves atop it, and began to chop.

Ten minutes passed before Holly came out of her shower and started laughing with Mattie. Georgia entered the kitchen, asking Ian if he wanted a glass of wine. She opened the bottle in a way that to him seemed remarkably graceful, filling his glass, handing it to him. She'd changed into a strapless ankle-length dress that was ivory colored and featured turquoise and blue tropical leaves.

"Thanks for today," she said, lifting her glass against his.

"I owe you the thanks."

She started to turn to the refrigerator but stopped, moving back toward him. "Ian?"

"Yeah?"

"It's nice . . . that we can be friends. I think Kate would want us to be close, to bring Mattie and Holly together, the way we used to."

"I reckon so," Ian replied, wondering how, at the end of her life, Kate had been able to think about bringing them together. "Kate always wanted what was best for everyone."

Georgia lifted her glass again. "To Kate."

To you, my luv, Ian thought, raising his glass.

"I miss her, you know," Georgia said, sipping her wine.

"I know."

"And I want to help. So please tell me how I can help with Mattie. And with you."

"You just helped her. You made her smile. And that makes me smile."

She nodded. "Good. Or as Holly would say, good, good, good."

"She's a fast talker, all right. Kind of like yours truly."

"Kind of. But without the funny accent."

"Or the facial hair."

Georgia grinned, turning down the music, listening to laughter emerge from the other room. "Amazing how they haven't hit a wall yet, isn't it?"

"They're making up for lost time," he replied, sipping his wine, feeling himself relax as the alcohol entered his system. He thought about what Georgia had said earlier, about their friendship. He'd been friends with many women in college and in Japan. But since he'd married Kate and started his company, those friendships had faded. He wondered if he could be close to Georgia, to someone who was bright and appealing. His yearning for the companionship of a woman had been so repressed that when he experienced a desire to reach for Georgia's hand, he didn't know what to do. She was lovely, and he sometimes felt so alone. He just wanted to hold her hand for a moment and talk with her. But he couldn't betray Kate in such a way, and so he smiled and returned to the cutting board, dicing the garlic.

Georgia watched him turn from her, thinking about Kate's final e-mail, about how she had said that he and Mattie might be coming. Did you send us on a path toward each other? she wondered, wishing again that she'd been able to see her friend before she died. Is that why you didn't ask me to be with you, at the end? Because you didn't want Ian and me to be together for your death, but for something else?

Removing the fish from the refrigerator, Georgia realized that she hoped to see Ian again, that she didn't want him to go. "You leave in two days?" she asked, setting the fish on the counter, seeing the gray in his sideburns and remembering when they were all so much younger.

"That's right. In two days we buzz off for Vietnam."

She nodded, waiting for him to say more, wondering if he would.

"It won't be easy . . . for Mattie to leave Holly," he added.

"I know. And I'm sorry."

"Reckon sometime you could come to New York? To visit us?"

She reached for the wine bottle and refilled their glasses. "I don't know, Ian. I really don't. But maybe."

"Mattie would fancy that."

She set the wine bottle down, feeling a familiar pain, a sense of loss. The sensation wasn't nearly as acute as it had been when she learned about her husband's infidelity, but nonetheless, she felt as if Ian were already stepping away from her. She started to reach for his fingers but stopped herself. He would leave her, she knew, but he wouldn't leave Kate. And she didn't want him to. Not for her. Not for Holly. Kate still dwelled in his heart, and Georgia couldn't ask him to turn from his true love. And so she sipped her wine, gathered her thoughts, and left him to go say hello to the girls.

THE FOLLOWING DAY, IAN AND MATTIE SAT in a dress shop. He had taken her there to buy her something pretty, to make her smile despite their looming departure. The shop seemed indulgent even by Manhattan standards. Standing beside the glass storefront were beautifully dressed mannequins, only these mannequins were living Chinese teenagers, who stood still and smiled for passersby. The girls seemed content, but Ian thought the display was bizarre. The rest of the store was equally ostentatious. The walls were black and lined with gold-framed pictures of women in flowing gowns. Crystal chandeliers hung from the ceiling. The dresses on display—those on the living mannequins as well as those hanging from silver stands—were fashionable and lovely. Ian wanted to see Mattie in one, to watch her face light up at the sight of herself.

But Mattie wasn't interested in the dresses. The artist in her admired their designs, but the little girl in her didn't want to be looking at dresses. She longed to be with Holly, to be laughing and playing Marco Polo. The thought of getting on a plane the next day and flying to Vietnam made her feel as if she was lying in bed with a fever. She had already said good-bye to her mother and to Rupee. And she didn't want to leave Holly. She didn't feel strong enough for another farewell, even with her father beside her.

Now, as he spoke with a saleswoman about the different dresses, about silk and size and style, Mattie did her best to keep her emotions at bay. She felt so tired, so weak. She didn't want to burden her father with her feelings, aware that he was trying to make her happy, that he was sticking to her mother's plan. Normally, she would have enjoyed picking out a dress with him. He'd never taken her to such a store, and she was glad that the idea had come to him. Only she couldn't focus on that gladness. Instead she thought about Holly, about how she wouldn't see her for many, many months.

An elegantly dressed woman asked Mattie to stand and started taking her measurements. Mattie held out her arms, watching how the mannequins smiled at one another, wanting to share their smiles but feeling her strength ebb away. Her hands began to tremble. She swayed unsteadily. Suddenly she lacked the stamina to stand, and stumbled toward a leather couch. Her father caught her, his eyes on hers, tears blurring her vision. He said something to the saleswoman, and picked up Mattie, carrying her outside, kissing her forehead. She wrapped her arms around him, pulling herself tighter against him, trying not to sob, but unable to stop herself from doing so. She buried her face against his chest, aware of the sun on her neck, of him taking steps. He didn't say anything, but kissed her again.

He must have walked a thousand steps, she thought, by the time she finally stopped crying. She opened her eyes and saw that he was carrying her into a park, into a place of tall trees and ornate bushes. He headed toward a granite bench and sat down, holding her on his lap.

"What hurts, luv?" he asked, stroking the side of her face.

"I . . . I don't want to go."

"You don't want to leave Holly?"

"No. Or to say any more good-byes. Please, Daddy, please don't make me say any more good-byes." She took a deep breath, feeling as if she wasn't able to fill her lungs properly. "I still . . . I still say good-bye to Mommy. Sometimes at night. But I don't want to. And I don't want to say good-bye to Holly either."

"Why, Roo? Why do you say good-bye to your mum?"

Mattie's tears began anew. "Because sometimes . . . sometimes she's here. And then she's gone. And I have to say good-bye all over again."

He pulled her tighter against him. "Oh, luv. You don't have to do that."

"Yes, I do."

He wiped away her tears. "Just say hello to her. When she comes. And the next time she comes, say hello again. You don't ever have to say good-bye."

She continued to cry, unable to stop, shaking against him. He watched her crumble, and the sight of that collapse beat him down, bringing his worst fears to life, his deepest sorrows. His baby girl was wounded so badly, and he didn't know how to stop her from bleeding. He kissed her painted pink fingernails, his stomach throbbing, his world on fire.

Ian looked up, searching for Kate, but seeing only the treetops. A wind tugged at them, a wind from the north, from China. The wind was humble, lacking gusts and spirit, yet it seemed to carry an answer to him—as if he had been spoken to, been given a gift from Kate. "Roo," he said, looking into her glistening eyes. "Write down what you want. About Holly. Write a wish down on a piece of paper."

"What?"

"Just do it, luv. Please do it."

Mattie sat up, wiped her eyes, and opened her backpack. She took out a piece of paper, wrote down that she wanted to see Holly again, and folded up the paper. "Now what?"

Ian pointed to an immense ficus tree. "Now climb up on that first branch. And leave your wish."

Nodding, she stood up, holding his hand, and walked to the tree. He lifted her from the ground until she was able to grasp the bottom branch. Pulling herself higher, she swung her legs over the branch, moving her hands to the trunk. Vines encircled parts of the tree, and she tugged at one, testing its strength. Deciding that the vine was sound, she tucked the folded paper between the vine and the trunk, closing her eyes, saying hello to her mother. She remained in the tree for a few minutes, silently repeating her wish.

Ian helped Mattie down from the branch and set her on his shoulders. "I can't promise what they'll say, Roo, but I'll ask Georgia if she and Holly would fancy meeting us in Vietnam. They could travel with us for a few days, and I'm sure we'd all have a beaut of a time."

"Really?"

"Aye, aye, First Mate."

"Really, Daddy? You'll ask her?"

"Absobloodylutely."

"Do you think she'll say yes?"

He pointed to where her note poked out from beneath the vine. "That's a wishing tree if I ever saw one, Roo. See how it spreads out, up high? How it has so many branches for people to leave their wishes on?"

"I do."

"That tree isn't going to let you down. And neither is your mum. She's seen your wish, and I reckon she'll make it come true."

Mattie lowered her hands around his head and squeezed him tight. "Thank you, Daddy."

"You're choking me, luv," he replied, smiling, wondering if Georgia would agree to meet them, praying that she would.

"Let's go call them," Mattie said. "Right now. Before they make other plans."

"No worries, Roo. But one thing first."

"What?"

"If they can't meet us in Vietnam, we'll just have to sit tight and do it another time. And even if they come, and we do a walkabout together, we'll have to say good-bye to them in Vietnam. Our trip's almost over."

"I know. I understand."

He kissed the back of her hand. "Your mum was always such a good listener. Just like you."

"So?"

"So, let's go find out what she's decided to do with that wish of yours."

VIETNAM

A Light in Her Eyes

"When eating a fruit, think of the person who planted the tree."

—Vietnamese saying

Following an hour's drive from the heart of Ho Chi Minh City, Ian and Mattie stepped out of a beat-up jeep, thanked their driver, and walked toward Cao Dai Temple. Ian had wanted to visit the temple because, a century earlier, its founders had created the Cao Dai religion—a combination of Buddhism, Islam, Christianity, Hinduism, Confucianism, and a variety of other worldwide faiths. He had remembered the site from his earlier trip to Vietnam and wanted to show Mattie.

The temple was a three-story yellow-and-pink building that featured two pagoda-like towers on either side of the front entrance. Holding Mattie's hand, Ian led her across a wide boulevard, which was almost vacant of traffic and completely unlike the streets of Ho Chi Minh City. At the opposite corner, a man dressed in white trousers, a black T-shirt, and a traditional conical hat held a bamboo birdcage. Inside the cage was a gray-and-white dove.

"You want to free bird, to bring good luck to you?" the man asked

Ian, stepping forward. "Only cost you five dollar. And five dollar for good luck is good, good deal."

Ian smiled at the stranger but shook his head, eager to enter the temple, the doors of which were open. Inside, the building was as he remembered—cavernous and full of light. Massive pink columns encircled by snakelike green dragons supported the roof. The dragons were openmouthed and seemed to grin. The blue roof was painted with clouds. Perhaps most striking was the floor, which contained no pews or places for people to sit but was wide-open and covered in elaborate brown and white tiles. Along the walls, images of a single eye with rays of yellow light shooting in all directions appeared to look down on hundreds of worshippers, who sat on the floor and were dressed in white, yellow, blue, and red robes. No one spoke, and the sound of cooing pigeons was all that could be heard.

Ian led Mattie forward a few feet, and then to one side of the structure. She had seen so many churches and temples that were magnificent, but almost inevitably dark and full of gloom. This place was open and inspiring and colorful. She felt as if she were inside a magical, wondrous box. The wall beside her featured a painting of three men dressed as they might have been when the temple was built. One man looked to be from Europe, one from China, and the other from Vietnam. The European and the Chinese were writing upon what appeared to be a window in a sky. Within the window, words were written in French and Chinese. Mattie opened a pamphlet that their driver had given them and found a picture of the painting. The words said, "God and Humanity, Love and Justice."

She thought about the words, then whispered to her father, asking him if she could take out her sketch pad and draw the inside of the temple. He nodded, sitting quietly on the floor, assuming the position of the worshippers in front of them. Mattie sat as well, putting her sketch pad on her lap and removing her colored pencils from their carrying case. Looking around, she wasn't sure what should be the focus of her drawing. The far end of the building seemed to have an altar of sorts, upon which rested an immense, emerald-colored sphere.

Mattie decided to start with the sphere, her fingers gripping a green pencil and moving instinctively. She wanted to create something beautiful for her mother, who had heard her wish and made it come true. Georgia and Holly would join them in two days back in Ho Chi Minh City, and then the four of them would travel along the coast and into the mountains. Holly had already been to Vietnam twice and knew exactly where they should go together. She'd been as excited as Mattie when Georgia agreed to the trip. The girls had held hands and danced in a circle while Ian and Georgia talked about how and where they might meet.

Her wish being granted was only one of the reasons that Mattie's hand re-created the scene before her. They had come to the temple because they hoped to open the remaining two canisters in a beautiful place. Mattie didn't want to read her mother's last words but needed to before Holly arrived. And whatever her mother said in those final words, Mattie planned to leave her a drawing, to show her how much she loved her.

Mattie sketched the temple with no sense of haste. She wanted her picture to be as good as she could make it. She liked how the worshippers had combined all the religions of the world, and felt that in such a place it might be easier for her mother to find her. "Can you see me, Mommy?" she whispered, drawing a dragon.

More than an hour passed before she was content with her drawing. She showed it to her father, who held it carefully, nodding, kissing her cheek. They stood up and walked along the edge of the room, coming to a side door, exiting into a garden crisscrossed with paved pathways. An arbitrary collection of trees, bushes, flowers, and grassy patches composed the garden. Mattie walked toward a shady spot and sat down on a cast-iron bench. She felt the canister's bulk within her pocket but wasn't ready to open it.

"Do you think she'll say good-bye?" she asked, looking above.

Ian shook his head. "No, Roo. Your mum would never say good-bye. Don't be afraid of that."

She wished that her heartbeat would slow. "Daddy?"

"What, luv?"

"The people in there . . . would they say that she's in heaven or reincarnated or something else?"

"I don't know. But we can ask."

"What do you believe?"

He motioned for her drawing, unrolling it, studying the movements her pencils had made. "I believe, Roo, that she's in you, that in some ways, you're her reincarnation. She helped you learn to draw, and you love to draw. She taught you how to swim, and you love the ocean. And she was kind and caring and beautiful inside, just like you."

"You really think so?"

"I reckon she'll always be in you."

Mattie bit her bottom lip. "Should we open them?"

"If you want to."

She didn't move right away, but soon her hand reached toward her pocket. The canister opened; the paper unfurled.

My Angel,

This will be my second-to-last letter to you. Another one awaits you, to find and be opened by you on your sixteenth birthday. But for now, for this trip, these are my last words.

I hope you enjoy Vietnam. It's a place that once knew only war and suffering but now is different. Now there is hope. And I think you'll see this hope, and learn from it.

I know that you believed that your trip would end in Vietnam, but this isn't the case. I would like you and your daddy to pick a new country, a place where he and I never traveled. I want the two of you to create your own memories, to walk through the wonders of a new city and to feel those wonders run from the bottoms of your feet to the tops of your heads. And I want you to tell me about those wonders, through your thoughts, your dreams, and your art.

Speaking of your art, will you do something for me, Mattie? Will you make an exhibit for your daddy and me? Of the places you've been? I want to see your first exhibit. I've wanted to for so long, but I'm not going to get the chance. At least not in this body. So please create an exhibit and know that I'll watch from above.

I am so proud of you, Mattie. I could not love you any more than I already do. Please don't be sad for me. I feel myself traveling somewhere beautiful. I don't know where I'm going, but I'm not afraid. I'll be fine. And I'll be with you when you graduate from high school, when you go to college, when you're out on your own. If you decide to marry, to have a child, I'll be with you then as well. Just like I'll be beside you throughout all the highs and lows of your life.

During the past month, I've read a lot about the journey I'm about to take. Do you know what Albert Einstein said about that journey? He said, "Our death is not an end if we can live on through our children and the younger generation. For they are us, our bodies are only wilted leaves on the tree of life."

With all my heart, Mattie, I believe in his words. I'll always be with you, my precious girl. Like the sun is with the sky. Like how green remains deep within the soil, all winter, and returns with the spring.

Be happy, Mattie. Let me see you dance and sing and smile. A mother and her daughter have a special connection, a bond that can never be broken. It may be tested. It may be pulled. But that bond will endure. Forever.

I love you, my delightful, wonderful child. Now go and laugh. Go and be free.

Mommy

Mattie let the paper coil back up. Then she read the letter two more times, tracing the final words with her forefinger. Finally she placed the note back into the canister. "She said what you did, Daddy."

"What do you mean, luv?"

"She said that she's in me."

He took her hand within his own. "Of course she is."

"Are you going to read your note?"

Nodding, he removed his canister. He looked to the temple, to the sky, to his daughter's face.

My Love,

Thank you for going on this trip, something I asked you to do, something that must not have been easy, but I hope was beautiful. I debated sending you on such a journey but, in the end, felt that I had no choice. You had to walk where we planned on setting our feet, where we once traveled. You had to live.

In my note to Mattie, I asked that you both go someplace new, after Vietnam. Will you do that? I want you to experience a country where we never traveled, where you and Mattie can create memories for the two of you to share. That's how I would like you to end your trip, before returning to America. Go somewhere wonderful and behold that wonder together.

This is one of my last notes to you. There will be one more, which will find you in the future. But for now, my pen will be put to rest. I'm so tired. I'm about to leave this body, which has served me so well. As I said to Mattie, I'm set to start my own journey. And though that journey may take me in a different direction from you, I'll see you and Mattie again. Love does that. It creates bridges. And I'll follow those bridges to you. I'll follow them to you, and I'll support whatever choices you have made, whatever destinations you have arrived at.

I'm going to put my pen down now, my love. I'm going to rest. But I'll leave you with one last poem. At least for now.

Two as One

Here he comes
Across the room.
His voice so strange
His hand outstretched.

Can love live at first sight?

I've only known one kind of love.
A love that he nurtured within me,
That was given light and water,
That was never taken for granted.
A love that grew,
Slowly at first,
Like the warmth of dawn.

He didn't capture me with his eyes or smile or strength,
But with that same warmth,
Which seemed to take flight,
As if the sun gave out wings.

My home became his,
His secrets mine.

We journeyed together,
Two as one.

Up and down mountains
Of stone and thought.

We created a life together.
Shared her triumphs and joys,
Witnessed beauty through her eyes,
Which saw what angels see—
Miracles that too often go unnoticed,
Flowering weeds in a bed of roses.

The years slipped by,
Too short and fast.

We argued.
Paid bills.
And fell into monotonous patterns.
But our cores remained merged,
Tethered to each other.

Love can be damaged, wasted, torn.
But ours was unbroken—
A sun not yet set,
A poem not yet read.

Even now,
As the lids of my eyes, my life, go heavy,
I feel one with you—
The father of our child.
The fabric of me.

You gave me so many gifts,
And for those I am grateful.
My fate is no longer bitter.
It is just that—my fate.

Mourn me no more, Ian.
Move on.
Ahead.
Into new places.

And if you hear footsteps
Or see shadows,
Know that I am still with you.
Throughout this life and every life thereafter.

I am yours as I always was,
As I always will be.
I love you,

Kate

Ian carefully rolled up the note and put it away, brushing away his tears. He didn't want to think about these being the last words that he would read from Kate for years. He longed to believe that he would hear her footsteps and see her shadow, but his faith in such things had been weakened, not strengthened, by her death.

He stood up, offering Mattie his hand. She took it and he led her away from the garden, from the temple where all religions were treated as one. In the distance he saw their driver leaning against his battered jeep. Ian started to walk toward it but noticed the man at the corner, holding his caged dove.

"Do you want to free it, luv?" Ian asked.

Mattie nodded. "Mommy would like that."

"Then let's make her happy."

They joined the man, and Ian handed him five dollars. The local smiled, revealing several missing teeth. "When you set bird free," he said, "you show your kindness to world. And then good luck, it come to you; it make you live longer; it make you happier."

The dove cooed, ruffling its wings, as if it knew that it was about to take flight.

Ian turned to Mattie. "Why don't you free her, Roo?"

She watched the bird, wanting to share the good luck with her father, wanting the world to know that he was kind. "Can we do it together?" she asked the man. "If we do it together, will we both get good luck?"

"Yes, I think so. A bird has two wings. So two people can release it."

"Will it fly high? To someone above?"

The man glanced up, squinting from the sun's glare. He then lowered his gaze to Mattie, appearing to study her. "Seven year ago, my father, he die. So, I go to river and let my favorite dove go free. I give him to my father. And that dove, he fly so high, like he want to meet my father. This make me happy. And this bird here, she strong. I think she do same thing."

Mattie smiled faintly, watching the dove, thinking about her mother's note. "Let's hold the cage high, Daddy. So we can help her fly high."

"Sure, luv. That's a great idea. A real beaut."

The man handed Mattie the cage, which she lifted until it was level with her eyes. The dove continued to coo.

"Can you open the door?" Mattie asked.

Ian put his fingers on the delicate bamboo. "Happily."

"Good-bye, little bird," Mattie said. "Fly high. Say hello to this man's father and . . . and to my mommy."

The cage's door swung open. For a few seconds, the bird didn't stir. But then it seemed to sense its looming freedom, leaping forward, spreading its wings. A feather fell as the dove took flight, rising above the street, a blur of white against a blue sky. Mattie reached for her father's hand as the bird continued to climb. He squeezed her fingers as it soared higher, heading straight to the south, as if it knew the way home.

The dove disappeared.

As her father thanked the man, Mattie bent down and picked up the feather. She opened her sketch pad and carefully placed the feather between two pages. I'll always keep you, she thought, closing the sketch pad and again taking her father's hand.

Two days later, Ian and Mattie waited for Georgia and Holly outside Ho Chi Minh City's airport. Though the airport was almost brand-new, and would have looked at home in any major city, nonpassengers were barred from entering it by a chain-link fence. Hundreds of locals were gathered behind this fence, awaiting the arrival of loved ones, friends, and business associates. People were orderly but tried to get as close as possible to the fence, stepping forward when spaces opened. Fortunately, Ian was taller than most everyone, and with Mattie sitting on his shoulders, they could stand in the back and still have a good view of passengers leaving the building.

As Ian waited, he wondered if he was crazy to be meeting Georgia. A part of him wanted to see her, but he also feared that the looming encounter would only further confuse Mattie. They planned to travel together for six days, and at that point, Mattie would be forced to again say good-bye. This time there wouldn't be a hello shortly afterward. He and Mattie would journey to a new country, as Kate had asked. And then they would return to America. Whatever bonds had been forged between Mattie and her new companions would be severed. Whatever steps forward she'd taken would be undone. Mattie wanted a sibling, but Holly wasn't her sister and never would be.

"Daddy?" she asked, leaning down from his shoulders.

"Yeah, Roo?"

"Is it . . . okay to be excited?"

"About Holly arriving?"

"Yes."

He looked up at her. "Of course, luv. What do you mean?"

"I mean, we read Mommy's last letter. And that made me sad. But now I'm excited."

"I'm glad you're excited," he replied, squeezing her leg. "That's a good thing."

"Why?"

"Because I reckon that being excited is one of the best feelings in the world. Right up there with love and joy. And after you've been kicked in the teeth like we have, well, we deserve to be excited."

"You are too?"

He smiled. "I am, my little question asker. We're going to have a bloody good time."

"Where are they? Shouldn't they be here by now?"

"Easy on, luv. We'll see them in a tick."

"I hope so."

Mattie drummed her fingers against Ian's shoulders, and he watched the pink nails of her right hand rise and fall, wishing that she hadn't discovered nail polish. He twisted to his left, looking away from the airport and into the darkening night. A nearby parking lot brimmed with battered taxis and motor scooters. Stainless-steel poles rose every fifty feet or so, topped by red flags with yellow stars. Though the sun had settled below the horizon, light still lingered, as if intent on illuminating whoever stepped from the airport.

Turning back toward the front of the airport, Ian studied the nearby locals. They were dressed more stylishly than he remembered from his earlier trip. Of course, a few conical bamboo hats perched atop the heads of the elderly, who tended to wear pajama-like pants and shirts. And many of the middle-aged women were covered from head to toe in formfitting traditional Vietnamese dresses. But members of the younger generation wore collared, Hawaiian-style T-shirts, jeans, skirts, and blouses.

Ian thought about how, fifteen years earlier, most everyone in Ho Chi Minh City rode bicycles. Now everyone, it seemed, owned a scooter. The black and red contraptions darted around the city like millions of water bugs released into a series of small streams. So many other things had changed as well. He remembered Ho Chi Minh City as having no skyscrapers or modern buildings. And though the city still didn't compare to Hong Kong in terms of architectural wonders, Ian had been surprised by the sight of a dozen high-rises along the banks of the Saigon River. Multistory cranes dominated other parts of the skyline as developers rushed to build hotels and business centers.

Georgia and Holly had already been to Ho Chi Minh City twice, so the plan was to meet, spend one night in the city, and then travel by car to Dalat, a popular destination in the mountains of southern Vietnam. Both Ian and Mattie were looking forward to being in the mountains again, to escaping the chaos of another large city.

As Ian wondered what had changed in Dalat since he and Kate had walked its streets, Mattie squeezed his neck with her knees and leaned forward, forcing him to step ahead or topple over. "There they are!" she said, pointing. "See them, Daddy? Right over there?"

Georgia and Holly emerged from the airport, each pulling a suitcase. Georgia was dressed in a simple white collared blouse and brown pants. Her red hair was pulled back in a long ponytail. Holly wore a white sundress with blue, green, and purple polka dots.

"Holly!" Mattie called out, waving wildly. "Over here!"

Georgia turned in their direction, followed a second later by Holly. Eyes met and hands gestured. Mattie asked to be put down, and as she jumped off Ian's shoulders, he had to keep her from slamming into the ground. They hurried to a gate where passengers were emerging. Holly let go of her suitcase and hugged Mattie. Georgia watched the girls, turned to Ian, and stepped ahead to embrace him. Their bodies didn't press against each other like those of the girls, and their hug was brief. But still, he kissed her cheek and she smiled. Pleasantries were exchanged as Ian helped them with their suitcases and headed toward a nearby taxi. He haggled with the driver, agreed to a price, and gestured for Georgia to take the front seat.

Holly, Mattie, and Ian settled into the back, and the taxi left the parking lot, soon merging onto a street inundated with trucks, buses, scooters, and bicycles. Ian thought that Georgia and Holly would want to check in to their hotel and freshen up, but Holly was eager to explore. As the girls chatted beside him, Ian asked their driver to swing by their hotel, where Ian handed the suitcases to a porter and inquired if someone could deliver them to Georgia's room. The man happily agreed, and soon the taxi was once again on the streets.

"Would you ladies fancy dining out this evening?" Ian asked, watching Georgia turn toward them.

Mattie nodded. "Where should we go?"

"Someplace fun?" Holly replied. "Maybe by the river?"

Ian unzipped his day pack so that he could reach his guidebook, but Holly leaned toward the driver. She started to speak in Mandarin, caught her mistake, and then said in English, "Excuse me, sir, but where should we go for dinner? What's a special, special place?"

The man glanced in the rearview mirror and smiled. "You want to eat Vietnamese or French food?"

"Can we have both?"

He nodded. "In that case, would you like to see the Temple Club?"

"What's the Temple Club?"

"An old Chinese temple," he replied, swinging the taxi around a broken-down bus. "It is now a restaurant. And very nice inside."

Holly looked at everyone else. "Sounds great to me. What do you guys think?"

Mattie agreed, as did Georgia and Ian. The driver turned onto a busy boulevard and began to tell them the history of the Temple Club. Outside their windows, Ho Chi Minh City pulsated, an eccentric mix of French Colonial structures, dilapidated apartment buildings, and modern high-rises. The sidewalks were lined with tropical trees and filled with tourists, merchants, and hustlers. A light rain began to fall. The driver turned on the windshield wipers and continued to talk.

A few minutes later, the taxi stopped in front of a two-story stone building that had been painted yellow. Ian paid and tipped the driver, and followed Georgia, Mattie, and Holly into the structure. The Temple Club wasn't tacky, as he had feared, but elegant and timeless. The exposed brick walls led to a high white ceiling. Oriental rugs partly covered a terra-cotta floor. Ancient stone statues of Buddha were present, as were hanging tapestries and ornamental lights. Jazz permeated the air.

A hostess seated the foursome at a wooden table with a white marble center. Ian helped Georgia, then the girls into high-backed teak chairs. A waitress clad in a traditional full-length Vietnamese dress appeared and handed everyone menus. Holly smiled, took her menu, and spoke again in Mandarin, covering her mouth when she realized her mistake.

"We're in Vietnam," Mattie said, grinning.

"I know, I know," Holly said, rolling her eyes. She looked up at the waitress. "I'm sorry. We just landed here from Hong Kong. That's why I spoke Mandarin to you."

The woman, who held her hands in front of her waist, smiled. "That okay. No problem. May I bring you some wine?"

Everyone ordered and soon was served their drinks. Other patrons, both foreigners and locals, occupied nearby tables, and a variety of languages echoed in the narrow room. Outside, scooters beeped amid distant thunderclaps. As Georgia and Ian began to discuss their itinerary, Mattie took Holly's hand. "I'm glad you came."

"I'm glad too."

"Our trip . . . it's almost over. Soon my daddy and I will be back in New York."

"I know. My mom and I were talking about that on the plane. How you'll be back with your friends, back in school."

Mattie nodded. "Can you teach me more Mandarin?"

"More?" Holly asked, setting down her drink. "You'll be home soon."

"Well, maybe I can . . . go to Chinatown, and talk to some people. And if my dad and I come back to Hong Kong to visit you someday, you won't have to do all the talking."

"I like the talking," Holly replied, smiling, pushing her bangs to the side.

"You're good at it."

"Nihao."

"What?"

"That means hello. Remember?"

"Ni . . . hao."

Holly shook her head. "No, no, no. Say the word like you fell and hurt your *knee* and then you ask *how*. Like this—*nihao*."

"Nihao."

"That's it! Perfect."

"Nihao."

"Say it to my mom."

Mattie turned toward Georgia, and repeated the word. Georgia smiled and complimented Mattie, who then asked Holly how to say thank you. As the girls worked on new words, dinner was served. Plates of roasted duck, grilled sea bass, and fresh vegetables soon occupied the center of the table. Everyone plucked morsels from each platter and deposited them on their own plates. The notes of Louis Armstrong lingered above the clink of cutlery and the collection of voices.

"Do you mind if I act like a tourist?" Georgia asked Ian, removing a small digital camera from her purse. She also took out a little mirror, and reapplied her lipstick.

"No worries."

When their waitress came by next, Georgia asked if she would take their photo. The woman smiled, and Ian and Georgia moved behind the girls. A flash illuminated the room twice, revealing a foursome of grinning faces. Then Ian and Georgia returned to their chairs. Ian asked Mattie how to say thank you in Mandarin, and Mattie pronounced the word just as Holly had taught her. Sensing that Mattie wanted to learn more from Holly, Ian turned back to Georgia, realizing how slowly she ate, how her fingers were long and slender.

He handed her a basket of fresh croissants. "Were you surprised that I asked?"

"To meet you in Vietnam?"

"Just that little thing."

She took a croissant and split it in half with a silver knife. "I don't know. Maybe. But I'm glad you did. I hoped you would."

"Why?"

The knife was placed carefully on the table. A pair of blond foreigners in the corner of the room laughed. "I . . . I can't say," Georgia replied. "At least not now. But I'm happy you called."

Ian took a bite of fish, thinking about her words, wondering if she hoped for anything else. He wasn't ready to fall for her, or to have her fall for him. "The mountains will be lovely," he said, smiling.

She noticed that the cuffs of his shirt were frayed and instinctively wanted to mend them, though she didn't know how to sew. "Are you taking care of yourself?"

"Oh, I'm all right. This old body isn't too particular."

"Kate would want you to take care of yourself."

Thirty minutes later, the platters were empty, and Ian and Georgia split the bill. They followed Mattie and Holly out of the building and into the street. Rain fell, slanting, from the dark sky. A young boy holding an umbrella hurried toward them, splashing in puddles. He was selling flowers, and Ian bought Georgia, Holly, and Mattie each a purple iris.

"Should we hail a taxi?" he asked, dangling his foot above a puddle. "Or walk back in the rain?"

Mattie glanced at Holly, who laughed and stepped into the same puddle.

"A walk it is," Ian said, putting his foot down, pleased to have the rain on his back.

As Vietnamese wearing ponchos sped past on scooters, Ian and Georgia followed the girls. He asked if she might like an umbrella, but she declined, preferring to get wet like Holly and Mattie. She remembered walking in the rain when she was young, when wetness was more a delight than a discomfort. She wanted to take Ian's arm, to stomp in the puddles with him. But knowing that she couldn't reach over and touch him, she simply walked ahead, savoring the sight of Holly and Mattie.

When they reached their hotel, Georgia checked in while Ian bought lollipops for the girls. As Mattie and Holly laughed and licked, Ian followed Georgia up the stairs, trying not to notice the curves revealed by her wet pants. Their rooms were on opposite ends of a hallway. Mattie hugged Holly and said good night. Ian leaned toward Georgia, sensed that she wanted him to hold her, but pulled away. "I reckon we're all a bit knackered, so sleep well," he said, nodding to Georgia and then to Holly. "We'll buzz off after breakfast."

Georgia wished that they were still walking in the rain, that his hand wasn't so near yet so far. "Good night," she said, opening her door, kissing Mattie on the cheek. Following Holly into their room, Georgia listened to Ian's footsteps fade away, not wanting to listen, but unable to help herself.

NINE HOURS INTO THE DRIVE TO HOI An, Mattie and Holly had become restless. Hoi An, a coastal city on the way to Dalat, was reached by a series of worn roads that ran through forests and valleys, as well as past stretches of coastline. For most of the drive, Ian and Georgia had played games with the girls. Four seats in the back of their van faced one another, and it had been easy to rig up a table between everyone's knees. Ian had taught Georgia and Holly how to play blackjack. Georgia had brought a magnetic checkerboard, which proved perfect for the swaying vehicle. They also listened to music, told stories, took digital photos of the countryside, and tried to nap.

Now, as the van descended a mountain toward a raging surf far below, Ian sipped from a bottle of water and watched the girls. For the first time since they'd been together, it seemed that they might argue. Both were tired, bored, and grumpy. Ian had already headed off several looming disagreements and didn't want to do so again. Turning around in his seat, he asked their driver if there was somewhere ahead where they could pull over and stretch their legs. The driver, a pleasant man named Khan, who might have entered his sixth decade, smiled and said that in twenty minutes they'd arrive at a suitable beach.

Ian looked around the back of the van, which was filled with their suitcases, pairs of crutches, and two crates of Tiger beer. The area that he shared with Georgia and the girls was cramped, and he wondered whether they might be happier if he sat in the front with the driver. "I reckon you ladies would fancy a break from all my yammering," he said, climbing into the front. "Talk about boys or something, will you?"

Georgia turned from the window and winked at Ian. "Did you hear, Mattie, about Holly's new classmate?"

Holly slapped her mother's knee. "Mom!"

"What?" Mattie asked, leaning forward. "What new classmate?"

"Didn't he pass you a note the other day?" Georgia added, catching Holly's hand as it descended again.

As Holly struggled against her mother's grasp, Ian settled into the front seat. The laughter in the rear of the van made him smile. Rolling down his window, he looked out at the verdant landscape, which was a combination of terraced rice fields, tropical trees, and granite crags.

"How far is it, Khan, to Hoi An?" he asked the driver.

Khan squinted, as if peering at their unseen destination. "Oh, not so far," he replied, his English well practiced and easy to understand. "Maybe two hours."

"Has it changed? Like Ho Chi Minh City?"

"Hoi An? Maybe a little. The way a daughter's face changes from year to year."

Ian smiled, liking Khan, who wore black-rimmed glasses and had a silver tooth. "Can I ask you something, mate?"

"Please."

"What are the crutches in the back for?"

Khan glanced in the rearview mirror. "I make those. And I bring them north every time I come."

"Why?"

"Because there are still many, many bombs in the countryside. Sometimes farmers or children step on them. And then they lose their legs. And so I leave crutches in villages."

Ian watched a section of jungle pass. "Can't . . . can't the bloody bombs be found and destroyed?"

"Impossible. Too many of them are left. There are as many bombs as stones. And the metal is worth money. So sometimes poor people try to find bombs, and sell the metal. And the bombs explode. Or sometimes children step on them." The driver shrugged, shaking his head. "So I make crutches and drive north. As often as I can."

"How many crutches do you make?"

"One pair every day. That is my goal. I want to make more, but wood is expensive, and my hands are old."

"I'm sorry."

"It is not your fault," Khan replied, squinting again as a truck approached. "Did you know, when I was thirteen years old, I helped Ho Chi Minh fight the Americans?"

Ian turned toward him. "How?"

"We made many secret trails so Ho Chi Minh could get supplies from Hanoi, in the north, to his men in the south, who fought against the Americans. These trails were very important, and the Americans knew this, so they bombed them. For six weeks, I worked on a bridge over a river. The Americans came in their planes every morning and bombed it. We rebuilt it every afternoon, and then at night, our trucks crossed it, going south. Then the Americans would bomb it the next day, and we would rebuild it, and so on and so on. Finally, we decided to build the bridge underwater, so the Americans would think it was gone. It took us eleven days to finish the underwater bridge. After that, the Americans did not bomb it because they thought we had tired of building it. But we had not. And every night our trucks went over it."

Ian tried to imagine what it would be like, to be thirteen and to watch bombs fall and things explode. "And now you build crutches?"

"Yes, because I know how to use wood. From my days of building the bridge."

The road dropped down to the edge of the sea, which was indigo colored and flatter than the pavement they followed. "What if I helped you?" Ian asked, looking at Khan's hands, which were thick-knuckled and scarred.

"What do you mean?"

"Might I send you some crutches, from America?"

Khan turned to him, lifting up his glasses and squinting once again. "Crutches from America? Really? That is not big trouble for you?"

"No worries, mate. I have your boss's business card. I could send them to his office."

The van coasted as Khan took his foot off the accelerator. "I need . . . more crutches. Would you do that, Mr. McCray? Would you send some to me?"

Ian stuck out his hand, which Khan grasped firmly. "I'll do it. I promise."

"Thank you. Thank you so much."

"I reckon I should thank you. For your deliveries. For trying to help."

Khan nodded, the van once again accelerating. "After the bridge, when I was older and fighting in the war . . . I made mistakes. I was not good. And I do not blame the Americans for everything. For what I did. So now I do my best to help. And I will make crutches until I die."

Ian started to ask him about the past but stopped. "I'll send you some crutches. Soon."

"You are very kind. Kind to an old man, and to the children. I will tell them about you. About the wonderful man who lives in America and sends them crutches."

"Thanks, mate. But really, you're the wonderful man. And you're still building bridges, you know. They just happen to let children walk."

The sea surged to their right, crashing against black rocks, filling the air with the scent of life and death. Ian glanced at Khan, who was smiling, his head moving up and down, as if he was listening to music.

In the rear of the van, Georgia was talking to Mattie and Holly about boys. Ian listened, interested in what advice she would give. She told them not to worry about such things, that they'd worry about boys for the rest of their lives and there was no reason to rush into such emotions. Mattie asked what to look for in boys. Georgia hesitated but soon said that Mattie should search for boys the way she might comb a beach for shells. Don't always seek out the most beautiful shell, she advised, but instead, the most interesting shell, the shell that you could always put to your ear and that would tell you a story, make you feel like you're still walking beside the sea.

Mattie and Holly kept asking questions, and Ian settled back into his seat and smiled. He was glad that Mattie could hear Georgia's perspectives on the confusing feelings brought to life by the opposite sex. If Georgia was jaded by the betrayal of her husband, she didn't hold that event against all men. At least she didn't verbalize such feelings. She didn't speak ill of boys, or tell Mattie to steer clear. Instead, she said that it took a long time to walk a beach full of shells, and that no one should prematurely decide on a favorite.

Squinting, Khan pointed to an empty parking lot near the sea. He pulled over, driving as close as possible to the water. Ian asked Mattie and Holly if they wanted a short break, and the girls jumped out of their seats, bobbing up and down, preparing to open the door.

Surrounded by rocks, the beach was about the same size as a basketball court. While Khan took a can of motor oil from beside his seat and opened the hood, Ian followed Georgia, Holly, and Mattie as they hurried toward the sand. The girls kicked off their flip-flops and stepped into the water. Georgia sat on a smooth and sun-bleached tree trunk that had washed ashore. Ian positioned himself beside her, handing over her camera, which she had forgotten on her seat.

"Thanks," she said, putting the strap around her neck and taking a picture of the girls.

"No worries."

Mattie splashed Holly, who started to chase her through the shallows. Watching the girls giggle, Georgia smiled, glad that they weren't talking about boys. She knew those days would arrive soon and she wasn't ready for them. "They act like sisters, don't they?" she asked, taking off her shoes, moving her toes through the sand.

Ian was tempted to join the girls in the water but decided to let them enjoy it with each other. "They were about to start fighting like sisters."

"Well, they were definitely pushing each other's buttons."

"They were going troppo, I reckon."

"Troppo?"

"Too much time in the tropics. Makes you crazy."

She smiled, still moving her toes through the sand. "You and your sayings. I don't know where in the world you come up with them. Maybe you're the one who's gone troppo."

"Me?"

"Yes, you."

He pretended to have a twitch near his eye. "Nothing wrong with a bit of madness, I reckon. Keeps things nice and interesting."

"You've always been that," she replied, her smile returning.

Holly shrieked as Mattie threw a fistful of seaweed at her. Ian picked up a stone and tossed it into the surf, remembering throwing stones in the Outback with his brothers. A return to Australia would be his next overseas trip, he knew. He'd show Mattie the Southern Cross, let her watch kangaroos bound over the desert and spend time with her cousins. He had thought on several occasions about adding Australia to the end of their trip but decided against it. His brothers were content and married to women they adored, and Ian wasn't sure if he was ready to see their joy. And though he loved his parents, they had never forgiven him for moving to America. To bridge the chasm between them, he needed to be farther from Kate's death, from such loss.

He watched Georgia's toes in the sand. They weren't pretty toes, having been held too tight together for too long by high-heeled shoes. She'd painted her toenails a shade of mauve that wasn't in stark contrast to her pale skin. Some of her calf was exposed, and he followed its contours upward until reaching the hem of her skirt. Realizing what he was doing, he looked toward the girls, sighing.

"What?" she asked, turning to him.

Holly caught Mattie and began kicking water at her.

"Do you reckon it's odd," he asked, "that we're traveling together?"

"Odd? You mean wrong?"

"No, not wrong. But . . . but why do you think we're here? For Holly? For Mattie? For something else?"

She watched the girls. "I don't know. I don't want to overthink things. You invited us, so we came. And it felt right to come, not wrong."

He glanced up, his mood suddenly less buoyant than a minute earlier, as if looking at Georgia's leg was tantamount to cheating on Kate. "I should have died, not her."

"Why in the world do you say that?"

"Because she was the best part of us."

Georgia shook her head. "That doesn't make sense. Us isn't something that's . . . made up of parts. It's made up of one."

Shifting on the tree trunk, he found her eyes. "Might I ask you something?"

"It's made of one, Ian."

He scratched at a mosquito bite, nodding. "I remember . . . when you left Frank. You were in so much pain. And now you seem so complete. How did you go from there to here?"

She closed her eyes for a moment. Nearby, a gull cried. "A day at a time," she replied, her feet moving again. "That's how I made it. I survived those early days, the worst days. I took life a day at a time, and then slowly, it got better. Because time was my friend. The days turned into weeks, the weeks to months, and everything just slowly improved. Not that my life is perfect. But it's good enough."

"He was crazy to hurt you. What a bloody fool. What a mongrel."

"He's still with her, so I don't know about the fool part. He seems happy. And I don't care about the mongrel part. I don't hate him anymore. I hated him for years, and that never did me any good. It certainly didn't help Holly, and it made me do . . . despicable things."

"You did nothing of the sort."

"I hurt him, Ian."

"No, you—"

"Yes, I did," she interrupted, shifting her gaze to the girls.

"How?"

She grew still. "You really want to know?"

"Only if you want to tell me."

A horn sounded in the distance. Georgia glanced toward the road, letting her memories unfurl, memories long ago suppressed. "It wasn't hard to hurt him. I let his key donors know, anonymously, through a fake e-mail address, what had happened at night . . . inside their museum, in his office, in storage rooms. You think they wrote their big checks after that? That I wasn't despicable? His donors left him, and he didn't last long. His dream job was gone. And I had my revenge. But I was even more miserable than before, because I ended up hurting other people at the museum. People whose jobs depended on those donations. And I can't make that up to them. Ever."

"You reacted to something horrible."

"But what I did wasn't right. And so I stopped hating."

"He's still a mongrel."

"Probably. But to me he's gone."

Ian slipped off his shoes. "I wouldn't have hurt you, you know. Never in a million years. Most men wouldn't have. Frank was a fool."

"Frank . . . was being Frank. I should have seen it coming. I was the fool."

Mattie and Holly had dropped into the water and were waving at

Ian and Georgia, yelling at them to come forward. "Reckon we should do a bit of wading?" Ian asked. "Might feel good on the old feet."

"Sure, let's wade."

Ian followed Georgia's footsteps through the warm sand, wondering why he'd just told her that he would have never cheated on her, why he'd placed them together. What the bloody hell am I doing? he asked himself, the water touching his toes, Mattie reaching out to him, pulling him away from shore. He smiled at her, kissing her wet brow, glancing at Georgia. She watched him and he turned to Mattie and picked her up, pressing his mouth against her neck and blowing.

Feeling as if he'd once again betrayed Kate, Ian turned all his attention to Mattie, continuing to tickle her, his emotions as mixed as the churning sand and water that surrounded his knees. He felt guilt and remorse, liberation and hope.

Holly ran forward to help Mattie tackle him, their legs twisting together, the three of them falling into the sea. Ian glimpsed Georgia staring at him, and their eyes met. Then the girls fell on him, pressing him into the water and sand, pushing him away from Georgia, in the direction that he needed to go.

LATER THAT NIGHT, AFTER THEY HAD CHECKED into their hotel rooms in Hoi An, the foursome walked along a quiet street. To their left stood a row of yellow two-story shops and restaurants with peaked tin roofs. Round red lanterns hung from below the roofs, glowing like embers. On the opposite side, a canal ran toward the distant sea. The canal was bound by granite blocks and held traditional Vietnamese boats, which were small, wooden, and featured flat bows.

Only a few cars and scooters navigated the street. Most Vietnamese walked or rode bicycles. The city, Ian knew, had been basically unchanged for the previous two hundred years. The architecture was an unusual blend of Chinese, Japanese, French, and Dutch structures—reflecting Hoi An's history as a once-famous city and harbor that attracted merchants from all over the world. At some point, Hoi An had fallen out of favor for ports to the south, and the city had all but disappeared from maps.

Though everyone was hungry after the long day in the van, Georgia and Ian had decided to surprise the girls with a trip to one of Hoi An's many tailor shops. Ian wanted to buy something pretty for Mattie and felt bad about her experience at the store in Hong Kong. Hoi An was well-known for its custom-made silk dresses and cashmere suits, creations that would cost hundreds of dollars in the West but ran ten or twenty dollars in this forgotten city.

As she had in Hong Kong, Holly led them forward, saying hello in Vietnamese to the locals she passed. Mattie did likewise, doing her best to keep pace with Holly's feet and grasp of languages. Mattie carried her backpack, as usual, but Ian hadn't seen her sketch pad emerge since the previous morning, which surprised him. For as long as he could remember, she had drawn at least one picture every day.

The girls were excited by the prospect of getting new dresses, which they planned to wear to dinner in Dalat. Still, Holly passed several tailor shops where men stood outside and tried to attract her attention. She didn't want to enter a shop run by men, as she believed that the men would focus on Ian. Questions would be directed to him. Tea served to him. And while Holly didn't need to be the center of attention, she wanted Mattie to receive that attention, not her father. Mattie was the one who needed a pretty dress, who had an eye for beautiful things.

Holly finally located a shop where two middle-aged women sat outside on plastic chairs. The women wore black pants and white collared shirts. They were sipping soft drinks and pointing to something in the distance. Holly greeted them in Vietnamese, which produced broad smiles. Switching to English, she asked them if they made dresses, and the women stood up as if they'd sat on thumbtacks, taking Holly's hands and leading her into an old wooden building.

As Holly walked, she told the women how Mattie needed a special dress, how they were all going out to dinner the following night. The room that Holly was led into resembled the interior of a temple. The ceiling, two stories above, was made of dark wood, as were the walls and the thick pillars that ran from the stone floor to the highest point in the peaked roof. Red lanterns, unlit but vibrant, hung from old chains, descending like spiders spinning webs. Teak shelves lining the walls contained bolts of brightly colored silk. Headless mannequins displayed a variety of traditional and modern dresses.

The women, who looked to be twins, stopped in the center of the room. "You like Vietnamese or Western dresses?" one seamstress asked in broken English, her eyes as dark as the ceiling and the large mole next to her nose.

"Wait, sister, wait," the other woman said, scowling. "First, we welcome you to our store. Would you like anything to drink? To eat?"

Holly looked at Mattie. "Do you want anything?"

"I'm okay."

"Are you sure?" Holly asked. "They're happy to bring us something."

Mattie looked at the women, who nodded. "Maybe a drink?"

The smooth-faced sister smiled. "A Coca-Cola? A Fanta?"

"A Coke, please."

The woman looked at Holly, Georgia, and then Ian. Everyone ordered a drink, and the seamstress hurried out into the street. The remaining proprietor lit a stick of incense and picked up a measuring tape. "My sister, Kim, she be back soon. My name Binh. No one come to our shop today, so since you first customer, that mean you lucky customer, and we give you good price."

Georgia saw Holly's glance and nodded, sitting down on a granite bench. Ian moved beside her, a cramp in his stomach, making him realize that he hadn't taken an antacid since arriving in Vietnam.

"What do you think," Holly asked Mattie, "a Vietnamese or a Western dress?"

Mattie looked at the mannequins. She walked over to a traditional

Vietnamese dress, which was almost ankle length and worn over white silk pants. The dress was blue, with buttons falling from the neck to the underside of a shoulder. The top half of the dress featured a variety of blurred colors, like a garden observed through rain-covered glass. Mattie thought that she saw roses, tulips, and a hundred other flowers. She liked the idea of being a walking garden and touched the soft fabric. "I love this one," she said. "Is it expensive?"

"No," Binh replied. "For you, only fifteen dollars."

Holly shook her head. "But we're your first customers, your lucky, lucky customers. I think for us, eight dollars is a better price. A much better price. With that price, more luck will come your way. So much luck that you'll make dresses for free."

"Eight dollars!" Binh repeated, feigning shock. "Twelve dollars for you. This my best price. Sure, sure."

"No, no, no. Nine dollars. That's my best price. Sure, sure."

"Ten."

"Nine."

As Holly and the seamstress haggled, Mattie saw a boy's suit and thought of Rupee. "Daddy, can we get something for Rupee?" she asked. "Something special?"

Ian followed her gaze to the suit, wondering how the other orphans would react to such clothes, and why he hadn't heard back from the orphanage's director, whom he'd e-mailed three days earlier. "I don't know, luv," he finally replied, "if the other blokes at the orphanage would fancy seeing Rupee in a suit. Maybe we could send them some soft blankets instead? Would that be all right?"

"As soft as this?" Mattie asked, again touching the dress.

"Aye, aye, First Mate. As soft as that."

Mattie grinned and thanked him as Holly and Binh finally agreed on a price of ten dollars. Glad to see Holly smile, and that they were going to buy blankets for the children at Rupee's orphanage, Mattie stepped forward as Binh pulled a measuring tape from her pocket. Remembering how she had fled from the seamstress in Hong Kong, Mattie stood straight, glancing at her father.

Rather than immediately take Mattie's measurements, Binh squeezed her arms, touched the contours of her spine, and traced the outline of her collarbones. Mattie felt as if she was in a doctor's office and looked to Holly, who smiled, placing a hand in front of her mouth as she laughed.

"You strong girl," Binh said, unwinding her measuring tape, clucking her tongue as she recorded the circumference of Mattie's neck and waist, as well as the length of her torso, legs, and arms.

Kim returned from the street and handed soft drinks to Georgia, Holly, and Ian. "Be careful my sister no choke you with measuring tape," she said, smiling.

Binh scowled, replying in Vietnamese, and then adding in English, "Kim good at making dresses, but better at talking. She talk all day and night if I let her. If you let her. Go, Kim. Go outside and get them food."

Still smiling, Kim turned to Ian and Georgia. "Binh not have many good ideas, but that one of them. You want something to eat? Some grilled chicken or squid?"

"Will this take a while?" Ian asked, gesturing toward Mattie.

"Oh, yes," Kim replied. "If we measure all of you, it take some time. Especially with Binh measuring you. She make many mistakes, for sure."

Ian set his drink aside. "I reckon I don't need to be measured."

"Yes, you do," Mattie replied, turning in his direction. "You're going to get a nice suit, Daddy. That you can wear to dinner tomorrow night."

"I am?"

"You certainly are," Georgia answered, stepping to a nearby shelf that held bolts of dark fabric and feeling the material. "A beautiful cashmere suit to wear with all your ladies."

Ian smiled. "Well, in that case, I suspect we could do with a bit of grub."

"I go now," Kim said. "Be back soon with delicious dinner. You make sure that my sister measure you right. Sometimes her eyes and brain not work so good."

Binh shooed Kim away, said something in Vietnamese, and the twins laughed. Kim left the room. After jotting down a few numbers, Binh walked over to Holly and repeated the process, continuing to cluck her tongue. Holly had watched the sisters with interest, deciding at the last moment that she didn't want a black dress, but one just like Mattie's. She hoped to be Mattie's twin, if only for a night.

It took another twenty minutes to measure Holly, Ian, and Georgia. Halfway through the process, Kim returned with skewers of roasted chicken and squid. She placed the food on wooden plates and served her patrons, making a point to show the steaming morsels to her sister, but offering her none. As Mattie and Holly began to eat, and Georgia stretched out her arm for Binh to measure, Ian motioned for Kim to follow him out into the street.

"You need something?" she asked. "A beer? A scooter? Maybe foot massage?"

He smiled, removing three pieces of sea glass that he had found on the beach earlier that day. The pieces were green and worn smooth by the passage of countless waves. They were about the size of his thumbnail and looked like precious stones that had been found deep in the earth. He handed the pieces to Kim. "Reckon you could turn these bits of sea glass into three necklaces? Or do you know someone who can?"

Kim placed the sea glass on her palm, moving the pieces around with her forefinger. "What kind of necklace?"

"Something to go with their dresses? Maybe . . . maybe a silver setting on a black leather cord?"

"My friend, she can do this. Make them very beautiful for your ladies. Cost you . . . twenty dollar."

Ian leaned closer to her. "Let's have a go at it, shall we? And if you keep it a secret, I'll give you some extra loot. But they need to be ready tomorrow morning. When we pick up the dresses, you can give them to me."

"No problem. I go to my friend right now."

He reached into his day pack and handed her twenty-five dollars. "Please tell your mate to make them special."

Kim pocketed the money but continued to hold the sea glass. "Your wife, she lucky woman."

Ian's smile faded. "Georgia? She's . . . she's not my wife."

"No?"

"No."

"Well, she still lucky. If you find beautiful thing and give it to her, then I think she lucky. Same, same for girls."

"Thank you."

"Okay, you go back inside, so they no wonder where you are, so they no think I am your new girlfriend. See you tomorrow."

"Good night. Thank you for the food."

"Good night, Mr. Sea Glass Man."

Ian watched the Vietnamese woman depart, wondering if all the locals assumed that he and Georgia were married. "Sorry, my luv," he whispered, looking into the night sky, which shimmered with starlight.

Back inside the dress shop, Binh had finished measuring Georgia and was talking with Mattie about silk blankets. Ian entered the room, leaned against a wall, and listened to his daughter and Holly haggle with Binh over the cost of blankets. Mattie wasn't a good negotiator, and Holly seemed frustrated when Mattie prematurely agreed on a price. But Mattie was happy, which prompted Ian's smile to return.

He handed Binh some bills and lifted a skewered squid from a plate. "Thank you," he said. "We'll be back tomorrow morning. Before we buzz off for Dalat. Reckon you can get the dresses done?"

Binh rubbed the bills for good luck. "We work on dresses all night, and we sleep tomorrow. This perfect for us. Especially for Kim. Now she can talk all night."

"Well, have a good chat."

"You too."

Farewells were exchanged, and Ian led Georgia and the girls out onto the street. He took a bite of the squid, which was warm and sweet. "Might I show you something?" he asked.

Everyone nodded, and he walked over to a pair of bicycle taxis. After telling the drivers his intentions, Ian and Mattie got into one seat, while Georgia and Holly occupied the other. The drivers pedaled hard, and the contraptions gathered speed, easing into the empty road. Two-hundred-year-old storefronts passed. Streetlamps flickered. Mattie and Holly reached out to each other and clasped hands. One driver smoked a cigarette while his companion spoke to him in Vietnamese.

The bicycle taxis turned down a dirt road, rumbling ahead like a pair of racing tortoises. As the lights of Hoi An faded behind them, the stars strengthened. Coconut trees bordered the road, rising high, their fronds whispering in the wind. Soon the surf could be heard. A beach appeared, gray and massive.

Ian paid the drivers and asked them to wait. Taking Mattie's hand, he led her forward, toward the sea. Georgia and Holly followed, talking about the beauty of the night, which seemed to increase with each passing step. Layers of stars, as countless as the grains of sand beneath their feet, sparkled in a sky that was filled with too much light to be considered black. A few hundred paces to their right, a group of Vietnamese had gathered around a bonfire and were singing. The bonfire partly illuminated the nearby sea. The singing mingled with the crashing of waves.

"Here's a beaut of a spot," Ian said, lying down on the sand twenty feet from the water and seemingly a handbreadth from the sky. "This is what we'd do in the bush," he added. "When my mates and I were young. Sometimes we'd light a campfire. We called it a bush telly. But it was better to watch the stars in the dark."

Mattie, Holly, and Georgia also moved to the sand, staring up. At first, no one spoke. The sky twinkled. Occasionally, shooting stars flashed past forgotten constellations, disappearing above the sea. Several satellites—no more than specks of light—drifted, their steel hulls reflecting sunlight from the other side of the world. No moon was present. Nor were any clouds. The sky was alone with its worlds and histories and monuments.

Georgia realized that her ex-husband, despite his role as a museum director, as someone who loved beauty, had never encouraged her to do anything like gaze at stars. "What do you see?" she asked, listening to the waves, watching a satellite.

Holly gathered sand in her hand and let it fall through her fingers. "I think the shooting stars are the best. It's like . . . an invisible giant is waving a bunch of candles above us. And they're going out, splash, splash, splash, when they fall into the ocean."

"How about you, Mattie?" Georgia wondered. "What do you see up there?"

Mattie saw her mother in the stars, saw the beauty and grace and strength of someone who had made her feel free. But she wasn't sure if she should say as much. She didn't want to make her father sad. On the other hand, she didn't want to lie to Georgia either. "I . . . I see my mother," she finally replied, tears gathering in the hollows below her eyes. She felt guilty that she hadn't thought about her mother all day. And now, looking at the sky, she feared that she would forget her mother's voice, her face. Feeling panic rise within her, she reached for her father's hand. He took her fingers in his, squeezed her flesh, and she knew that his thoughts followed in the footsteps of hers.

"Your mum was beautiful," he responded, unsure what to say in front of Georgia and Holly. "And you're right. She was just like this sky. She wasn't a single star, but a heap of them."

Mattie blinked, her tears stinging. "All of them."

"You know what else is beautiful, luv?"

"What?"

"The four of us, lying here next to the South China Sea, looking at this lovely sky. We're four friends. Four mates, really. And I reckon that's a beautiful thing too."

Mattie nodded, squeezing his fingers. "We're . . . kind of like a family."

He stiffened, turning toward her. "A family of friends."

Georgia, who lay on the other side of Mattie, wished that she could see Ian's face, that he would build a campfire with Holly's help, and that the girls could throw sticks into it while she rested her head on his chest. Yet she would never encourage him to touch her, no matter that the more time she spent with him, the more she wanted to feel him. "I don't like the circumstances that brought us together," she said, her heartbeat quickening. "But I'm glad we're together. There's no place I'd rather be right now, no people I'd rather be with."

"Me too," Holly said, rising to her knees and moving closer to Mattie.

As Holly reached out for Mattie, Georgia asked herself if she had said too much. Can he sense what I want? Is it awful for me to think about him when Mattie's so close to tears?

When Ian made no reply, she wondered where his thoughts were wandering. She mused over what he'd said, and the silence that now lingered. Unable to bear such silence, she sat up. "Do you want a fire, Mattie?" she asked. "Like those people down there? Let's build a fire and tell stories."

Mattie stood up. Ian moved more slowly, but his eyes found Georgia's in the darkness, and she thought his gaze might have lingered. Why it lingered, she wasn't certain, but she didn't turn from him, and for a moment she felt exposed, as if she were lying naked in a bathtub before him. Something seemed to briefly connect them, to draw them together. Then he turned toward the girls and that something was gone.

THE FOLLOWING DAY, THE FOUR TRAVELERS SAT in the rear of the van, watching the Vietnamese mountains pass. As they neared Dalat, the mountains grew—full of towering evergreens, rivers, waterfalls, and wildlife. The air smelled like pine and sap. The road was empty, the forest unblemished. Georgia, who had explored the mountains outside Seattle, felt as if she was in the Pacific Northwest. She had never seen this side of Vietnam and was glad that they'd decided to travel to Dalat, which had long been a summer destination for wealthy Vietnamese.

They'd stopped twice on the way, and Khan had left crutches with someone he trusted on each occasion. Everyone was saddened by the thought of children needing the crutches. They had met two such children—young boys injured by the same bomb. In a way, the boys were lucky. The bomb had taken only a foot from each. With crutches they would be mobile. They could live their lives. As Khan had explained to them how to use the crutches, Mattie had led Holly into a nearby store, where they pooled their money and bought two fishing poles. The boys could hardly have acted more surprised to receive the gifts.

Now, as Khan headed up the mountains, only three sets of crutches remained in the back of his van. Mattie found it hard to believe that bombs existed in the beautiful forest around them. She had asked Khan where the bombs were, and from time to time he squinted and pointed out craters in the landscape. Some of these were old and overrun with foliage. On her own, Mattie would never have noticed the dimples in the earth, most of which were filled with water and looked like small round ponds. But other craters were obviously of a more recent origin. Khan told her that long ago the area around Dalat had been cleared of such ordnance, but that in the wilderness, countless bombs remained.

Mattie knew that the Vietnamese believed in ghosts, and as she looked into the forest, she wondered if the dead might still inhabit the woods. She wasn't sure what to think. The mountains were so beautiful and lush. She had never seen so much green, and surely the fields and valleys, streams and waterfalls were places where life flourished. Yet these same places had seen a war, and though Mattie didn't know much about war, she was certain that dying so suddenly and painfully might trap someone between worlds. Her mother, she knew, had time to plan for her death, to understand it. And her mother hadn't been afraid. She had told Mattie as much many times, and Mattie had believed her. But dying in a forest with explosions and pain and sadness must have been even harder than what her mother had faced.

Taking out her sketch pad, Mattie outlined mountains and pine trees in black pencil and then filled them in with green. She didn't draw any ghosts but added footprints to the bottom of her image, as if someone had walked through the woods. Though she was unsure why she had included the footprints, it felt right to put them in her drawing. The forest hadn't always been so empty. And to make it appear empty felt wrong—both in terms of the people who had died within it and because she believed that her mother wasn't gone.

Dalat materialized through her window as they reached a summit. The van dipped and the city vanished, reappearing a few minutes later. A river ran beside the road, churning over boulders, falling straight down a cliff face in a massive exhibition of strength and sound. Mattie had never seen such a waterfall, not even in the Himalayas. The air felt cooler in its presence, and she breathed deeply, drawing moisture into her lungs.

In its lush mountain setting, Dalat looked far different from the other Vietnamese cities Mattie had visited. Though the architecture was similar—with a variety of white three-story buildings comprising the city center—the nearby forest seemed to dominate the concrete structures. Ponds, streams, and pines were also an integral part of Dalat, creating multiple havens of green.

They drove to a hotel where Ian had made arrangements. The four travelers removed their luggage from the van, thanked Khan, and checked in. Since it was midafternoon and everyone was tired from the long drive, they retired to their two rooms, located across the hall from each other. While Ian and Mattie worked on fractions, Holly practiced her Mandarin and Georgia took a bath. Outside their hotel, scooters beeped, red flags flapped, and uniformed children walked home from school.

Ian showered, shaved, and put on a white dress shirt and his new olive green cashmere suit. He slipped the three sea-glass necklaces into his pocket. While Mattie changed, he looked out the window, thinking of Kate, of how he regretted having taken her for granted. He hoped that wherever she was, she forgave him.

Soon Mattie stepped from the bathroom, wearing her new dress, and looking to Ian like a reincarnation of everything beautiful in the world. He told her as much and they embraced. Taking a comb, he carefully drew it through her hair, moving as he'd seen Kate move, remembering his loved ones together. Only when Mattie's hair was perfect did he set down the comb. She looked lovely and precious and somehow too old. He kissed her brow, holding her with both of his hands, as if she would otherwise take flight.

They met Georgia and Holly in the lobby. Though no one would ever be as beautiful to Ian as his little girl, Georgia was striking in a violet sleeveless dress, and Holly's smile seemed to brighten the room. Ian held out his hands, which Mattie and Holly took. He led them outside, to a waiting taxi. After helping Georgia into her seat, he moved to the front and told the driver where to take them.

As Georgia and the girls talked about their dresses, Ian watched the city pass. He twisted around, wanting to see their faces behind him. Georgia asked Mattie if she needed any makeup, and seeing that Holly wore lip gloss, Mattie said yes. Rather than handing Mattie the gloss, Georgia dipped an applicator into the opaque liquid and made smooth and steady strokes on Mattie's lips.

The driver turned down a freshly paved road. The city seemed distant, and the road was lined on both sides by pine trees. After a few minutes, they came to a wooden two-story restaurant on a hill overlooking a lake. The shoreline was surrounded by flowering trees and grass. In the distance, green mountains reached for the sky, which had turned a deep blue as dusk approached. The lake was the shape of a turtle. Drifting on its surface were paddleboats designed to resemble swans, most of them filled with parents and children, though several contained couples who sought distant stretches of water.

Ian led Mattie, Holly, and Georgia into the restaurant. A hostess greeted them, offering a table on the upstairs veranda. Most of the outdoor tables were already occupied by well-dressed Vietnamese, who faced the lake and sipped various drinks. Ian helped Georgia, then

Holly and Mattie into their chairs. He sat opposite Georgia and was the only one who didn't have a view of the lake.

After a waitress came and took their drink orders, Ian reached into his pocket. "I've got something for each of you. Something I found on the beach yesterday. A keepsake of our walkabout together." He handed Mattie, Holly, and Georgia each a necklace, being careful to give the right item to the right person. Whoever had made the jewelry had wrapped the top and bottom of each piece of sea glass with a strand of silver wire. As Ian had suggested, a thin strap of black leather allowed the sea glass to hang around the wearer's neck.

Mattie was the first to put on her necklace, and she lifted the sea glass, inspecting it carefully. "I love it, Daddy," she said, stroking the glass. "You found it? Really?"

"Yeah, luv. When you ladies were frolicking in the water."

Georgia draped her present around her neck. "They're wonderful, Ian. Just wonderful. Thank you so much."

"It's my pleasure. A real honor."

Holly, who had never been given a piece of jewelry by anyone other than her mother, continued to hold her necklace. "You . . . you got this . . . for me?" she asked, her fingers still, her gaze on Ian.

"Of course. You're Mattie's mate. And mine too."

She focused on the sea glass, unaware that her eyes glistened. "But it's so . . . beautiful."

"As are you, Holly. As are you."

Georgia smiled, helping Holly put on the necklace. "It goes perfectly with your dress. With both your dresses."

Holly's fingers remained on the necklace. She felt its contours, using her feet to shift her chair closer to Ian's. "Thank you," she said, her voice softer and slower than usual. "It's perfect. You found a perfect necklace for me."

"Sea glass won't be around much longer," Ian replied. "Everything's plastic these days. And plastic thrown into the sea never turns into anything beautiful. Unlike what I found on that little beach."

Mattie turned toward her father. "But we didn't find anything for you."

"That's all right, Roo. You've already given me enough."

Their waitress returned with their drinks and a small mesh cage that resembled a lantern.

"What's this?" Mattie asked.

The woman gestured toward the lake. The sun was setting and the lights of fireflies pulsated above the water and nearby shore. "See the children?" she replied. "See them catch the fire bugs? You can catch them down there too, then bring them back up to your table."

Mattie saw that groups of children were chasing the fireflies and putting them into similar cages. She stood up. "Can we go, Daddy? Please?"

"Let's all go. It looks like a heap of fun."

Ian took off his suit jacket, hung it over his chair, and followed the girls and Georgia to the stairs. Holly turned around, smiling at him, still touching her necklace. He winked at her, carrying the mesh lantern, glad that the hotel manager had told him about the restaurant. It seemed perfect, and his spirits soared as he watched Mattie and Holly hurry toward the lake in their new dresses. The land had been carefully manicured—the grass cut thick and short, clumps of flowering bushes planted next to smooth boulders. Fireflies were everywhere, lighting for a second or two, then becoming almost invisible in the growing darkness. Children chased the insects, while parents helped collect them, putting the fireflies into glass jars or lanterns from the restaurant.

Mattie and Holly began to pursue a pair of fireflies that hovered near the base of a flowering tree. They laughed as the insects evaded them, disappearing and then reappearing in a flash of light a few feet away. Ian chuckled, thinking that neither Mattie nor Holly had chased many fireflies. Growing up in Manhattan and Hong Kong didn't provide an abundance of such opportunities.

Holly was the first to snare a firefly and she ran to Ian, giggling. He opened a miniature door on the bottom of the lantern and she shook her hand until the firefly flew into the cage. Mattie hurried over, repeating the process, trying to move quickly while Holly ran toward a group of fireflies that a Vietnamese toddler was chasing without success.

As the girls stalked more fireflies, Georgia shifted closer to Ian, lifting her camera. She took several pictures of Holly and Mattie, then turned to him. "Let me get one of you," she said. "In your fancy new outfit."

He grinned and reached for a firefly, jumping as it rose above his outstretched hand. "Look at her go," he said, stepping to his right, staying beneath the firefly. "What a little beaut."

Georgia captured his smile and lowered the camera. "I don't think she wants to be caught."

"Hats off to her." Holding out the lantern so that Mattie and Holly could stick more fireflies into it, Ian nodded at Georgia. "Might I snap one of you?" he asked as Mattie and Holly ran back toward the lake.

"Of me?"

"That's right."

She reached into her purse and removed a little mirror. "Just a second."

"You don't need that. Not one bit."

Remembering how Frank had told her that he no longer found her attractive, that pregnancy had made her face too full, she pushed her hair into place. "Sorry," she said. "A bad habit, I guess."

"An unnecessary habit. Might as well repaint a schooner every time it heads out to sea."

"A schooner?"

"An old sailing ship."

Her brow furrowed as she smiled. "So I'm an old ship headed out to sea?"

"Well . . . something like that. But let's strike the old part."

"Strike away."

Her smile lingered and he took her picture, framing it with the lake on one side and the distant forms of Mattie and Holly on the other. He handed the camera back to her. "It's a beaut of a night, isn't it?"

"It's more than that."

"You reckon?"

Georgia took another photo of the girls. "Look at them. Look at Mattie. She's dancing around like the fireflies she's chasing."

"There's a hop in her step—that's for sure. She's like the old Roo."

"A big hop. So the next time you're worried about her happiness, remember tonight. She hasn't forgotten how to be happy. And neither have you."

He caught a firefly, watched it glow within his cupped hands, and set it free. "I want to believe . . . those things."

"And you should."

"You do?"

She stepped closer to him, trying to stop the feelings that were flooding into her, but unable to deny them. "Can I . . . take your hand?" she asked, her pulse quickening, her voice unsteady. "Just as a friend? And nothing else? I just want to take your hand and walk beside the lake while our girls catch fireflies. That would make a beaut of a night . . . a perfect night."

He studied her face, saw how she was no longer the confident woman who looked so at home on the streets of Hong Kong. "Let's make it a perfect night," he said, reaching toward her. "There's no reason that mates can't hold hands and have a walkabout."

"Thank you, Ian."

"No worries. And I should thank you. Not the other way around."

Georgia smiled, his hand warm against hers. She felt as if she were suddenly decades younger. The sun had set and the lake was no longer afire with its reflection. The world was growing more subtle. Mattie and Holly ran back to add four or five fireflies to the lantern. "Look at you both," Georgia said. "In your beautiful dresses. I just said that you remind me of the fireflies you're chasing."

Holly laughed. "They're bugs, Mom. We're girls."

"True," Georgia replied, still conscious of the warmth of Ian's fingers. "But that doesn't make you so different."

Mattie nodded as Holly shook her head. The girls then turned and hurried back up the hill toward the restaurant, where a few fireflies were evading the outstretched hands of the local children. Ian and Georgia followed, neither talking, both content to watch their daughters. At first Ian felt guilty about holding Georgia's hand, as the act seemed intimate. But soon his emotions shifted. She needed him and he needed her. And friends ought to be able to hold hands. If friends couldn't hold hands, what good were they to each other?

Fireflies continued to escape or be caught. Though Mattie was more than a hundred feet from Ian, her laughter drifted to him, infusing him with her joy and spirit. She climbed onto a stump and jumped off it—twirling and soaring and undergoing what seemed to be an almost metamorphic change. Her colorful dress billowed outward and she appeared to take flight, and this instantaneous journey lifted Ian skyward, turning his fears into hopes, his sorrow into elation. Without thought or concern or reservation, he lifted Georgia's hand and brought it to his lips, kissing the back of her wrist, holding her flesh against his as Mattie caught a darting source of light.

The girls turned toward him, and he lowered Georgia's hand. She squeezed his fingers, leaning toward him, starting to speak, but closing her mouth, her lips forming a smile. Mattie's firefly was set within the cage, and in the strengthening darkness the foursome walked back into the restaurant. Ian tightened his grip on Georgia's hand, then released her fingers, carrying the lantern upstairs, setting it on their table. A dozen other tables held similar lanterns, and hundreds of fireflies appeared to beckon to one another on the veranda.

Their waitress took everyone's orders, and as Georgia and Ian smiled and spoke about the coming day, Holly and Mattie watched their fireflies, trying to count them. All the other patrons at the restaurant were Vietnamese, and the sounds of the old language seemed to echo into the night.

Before long their waitress returned with platters of steaming food. The companions shared their entrees as if they were locals, passing plates, mixing sauces that were sampled by all. Throughout the meal, their fireflies flickered. Only when dessert was served did Mattie and

Holly tip the lantern to its side, open the door, and watch the fireflies depart.

As Holly led them to a taxi, everyone agreed that the restaurant was one of their favorites. Georgia seemed to be in particularly high spirits, which, to Ian's surprise, comforted him. He hadn't expected to ever make another woman happy, and the knowledge that he could warmed him. He wasn't broken, as he had feared. Not completely lost.

Turning in the front seat, he realized that no sight could have pleased him more than that of Mattie sitting between Holly and Georgia, smiling as Georgia took her picture and asked what her favorite part of the day was. Of course, Mattie's answer was the fireflies they'd chased, and how she was going to draw Rupee a sketch of them. Mattie wasn't sure if there were fireflies in India and she wanted Rupee to see what she had seen. As Mattie spoke, Ian thought he detected a new self-assurance in her voice. He didn't know if this confidence stemmed from her time with Holly or Georgia or from something else altogether. But it seemed to arise when Georgia asked her questions, when her mother's best friend treated Mattie as she did Holly.

Ian was aware that during their time together, Georgia had tried to connect with Mattie, to make her smile. And he was grateful for those efforts, so grateful, perhaps, that he had kissed her wrist, that he had wanted to share his happiness with her. Not including his moments with Mattie, kissing Georgia had been the most pleasant thing he had done in months. He wanted to do it again.

He smiled at something Mattie said, watching her, then shifted his gaze to Georgia's face, which wasn't bordered by laugh lines or defined by the softness of an easy life. Her face wasn't proud or all-knowing or free of doubt. Rather, it exuded a combination of compassion and wisdom and hope. Suddenly Ian longed to kiss her lips in the same way that he'd kissed her wrist. He didn't want to feel alone, even though he had tried to bury such loneliness deep within him. He had done so for Mattie's sake, but now, as he looked at Georgia sitting next to his little girl, he knew that he'd failed. As much as he adored Mattie, he needed more than she could give. And he knew that she would be happier if his spirits were lifted.

The taxi turned into the heart of Dalat, passing through an older part of the city. This area was where he and Kate had stayed. Though some things had changed, most of the weathered buildings looked familiar. Ian was about to turn from this view, and back to that of Georgia, when he saw an ancient stone bridge that spanned a river. A memory flooded back to him—a vision of Kate and him standing at the side of the bridge, late at night. She had thought of a poem about the bridge, something about how it was tired from the passage of countless feet. He'd grabbed her before she finished, holding her tight, laughing as she tried to complete her poem. As she had protested, he had picked her up and carried her across the weary bridge, moving into their guesthouse, up the cement stairs, and into their room. They had made love on a thin mattress, surrounded by a mosquito net, a ceiling fan wobbling above them.

He stared at the bridge until it was gone. Then he looked forward. The city that had seemed so alive a minute earlier now appeared to be dead. Everything was dark and dreary and spotted with age. Rubbing his brow, Ian wished that he had let Kate finish the poem. He wanted to hear it now, to listen to her voice once more. He had always loved the sound of her voice, whether in person or over the phone or across a street. Her voice was like a river, full of currents and the ability to sweep him away. But now it was gone, departed even before the ancient bridge that she had so sympathized with.

You should be here now, he thought. I want you to see your bridge. It hasn't changed a bit. And you never told me the end of your poem. I ruined it. I took you for granted. And I'm so sorry, my luv. I should have let you finish. I should have sat and waited for the proper words to come to you. I was a bloody fool.

Ian sniffed, his stomach aching for the first time all day. Georgia asked him if everything was fine. He nodded but remained silent, fearing that his voice would betray him. He didn't want to hurt her, though he knew he would, because he wouldn't kiss her again, wouldn't walk her to her room and hug her as he said good night. He had wanted to do those things just a few minutes earlier, but the sight of the bridge had reminded him that Kate had been torn from him, had died in pain. And it didn't feel right, that he should be happy with her gone. It felt as wrong as anything he had ever experienced.

Finally, he turned to Georgia. "Would it be all right . . . if Mattie slept in your extra bed tonight? The girls would enjoy that, I reckon. And I'd fancy a walk, if that's all right with you."

"A walk?"

"A stroll around town. Just to stretch my legs."

As Mattie and Holly talked excitedly about the prospect of sleeping together, Ian saw Georgia looking at him, her eyes questioning, her lips silently mouthing, "Why?"

But rather than answering, he shook his head and turned away, staring at his feet, afraid of what else he might see in the old part of the city.

MATTIE AWOKE THE NEXT MORNING NEXT TO Holly. She was used to sleeping with her father and felt disoriented without him. Though she'd enjoyed whispering with Holly deep into the night, she was lonely after realizing that her father was in the room across the hall, all by himself. Thinking about him, and her mother's request for an art exhibition, Mattie dressed and walked to the corner of the room, where Georgia sat in a robe, staring out the window.

"Good morning," Georgia whispered, glancing up, reaching for Mattie's hand.

"Good morning."

"Did you sleep well? I heard you girls whispering late. Maybe too late."

"Holly was being silly."

"She usually is."

"Thank you for letting me stay in your room."

"You're welcome," Georgia replied, giving Mattie's hand a squeeze.

Mattie sat down in a nearby chair, careful to be quiet. "Can I ask you something?"

"Sure."

"Why did my dad go for a walk last night? Why did he leave me?"

Georgia started to speak but paused, collecting herself, controlling her hurt. "I don't know, Mattie."

"But why do you think?"

Shaking her head, Georgia looked out the window again. The city already teemed with pedestrians and scooters, moving like a kaleidoscope turned round and round. "You have your drawings," she finally replied. "And your drawings give you . . . time to escape. They do that, don't they?"

"Usually."

"Well, your dad needs some escapes too. And he can't draw. So he . . . took a long walk. And however he was feeling, that walk made him feel better. Just like your drawings make you feel better."

Mattie nodded. "I guess . . . if I couldn't draw, I'd want to walk too. I'd walk so far. My shoes would wear out."

Georgia moved closer to Mattie. "You have to remember that you have a lot of gifts. Your drawing is a gift. Your father is a gift."

"My mommy . . . told me that once."

"She was right."

"She was a gift too."

Georgia squeezed Mattie's fingers. "For both of us."

"Can I ask you something else? It's about her."

"What?"

Mattie pulled one of her braids to her mouth, biting it. "In her last letter to me, she asked if I'd do something for Daddy and her."

"Do what?"

"She wanted me to create an exhibit, an exhibit of my drawings. Things I've seen on our trip. Things to show my dad . . . and to show her."

"And . . . and you want to draw them here? In our room?"

Mattie continued to bite her braid, which had come loose during the night. "She can't see them here. They need to be outside."

Georgia forced her thoughts of Ian away, leaning forward so that she could rework Mattie's braid. "Outside? But where?"

"By that waterfall with the big boulders around it," Mattie replied, hoping that Georgia would say yes, worried that she wouldn't. "I want to go there and use my chalk on the boulders. I want my first exhibit to be near that waterfall, where Mommy can see it."

"And you want Holly and me to go with you?"

Mattie nodded, enjoying the feel of Georgia's hands on her hair. "Please. Just for a while. Then my dad will come . . . and you can do whatever you want."

Georgia rewound three strands of hair, creating a tight braid. "Of course we'll go with you. We'd love to."

"You would?"

"You know, Mattie, your mom was my best friend. We laughed like you and Holly laugh. And I . . . I want her to see your drawings. And I want to see them too. I'd love to see them. So let's go. Let's wake up Holly and go. Right now, before it starts to rain or something."

Mattie moved closer to Georgia, smelling her perfume. "Do you miss my mom?"

"I'll always miss her. Best friends shouldn't have to say good-bye to each other, just like daughters and mothers shouldn't."

"I don't want to say any more good-byes."

"Neither do I," Georgia said, stroking the back of Mattie's head. "You've got beautiful hair. Hair that reminds me of Holly's, when hers was long, before she met all the Hong Kong girls and wanted it short like theirs." She kissed Mattie on the forehead. "Now let's go wake her up. And then we'll tell your dad where we're going, and that he should take a taxi to the waterfall in—what? Two hours?"

"Maybe three."

"You go tell him. I'll wake up Holly, and we'll hurry and get dressed."

"Thank you."

Georgia squeezed her shoulder. "I'm excited about your first exhibit, Mattie. Thank you for inviting me, for making me a part of your big day."

Mattie smiled, leaving the room, knocking on her father's door. He must have awoken some time ago, because he opened the door right away and was already dressed. He dropped to his knees, hugging her tightly. His eyes were bloodshot, but he kissed her on the cheek and smiled. "Morning, luv," he said, kissing her again. "Did you sleep all right with Holly?"

"We talked late."

"You did? Well, that's what mates are supposed to do."

"She likes to talk."

He ran his fingers down her cheek. "Were you okay, sleeping in their room? I thought you might fancy it."

"Daddy?"

"What, luv?"

"Georgia, Holly, and I are going out for a while. I'm surprising you with something."

"You are? And I can't go with you?"

"It wouldn't be a surprise, silly, if you went with me."

He poked the end of her nose. "What am I supposed to do, Roo? Just wait here? Paint my nails pink like you did?"

"Wait three hours. Then take a taxi to the big waterfall, just outside town."

He was about to ask her another question when Georgia and Holly appeared at the door. Georgia said good morning to him, her smile weak and forced. As they spoke, Mattie hurried into her room, picked up her backpack, and gave him another hug. He kissed her, finding it hard to let her go. "Be careful, luv," he said, his eyes on hers. "Stay with Georgia and Holly. I'll see you all soon."

Mattie said good-bye and followed Georgia and Holly down the hallway. As they got into the elevator, Georgia explained to Holly where they were going and why they were going there. After swinging by the hotel's restaurant so that she could take a few croissants and bottles of water, Georgia led the girls outside and hailed a taxi. She asked the driver to take them to the waterfall, and the city drifted past. She saw the old bridge and thought it was beautiful. The forest came next, the pines more fragrant in the morning, before breezes carried away their scents.

The taxi left them a few hundred paces from their destination. As they followed a trail, the waterfall soon loomed ahead, much larger than Mattie remembered, emerging from a ledge above, trees and bushes on either side. The waterfall was at least fifty feet across and another fifty feet high. Below it, moss-covered boulders the size of trucks were pounded by the water.

Mattie thanked Holly and Georgia and began to walk toward the rocks. She thought about her mother's request, her mind serious, her steps steady. She wanted to create something beautiful, something that could be seen from the ground as well as the sky. The previous night, after Holly had finally fallen asleep, Mattie had mused over what she would draw. And visions had come to her, wondrous ideas that flowed into her in the same manner that they did every great artist. She saw splendor, knew that she could re-create it, and now, as she neared the boulders, her feet moved faster. Dropping her backpack, she reached inside, removing a case of colored sidewalk chalk. After wiping off a dry boulder until it was free of twigs and debris, she leaned close to it, tracing its contours, feeling its texture.

The first image that Mattie created was simple—a cherry tree, full of blossoms, leaning over a river. As she worked, she saw that Holly and Georgia had moved to nearby boulders and were wiping them clean. Mattie smiled but said nothing, her hand in constant motion, chalk coloring the boulders and her fingers. In her mind's eye, she saw the tree in Kyoto, near the river, and she brought that tree back to life. It dominated the rock, her pink petals full and falling, her river catching their reflections.

Mattie moved to the next boulder, taking out a thick, brand-new piece of white chalk. She closed her eyes, imagining the Taj Mahal—the dome sparking in the sun, the sky blue and ancient. Her hand began to move again, almost of its own accord, and the Taj was rebuilt, section by section, dream by dream. She smiled as she worked, believing that her mother was watching her, guiding her. That was why her hand moved so freely, like the dove that they'd let go.

The mountains of Nepal came next, their peaks topped with snow, their bases dominated by fields of green and drifts of flowers. Mattie then sketched the longboat in Thailand, the girl they had helped perched in its bow. Rupee was her fifth creation. She drew him in his new clothes, sitting on a tree branch and smiling at her. She couldn't be too detailed with the chalk, but she captured his smile, the joy that shone from his face.

She stepped onto a massive boulder that Georgia and Holly had just cleaned. As Mattie settled in front of the boulder, Georgia knelt down and positioned a white wildflower above Mattie's ear, then kissed the top of her head before moving back.

Mattie's sticks of chalk were shrinking to stubs, so she decided to merely outline the city of Hong Kong, as seen from the mountains above. The harbor, the skyscrapers, the majesty of the city were reincarnated on the rock. Finally satisfied, Mattie moved to another boulder, on which she drew a lake. She then added dots of yellow—fireflies created from her memory, from a night that would always remain with her. Four figures came to life near the lake. Two leapt for fireflies and two held hands.

Mattie was still working when Ian crept up behind her. He studied the boulders, saw how her memories had blossomed—good memories, recollections of beauty and joy. Though he had always known that Mattie was talented, as he stood there, he realized that her skills went beyond what he had imagined. She had a gift far exceeding anything he might grasp. Though her Taj Mahal might not have been perfectly shaped, she had captured its soul. Though Rupee's features weren't quite right, his smile was angelic.

Ian knelt behind Mattie, kissing the back of her head, drawing her against him. She turned, and he nodded, again and again. Her chalk-covered hands went around him. He squeezed her, for the first time since Kate's death believing that she could actually see them. Kate had asked Mattie to create something beautiful, and she had. And there was no way that her mother wouldn't be watching her right now.

Thirty feet away, Georgia and Holly stood hand in hand. Holly, who had been so hurt by her father's neglect, by his preference for a museum over her, had never expected to like a painting or a sculpture or a poem. But she was entranced by what Mattie had done. And Georgia kept staring at the rock with the fireflies, the rock that showed the two adult figures holding hands.

Mattie kissed her father's cheek. She picked up a piece of red chalk and walked to another boulder. She climbed to the top and drew an immense red heart. Under the heart, in white lettering, she wrote, "We love you, Mommy. And I love you, Daddy."

Ian stepped to the boulder, helping her down, holding her against him. He kissed her forehead, touching her tears, which were joined by his own. But then she smiled. And in her smile existed such goodness and hope and pride that he lifted her higher, so that she could see all of her work. He turned her around, still holding her up.

He looked up at the sky, telling Kate that he loved her, that Mattie loved her. Then his feet began to carry them toward Georgia and Holly, toward where he knew Mattie wanted to go. Though his own thoughts were still unformed, his steps were steady, and the two groups came together as one.

TWO DAYS LATER, AFTER TRAVELING BACK DOWN the coast with Khan in his battered van, the companions walked through the zoo in Ho Chi Minh City. Though not large, it had a variety of animals and exhibits. Like most zoos in the West, it featured boulevards to walk on, immense shade trees, ponds, and colorful gardens. Since it was a Sunday, the site was packed with Vietnamese—parents pulling children in wagons, couples seeking secluded benches.

The smiles shared by Mattie, Holly, Georgia, and Ian had departed. Holly and Georgia were leaving in a few hours and had brought their bags to the zoo, which was on the way to the airport. Mattie moved like the caged tigers and lions—listless and without purpose. She held Holly's hand, and they headed toward the elephants, which Holly remembered from an earlier trip. Though Holly was sad about her looming departure, she held herself straighter than Mattie. She didn't walk as if she was inside a cage. She had spent her whole life learning to move this way, and even though sadness gripped her, she continued onward. As she often did when she was unhappy, she recalled watching the play *Annie* with her mother when she was younger. Annie had believed in a better tomorrow, and so did Holly.

Holly told Mattie about a baby elephant that had been born in the zoo a year earlier. She wanted to see the elephant, wanted Mattie to smile at the sight of it. But Holly wasn't sure if her friend would smile at the zoo. Mattie seemed beaten, and Holly wondered if she had ever seen *Annie*. Probably not, which made Holly sad.

"Did you ride an elephant in Thailand?" Holly asked. "I did. And I even got to feed a baby."

Mattie glanced up from the pavement. "No, we didn't see any elephants."

"Well, maybe next time you will. And if you do, you should ride one. Ride one and give him little bananas afterward. Juicy little bananas that will make his trunk twist and curl."

Thinking that she'd be back in Manhattan in about ten days, where she could never ride an elephant, Mattie nodded. "Maybe someday . . . we can meet in Thailand."

"We will, Mattie. We will."

"I hope so."

About twenty feet behind them, Ian pulled Georgia's suitcase and watched Mattie and Holly talk. He noticed that Mattie seemed to be much more affected than Holly by thoughts of the future. He wanted to lift his little girl, to put her on his shoulders and tell her that she'd see Holly again. But he had the suitcase, and he was also tired. The best week they'd had since Kate's death was about to end.

Though she kept her emotions hidden, Georgia was also disheartened. She saw how Holly and Mattie were holding hands, and she longed to do the same with Ian, to feel him once again. But they hadn't touched since that night by the lake, and she didn't expect to ever hold his hand again. He was still in love with Kate, still one with her. And she wasn't going to try to disrupt that connection.

Yet, needing to hear his voice, Georgia turned to him. "What will you do . . . in Egypt?"

Ian knew that she wanted him to touch her, but he thought again about the bridge, about how Kate had died with tears in her eyes. "We've hardly talked about it," he replied, moving closer to Georgia. "I don't know much about the place. I reckon we'll start in Cairo, have a gander at the pyramids, and maybe buzz off for the Nile."

"And it's your last country? Then you'll go home?"

"Our walkabout will be over."

"Well, I think you made the perfect choice. Mattie will love Egypt."

Ian glanced at his daughter, unaware of the monkeys to his left. "She seems awfully down, doesn't she?"

Georgia saw the concern on his face but couldn't tend to it as she wanted to. "She's still finding her way. But she won't always be."

"She won't?"

"No. Not at all. Just think about what she's done on this trip. How brave she's been. And she talks about Rupee constantly. She wants to help him. And that's not what someone does when she can only think about herself, when sadness is in the way of everything else."

Ian nodded, wondering again why his e-mails to the orphanage's director were not being returned. The lack of a response unsettled him. "I'm proud of her . . . for that."

"And you should be. And that's a reflection not just on her, but on you."

"Me?"

"Yes, you," Georgia replied, pushing her bangs back so that she could see him better. "Like I said, she's finding her way. But you're showing her the way too. I know about that. I know how it works. And you're doing a wonderful job."

"You're a lovely friend," he said, taking her hand, surprising himself once again. Even though he often thought about the bridge, he wasn't ready to say good-bye to Georgia. "A lovely mate. I'm sorry that we'll soon be so far apart."

"Me too," she replied, thinking about his lips against her skin, wanting to walk all day, hand in hand, in the footsteps of their children.

"I reckon the world's too big for us, isn't it?"

"What do you mean?"

"I mean, I'll be in Manhattan; you'll be in Hong Kong. And that's a lot of space . . . even for mates."

"Space is only as big as you make it."

He glanced at the sky, his feet feeling heavy. "That's true. But . . . but to be honest, Kate's still a part of my world. Of my space. And no matter how I'm feeling . . . right now, I'm not ready to leave her. I can't . . . leave her."

Georgia shook her head. "No one's asking you to leave anyone. Don't put words in my mouth."

"I didn't mean it that way."

"I would never ask that. I wouldn't even think it."

He stopped walking, turning to face her. "I know. And I'm sorry."

She squeezed his hand. "Don't forget that I loved Kate too. I wouldn't ever want you to leave her."

"Sorry. I said something stupid. It came out all wrong."

Georgia saw how Ian had slumped, how his face seemed to have aged. Even though he had just hurt her, she didn't want to do the same to him. "You know, Kate used to tell me all about you, about not wanting to ever leave you. She adored you so much. Sometimes I'd kind of laugh to myself about how head over heels she'd fallen for you. It almost seemed . . . childish. Or maybe naive. But now I know. I know why she felt that way."

"Why?"

A group of children passed, holding balloons, rushing toward a stray peacock. Georgia watched the children, then turned back to him. "I'm not going to say much, Ian. Not now. But I'll say this. You make me feel young. And that makes me happy."

He looked at her eyes, aware of how frail they seemed—faint green orbs, sheltered by thin lashes, surrounded by so many harsh elements. He wondered what would happen if he had another month to spend with her. Would memories of the bridge fade? Would he want her lips on his?

"I . . . I don't fancy going home," he said, aware that the girls had finally reached the elephants and stopped. "But I have to."

"I know," she replied, squeezing his hand once more and then releasing it, seeing his face soften, seeing his hurt.

"I'll miss you," he whispered.

"And I'll miss you."

Ian watched her step to the fence and ask Holly and Mattie what they thought of the elephants. She's so bloody strong, he thought. So strong and wonderful.

At the fence, Mattie and Holly gazed at an adult elephant rubbing its head against a tree trunk. The baby elephant was nowhere to be found, which disappointed Holly since she wanted Mattie to see it. Holly saw her mother point to her watch and knew that they didn't have much time left. Soon they would be back on a plane, back in Hong Kong. And everything would be like before.

"Do you think you can visit again?" Holly asked, her fingers on her sea-glass necklace. "I really hope you and your dad can come back."

Mattie shrugged, wanting to free the elephant just as she had freed the bird. "I wish we could live in Hong Kong. Then you and I could be best friends. We wouldn't have to say good-bye."

"Maybe you can. Maybe he can get a job there. And you could go to school with me."

"No."

"Well, maybe we . . . we can go to the same college. You could study art. And I . . . could study banking, like my mom. Then we could still be best friends."

"That's too far away," Mattie replied, feeling trapped like the elephant and longing to run.

"We can e-mail each other. I'll teach you one word in Mandarin every day. And you can send me pictures of your drawings."

Mattie looked at the elephant, then at the pathway leading away. Her legs trembled. Her breaths were shallow and frequent.

"You'll have fun in Egypt," Holly added. "So much fun."

Holly said something else, as did her mother, but Mattie didn't hear them. Instead she hugged her friend, holding her tight. She started to cry, even though she tried to hold back her tears, wanting to be strong like Holly and Georgia. But she couldn't stop, and her tears continued to fall. She heard Georgia's voice, saw her father's arms encircle her, and yet she still felt alone. Watching the elephant, wishing she could climb onto its back and that together they could charge away into a jungle, she tried to set herself free.

But she failed. And the elephant turned away, moving toward the other side of its enclosure, where the dirt was trampled by the passage of countless footsteps, where human voices were more distant, and where the wind rustled the leaves of nearby trees.

EGYPT

The Choice

"Friendship doubles joy and halves grief."

—Egyptian saying

From twenty stories up, on the balcony of a modern hotel, the Nile still looked ancient. The immense brown river dominated Cairo, dividing the city in half. Barges, passenger vessels, and traditional sailing boats known as feluccas drifted over the water, passing in front of a skyline so colorless it was as if the nearby desert had long ago covered Cairo's buildings in dust and sand.

Though the streets below the hotel were inundated with throngs of people and battered and beeping cars, from up here the city seemed still, perhaps paying its respects to the pyramids, which stood only a few miles away. Where modern-day Cairo ended, the desert began, and the pyramids rose, overlooking the city, seemingly impervious to the elements of time that besieged steel, glass, and cement.

Mattie and Ian sat on a pair of faded wooden chairs, watching the sun set over the Nile. Ian lifted a bottle and poured a half inch of wine into a glass that Mattie held. "Most people," he said, "would call me a scoundrel for doing this. But you deserve a sip or two."

She smiled, remembering how he had often filled her mother's glass. "Does it taste like juice?"

"I reckon not, Roo. It's a heap more bitter." He raised his glass to hers. "Cheers, luv. To you. And to Egypt."

Her lips touched the wine and she took a sip, surprised by the strength of the drink. She started to grimace but stopped herself, knowing that her mother had loved wine. "It's . . . good," she said, setting her glass on a table.

He grinned. "You're not much of a liar, luv."

"No. I like it."

"You do?"

"It's kind of . . . tangy."

"Tangy?"

"It makes my tongue tingle."

A jet entered Ian's field of vision, directing his gaze to the south, where the Nile began. He stroked the soft silk of a violet-colored tie that Holly had snuck into his backpack. He wasn't sure when Holly and Georgia had bought it or the compact binoculars that hung from Mattie's neck. Holly had written them each a note and hidden her gifts within the folds of their clothes. They hadn't found the tie and binoculars until landing in Egypt. "I'm glad, Roo, that you're feeling a bit better about Holly," he said, studying the tie, smiling at the thought of Holly picking it out for him, of her sneaking it into his backpack.

Mattie wasn't feeling better at all, but she pretended to be. "Well, you promised we'd come back in a year."

"We will."

"Pinkie swear?" she asked, sticking out her finger.

He wrapped his pinkie around hers and squeezed tight. "Pinkie swear."

"Thanks, Daddy."

Watching her face, he realized that it was tan, like the city and river below. "Your skin is getting dark. Too dark. Tomorrow I'm going to cover you in sunscreen. And you need to wear your sunnies."

She sipped her wine. "Did you ever have to say good-bye to your friends?"

"Sure, luv."

"When?"

"When I was eighteen, I left the bush, left my family and my mates. I moved to Sydney and went to a uni there. Then, after graduating, I buzzed off for Japan."

"Wasn't that hard?"

"It was hard on my mum and dad. They're still as cross as a frog in a sock about it."

"A frog in a sock?"

"That's right, luv. They aren't too pleased." He watched birds ride on an updraft, soaring above a nearby building. "Change like that, like saying good-bye to Holly, can be a real kick in the teeth."

"It is."

"I agree, Roo. But do you know what?"

"What?"

"Those changes, the ones I made, led me to your mum. They led me to you. If I had never left the bush, you wouldn't exist. And I wouldn't have created the loveliest thing to come out of my life."

"But you might have had another girl."

"Maybe. Maybe not. But I reckon that doesn't matter. Because there's only one you, and I don't fancy anyone else."

"And I don't fancy another daddy."

"You won't have one, luv. You're stuck with me, I'm afraid. Like a dingo with his looks."

On the Nile, a mighty rust-stained barge sounded its horn, shooing feluccas away. She lifted her binoculars and watched the barge force its way up the massive river. "Daddy?"

"What?"

"I'm sorry I've complained on our trip. I'm trying not to. Even though I don't always like the food or all the mosquitoes or saying good-bye to my friends."

"You don't need to—"

"Thank you for taking me."

He put his hand on her knee, stroking an old scar, remembering how she had fallen off her bike. "You're welcome, luv. And thank you. Thank you for being a perfect traveling companion."

"Can we go down and check your e-mail? Maybe there's a message from Rupee or Holly. Or maybe Leslie sent us another picture from Nepal."

Ian finished his wine, and hers, then glanced at the river, wondering what Kate would think of it, wishing she had seen it. She had always loved water, whether it was salt or fresh, blue or brown.

After putting on his shoes and grabbing his wallet, Ian followed Mattie out the door. She walked down the hallway with purpose, eager to see if her friends had written. Ian knew that she wasn't as content with their situation as she pretended and figured that she was embarrassed by her breakdown at the zoo and was trying to act older.

The main floor of the hotel was populated by people from all over the world. Men in Western-style suits or long tunics sat in front of low tables and talked business. Women, some wearing a head scarf and some not, soothed babies and kept track of giggling children. An adjacent, ornately decorated room revealed groups of men surrounding giant water pipes, know as hookahs, which were made of silver or brass and had bowls at the top that contained smoldering tobacco. The men sucked on colorful hoses, clouds of smoke escaping from between their lips.

The business center contained several desktop computers, chairs, and a printer. Ian and Mattie sat at the farthest monitor from the door, and Ian got online and opened his e-mail. He, too, wondered if anyone had written. To his disappointment, there was no e-mail from the orphanage's director, which caused his stomach to clench. He didn't understand why the director wasn't responding and vowed to make a phone call the next morning, to call and call until he heard that Rupee was fine.

Balancing out his mood was an e-mail from Georgia. He opened her message and moved aside so that Mattie could also read it.

Dear Mattie,

This is Holly, and I am typing on my mom's computer at her office. We've been home two days now, and I miss you and Vietnam. I wore my new dress again last night, and the necklace that your dad had made for me. I showed his necklace to my friends at school and they loved it. I do too.

I wish we could go swimming again in the ocean. There are beaches here, but not like what we saw in Vietnam. And there are almost no stars in Hong Kong. The city lights make them go away.

I asked my mom if we could travel to New York someday to visit you. She said if my grades were high that we could probably go. Maybe at the end of the summer. I plan on working hard because I want to see you again.

My fingers are tired from all of this typing, so I am going to say good-bye. My mom attached some photos from our trip. They make me smile. Please send me a drawing from Egypt. I have never been there.

By the way, my mom says hello to your dad. She had a good time with him, I think.

Your friend,
Holly

Mattie reread the e-mail, then asked Ian to open the attached photos. First was an image of Mattie and Holly ankle deep in the ocean. Next came a shot of the four of them at the Temple Club in Ho Chi Minh City. The third photo was of Mattie and Holly chasing fireflies. And the fourth was of the girls in their new dresses.

Mattie leaned forward. Ian did likewise, seeing how Mattie smiled in the photos, how she looked more like a little girl than she did at the moment. He also appeared happy in the photo at the restaurant, seated beside Georgia. He saw Georgia's hand on the table, remembered holding it, remembered the warmth of her skin against his.

After replying to Holly, and sending the orphanage's director another message, Mattie and Ian went back to their room, put on their pajamas, and climbed into bed. He told her a story about a little girl who nursed a battered falcon back to health. Then he kissed her good night, smiled when she put her head on his chest, and tried to convince himself that everything was going to be all right.

ABOUT FIVE HUNDRED MILES SOUTH OF CAIRO, and only a few miles downstream from the massive dam at Aswan, Mattie and Ian sat on the top of a weathered hundred-passenger cruise ship. The roof held a few tables and chairs, as well as green synthetic grass similar to what would be found at a miniature golf course. The grass was faded from the unrelenting sun, as was the rest of the ship. Little more than a white rectangle with a pointed bow, the vessel was two stories above water, featuring private river-view rooms and a large dining and entertainment area. A belly dancer amused passengers below, while other tourists were gathered on the roof—taking pictures, sipping drinks, holding their hats in place as a warm wind buffeted the ship.

The Nile near Aswan appeared far different from the way it did in Cairo. The river here didn't look bigger, but the water seemed deeper and was the color of twilight. About a half mile wide, the Nile was flanked by a verdant landscape full of fields and palm trees. This area, watered by millennium-old irrigation systems, extended a stone's throw from the river. Where the irrigation systems stopped, the desert immediately began, lush fields turning to sand within a handful of paces. Barren hills, brown and crumbling, rose in the distance. Though sandstone homes, as well as farmers and fishermen, could be seen along the river, nothing appeared to exist in the hills. They were as dead as the Nile was alive.

Scattered over the water were feluccas, which looked to be as ancient as the five-thousand-year-old civilization that still flourished there. The feluccas were wooden, their single masts sprouting forty feet high and holding narrow canvas sails. Though the boats looked ungainly and were cluttered with ropes and supplies, they prowled the Nile gracefully, sailing up- or downstream with ease. The boats didn't appear all that different from the camels at the river's edge—both were brown creatures, burdened with gear, worn and frayed and yet a part of the desert landscape.

Though Mattie had enjoyed the pyramids, which were immense and magnificent, she preferred to be on the Nile, looking out over the desert. The pyramids were full of tourists, hustlers, and security guards holding automatic weapons. While she had marveled at the sights, she'd also felt rushed and harassed, and hadn't experienced any desire to pull out her sketch pad.

On the Nile, though, she felt as if she had truly stepped back in time, more so than at any other point on their trip. The Nile must be as old as the world itself, she was certain, watching camels drink from a distant bank. She thought of the Ganges River and remembered how the Hindus pushed the ashes of their loved ones into its waters, so that the journey toward rebirth could begin.

"Do the Egyptians put people's ashes in the Nile?" she asked, turning toward her father, glad that they would spend several days and nights on the ship, traveling north back toward Cairo and stopping at famous temples and tombs.

He tilted his traveling hat higher, so that he could see her better. "No, luv. I haven't heard that."

"Why not?"

"I don't know. But I reckon that the river is still sacred to them. They've worshipped it for thousands of years. The ancient Egyptians had a god that governed its waters."

Mattie leaned forward in her chair, thinking about her mother. "What else?"

"Well, I read somewhere that the pharaohs believed life began on the east side of the Nile, and ended on the west side. That's why all the tombs are on the west side."

"Why would they think that?"

"Because of the sun. It's born in the east, and it sets in the west."

Mattie lifted her binoculars and scanned the horizon for tombs, wondering if her mother might also be in the west. "Maybe the ancient Egyptians were right."

"Maybe, Roo."

Mattie continued to search the horizon. "Why did Egyptians build wonderful tombs for the people they loved, and back home we don't build anything?"

"I—"

"Shah Jahan built the Taj Mahal for his wife. The Japanese have their shrines, right in their houses. But we didn't do anything for Mommy. All we did was bury her. And I don't think that was enough. I don't think that was enough at all."

Ian moved his chair closer to hers, putting his hand on her knee. "Easy on, Roo. We loved your mum as much as we could. As much as anyone has ever loved another person."

"Then why didn't we build anything for her?"

"Shah Jahan was the emperor, luv. He could spend whatever money he wanted to build the Taj Mahal."

"So? He still did it. And we have money too. I've got more than four hundred dollars in my bank account. And I know that you have a lot more than that."

Ian leaned forward, kissing her brow. "You fancy the thought of building her a shrine, right in our home, like the Japanese?"

"Yes. Just like them. With her picture, and a place for us to kneel and pray for her."

"Then that's what we'll do, luv, when we get home. We'll build her a lovely shrine."

She nodded, removing her great-grandmother's ring from her pocket, a dash of sunscreen still visible on her freckled cheek. "Thanks, Daddy."

"Thank you, luv. It was your idea. And it's a keeper."

Mattie rubbed the ring, wishing that her fingers weren't so small, wanting to wear what her mother had worn. A felucca passed in front of their ship, drifting toward the western shore, its captain a young man dressed in a white tunic. The sight of him and his boat, with the palm trees and desert behind him, prompted her to put the ring on her thumb and pull out her sketch pad. Within a minute she was drawing with a blue pencil, creating an outline of the Nile.

Ian watched her work, loving their moments together but also understanding that she needed more than just him. And, if he was honest with himself, he needed more than just her. She was his life, for certain, his reason to arise each morning. But one day she would grow up, fall in love, and leave him. He wanted her to be happy, of course, but the thought of that day saddened him. No matter how hard he tried to deny it, to remain loyal to Kate, he didn't want to be alone. And when Mattie grew up, he would be.

As Mattie began to sketch the felucca, Ian thought about Georgia. He missed her. She had a steady, calming influence on him. She'd wanted to hold his hand, to touch him. She wasn't intimidated by his enduring love for Kate. On the contrary, Georgia respected that love, and his efforts to honor it. She hadn't pursued him, even though a part of her obviously wanted to.

Reaching into his day pack, Ian withdrew an antacid and popped it into his mouth. The Nile was widening as they headed farther downstream. The ruins of sandstone structures dotted the distant shore, and Ian found himself wishing that not only could Kate see the sight, but that Georgia and Holly could also share in it. He looked to the west and shook his head. Why, luv, he thought, did you send us on this walkabout? To bond? To make new lives? To spend time with Georgia and Holly? Did you want me to fancy her, like you said in your poem? I know you wrote those words, that your strength, your will put them on paper. But is that how you really felt? I started to fall for her, but then I saw our bridge, where you tried to write your poem. I can't stop thinking about that bloody bridge. Was it a sign? If it wasn't, will you please give me one? Will you let me know what to do? I know Roo wants to see them again. And a part of me does too. But I'm not ready to step away from you, my luv. Even though I enjoyed holding Georgia's hand . . . kissing her hand . . . I can't let go of yours.

Mattie finished her sketch and held up the paper so Ian could see it. "That's a real masterpiece," he said, seeing how she had brought the river to life, and how the desert loomed above everything else. "I fancy the boat. It seems to be sailing."

"Thanks, Daddy."

"Good onya, luv. You've got heaps of talent, you know. And you didn't get that from me. Not that kind of skill. I was born with ten thumbs."

Mattie nodded, putting her pencils away. "Daddy?"

"What?"

"I've been thinking."

"Tell me what you've been thinking."

"I don't want to go back to New York in a week. That sounds terrible."

Ian lowered her picture. "Terrible? Why would it be terrible? Our home is there. Our mates. It's a beaut of a city."

"I don't want to see our home, or my friends. That's too many memories for me."

"I feel the same, luv. I understand. I do. But we don't have a choice. We've been gone too long and we have to go back. I need to find a new job. You have to go to school."

"But we could do that in Hong Kong. Like Holly and her mom."

He dropped to his knees, setting her sketch pad aside and holding her hands. "We have to go home, Roo. Hong Kong isn't home for us. It's a place to vacation, to see our mates. And we'll do it again next year."

"That's too far away."

"No, it's—"

"You just want to be sad," she replied, shaking her head, pulling the ring off her thumb and holding it tight. "That's why you want to go home. So you can be sad. And you can work all the time, like you did before."

"So I can be sad? What are you talking about, Mattie?"

She pushed his hands away and stood up. "You don't want me to be happy. You want me to be sad like you. That's why we're going back to New York."

"You don't know what you're talking about. Not a bloody word of it."

"You're wrong! I do know! It will be the same as before, only now I won't have Mommy. I'll be all alone!"

"Mattie."

"There will be no one!"

"What—"

"You'll have your meetings and your business trips and your stupid phone, and I'll be all alone!"

"No. That's not—"

"Let go of me!" she shouted, pushing his hands away, running from him toward the staircase leading below.

He started to call after her but saw that one of her tears had landed on the back of his hand. It glistened in the Egyptian sun, the sight of it wounding him, causing his aches to rise up as if they'd been doused with gasoline and set afire. In her tear he saw the failures and heartaches in his life, and worse, in hers.

Picking up her sketch pad, he hurried after her, heedless of the stares of other travelers, of the wondrous temple rising to his right.

THE FOLLOWING DAY, MATTIE AND IAN WALKED over a gangplank from their ship to a stone pier at the edge of the Nile. Their ship had docked at the ancient city of Luxor, which was famous because of Karnak—a colossal complex of temples, obelisks, sphinxes, and chapels, some of which were almost four thousand years old.

As Mattie and Ian walked hand in hand toward Karnak, she did her best to act excited. Though she had been angry the previous evening, she had later heard her father in the bathroom, in the middle of the night. He'd remained there, with the lights off, for more than two hours, and she hadn't slept until he finally returned to bed. Guilt had consumed her about getting mad at him, about running from his outstretched hands. She'd made him retreat to the bathroom, where he was always miserable.

Mattie had apologized the next morning, but he told her not to worry, which made her feel even worse. It would have been better if he'd gotten angry, cast his frustration on her in the same way that she'd attacked him. But he hadn't. Instead he hugged her and told her that it was all right for her to get upset, that in some ways it was good. He had kissed her forehead, held her tight, and she had felt about two inches tall.

Now, as they neared Karnak, Mattie led him forward, moving faster than the other tourists from their boat. The main gate soon materialized—an immense rectangle of sandstone with a hollow middle. As her father paid for two tickets, Mattie continued to hold his hand. Soon they were inside Karnak, and all thoughts of her guilt and sadness fled—replaced by awe and reverence.

Karnak rose from the desert floor like a mirage or, better yet, a miracle. The complex was so massive and ancient and wondrous that it looked prehistoric. The thick walls were covered in hieroglyphics that depicted life on the Nile millennia ago, and were still faintly highlighted by green, blue, brown, and yellow hues. Between the walls ran dozens of towering stone columns, each as thick as a redwood tree. The open-aired room was larger than anything Mattie had ever seen, even Grand Central Station. In the distance, rows of ram-headed sphinxes looked ready to spring to life. An obelisk the height of a ten-story building cast a long and pointed shadow.

Mattie wanted to sketch something from Karnak, but where could she possibly start? The place was too immense, with too many spectacular sights. She could spend a year sketching here and still not draw everything she wanted. Looking at a hieroglyphic, which showed a bird with outstretched wings, she wiped her brow and tried to understand the magnitude of what she was seeing.

As Mattie imagined someone carving the ancient bird into the column, an Egyptian man slowly approached. He carried a sun-bleached walking stick and was dressed in a dirty blue robe that fell from his shoulders to his ankles. A white turban shielded his face from the sun. The man's wrinkled skin was much darker than the nearby stone, though his eyebrows were white. "Hello, kind sir and miss," he said softly in English, bowing. "My name is Rashidi. May I ask yours?"

Ian started to speak, but thinking about how Georgia encouraged Holly to interact with the locals, he motioned for Mattie to answer him.

"I'm Mattie," she replied, dipping her head in return. "And this is my dad. His name is Ian."

Ian smiled. "G'day."

The Egyptian continued to stand in the sun, his face void of the sweat that dripped from Mattie's skin. "Did you know, Miss Mattie, that Karnak is the largest place of worship in the world? That it covers two hundred acres and that fifty European cathedrals would sit easily inside it?"

Mattie glanced around her, wondering what was beyond the towering walls. "I didn't know that. What . . . what else don't I know?"

"That column next to you, Miss Mattie, with the birds and crocodiles, took generations of carvers to finish. Men would work from when they were young until they died on only a section of stone."

"So they never saw it finished?"

"No," Rashidi replied, gesturing around him. "It took thousands of years to finish Karnak. Do you know, Miss Mattie, that once, eighty-one thousand slaves worked here? Think about that number." He paused, his smile revealing crooked and stained teeth. "They were slaves, and they were beaten. But people come here from around the world to see what they built. People don't see what the rich built, with their words. People see what the poorest of the poor built, with their hands."

"Oh," she said, thinking about Rupee, how he was little different from the slaves who built Karnak. Suddenly she felt foolish for crying on the boat, for running from her father. At least she was loved. She didn't have to swim in a filthy river and look for gold teeth. She had never been a slave and she never would be.

"Would you like, Miss Mattie, for me to be your guide?"

Mattie pulled her thoughts to the present, looking from the Egyptian to her father. "How . . . how much will that cost?" she asked, knowing that Holly would expect her to bargain.

"Whatever you like. I am as old as the sand, and money is of little use to an old man."

"Where can we go?"

Rashidi stood straighter. "Come. I will show you something. And you too, Mr. Ian."

Ian thanked Rashidi, happy to follow Mattie, glad that she possessed enough confidence to talk with a stranger wearing a turban.

As they walked, Rashidi leaned closer to Mattie. "Do you know what 'Karnak' means?"

"No."

"It means the 'Most Perfect of Places.'"

"Really?"

"Wait and see, Miss Mattie. Wait and see."

They rounded a corner and walked past statues of men and animals. "How many statues are here?" Mattie asked, taking her father's hand.

Rashidi turned around, squinting, his white eyebrows long and disheveled. "How many statues? you ask. I do not know, Miss Mattie. Maybe ten thousand? The pharaohs loved their statues. They made them of their favorite gods, of themselves." Rashidi twisted into a narrow roofless passageway full of hieroglyphics that showed armies at war. On the other side of the passageway was an obelisk that had toppled to its side. "I am sure, Miss Mattie, that you will like this."

Mattie looked at the obelisk, which was mostly undamaged, despite its great fall. "What does it mean?"

"More than three thousand years ago, Egypt was ruled by Queen Hatshepsut, who built this obelisk, and the other, which still stands. She ruled for more than twenty years and was one of our strongest pharaohs. She built many temples, planted forests of trees, and made Egypt rich from trade."

Ian watched Mattie nod. "I reckon, luv," he said, "that you should sketch her obelisk."

"Which one?"

"Which one do you think?"

"The standing one."

"Well, then we'll sit beneath it, in the shade, and you can work your magic."

Rashidi stepped closer. "You could draw this?"

"She's quite good," Ian replied. "Queen Hatshepsut would have found a heap of work for her."

The Egyptian smiled. "Queen Hatshepsut would have made a statue of her, to celebrate her gifts to the world."

Mattie looked over the obelisk, and saw something blue. "What's that?"

"You see the Sacred Lake," Rashidi replied, grunting as he moved forward, his walking stick stirring up dust. "Come, let me show you."

The lake, Mattie soon saw, was rectangular and lined with sandstone. At several places, stairs descended into the water, which was indigo and home to a flock of geese. Near a corner of the lake, a group of squat palm trees swayed in a gentle breeze.

"Tuthmosis the Third built this lake," Rashidi said, his eyebrows moving as much as his mouth and dark eyes. "Priests used its water for rituals and would dress as gods and travel across it on golden boats. Also, Miss Mattie, every morning the priests would set a goose free on the lake at sunrise. They did this to please the god Amun. As you can see, the geese are still here."

Mattie stepped closer to the water. "Do they ever leave?"

"No. They were here when I was a boy and will be here long after I am sand."

"How . . . deep is the water?"

"Only Tuthmosis and his slaves know that. But it is deep. Very deep. Some people believe that the dead rise from its waters, late at night, and journey from side to side in their golden boats."

Mattie took a step closer to her father. "Can I ask you something, Mr. Rashidi?"

"Ask whatever you wish, Miss Mattie. My ears wait for your voice."

"Do you want to be buried on the west side of the Nile?"

Rashidi scratched his chin, his fingers unsteady. "When I can no longer work, when I am tired, I will walk west, from the river. I will walk into the desert, far into the desert. And at night, I will light a small fire and look at the same stars that the pharaohs saw. And then, the next day, the heat will carry me away."

"But . . . but what about your children? Won't you want to say good-bye?"

"I do not have children, Miss Mattie. So I will say good-bye to Karnak, and then I will try to find my god. No one will need to remember me. No tears will be shed."

Mattie studied the old man in front of her. Though he was smiling, she felt sorry for him. "I'll remember you," she said, nodding, looking into his dark eyes. "I'll remember what you told me about the queen and the geese."

"You are most kind, Miss Mattie."

"I'll think about you . . . when you're in the desert."

Rashidi's smile broadened. He bent lower, his robe scraping the dusty ground. Reaching into his pocket, he removed a stone beetle and offered it to Mattie. "The scarab beetle is precious in Egypt," he said, almost kneeling before her. "The beetle comes from the earth, from a pile of dung. It is born, and it walks the desert. It comes from nothing, and it dies, but it always returns, like the sun."

When he gestured that she should hold the beetle, she did, surprised by its weight. "It's beautiful."

"Please keep it, Miss Mattie. Now you have something else to remember me by. And when I am in the desert, I will think of you holding it. And that thought will bring me much peace; may God protect and preserve you."

AFTER SPENDING THREE DAYS ON THE NILE, and seeing a breathtaking variety of riverside temples and monuments, Ian and Mattie finished their cruise and took a small plane to the resort city of Sharm el-Sheikh, located on the Red Sea. In many ways Sharm el-Sheikh resembled an oasis—materializing in the heart of the desert, surrounded by palm trees and perched on the edge of the vast Red Sea. The city was composed of international hotels, dive shops, casinos, stores, and markets. At the edge of the concrete—where the desert began—colorful Bedouin tents kept the relentless sun at bay. Camels and robed figures stood near the tents, hooves and feet moving back and forth on the hot sand. Several miles in the distance, barren mountains rose to touch the belly of the sky.

The Red Sea wasn't red, but a deep blue. It had been navigated for thousands of years, with Egyptians, Persians, Romans, and Chinese using the waterway for a trade route between Africa and Asia. Moses was said to have parted the Red Sea so that the Israelites could escape the Egyptian army. Napoleon had tried and failed to take control of the Red Sea. Though the waterway had lost some strategic importance in recent times, it was still a major shipping route.

Reading from a guidebook, Ian had explained the history of the Red Sea to Mattie. Now, as they sat on plastic beach chairs near the water's edge, Mattie found it hard to believe that men like Moses and

Napoleon had seen these same sights. The resort they were staying at seemed so modern—full of businesspeople who worked on laptops and tourists who went scuba diving or parasailing. The four-story hotel was white, with seaside rooms, a lush garden, a disco, and an immense pool.

The beach was wide and quiet, though filled with hundreds of people. Umbrellas rippled in the wind. Powerboats pulled water-skiers. Families from around the world enjoyed the sun—toddlers playing in the sand, teenagers throwing and kicking balls, parents reading and resting.

Savoring the scene, Mattie removed her sketch pad from her backpack. Soon her pencils drifted across a blank page, adding forms and colors, highlighting features that most people wouldn't see. She worked with care and patience, hating mistakes and taking her time.

Ian adjusted the umbrella that rose between them, tilting it over Mattie, thrusting its pole deeper into the sand. She wore a yellow bikini that he had purchased from a nearby store, and he still wasn't used to the sight of her in a two-piece suit. Her belly button was exposed, her hips too visible. He didn't like the thought of her growing up, and the bikini seemed to be a leap in that direction. But its purchase had made her smile.

Her blue pencil pausing, Mattie glanced around and noticed that he was watching her. "Daddy?"

"Yeah, luv?"

"When we were at Karnak, I was thinking about you."

"How so?"

"Well, I was thinking about Rashidi and Rupee, and how they didn't have anyone. How Rashidi was going to walk alone into the desert, and how Rupee was alone in the river."

Ian nodded, his body relaxed, his stomach free of pain, and his mind repeating the words of the orphanage's director, who had finally e-mailed him back, apologized for problems with their Internet connection, and said that Rupee was well. "And?"

"And I used to feel lonely, and I still do sometimes, but I know that I've never been alone, and I won't ever be."

"That's right, luv."

Mattie reached for his hand. "You . . . you know how to make my loneliness go away. And I'm sorry that I got mad at you on the boat. You're my daddy and I love you so much. Whatever Mommy said to you in those poems, I want to say the same things. I'll always think the same things."

Ian moved to his knees beside her. He kissed her forehead, drawing her tight against him. "Whatever I've done for you, luv, you've done for me over and over. You know that? If I've put a smile on your face, you've put one on mine. If I've taken your loneliness away, you've done the same for me. We're a team. The best kind of team. And I reckon that's how teammates work. They lift each other up."

"Thanks, Daddy. Thanks for lifting me up."

"Thank you, Roo."

He kissed her again, full of energy, of life. After reapplying sunscreen to her neck and shoulders, he leaned back in his chair, watching the waterline. Couples walked hand in hand. Naked babies sat in the shallows with their nearby parents. Children splashed one another and found smooth rocks that would be ultimately churned to sand. The weather was nearly perfect—not hot, but sunny, with a dry, gentle breeze that kept insects at bay.

As Ian watched the families, he was reminded of his day with Mattie, Holly, and Georgia at the pool. They had laughed so much. His sadness was at least temporarily forgotten. A simple game of Marco Polo had made him feel young again, had made him revel in Mattie's joy. And he had felt close to another woman for the first time since Kate's death. Georgia had captured him, even though he hadn't known it. He'd seen the promise of her, seen how his family was made better by the presence of hers.

Thinking about what Kate had written to him, that he needed to find new memories, he unzipped his day pack and searched for the film canister that he'd placed within it earlier that morning. Finding and opening it, he pulled out the little scroll and unrolled it, skipping immediately to the end of the poem that Kate had written.

Love like ours never dissipates, never wavers.
We were one and we will always be one—
Pages within the same book.
But life is long and you should not walk alone.

Please don't walk alone.
Find happiness again.
Find a version of us.

And within that version,
Celebrate what we were,
What we created,
The path that we took.

Only through happiness will you ever again smile at the memory of us.
And I want to watch your smiles from heaven.

I want to see you reborn,
Fashioned together with memories,
With joy,
And with hope.

Remember . . .
Love is a wilderness untamed,
A river uncrossed,
A promise unbroken.

I love you.

Ian closed his eyes, still holding the paper, repeating Kate's words, amazed by her foresight and strength. His eyes grew moist and he wiped them, believing that the road to ultimate happiness might start with Georgia and Holly. We shouldn't leave them, he thought. Not now, not when there seems to be such a lovely connection between us.

Ian took off his sunglasses and looked up into the cloudless sky. How did you know, my luv? he asked, thinking about how Kate, on her deathbed, had sent him toward another woman. And how did you do it? You're so bloody strong and selfless. I wouldn't have been stout enough, if things had been reversed. I couldn't have survived the thought of you with another bloke, even if he would have brought you joy. I'm so sorry, but it's true. I would have failed you.

He wiped his eyes again. I love you so much, he thought. You are, and always will be, the love of my life. As I've told you a heap of times, I don't put much trust in God. To me, he's been about as useful as an ashtray on a motorbike. But they say Moses parted these waters, and maybe he did, because someone brought you to me. Someone brought you to me, and that was the greatest gift of my life—because the crossing of our paths gave me you, and you gave me Mattie. And without the two of you, I'd be nothing.

"Daddy?"

Ian looked down, glanced to Mattie. "Yeah, Roo?"

"Are you crying?"

He shook his head. "No, luv. Just . . . a bit of sunscreen in the old eyes. Stings like the bite of a fire ant."

"Maybe you should wash it off. In the Red Sea."

"Will you go with me?"

"Sure."

Ian picked up their masks and snorkels, took Mattie's hand, and walked toward the water. It was cooler than he expected, contrasting with the fierce sun and nearby desert. Continuing to hold Mattie's hand, he waded deeper into the water, small waves tumbling into his calves, then his thighs. He handed Mattie her mask and snorkel, glad that her freckled face still looked young.

She put on her equipment. "Where should we go, Daddy? Do you think they have a Shark Point here?"

"No, luv. I reckon not. But let's . . . let's find something beautiful. Something for Holly."

"And we'll mail it to her? Maybe something each for Holly and Rupee?"

He adjusted the top of her bikini, trying to cover more of her flesh. "How about giving it to her, Roo? Would you fancy that?"

"Giving it to her? You mean, next year, when we come back?"

"I mean next month. When we return to Hong Kong."

"What?"

"Do you still want to go back, luv? I could work there, for a few ticks of the old clock, and we could see what happened. We could leave Egypt, go back to the States, say hello to our mates and loved ones, and then buzz off for Hong Kong."

She took off her mask. "Really? Really, Daddy?"

"If that's what you want."

Mattie dropped her mask, jumping up through the water, wrapping her arms around his neck. "That's what I want. It is. It is."

"I reckoned as much," he replied, holding her out of the water, her body so light against his.

"But is it . . . is it what you want?"

"Aye, aye, First Mate. And I think your mum wants us to go back too. I think that's one of the reasons she sent us on this walkabout."

Mattie looked around. "Which way is the west, Daddy?"

He pointed, still holding her. "Over there."

"Can we swim in that direction? I think we'll find the most beautiful things over there."

"Let's swim to the west."

"And when we swim . . . will you hold my hand? Like you always have?"

"I won't ever stop holding your hand, Roo."

"You won't?"

"No, luv. Not ever."

"Promise?"

He wrapped his pinkie around hers. "Promise."

Smiling, Mattie reached down, picking up her mask and snorkel from the sandy bottom. Soon she was swimming, holding her father's hand, watching green and blue fish, looking for treasures that she would find for Holly and Rupee, and that she would place in a wishing tree, a tree that stood on the west side of the Nile, where spirits rested, where her mother could easily see what she had done.

MUCH LATER, AFTER THE SKY HAD DARKENED and the moon arisen, Ian sat on the balcony of their hotel room. Mattie was asleep inside, and Ian had drawn the curtains and stepped into the night air. He had propped a flashlight on a chair beside him, and it cast a weak light on the notebook he held. As he wrote, he glanced at a large tropical tree that brushed up against the balcony. The tree must have been present long before the hotel. Its thick branches were gnarled and needed trimming. Yet fresh leaves emerged in places, as if the tree's will to endure was as strong as, or even stronger than, ever.

Ian finished taking notes, set the page aside, and started to write on a fresh piece of paper.

> *Kate,*
>
> *I'm no poet, my love, but I'll tell you this—you always made me want to be one. You made a believer of me in the beauty of words and thoughts. And now, I believe in so many things. In you. In love and goodness and forever. In that we were drawn together for reasons.*
>
> *I touch our daughter's face, and I see yours. I hear her laugh, and I listen to you.*
>
> *You're right—something can't be pulled from you if it's a part of you. And you're a part of me. And I will*

always cherish this oneness, just as the sun must cherish its unity with the sky.

I know, my love, that I don't need to ask your forgiveness for what I'm about to do, for opening my heart. I know that you led me down this path, and why you did so. You took my hand and guided me toward a source of light, a new beginning. Not away from you, but toward you, toward that oneness, that sense beyond self.

I love you so much, Kate. I always have and I always will. You created us, and from us, such wonder has happened. Mattie will be happy. Content. And loved. You saved her. And me. And we're going to save a child of the streets. A boy who was lost, but soon will be found.

We've lived so many lives together, you and I. And we'll keep living them, not in flesh, but in spirit. And then, one day, I won't need wishing trees to talk with you. I'll go where you've gone, where beauty seeks refuge, where bliss becomes eternal, and together we'll watch goodness unfold—like one of Mattie's drawings, full of so much splendor and hope and love. So much wonder.

Look at what we've done, my love. Look and be happy. I love you. I love you. I love you.

Ian

He folded the paper carefully. After making sure that Mattie was still asleep and that the room's door was locked, he crept to the edge of the balcony. The ground was about twenty feet below, and the beat of his heart quickened as he eyed a nearby branch, which was almost an arm's length away and as thick as his thigh. Certain that the branch would support him, that the old tree wouldn't fail him, Ian tucked his letter into his pocket. He climbed over the railing and stood on the edge of the balcony, holding the metal behind him.

After taking several deep breaths and studying the branch, he leapt for it, his arms wrapping around it, his skin pierced and torn in several places, but his mind unyielding. Grunting, he pulled himself up, swinging his leg over the branch, twisting so that he was atop it. Scooting forward, he reached the trunk of the tree and began to climb. He took pleasure in the task, as if he were drawing closer to Kate. And he went up, higher and higher, until the tree swayed beneath him, and distant lights on the Red Sea shined like fireflies.

A breeze arose, causing leaves to move and chatter, the tree to come alive. He watched the stars, the gathering of worlds. He thought of Mattie sleeping below, of how they would explore more peaks and valleys, seas and sketches. His life wasn't over, he knew, though not long ago he had feared that it was. In so many ways, he was like the tree, whose ancestors might have shaded Moses. The tree had been wounded in places, with stumps where branches had been, with cracks in once-smooth wood. Yet the tree was unquestionably alive, and supported life. Insects crawled about it. A bird's nest was near. The tree still knew how to sing in the wind.

Ian found a crevice in the trunk, which held old leaves and a fine layer of sand. The sand must have arrived before the hotel was built, when storms carried the desert toward the Red Sea. Careful not to disturb the sand, Ian tucked his note into the crevice. The act of seeing the ancient sand, of leaving Kate a note, felt holy. At no point since her death had Ian felt closer to Kate than he did now. He believed in the wishing tree. He believed that she could see him on it, and that she would read or hear or somehow sense the words that he had written. She had spoken to him from the dead—leading him here, to a place where he could rise anew, where the Nile flowed, millennium after millennium, carrying silt and moisture to soil that brought life to the desert, to a place of memories, of histories, of dynasties that would continue to be discovered and celebrated.

The river still flowed, its waters not yet gone, its stories not yet fully told.

HONG KONG

The Smiles of Strangers

"A BIRD DOES NOT SING BECAUSE IT HAS AN ANSWER.
A BIRD SINGS BECAUSE IT HAS A SONG."

—CHINESE SAYING

An old man removed his thick glasses, cleaned them on his shirt, and then settled back on the bench. He had been coming to the park since childhood, and though the city below it had changed, the park hadn't. The boulders were the same, as were the wide stretch of grass, the laugher of children, the way the sun felt on his skin.

As he had many times over the past year and a half, the old man watched a family of Westerners, their words incomprehensible to him, but their faces familiar and welcome. The family sat on a picnic blanket and savored the day. A girl with light brown hair lay on her belly, drawing in a sketch pad. Another girl, about the same age, laughed with a dark-skinned boy who had only recently begun arriving with them.

The old man didn't understand the appearance of the boy, who looked so different from the girls and the man and woman, who often held hands. The boy always sat near the girls and played with them as if they were his siblings, even though they did not have the same flesh and blood.

As the sun climbed higher, the old man continued to watch the family, savoring their joy, reminded of his own brothers and sisters.

The father removed a soccer ball from a backpack, and soon he and the woman were chasing the ball, and the children ran and laughed, kicking and falling and giggling and making the old man smile so many times.

Dear Reader,

I want to take a moment to thank you for reading *The Wishing Trees*. Countless wonderful and deserving novels exist, and I'm grateful that you set the time aside to read my book. I hope you enjoyed it.

The Wishing Trees follows in the footsteps of my third novel, *Dragon House*, and I'd like to update you on the street children that *Dragon House* is helping. The success of that novel, along with direct donations from readers, has allowed us to buy sets of schoolbooks for about eight hundred Vietnamese street children over the past year. I'm so grateful for this outcome and am indebted to readers, librarians, and booksellers for their encouragement and generosity.

I also want some good to come out of *The Wishing Trees* and plan to donate some of the funds generated by my book to support the Arbor Day Foundation. So, if you've purchased *The Wishing Trees*, or told a friend about it, know that you've helped plant a little tree—a wishing tree, as I like to think.

As always, feel free to contact me with questions or comments. I can be reached through my Web site at www.johnshors.com.

Be well.
John

Acknowledgments

The Wishing Trees would not have been possible without the support of my wife, Allison, and our children, Sophie and Jack. Thank you for letting me live my dream. I love you all.

I'd like to express my gratitude toward Ellen Edwards, my wonderful editor, as well as Laura Dail, my agent extraordinaire. Thanks also to my parents, John and Patsy Shors; my brothers, Tom, Matt, and Luke; as well as Mary and Doug Barakat, Bruce McPherson, Dustin O'Regan, Amy Tan, Wally Lamb, Mahbod Seraji, Kara Cesare, Michael Brosowski, Pennie Ianniciello, Clover Apelian, Shawna Sharp, Sarah Streett, Bliss Darragh, Diane Saarinen, Amy Cherry, Kara Welsh, Craig Burke, Kaitlyn Kennedy, and Davina Witts at BookBrowse.com.

Photo by Jim Barbour

John Shors is the bestselling author of *Beneath a Marble Sky*, *Beside a Burning Sea*, *Dragon House*, and *The Wishing Trees*. He has won numerous awards for his writing, and his novels have been translated into twenty-five languages.

John lives in Boulder, Colorado, with his wife and two children. For more information, please visit www.johnshors.com.

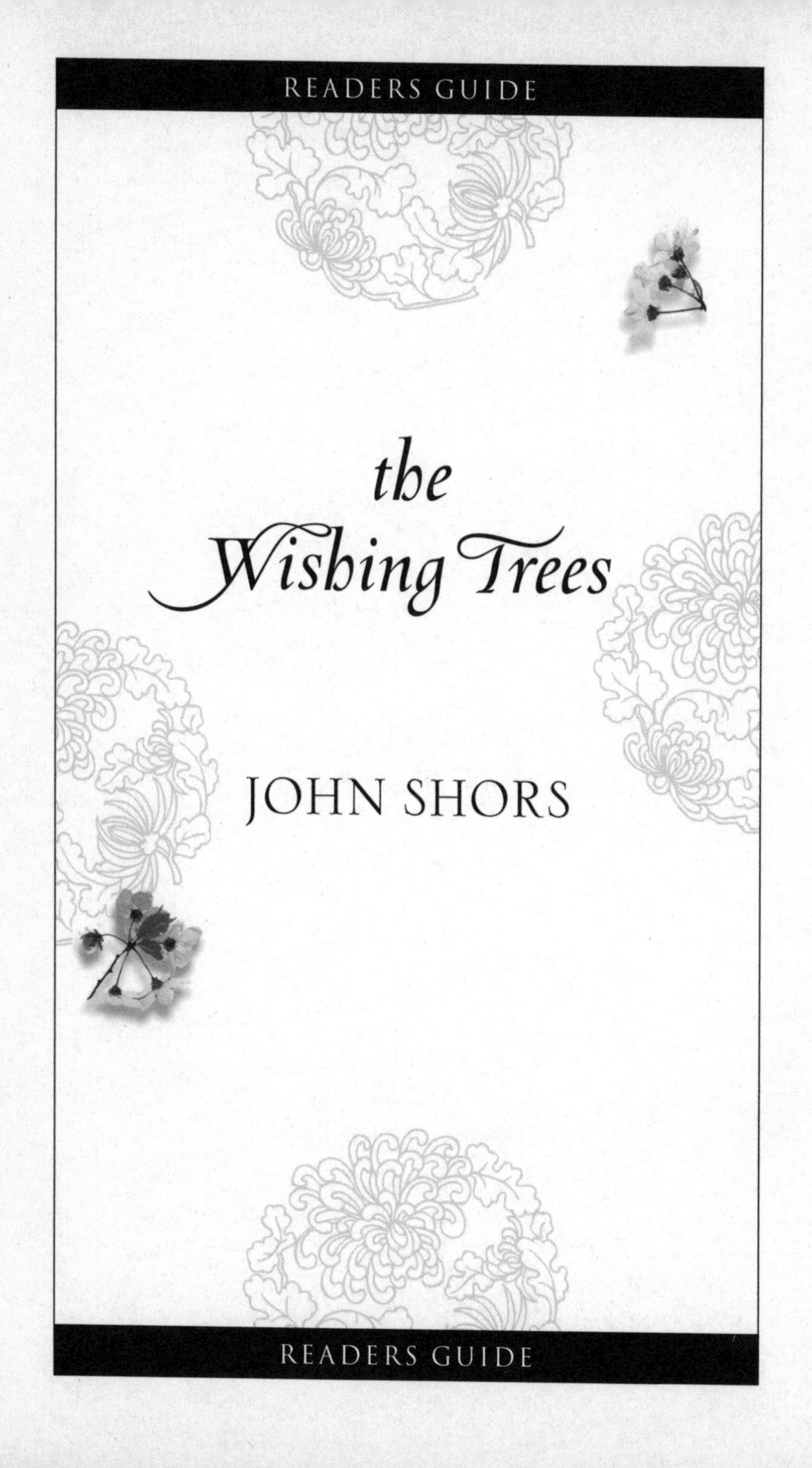
READERS GUIDE
the
Wishing Trees
JOHN SHORS
READERS GUIDE

A CONVERSATION WITH JOHN SHORS

Q. At the heart of The Wishing Trees *is a touching father-daughter relationship. How much did you draw upon your relationship with your own daughter in creating the interactions between Ian and Mattie?*
A. I try in all my novels not to base characters on the people in my life. I prefer to create characters from scratch, to watch them grow, draft by draft. Having said that, certainly my experience as the father of a young girl and boy was crucial for this novel. I could put myself in Ian's shoes, and make him believable, because of this experience. Also, having young children made it easier for me to write from Mattie's perspective.

Q. What particular challenges did you encounter in writing about two people grieving for the wife and mother whom they loved?
A. Obviously, two such people are going to have a great deal of sadness in their lives, and I needed to honor that sadness. But I didn't want to dwell on it too deeply. I wanted to also give my characters hope and humor, compassion and joy. Finding a balance between sorrow and celebration was a difficult process.

Q. Describe your experience with "wish trees."
A. After graduating from college, I moved to Kyoto, Japan, where I

taught English for several years. I have vivid memories of wish trees, which were often located in popular parks. The trees tended to be old—propped up with bamboo poles and rope. During holidays and busy weekends, the trees were covered with thousands of small white pieces of paper that contained people's wishes. I loved the sight of these trees, and the thought of wishes being fulfilled.

Q. Did many of the scenes in The Wishing Trees *come from your own personal experience?*
A. While teaching in Japan I managed to save enough money to backpack throughout Asia. I was fortunate to spend a significant amount of time in all of the countries depicted in *The Wishing Trees*, and many of the scenes in the novel are based on my own experiences. For instance, I swam with the sharks at Ko Phi Phi, I helped a Nepalese girl carry her firewood up an endless series of stone steps, and I went on a self-propelled roller coaster in India. I am the type of writer who needs to live in a place to bring that place to life on the page. There's no way I could have written this novel without having first visited the cities, mountains, and coastlines portrayed within it.

Q. What fuels your passion for travel? And what are your favorite countries to visit?
A. I love being in a new place and exploring. To me there are few experiences as exhilarating as making discoveries. Sometimes I'm amazed at what can be found near my home in Colorado. Sometimes a journey takes me overseas. Whatever the case, I'm always looking for new experiences, which make me a better writer. In terms of my favorite destinations, I have a strong attachment to Asia. Perhaps this kinship is bred from familiarity. I feel as if I understand the region well. I admire its cultures and its people and its natural wonders. Of course, I hope to travel more extensively to other continents, and to get to know those places as well. Every country, I believe, has something to offer.

Q. As an armchair traveler, I would enjoy hearing about a particularly good travel experience and a particularly bad one, if you'd care to share.

A. I've been blessed with a lot of wonderful experiences, but one stands out. While living in Japan, two friends and I rode our mountain bikes across a mountainous part of the country. We didn't have much money, and one evening we opted to sleep in a city's park—not eager for a cold, damp, and uncomfortable night, but without much choice. As we were setting up our sleeping bags, an old woman walked past us. She was probably in her late eighties, and couldn't speak a word of English. But through a series of friendly gestures, she invited us into her nearby home, where we bathed as she cooked us an enormous meal. We later drank sake and danced with her, and slept in the beds that once comforted her children. By the end of that night, I realized just how deep a capacity the human heart has for goodwill, and that realization continues to resonate within me today.

Now, in terms of bad experiences, I've some of those too. Once, in the slums of a large Asian city, some men tried to rob me, and instead of giving them what they wanted, I ran away, which wasn't a wise move. I was caught a few minutes later, and found myself fighting off a bunch of angry thieves. I would have been in big trouble had not a local television reporter happened on the scene and come to my rescue.

Q. Why does The Wishing Trees *span so much of the globe?*

A. I wanted Ian and Mattie to take an emotional and spiritual journey as well as a physical one. These two ideas went hand in hand. One of my goals was to have my characters learn from the people they met, and that needed to happen in a variety of countries and cultures, where attitudes toward life and death vary enormously. I believe we can all learn from one another, no matter how different, even incompatible, we at first appear, and I hoped to show that in *The Wishing Trees.*

Q. Which character was the hardest to write and why?

A. I'd say that Ian was the toughest, because of his vernacular. I thought that an Australian character would add a dimension to the novel and was intrigued with the idea of bringing Ian to life. But Australians use as much slang as any group of people in the world, and I was a bit nervous about making his voice believable. I didn't want to go too far in one direction or not far enough in the other. So, I studied Australian slang and had an Australian friend read an early draft of *The Wishing Trees*. I was also fortunate to have traveled to Australia, and have always had some of their colorful expressions stuck in my head. Sometimes, for instance, I find myself saying, "I reckon," when other people would just say, "Yes."

Q. Your previous novels have had many characters and various subplots. Why did you decide to switch things up in The Wishing Trees*?*

A. I'm not particularly interested in writing the same kind of novel over and over. What I'm interested in is challenging myself and providing readers with fresh stories. For instance, in *Beneath a Marble Sky*, I wrote in the first person, bringing to life the voice of a seventeenth-century Indian princess—not an easy task for a guy sitting in his office in Colorado. In *Beside a Burning Sea*, I began each chapter with an original haiku. *Dragon House* is a tale about some remarkable homeless children. In many ways, *The Wishing Trees* is a departure from my earlier work. There are only a few characters. There's no villain. And there's no dominant love story. In my future novels, I'll continue to pursue different themes and experiment with structure, point of view, and other writing techniques.

Q. What's the hardest aspect about being a writer?

A. Well, of course there are deadlines and pressures, which can rule my day-to-day existence. But what I think is toughest is the lack of camaraderie that's so often found in other professions. Rarely do writers have brainstorming sessions, go out to lunch together, or enjoy an after-work cocktail. Writing is a very solitary affair. Sometimes that's wonderful. But it can also be a bit too quiet. And when that silence starts to settle in, I find it necessary to go out for a walk, to somehow interact with the world.

Q. Why do children play such big roles in your novels?
A. I want to bring diverse points of view to my books. That diversity can be defined by age, race, personal attributes, and so forth. For me, children are a means to add different voices, and very compelling voices at that. I think children often interpret the world in ways that adults don't, and it's rewarding to open myself to their way of seeing. My own children, for example, often take pleasure in experiences that I might rush past—the sensation of stepping into mud, the texture of a feather, the sight of something small and wondrous.

Q. It's absolutely amazing that you've spoken to almost twenty-five hundred book clubs around the world, both in person and via speakerphone. Why have you made such efforts, and why do you think so many people are involved in book clubs?
A. Once my first novel, *Beneath a Marble Sky*, took off internationally, selling well in many countries, I decided that I wanted to give something back to readers. If people were going to support me—reading my novels and telling their friends about them—then I needed to support them in return. Communicating with tens of thousands of readers via e-mail and through book club talks requires a lot of work on my part, but it's worth it. Readers deserve such interaction, and I'm honored to reach out to them.

I believe that books are not an endangered species. There's so much talk these days about the demise of books, about the end of reading as a leisure activity. But I think there is some false drama built into these conversations. Books are vehicles that take us to magnificent destinations; they're irreplaceable. The fact that I'm still speaking with several book clubs every night further convinces me that the love affair with the book has not ended. Book clubs symbolize this communal, continual love.

Q. Tell us about your next novel.

A. My next novel is set in Ko Phi Phi, Thailand—an island paradise that was hit hard by the tsunami in 2004. In the book I bring together three Americans—two brothers and the woman who loves them both—and a local Thai family that depends on Western tourism while also disliking many of the changes it produces. As this mingling of cultures and personal relationships creates growing conflicts, a disastrous event threatens my characters' lives, challenges their loyalties, and turns their expectations upside down. I'm already deep into the story and am excited about the way it's unfolding.

QUESTIONS FOR DISCUSSION

1. Had you heard of "wish trees" before? If not, did you enjoy being introduced to them? Is there anything similar in your country?

2. If you were Ian, would you take Mattie on the trip? Where do you draw the line between offering your child new experiences and providing for her/his safety?

3. Would you like to travel like Ian and Mattie do? Which country did you enjoy the most, and what about it appeals to you?

4. What did you think of Kate's character, and her letters? Did you find Ian's and Mattie's reactions to her death believable and moving? Are they similar to your own experiences of loss?

5. Did everything ring true within the relationship of Ian and Mattie?

6. Who was your favorite character and why?

7. What do you think of Rupee, and how did he contribute to the story?

8. What do you think will happen to the young sex worker, Jaidee, when she returns home? Was Ian right to try to help her?

9. What was the most memorable moment of the book for you?

10. Ian and Mattie feel compelled to help the needy people they meet during their travels. Do you think people in wealthy countries have a moral obligation to assist the poor and suffering elsewhere in the world? To what extent? What sacrifices are you willing and not willing to make?

11. At the end of the novel, Ian and Mattie choose to settle in Hong Kong. How do you feel about their decision?

12. John Shors is supporting street children in Vietnam through his previous novel, *Dragon House*, and in conjunction with *The Wishing Trees* he is donating some of the funds generated by the book to the Arbor Day Foundation to plant trees. Do you think it's important for writers to take on such causes?

13. What do you think are the key messages of *The Wishing Trees*?

14. Which of John Shors's novels have you enjoyed most?